UNDEAD ASSIMILATION

AN APOCALYPTIC THRILLER

MATTHEW DOGGETT

FIVE BROTHERS PUBLISHING

CONTENTS

PROLOGUE

J oseph burst out onto the roof, sweat glistening on his balding pate, breath hissing between his brown teeth. He surveyed the rooftop of the building quickly, noting without interest the concrete dome in the middle. A demented smile cracked his only-a-mother-could-love face as he placed grimy hands on the strap across his chest. He ducked his head, pulling the strap off and the Remington 700 rifle to which it was attached.

He walked toward the edge of the building, glancing down at the errant bird feathers that scattered the roof. He frowned slightly, his eyebrows momentarily joining to make one long, angry, black caterpillar. *They're for the birds*, he thought of the feathers, and laughed at his own awesome wit. The strange smattering of feathers quickly left his mind as he approached the three-foot rim of the roof, crouching as he neared it.

The sun was touching the horizon to his left, but it wouldn't be a problem. He knelt down and pulled the 700 to his shoulder, angling it right, away from the sun. He peered through his scope, made a few adjustments, and silently thanked his former employer, the city police department, for providing him with his toy.

It had been nearly a month since the apocalypse began, and Joseph had been having himself a good old time. He'd killed a few blacks and

Hispanics during his short tenure as a police, but the end of the world provided him with so many excellent opportunities to have his fun. And without all the paperwork and investigations and bullshit that came with shooting someone as a cop.

He had never—not even for a second—regretted his decision to strike out on his own, here in the outskirts. The way he saw it, there was really no choice. Stay in the safe zone and risk getting caught for killing people, or put up with the dangers of the outskirts and kill as many people as he wanted?

There had never been an easier decision.

Now, as he knelt in the fading daylight on top of the Paredo building, he thought back to his first kill as a free man. Or, rather, his first several kills. He'd gotten the first few with his trusty 700, from a roof not unlike the one he was on now. A couple of big, tattooed guys with guns walking down the sidewalk like they owned the city. He got one in the neck and the other in the head. *Bam, bam.* Then a third guy, too. There were two women with them, which he had hoped to get alive, but that hadn't worked out. Too bad. They had been lookers.

Then, his favorite part happened. His partner, whose name he couldn't remember now, got all bent out of shape about it. Like the world hadn't already gone to shit. Like there were still rules. Like fucking zombies weren't roaming the goddamn streets. But he had taken care of that little bitch with a nice shove off the roof.

Joseph got a little excited as he thought about the noise the guy made as he hit the concrete. *Best day of my life*, he thought. *But maybe today will take its place.*

He had one eye to his scope as he relived that day, Z-Day, as it was now known. The first day of the new world, where zombies roamed the streets and chaos reigned supreme.

The zombies were easy to handle. It was the gangs that you had to worry about.

And the do-gooders.

Presently, Joseph's breath caught as he saw movement through the scope. *Here they come. Too far to shoot, though.* He would have to wait for them to get close. It was a rather large group of people, clearly not familiar with the city, because they were going the wrong way. Of course, it helped that Joseph had moved the signs that the do-gooders had put up to lead people to the safe zone. He liked corralling people into his little traps.

Watching through the scope, he debated which one he would get first. It looked like two families traveling together. Five adults and six kids. He debated killing the smallest of the kids first. They were harder to hit; small, quick bodies that could easily hide once they realized what was happening.

He finally decided on who to shoot first when he heard something like the creaking of a rusty hinge. He looked up from his rifle, toward the domed structure. From his angle near the corner of the roof, he could see that the door was open. *Was that door open when I came up here?* He couldn't remember. He'd been so excited about this current batch of victims . . .

It must have been open, he decided, looking back through his scope. They were almost in range. Joseph started slowing his breathing in preparation, getting his mind into shooting mode. No need to load a bullet; he always had one in the chamber.

He set his crosshairs on the gray-haired man in the middle of the group. The bullet would drop a little and move slightly to the left, catching the kid holding the old man's hand as they walked. That kid looked fast. Best to get him first. The adults would be so concerned that they would all bunch up around the dead kid. Maybe he could even get two-for-one today. He'd always wanted to do that.

Joseph moved his finger inside the trigger guard, his breath slowing, his mind zeroed in.

A scrape sounded close by on the roof, causing Joseph to jerk his head away from the scope and look. A badly deformed man in a plaid shirt, jeans, and sneakers stood an arm's length from him, staring with wide, bloodshot eyes. One of his arms was canted at a bad angle in the middle, and the fingers of that hand pointed in all directions.

The man opened his mouth, his eyes going wider, and reached toward Joseph with his good hand. Blackness seemed to pour out of the guy's mouth. Joseph stood up and swung his rifle toward his attacker. The man yanked the rifle out of his hand, turned it around, and jammed it through Joseph's right foot. Joseph screamed in agony as the blunt barrel smashed through skin, muscle, tendon, and bone. It passed through his foot, through his boot sole, and into the hard scrim of the roof, pinning him in place. The deformed man let go of the rifle, which stayed upright, swaying slightly.

"Oh god, oh god, oh please, what do you want?" Joseph said as the man reached for him. Joseph put his right hand out, an unconscious gesture of pleading.

"Duuuude," the man said, just before chomping down on Joseph's trembling, pleading hand. Joseph screamed as the man's teeth snapped and separated three of his fingers from his hand.

By the time Joseph finally lost consciousness, he'd decided that this was the worst day of his life.

Of course, who can blame him? It's hard to stay optimistic when you're being eaten alive by an unlikely monster.

Or, for that matter, any kind of monster.

Avoid it if you can.

***

When the monster, whose name was Buck, finished picking Joseph's bones clean, he spoke. "Much better than pigeons," he said to himself as his broken arm began to heal. "Now, where the fuck is that asshole detective who brought me up here? We're going to have words."

A voice answered that only Buck could hear, and he nodded in response as he walked toward the door that led to the staircase. The sun was a thin slit on the horizon, and Buck felt better than he had in days. He felt alive. But, most of all, he felt a righteous fury expanding in him like an oxygen-starved fire swooping through a newly opened door.

That fury had one person and one person only in its sights.

CHAPTER ONE

A NEW BREED

D etective Kurt Atticus Weller pulled his left hand out of the hole in the wall. His teeth were clenched in pain and anger. The dark skin of his hand was spotted with blood and powdered with drywall dust. The sight of blood on his hand made him even angrier, and he headbutted the wall, denting it inward and sending a wave of pain through his skull. He stumbled backward and sat on his bed, jarring his slowly healing cracked ribs.

If you're not careful you'll break your other hand, he thought to himself, looking down at the cast on his right arm. Technically, his right hand wasn't broken. It was both the bones of his forearm that had been snapped three weeks earlier. Still, it hurt to use his right hand for anything, much less punching a wall, which was a habit of his lately, as evidenced by the dozen or so holes in his bedroom walls.

He wiped his forehead off with his left hand and got up, dressed only in his boxer briefs. He walked out past the kitchen and into the living room, glancing at the clock on his wall, not surprised to find out that it was the middle of the damn night. Sleep was ever elusive for the detective, no matter how he tried, which was one of the many reasons he felt obliged to put holes in his walls.

He resigned himself to another sleepless night and picked up a small silver analog recording device with his left hand, ignoring the drying blood and white dust still stuck to his skin. He pressed the appropriate buttons and brought it to his mouth, clearing his throat as he did so.

"Okay, where was I?" he asked the recorder. He wasn't about to rewind it and listen to his own voice from the previous night. Not because he didn't like his voice, but because he barely knew how to operate the damn recorder. "For my ex-wife JayLynn Whittaker, formerly JayLynn Weller, in case I die, blah, blah, blah. Apocalypse, bombs falling, zombies roaming the streets, we're all infected, yadda, yadda, yadda. Oh yeah. I was getting to the vampires. Yes, they exist. So far as I know, I'm the only living human who has been trusted with that most unholy knowledge. And these fuckers are old. Unlike the zombies, they aren't a product of the apocalypse.

"Plus, there was this crazy big guy named Merek who used to be a vampire, but he turned into something else. Like a vampire who fed off vampires. And he was on a mission to kill all the vampires here. Again, nothing to do with the apocalypse. Just bad timing. He's the one that broke my damn arm and ribs." Weller paused, his eyes focusing on the memory that wasn't even three weeks old yet.

"It could have been worse, I guess. And before that, there was this guy named Buck. A real grunge-type loser, but he wasn't all that bad. Anyway, I accidentally got him killed. Which was kind of all for the better, because he was some sort of weird zombie-vampire hybrid. He tried to eat me the first time we met. Like he was in some sort of fugue state."

Weller paused again, looking at his ceiling while the spindles in the recording device spun. "Oh shit, I forgot to tell you about Diirek. He's the first vampire I met. His wife or girlfriend or whatever got killed by Merek, so he's out wandering the wasteland like some sort of depressed messiah . . . I guess that's redundant. All messiahs are pretty depressed.

"He told me he's trying to figure out what caused the apocalypse because no one knows, but I think he's just writing emo songs about his dead girl and crying blood tears. You know, because he's a vampire.

"Anyway, I said I'd watch over his little group of twenty or so vampires here in the safe zone in exchange for information. I don't know how he'll get that information to me, though, seeing as how we don't have working cell phones or internet. Or even damn landlines. Maybe he can turn into a bat. He told me he couldn't, but maybe he was lying."

Something occurred to the detective, and his dark face narrowed. "I can't remember the name to this song I have stuck in my head. That's neither here nor there, but maybe you can help me figure it out. Well, actually you'll only listen to this if I'm dead, I suppose. By then I won't have a head for a song to be stuck in. At least I don't think so." He paused.

"If I die without knowing the name of this song, I'm gonna be pissed. The chorus goes like this—"

A sound like a bucket full of rabid cats being tossed on an angry hippo assaulted him from the street. (It was a better sound than would have emanated from Weller's mouth, so we'll just call that good timing.)

"What the hell?" Weller jumped up, tweaking his ribs in the process. He arrived at the window in time to see a blue-gray figure tear down the street in a frantic blur, four floors below. "Dammit," he yelled to his empty apartment. "What the shit is it now?" Then something caught his eye in the other direction. It was a goddamn vampire, sitting in the street.

Weller couldn't see his face, but he thought he recognized the vamp. He stepped back from the window and walked backward to the couch. He sat down when his calves touched imitation leather. He still held the recorder, spindles turning the seconds away. "I'm so sick of this shit," he said to the silver device. His eyes were wide, staring at nothing. "Why can't I just get one night of decent rest? It's always something. Things were bad enough when it was just humans fucking up the world. But now . . ." Weller trailed off. He forced his eyes to focus and looked at the night outside his window.

He clicked off the recorder and threw it at his couch as he stood up. "Goddammit," he said, stepping behind the couch and grabbing his Sig Sauer P229 9mm pistol from his shoulder holster on the back of a chair. He was out the door before he realized he was only wearing boxer shorts and a cast. By then it was too late to turn around. He knew that if he went back into the apartment, he wouldn't be able to force himself out again.

The late-spring night was pleasant, and the breeze felt good on his skin and through the thin material of his purple-and-white striped boxers. Half of the streetlights were out to help conserve power for the safe zone. There wasn't another soul on the street. Including the vampire, if the lore was correct. For his part, Weller didn't know if he believed in souls or not, but he sure as hell believed in vampires. Seeing is believing, after all.

The night was quiet now. The strange sound had apparently been an anomaly.

He approached the vampire, his bare feet padding along the sidewalk. As he got closer, he knew something was wrong. He *did* recognize the vampire. His name was Ricardo, and his eyes were wide open, as if in surprise, staring the way the blue-gray blur had gone. He sat in the middle of the street, his feet splayed in front of him, his pale skin glowing in the light of the moon.

"Yo, Ricardo," Weller said.

"Ahhh!" The vampire twitched violently and looked accusingly at Weller. "What the hell, man? You know how dark you are? You're like a cast, a pair of boxers, and a gun floating through the night. Scared the hell out of me."

"Oh, a joke about a black guy at night. Real original, jackass. Plus, you're a goddamn vampire. How is anyone going to sneak up on you?

When—" Weller stopped, noticing something. "What the fuck is that?" he said, pointing to the right side of the vamp's chest. Just under his pectoral muscle was a dent about the size and shape of a fist. The vampire's black T-shirt was stuck in the dent, making it visible to Weller.

Ricardo looked down. "Oh, that's what hurts. Damn, that thing was fast." The vampire got up off the ground. As he did so, Weller could hear his smashed rib bones grinding together like a rock polisher.

"Ah, man," he said, wincing. "And I thought *my* ribs hurt. Wait—what 'thing' was fast?"

"I don't know. Whatever it was that punched me and took off down the street. If I knew what it was, I wouldn't say 'thing' now would I? I'd say, 'that kangaroo was fast.' or, 'that heavyweight boxing champion was fast.'" Ricardo clutched his damaged ribs as he straightened and then pulled his plain black t-shirt out of the dent.

"Don't tell me we have another vampire-hunting monster in the city. We just finished with that bullshit."

"No, I don't think so. This thing was fast, but not as fast as Merek was—or as powerful. I thought it was a zombie at first. I was on my way over here when I saw the thing. It kind of looked like a zombie, but it wasn't moving like one. And it seemed . . . almost intelligent. Anyway, it was just strolling along. So I followed it for a little while, then I guess it noticed me because it started running, so I chased it. Then it stopped, turned, and came at me. And punched me."

"I heard some kind of crazy noise. Was that you?"

Ricardo looked defensive. "I was scared and hurt. That thing was crazy. You'd be scared too. Just get off my back already," he said, rapid-fire.

"Oh, Christ," Weller said, throwing his hands up, one of which still held his pistol. "Can't we just have a nice quiet apocalypse for a change? I've got other shit to deal with."

"Whatever. You love it, you sick bastard. Oh, hey, you think I can get some blood? I gotta heal this thing. Hurts like a bitch." Ricardo gestured at his now-hidden wound.

"What? No. Go find some asshole in the outskirts and do the world a favor."

"C'mon, Detective, why do you think I was coming here in the first place? It's a quiet night everywhere. Unless you'd like me to break into one of these brownstones and drink some innocent blood . . ."

"What do I care? You guys are half-feeding anyway, right? If you're not, I'll know. I start finding dried-up bodies, I know where to look."

"Alright, if you say so, Detective." Ricardo started walking away, backward, smiling at Weller. "Where does your ex-wife live again?"

Weller glared at the vampire. "Alright dammit, come on," he said, turning back toward his apartment building. "I have some blood in the fridge. But this is not a regular thing. And my ex is off-limits. And after this you go find whatever the hell that thing was that punched you and, I don't know . . . Figure out what it is. And let me know."

"Oh, Detective, you love us, don't you?" Ricardo said in a high, dramatic voice. "You keep blood in the fridge for vampires, don't you? I knew there was a reason we all liked you. You're a celebrity in the Underground, you know that?"

"Whatever. The blood is for emergencies only. This will not become a habit."

Weller scowled. Ricardo smiled. They headed into the apartment.

CHAPTER TWO

WAKE UP, GOD, IT'S ME, DIPSHIT

"What is it?" Dipshit asked, trying to sound calm.

"I don't know," Sicko said, out of the darkness beside him. "Probably nothing, but the alarm was tripped. Maybe it's just a walker."

Dipshit peered out through a crack between the boards covering the window of the old farmhouse. "I don't see a walker. I don't see anything out there," he said. "Where was the alarm tripped?"

"Damnation, Dipshit, just think for a minute, will you? It was the front alarm. Why else do you think I would be here looking out the *front* of the house?"

"Sorry," Dipshit said, casting his eyes down. His real name was Fred, but no one called him that at the farmhouse. He had turned seventeen two days before the apocalypse, and although he'd done a lot of growing up in the month since, he still felt like a little kid. Especially around the tough grown men at the farm. He admonished himself silently for asking such a stupid question and affirmed that he deserved the name bestowed upon him by Sicko and the others.

He looked out the crack again, tracking along the coiled barbed wire that sat on this side of the farm's short wooden fence. Sometimes a walker would manage to get over the fence and caught in the wire, triggering the alarm, ringing one of six bells inside the house. He'd never known a walker to get back out of the barbed wire, though. The fact that he didn't see anything out there made him uneasy. He gripped his .22 hunting rifle tighter.

The shrill insistent ringing of another bell blasted Dipshit's ears. He and Sicko turned around, the latter clicking a flashlight on and shining it at the six bells fastened near the ceiling of the living room. The one that was ringing had a label under it that read "backyard."

"Wake the others," Sicko said, heading to the viewport at the back of the house.

Dipshit set his rifle against the wall and then hustled down the hall while digging his own small flashlight out of his pajama bottoms. He burst into the master bedroom and started shaking the man lying on the bed there.

"God? Wake up, God. Sicko said to get everyone up. Two alarms have gone off," he said in a high, hurried voice.

God, who didn't look anything like the God Dipshit had grown up learning about, opened his lids, revealing striking and cruel green eyes. The man tossed the sheets off with one hand and swung his unusually hairy body up to sit on the edge of the bed. He stood, the elastic of his stained white underwear struggling to stay put under his giant, ripe beer belly and over his nonexistent ass. Dipshit stood there, a full head taller than God, his mind a blank like it nearly always was lately.

"What the fuck are you still doing here?" God said in his reedy, un-godlike voice. "Go get the brothers up, Dipshit."

Dipshit's mind snapped back to attention like an old rubber band, and he headed out of the room and across the hall. He opened the door to the other bedroom and started yelling as politely as he could at the two men sleeping in the wooden bunk beds.

"Dementor, Scorpion, wake up! The alarm's going off. Someone's trying to get in."

The two brothers shook the sleep off and got up while Dipshit headed out of the room. As he stepped into the hallway, he heard glass breaking and wood snapping. He ran down, snagged his rifle from where he'd propped it, and headed to the back. The alarm bell had stopped ringing, but Dipshit couldn't recall exactly when.

He ran through the living room and around the corner to the den, to where the viewport was. He stopped short when he saw the state of the boards that had been covering the window. Most of them had been broken. There was a hole large enough for a man to fit through.

"Sicko?" he said, quietly. His heart jangled like an alarm bell in his chest and his vision started to narrow as he crept to the window, his rifle at his shoulder, the flashlight held against the barrel with his left hand.

The only illumination was from his skinny flashlight and the half-moon that floated crooked over the earth. The back lawn had been cleared of all the paint-chipped metal barrels, rusting farm equipment, and overgrown bathroom fixtures that had littered it when God and his crew had arrived. It was Dipshit's job to keep the lawn trimmed, which he had only done once since he'd been conscripted into God's service just under two weeks earlier. The fence was backed with rolls of barbed wire here, too. As was the case all around the farmhouse. Beyond the fence was a small copse of trees, lush with greenery. The deep shadows under the foliage made it impossible to see what may or may not have been lurking there.

Dipshit leaned out the window and pointed his flashlight down to see if Sicko was there. He wasn't, but there was a small amount of blood marring the short grass. Dipshit gulped. A branch snapped off in the distance, causing the boy to jerk his gun up and shine the flashlight futilely at the trees.

Nothing.

"What is it?" God said from Dipshit's elbow, causing the teenager to jump and swing his gun at the small man. God, now dressed in grimy shorts and a matching t-shirt, grabbed the barrel and shoved it away. "You do that again I'll kill you myself, you fucking Dipshit."

Not for the first time, Dipshit thought that this God *did* share some traits with the one he'd learned about—the one from the Old Testament, anyway. This small, hairy God wasn't one to forgive and forget, that was for sure.

"I—I—I heard a branch snap," Dipshit said, visibly shaking, as God looked out the smashed window from behind the barrel of his AR15.

"I don't see—" God's voice was interrupted as Sicko came swinging down from the roof above the window, face-first, his hands fastened behind his back. Sicko's forehead and nose smacked the still-intact bottom board nailed across the window. The momentum carried the rest of Sicko's upper body through the hole there. God and Dipshit watched as the man's neck folded nearly in half backward, hearing vertebra and something else—the rain gutter maybe—crack and snap. It was clear that Sicko's feet were fastened to the roof somehow. His body swung back out, allowing his neck to straighten, then it came back, and his neck folded again, this time with less force.

Dipshit realized with horror that the other snapping sound was that of Sicko's knee joints folding the wrong way as they met the framing above the window. The boy looked away as God cursed and started gibbering.

Dementor and Scorpion came running into the den, all eyes and automatic weapons.

"What in the Sam Hell?" the brothers said together.

"Battle stations," God yelled, looking smaller than ever.

Dementor and Scorpion looked at each other, then they looked back at God, their brows furrowed. "'Battle stations'? What the hell are you talking about?" Scorpion asked. Dipshit didn't have any idea, either.

"Just find a window and protect it. Dipshit, you stay here and guard this window."

The teenager's eyes went wide. "What? N—No way!"

Sicko's body started twitching at the window. The three men and the boy froze, looking over in shock. Their compatriot's body was jerked out into the night by some unseen force. It tumbled through the air and landed on a roll of barbed wire against the fence, ringing the backyard bell once before the weight snapped the line.

God stepped up to the window and started firing wildly. "Fuck you!" he screamed into the night.

Dipshit backed away from the window.

A sound of smashing glass issued behind him, barely audible over the firing AR15. He spun around to see a pale face floating in the darkness of the living room. Scorpion and Dementor had been shoved headfirst into the previous owner's china cabinet. Scorpion in the plates, Dementor in the bowls and teacups. They both lay there, bleeding, limp, and unconscious—possibly dead.

Scorpion groaned and the pale man turned from Dipshit and kicked the noisy brother, launching him into the nearby wall. Scorpion came to rest covered in pieces of broken drywall, his face a mess of blood and china shards.

The pale face came toward Dipshit, who was praying to God (no, the other one) for a swift and painless death. The terror expanded in him, and he felt a blubbering hysteria gather in his throat. But he wouldn't cry. He refused.

God stopped firing the AR15 as the pale figure approached the teenager, who closed his eyes and waited.

And waited . . .

"Gahh! What the hell?" God said from behind Dipshit. The boy opened his eyes and turned around to see the pale man lifting God off the ground. With the moonlight shining through the window, Dipshit noted with something resembling relief that the man wasn't just a pale floating face. He had a body; it was just dressed in the blackest of black clothes.

"Hello, God," the pale man said. "My name is Diirek. And I will be the one judging *your* sins tonight."

CHAPTER THREE

A FEW MINUTES ALONE WITH GOD

"Open it," Diirek said to the small man cowering at the door.

Dipshit was still feeling rather trepidatious about the whole situation, but he was keen to see what was behind the forbidden door. Since he'd come to the farmhouse, he'd been told to steer clear of the heavily padlocked portal. Dipshit was smart enough to know that the door led to a basement, but he couldn't imagine what was down there, although he had heard some strange, muffled sounds emanating from the forbidden subterranean room on occasion. Typically he'd heard these noises when one of the four men went down there, which happened at least once a day since he'd been here.

While God worked to open the door, his hands shaking and beads of sweat lazily traversing the hair-maze covering his body, Dipshit studied Diirek. The pale man had paid him no mind at all, besides saying, "Don't go anywhere," when they'd reached the basement door.

Mostly the seventeen-year-old was in awe of this man who couldn't be a man, not really. He was more like a superhero. He had, after all, taken out the bad guys. That's what the boy had come to see his four roommates as during his short stay at the farm: bad guys. They had all started out nice enough, but that had changed quickly. Pretty soon they were making Dipshit do all the household chores, cleaning, cooking, and even fetching water from the hand pump in the back. He mowed the lawns and tended to the garden. If he didn't do any of the chores to their liking, they took a belt to him. Really, it wasn't all that different than the way his dad treated him before the world ended. Only instead of one father, he had four.

Meanwhile, God and the others sat around playing cards, drinking, smoking, and making visits to the basement, sweaty and out of breath when they came back up. At first, he thought they were exercising, but that didn't make much sense when he really got to thinking about it. He wanted to leave them, but he'd barely survived the few days out amongst the walkers before the men found him. At least he had a place to sleep and food to eat.

Presently, he made a guess about what he'd find in the basement and hoped he was wrong. God finally got the door open. Diirek shoved the small man, who disappeared into the darkness engulfing the old wooden staircase, the only evidence of his existence the screaming, thumping, and the occasional dull snap as the man tumbled down the stairs.

Diirek turned to Dipshit, his eyes seeming to glow in the darkness, and spoke. "I know you were not involved with this, which is why you are still alive. But you should see what these so-called 'men' were doing down there." He gestured at the dark stairwell. Dipshit brought his still-lit flashlight up and realized that he was still holding his .22 rifle in his right hand. He propped it against the wall and started down the stairs, Diirek's luminous eyes watching him as he went.

His flashlight beam found God at the bottom of the stairs, groaning and rolling his eyes. The small man's right arm was twisted impossibly behind his back, bringing new meaning to the term "patting yourself on the back," which was something that God had done often, if not literally. A shard of pink bone stuck out of the front of one of his shins under the grimy shorts he wore. Dipshit looked away from the horrid sight, ambivalent about the state of the man.

The boy stepped further into the basement, the cracked concrete floor covered in dirt and grime. He swung the flashlight up ahead of him and jumped when the beam landed on a woman's face. She sat on a bare mattress, a ball-gag in her mouth and her arms cuffed and chained to the wall above her. She made a pleading sound and sat up straight, her eyebrows separating in hope and desperation. Dipshit realized that she was only wearing a bra and panties, and he shifted his gaze and the flashlight away, but they landed on another woman who was wearing even less.

"Oh my..." He didn't want to say God, but it would have been appropriate in more ways than one.

"Here," Diirek said from just behind him, causing the boy to jump again, revealing yet another bound and gagged woman with the light. Dipshit turned around to find Diirek standing there, God's keys resting on the palm of his gloved hand.

Dipshit looked at the keys, at Diirek, and then at the still-moaning God a few feet to the left. He felt as if the pale man were giving him his strength because what he did next surprised him.

Dipshit narrowed his eyes, grabbed the keys, stepped over, and knelt in front of God.

"Which ones unlock them?" he asked, shoving the keyring in God's face.

"Help me, Dipshit," God pleaded. Dipshit stood up.

"My name is *Fred*," he said, kicking God in the stomach to drive home the point. It felt good. The small man screamed and writhed on the floor as Fred knelt again and repeated his question. God took the key ring tentatively in his good hand and separated 4 brass keys from the others. Fred yanked them away, realizing there was a fourth woman he hadn't seen.

As the boy stood up, he heard the sudden sound of concrete breaking. He shined the light toward the noise, illuminating Diirek, who had just torn two of the metal anchors out of the wall. He dropped the anchors—which still held the chains—onto a mattress next to one of the women. He moved to the other two anchors and yanked those out, too.

"You were taking too long," the pale man said. Fred would still need to unlock the shackles, but at least the women could move out of the basement now, albeit dragging chains and anchors with chunks of concrete still attached.

"Mmmm," one of the women said as she stood up. Fred stepped toward her and unclasped the ball-gag.

"Thank you. We'll be up in a minute," the near-naked blond woman said to Fred, but her eyes were fixed on the barely visible figure of God next to the stairs.

"Okay?" Fred said, unsure. "Do you want me to unlock the shackles first?"

"No," the woman said, glancing at the three others moving into the small circle of light cast by Fred's flashlight. "I think we'll find them useful for a good little while," she said, gathering some of the chain in her hands and hefting the anchor hanging there, as if to test its weight.

Diirek quickly unfastened the other three women's gags and nodded for Fred to go upstairs.

"Leave the flashlight," another woman said. Fred handed it to her.

"Go on now, hear?" the blond said.

Fred did as he was told. Diirek seemed to have disappeared into the shadows, leaving the women to do what they would with God.

This time Fred knew what was causing the sounds coming from the basement.

He didn't mind.

CHAPTER FOUR

DEATH BY BATMAN

"**M**aster, you need to see this," the hunched man said in a rasping voice. He limped up to the comically large wing-backed chair that sat in front of a fireplace designed to look like a bat. The hunched man's name was currently Slave One, or simply "One". He had heard tell of a slave who had, some years previous, remarked that the fireplace looked like the Batman symbol. Apparently, the idiot had done this while the Master was still in earshot.

One version of the story went that the Master had had the man thrown into the fireplace. He had sat down in his oversized chair and watched as the man screamed and burned. Every time he tried to crawl out, a slave shoved him back in.

Another version said that the Master had chained the offender up with the colony of vampire bats he had on the grounds, sealing the cave so that the bats eventually drained the man's blood.

Yet another version postulated that the Master had dressed the guy up as Batman and shoved him off the roof of the mansion.

The version that seemed most likely to One involved the massive movie theater in the east wing. The offending slave had been chained to a seat. Every night, the Master came in and sat beside the slave to watch a movie. They started with the first Batman movie, starring Adam West and Burt Ward. The Master talked over the movie, explaining in detail why Batman was a terrible hero and who could beat him in a fight. They then moved on to the 1989 Batman film with Michael Keaton and Jack Nicholson.

They continued nightly, moving through the films in sequential order. The Master deconstructed each film from top to bottom, leaving no inconsistency untouched and no special effect unscrutinized. Between the films, while the slave was chained up alone in the theater, the various Batman shows, both live-action and cartoon, played on repeat.

For his part, the slave made a valiant effort of it. Or so the story went. Random pieces of popcorn the Master offered him comprised the entirety of his sustenance. He would beg the Master to stop every night, and every night he would receive little electric shocks to keep him awake, listening to the man beside him drone on and on.

Finally, in the middle of *The Dark Knight Rises*, the slave managed to break his own neck by whipping his head violently back and forth, using the back of his seat as a leverage point to end his life.

While the slave was in the process of killing himself, the Master apparently said, "It's bad, but it's not *that* bad. We haven't even got to *Batman v Superman*."

These stories, whether true or not, served as a reminder for One. A reminder to keep his mouth shut and do his job. And to never, ever mention Batman. He thought about these tales of woe every time he entered the study to fetch the Master.

Presently, One brought his gaze from the fireplace to the chair. He'd heard no answer to his initial insistence.

"Master?" he said tentatively as he rounded toward the front of the chair. The Master's skinny legs were splayed out in front of him, his blood-red satin pajama bottoms shining with reflected firelight. Upon his lap lay a book. One of the Master's slender, pale fingers bisected the pages. One chanced a look at the Master's face, something he wouldn't have done had he not been certain that the man was asleep. Sure enough, his eyes were closed under a smooth forehead and black widow's peak.

One stared for a minute, taking the opportunity to study a face he only ever saw in quick glances; Master didn't like his slaves looking him in the eyes. The man's long face, wide nose, pronounced cheekbones, and fragile lips spoke to excellent breeding. His upper body bulged in the satin pajama top, his biceps and shoulders close to stressing the fabric.

A log in the fire crackled behind him and One jumped slightly, coming out of his hunch, and looking behind him for a second. He looked back at the Master, whose violet orbs were open, staring into One's hazel eyes. The slave quickly looked down at the floor and settled into his practiced hunch.

"Master," he said to the expensive rug underneath his feet. "You need to see this."

"How long have you been standing there, One?" The Master didn't sound mad as he said this, but it was hard to tell. His nasally effeminate voice was often without emotion.

"Not long, Master. I spoke when I first came into the room but received no answer. So, I came around to wake you."

Master set his book down on the side table and stretched his muscular arms up before rising to his full six-and-a-half feet. One limped toward the door to the study and paused, waiting for the Master to come up behind him before continuing.

"This better be good, One. I was having a great dream. Is the field trip ready, yet, by the way?"

"Not yet, Master. Tomorrow, it will be ready. Tomorrow. But I think your plans may change after you see this." One smiled as he walked, leading the way. He heard the Master stop.

"Really?" the tall man said, his voice hopeful like One had never heard it.

One half-turned and looked back at the man's knees. "Yes, Master. I think we may have found what you're looking for." One turned back around and dragged his left foot down the hall a little way. Ornate stone walls bordered the hallway. A runner traversed the length of the hall, its design a match for the rug in the study. Flickering fake torches lined the walls, providing de facto illumination to the area. Hidden track lighting did the bulk of the work, shining inconspicuously out from recesses in the floor and ceiling.

One stepped up to an electronic screen mounted in the stone wall exactly 25 feet from the doorway to the study. The Master would have no electronics any closer to his sanctuary than that. With practiced fingers, the hunched slave swiped and tapped the screen in the wall, bringing up a frozen image with a play symbol in the middle. The Master squared his shoulders to the screen and put his hands behind his back. One pressed the white triangle in the middle of the screen and the frozen image started moving. The slave stepped aside. He'd already watched it. Numerous times.

The footage was colorless, grainy, and shot from a vertiginous angle. It was clear that the camera capturing it was located on the top of a three- or four-story building. Nearly all of the picture was filled by a sea of writhing bodies. Zombies. Hundreds of them—maybe over a thousand. At the left side of the screen was a slim patch of road, the edge of the zombie horde.

One glanced at the Master's face quickly, seeing no change. Nor did he expect to. Not yet. Something happened on the screen and One turned to watch it, if only to try and see it through the Master's eyes, to feel what he was about to feel. To share the experience.

A pale man took two lunging steps onto the screen and fell near the edge of the zombies as something hit him. The Master sucked in breath as a huge and strangely muscled thing came into view, approaching the man on the ground. It looked like this thing—this monster—had a pole through its chest and was carrying a slender piece of metal. Part of a street sign, One had surmised after studying the footage.

Another figure—a woman—materialized and was quickly dispatched by the muscular being, her head chopped off by the hurled street sign. Then there were suddenly men and women running through the frame as the muscular thing chased the pale man into the crowd of zombies. These men and women moved impossibly fast. They were agile and strong and driven. The zombies seemed to pay them no mind as the figures threw pouches of dark liquid onto the giant.

The Master stepped toward the wall, his eyes wide and his hands coming up to rest on the stone to either side of the screen. One smiled.

The rest of the footage played out. The zombies attacked the giant. It looked like he was finished, but then he jumped out of the crowd, torn to pieces but still clearly incredibly strong. Then he was gone. Off-camera. The screen went black and a second later the first frame appeared again, the play button sitting in the middle of the screen.

"Is there any more? Did you see what happened after that? Were there any more cameras in the area?"

"No, Master. No more cameras in the area. Not aiming at the rooftop. But I have people going over footage from that city right now. Looking for these . . . beings."

The Master laughed and looked into One's eyes, the joy shining out from him and directly into the slave. "It worked! It worked! I've done it." The laughter fell out of the tall man's mouth as if it had been building there for years, waiting to escape.

"How old is this footage?" he asked One when he finally caught a breath.

"Nearly three weeks Master. This wasn't one of our likely targets, so we didn't prioritize it."

"No matter. No matter," The Master said, waving a hand at One. "There were so many of them. I'm sure they're still alive. They must be. That giant . . . thing, whatever it was, may not be. But that doesn't really matter. It was ugly. No, no, no. What matters is that I've done it. It worked. I *knew* it. Vampires are *real*." The Master paused, seeming to revel in those three words for a long moment. "And I know where to find them."

CHAPTER FIVE

YOU GOT SOME 'SPLAININ TO DO

D etective Kurt Weller, now dressed in T-shirt and sweatpants, paced back and forth in his living room, flexing his sore left hand, waiting for Ricardo to return. The vampire's nonchalance had rubbed off on him, but after the fiend had left, Weller's hamster wheel of a mind started turning and turning. He looked at his Sig, hanging in his shoulder holster on the back of a dining room chair. Then he looked down at his right arm, willing it to heal so he could take this damn cast off. And so he could stop feeling so . . . useless.

The darting figure he had seen began to worry him more with every tick of the clock. Anything that could punch a dent in a vampire's chest wasn't to be taken lightly. The safe zone was precarious enough as it was. The last thing the city needed was some kind of smart zombie running around. Modern weaponry could only do so much. Weller recalled shooting Merek, and how it had been about as effective as throwing a pebble.

Weller kept pacing, trying and failing to keep his blood pressure down. He felt sick to his stomach. Not for the first time, he thought about Direk. It had only been two and a half weeks since the vampire had left the city and the detective already missed him. They had formed some small amount of trust during their time together, and Weller wasn't ready to extend that same courtesy to the other vamps in the Underground, although he realized with some surprise that he trusted the vamps more than 99% of the humans he knew. At least, ever since they had eliminated the tyrants that had been running their little society before the world ended.

Knowing he wouldn't be able to sleep, Weller changed into one of his many khaki suits. He draped the jacket over a chair in the kitchen, as was his habit. He stepped to the bathroom and looked in the mirror, straightening his black tie, and noting the bags under his eyes. He ran a hand across the minuscule stubble on his head, cheeks, and chin. He didn't have the energy to shave any part of his head, so he washed his face and headed back to wear out the carpet in his living room.

Darkness still reigned supreme outside and would for a few more hours. Still, he grabbed and donned his shoulder holster, the weight of his pistol under his left armpit doing little to put him at ease, as it had so many times in the past. He walked to the front window and glanced at the street below as he put his suit jacket on to complete the ensemble. There was a figure standing in the middle of the road, seeming to stare at his apartment window. At first, it didn't register, and Weller's eyes swept up the street. Then they went wide, and he looked quickly back to the area where the figure had been.

Nothing.

The figure was gone. Disappeared like some wraith in the—movement directly below caught his attention. He leaned his forehead against the window to look down. There was a small, redheaded man dressed in a plaid shirt and jeans trying and failing to hide among the small bushes that lined the front of the apartment building.

"Holy shit. Buck?" Weller said.

The man looked up as if in response, the dumbfounded look on his face unmistakable. Sure enough, it was Buck. A man—or thing, rather—that Weller had assumed was dead. Killed by Merek after Weller had dragged Buck out of bed to help him find the monster. He'd felt bad about it, he really had. But, then again, Buck tried to eat him the first time they'd met, so he didn't really beat himself up about it. Buck was some sort of alcoholic zombie-vampire hybrid. To be clear, he was an alcoholic before he'd been turned. Couldn't blame that on the apocalypse.

Presently, Buck's face changed, the dumbfounded look turning to one of pure anger. His mouth moved, but Weller couldn't make out the words. Weller gestured with his index finger, mouthing the words, "Wait one," before stepping back from the window. In all honesty, he was glad to see that Buck was alive, if only because it took his death off Weller's conscience. He stepped out the front door for the second time that night and walked down the stairs.

Buck was standing in the middle of the street when Weller stepped outside into the pleasant night. Weller opened his mouth to speak a greeting, knowing he had to tread softly. It was clear Buck was mad at him. Before he could speak, Buck yelled, "Don't you fucking speak to me. Not until I've had my say."

Weller shut his mouth. He couldn't blame the little guy. Technically, he had gotten him killed—or at least maimed. But the redheaded man looked no worse for wear. His clothes were a little torn and bloody, but otherwise, he looked fine.

It looked as if Buck was about to speak, but instead, he turned and looked down the dark street. Weller followed his gaze and saw two figures running straight toward him on the sidewalk. And coming fast.

Weller stepped off the sidewalk, keeping his eyes on the fast-approaching figures. He pulled his pistol out of his holster with his right hand, wincing as pain shot up his forearm. Buck moved, causing Weller to glance his way. He was no longer standing where he had been. Weller turned his head more and saw the small man receding in the middle distance, running away from Weller and whatever was coming to greet him.

By now the slapping footsteps were close, so Weller turned his attention back to the figures. They were close enough for Weller to see that it was Ricardo chasing a weird-looking zombie. The thing looked like it had been born of a man who had died from a steroid overdose. Its skin, mottled blue, gray, and green, stretched over bulging and pulsing muscles. Although it was clearly a zombie, the look on its face wasn't blank like those of its brethren. It was a twisted sneer of effort as it ran away from Ricardo.

Ricardo, for his part, looked like he was running a marathon. He wasn't sweating, but he looked about at his limit. "Shoot it," Ricardo said as they closed the distance. The zombie shifted its eyes to Weller and then changed direction, heading straight for the detective.

"Oh, shit," he said.

"Oh, shit," Ricardo said.

The zombie said nothing, but its intentions were clear.

Weller brought his Sig up and pulled the trigger, catching the zombie in the chest, which was his intended target. He wanted to slow the thing down so he could shoot it in the head. It kept coming.

"Move!" Weller yelled at Ricardo, who had followed and was directly behind the zombie. The vampire veered off to get out of the line of fire. Weller opened up even as he backpedaled to keep some room between him and the zombie. It took all his bullets to put the thing down, even with several headshots. The zombie collapsed and slid to a messy stop at Weller's feet, its head mostly gone.

Ricardo slowed to a stop nearby.

The detective and the vampire looked at each other.

"You got some 'splainin to do," Weller said, mostly because he'd been wanting to say it since he'd met Ricardo, but also because he wanted to know what the fuck he just killed. It was no regular zombie, that was sure.

"I didn't do this," Ricardo said, bringing his palms up.

"First we get super rats dragging pizza around, and now a super zombie. I don't like this. At least we got him."

Ricardo made a face.

"What?" Weller asked.

"Well, you're not going to like this either," Ricardo began. "That's not the same one that punched me. I just stumbled across this one while I was looking for the other one."

"You're shitting me."

Ricardo shook his head. "And . . ."

"And what? There's more?"

"Yeah. You see, this isn't the only one I stumbled across. There were several more. Like six more. They scattered when I came up on them. They all looked . . . Weird . . . Like this one."

Weller stared at Ricardo, his mouth open.

"Oh, yeah," Ricardo continued. "And I think I recognized one of them."

CHAPTER SIX

NOTHING MORE TO SAY

T he teenager formerly known as Dipshit stared with wide eyes and stirring loins at the women. He could no more help these reactions than he could throw a grown man into a china cabinet. It was no use trying.

They were in the living room, a camping lantern on the coffee table, illuminating the four barely dressed women and one teenage boy.

It was clear that these women had bonded during their experience. Only two of them, Rachel and Dena, had known each other before the end of the world. In fact, the way they embraced and kissed after the whole ordeal in the basement told Fred that they were very well acquainted. This scene was a major factor contributing to the awakening of a certain part of the boy's anatomy. Luckily, there was a couch nearby, to which Fred walked awkwardly. He sat down and grabbed a throw pillow, which he slammed on his crotch as if to smother the thing currently seeking escape from his pants. Shame flooded the boy and began to war with his hormones in an unwinnable battle.

It became clear that the other two women, Sharon and Shirley, had lost their husbands to the apocalypse. Sharon's husband had been bitten by a walker, while Shirley's had been killed by God and his crew—the God that lay dead in the basement, not the other one, although He may have had something to do with it. Shirley had lost her only child years before to a car accident. Sharon never had children.

Now, all the women had was each other. And for the time being, they decided to stay at the farmhouse. It was defensible and there was plenty of land on which to plant food and hunt. They didn't pay Fred much mind except to throw inscrutable looks his way from time to time.

They didn't talk about Diirek at all, and Fred hadn't seen him since he'd left the basement. The fact that the pale man had done the impossible by ripping those concrete anchors out of the wall didn't seem to matter to them. They were free, and their captors were all dead. Everything else could be overlooked, apparently.

Fred sat as still as a statue on the couch for what seemed like an hour but was only five or ten minutes. He felt profoundly uncomfortable and wished the women would put on some more clothes so he could stop feeling such. Soon enough, as their rushed conversation and nervous energy began to abate (as the adrenaline slowed to a trickle), Rachel went to find clothes.

Most of the previous owners' clothing had been torched by the rapists that had commandeered the house. As a result, there were no women's clothes there, save the torn tatters the women had been captured wearing. Still, they all dressed in ill-fitting jeans and t-shirts, helping Fred quell his overactive libido for the time being.

The door to the basement opened and five sets of eyes turned to the tall, handsome, pale man stepping out of the darkness. Diirek had God's body over his shoulder. He had put an old trash bag over the man's ruined head to keep from making a mess. He didn't look at any of them as he walked to the front door and opened it to step outside. He came back half a minute later and headed to Scorpion and Dementor's bodies.

When he reached them, in the adjacent dining area, he stepped back to the living room.

"Did you shoot them in the head?" he asked Fred.

The boy nodded. "While you all were in the basement. I didn't want them coming back."

Diirek dipped his head slightly and gathered Scorpion up, walking the corpse to the nearby broken window. He tossed the dead man out like he weighed nearly nothing, and then proceeded to do the same with Dementor's body.

All five people watched this process, curious. Diirek tracked through the living room again, and walked out the front door, shutting it behind him.

Fred looked at the women, who all looked back at him, faces unreadable. He removed the pillow from his lap, stood up, and headed out the front door, grabbing his rifle on the way.

"Hey," the boy said, catching up to Diirek, who was carrying God's body around to the back of the house. Diirek looked at him but didn't say anything.

"So . . . how come you're so strong?"

Nothing.

"Where'd you come from? I lived in a little town east of here about thirty miles. But I was out riding my bike when the bombs started falling. I was riding to town to drive my dad back from the bar in his truck. I don't have a permit or anything, I just learned on my own. Anyway, I was almost there when the bomb fell. It knocked me clean off. Like I was just a leaf in a stiff breeze." Fred didn't know why, but he couldn't help himself from talking. Maybe it was the fact that nearly every time he'd talked to any of the men that now lay dead in the backyard, they told him to shut up either with their hands or their words. He'd always been kind of a talker, just never really had anyone to talk to. His had been a lonely life even before the apocalypse.

Diirek looked at him, then turned his attention back to the task at hand, which was searching through the dead men's pockets.

Fred continued. "So I knew my dad was dead, then, because he was at the bar when it happened, and the bar was right in the middle of town." The boy paused, waiting for Diirek to speak. He didn't.

"Well, my mom, she died in a car accident when I was no bigger than a pup. That's what my dad used to say, anyway. Before he started drinkin' and turned mean. I don't remember her at all. Although I think I see her in my dreams from time to time." What Fred didn't say was that it wasn't dreams in which he saw his mother. It was nightmares.

A moan sounded from far off in the yard and Fred raised his rifle, squinting into the dark and breathing fast. Diirek stood up, put a gloved hand to the rifle barrel, and pushed it gently toward the ground.

"It is just Sicko," Diirek said. "I will get him. Stay here."

Fred noticed a faint accent as Diirek talked, and he found it funny the way he pronounced every part of the words he spoke. The pale man started toward the back of the yard, and the boy followed, ignoring the man's command.

"The way his neck folded back, that was wild. You did that on purpose?"

Diirek glanced back. Something in his eyes made Fred cease his speaking.

They came upon Sicko, who had somehow managed to stand up in the middle of the two rows of barbed wire. The man's head was hanging loosely between his shoulder blades. He was trying to walk out of the barbed wire that had snagged him.

Diirek walked up and reached over the wire. He grasped Sicko's shoulders and turned him, so the lolling head was facing him. The cloudy eyes went wide, and another moan issued from the badly damaged vocal cords. The pale man grabbed the head in both hands and yanked down and back. A crunching, tearing sound made Fred grimace.

The movement pulled Sicko's body with it, which ended up on its back near Diirek's feet, half in and half out of the barbed wire. A stubborn bundle of tendons or nerves still connected the head with the body, but another swift yank took care of that.

Diirek set the head on the ground much like Fred had seen his father do with an empty beer can. The pale man lifted his right foot up and brought it down on the top of the head, which exploded outwards with the impact. Fred looked down at his shoe to see one of Sicko's ears resting there, as if ready to listen in death in a way that he never had in life. The boy kicked it off. There was nothing to say to Sicko or any of the other men. Diirek had said it all.

The duo walked back to the other three bodies. After Diirek searched each of them, he grabbed them by the legs, spun around a few times, and launched them into the darkness past the back fence.

Fred watched in amazement.

Finished, Diirek headed back toward the front of the house, uncovering and checking a watch as he did so. Something suddenly occurred to the boy as he followed.

"Did you ever fight a werewolf?" he asked. Diirek stopped. So did Fred, two paces behind him. Slowly, the pale man turned to face Fred.

"What did you say?"

"A werewolf. Did you ever fight one?"

"There is no such thing as a werewolf," Diirek said, but he didn't look sure.

"There is now. I saw two of them before I found this place. They were fast. And big." Fred looked at the bit of blood on his shoe, leftover from Sicko's ear. "I bet you could take them, though. The other guys, they didn't believe me. But I'm sure. I can even show you where I saw them."

Diirek looked stunned. His pale face seemed to grow even paler. Finally, almost inaudibly, he said, "I knew it."

Chapter Seven

GETTING GRAY MATTER TO MATTER

"Everything is shit. I need a vacation," Weller said, his mind trying and failing to get into gear. His thoughts were scattered and unfocused. *I need some goddamn sleep*, he thought, before an incessant jingle barged into and took over his gray matter.

"You're weird," Ricardo replied, licking a blood mustache from his upper lip. They were back in Weller's apartment for the second time in two hours, and the vampire was enjoying a mug of blood, given reluctantly by the detective after saying, once again, that it wouldn't become a habit.

"So," Weller began after collecting himself. "Your theory is that all those zombies that ate Merek have somehow absorbed his power. And you think this because you recognized one of the buff, discolored zombies when you stumbled on a group of them. Do I have that right?"

Ricardo, who was in the middle of an orgasmic draft of blood, finished up, smacked his lips, and released a contented sigh before speaking.

"Wow, you're some detective. You remembered what I told you thirty seconds ago and repeated it back to me using different words. I'm in awe of your powers."

"Everything is shit," Weller said again, pointing a finger at Ricardo.

"You said that already."

Weller paced while Ricardo rinsed his mug at the sink. "You know, considering the world got blown up, it's amazing that we have power and running water," the vampire said. "It's almost like they missed us on purpose. And the fact that there are cameras still working in the outskirts is weird. I just noticed that the other day. Why do you think that is when the rest of the outskirts doesn't have any power?"

The detective continued pacing, ignoring the blood-drinking fiend. Ricardo sat down at the second-hand dining room table and stared at Weller.

"Shit, shit, shit, shit." The detective stopped pacing and stared into space.

"What now? Do you have a plan yet?"

"I can't remember the name of this goddamn song. It's bottling my mind."

"Did you just say bottling—"

"Fine, I'll do just a little bit of coke." Weller made this declaration apropos of nothing and stomped to his bedroom.

"Uh, what?" Ricardo asked the empty room.

Weller returned shortly with a sandwich bag full of coke, smacking it down on the table.

"Holy crack, man. Should I call you Carlito? Or maybe Tony Montoya? Eh? Maybe 'American Gangster'? No, that was heroin. I can't think of any movies about black coke dealers."

Weller looked at the vampire, whose eyes were shining, while he gathered supplies on the table. "Can you even get high?" he asked when it was clear that Ricardo was all but snorting lines with his eyes.

"Pssshhh. I can get higher than you. The last time I did coke was in the 80s—the 1880s, that is."

"Yeah, I get it, you're fucking old. Now shut up and snort some drugs. I gotta figure out what the hell this song is. Then I can focus on everything else." Weller handed the vampire a rolled-up hundred-dollar bill that was now only good for snorting coke since money was on hiatus and wouldn't be back soon.

The vampire arranged and subsequently inhaled through his nose a thick line of the white-yellow powder and handed the makeshift straw back to Weller, who did the same.

Much like Ricardo had done with the blood, Weller now did as the coke hit his bloodstream. "Ahhhhhh," he said, leaning his chair back onto two legs and closing his eyes. He waited for his brain to start working as he knew it could. Pale neon ghosts floated across the backs of his eyelids. A song started playing again, in his head.

"Fuck you," the irate detective said, slamming his chair down and opening his eyes.

"I didn't even say anything," Ricardo said.

"Not you. Me. Fuck me. Hey, do you know what song this is—" As Weller opened his mouth to start singing the melody, a brick smashed through his window and embedded itself in the drywall with a thunk.

Weller moved almost as fast as Ricardo, who made it out the front door first, nearly pulling the barrier off its hinges as he yanked it open. The two men ran down the stairs, Weller with his gun in hand, Ricardo moving with a dangerous fluidity that only vampires and jungle cats possess. Both men were high as hell.

Ricardo stopped on the sidewalk. Weller, coming out behind him, didn't see anything at first. He stood a little way behind the vampire and looked left, then right.

"Detective!" a familiar voice yelled from what seemed like straight ahead. Weller stepped one pace to the right, and Buck became visible, his body previously hidden by Ricardo and the angle at which Weller had been standing.

Buck's fists were clenched, his jaw set under his scruffy red beard. Ricardo looked back at Weller with a question that seemed to say, "Who the hell is this little dude?"

Weller had been expecting to see at least one buff blue-green zombie, but here was Buck, looking like an angry child. Relief poured into the detective's exhausted mind and he started laughing. He couldn't help himself. The drugs and the lack of sleep and the whole apocalypse crowded in on him and he laughed harder. Although it sounded like a laugh of joy, Weller felt no joy as he cackled. It was as if he were standing outside his body, watching himself, out of control and powerless.

For whatever reason (probably the drugs), Ricardo started laughing, too. Pretty soon they were both doubled over, cackling like coked-up hyenas. Finally, after what seemed like a week, Weller managed to get himself under control.

"Bu—Buck. I—I'm sorry, man," he said between exhalations of dying laughter. He cleared his tear-filled eyes and looked at where the small man had been standing in the street. He was gone.

"Buck? Where'd you go? Hey, listen, I wasn't laughing at you." He spun around slowly, looking for the strange little guy.

"Wow, that guy's funny," Ricardo said, holding his abs. "I haven't laughed like that since the 90s—the 1890s, that is."

Weller shook his head, no longer laughing. "I hate you."

CHAPTER EIGHT

GOOD ZOMBIE

B uck stalked through the safe zone, his fists still bunched, his fingers piercing the skin of his palms and assaulting the tendons underneath. Weller and the other man's laughter echoed through his head, causing him to see only red. When he'd showed up the first time, all he wanted was an apology from the man for getting him killed. Maybe throw a couple of f-bombs the detective's way. Mostly, he wanted to know that Weller felt guilty about leading him to die at the hands of that freak Merek. Then those figures had come running up and Weller pulled out his gun . . . that was when the voice that wasn't really a voice told Buck to go. It seemed to tell him to bide his time.

The brick through Weller's window felt good, but that feeling hadn't lasted. They laughed at him. They laughed and laughed, bringing Buck back to his youth. The runt of the litter, he'd grown up with two older half-sisters and a little half-brother who was much bigger than him since Buck had been nine and his brother, Bobby, seven. He'd gotten it from all sides. Always getting picked on and laughed at. Even his stepdad joined in.

He thought of his friend Charlie, who wasn't much bigger than himself. It seemed like Charlie was the only one who never picked on him. And Buck hadn't even gone to see his old pal yet. Surely, he would be worried. After all, Buck had been gone for a while, eating pigeons, and slowly regaining his strength—and his sanity—in that concrete dome on the Paredo building.

Then that guy with the sniper rifle had stumbled upon the roof to provide him with a real meal. His body finally fully healed after that savory snack. And the first thing he did was find out where the detective lived. Never mind that he had to torture a police officer to do it. And once the torturing was done, he didn't really have much of a choice; he had to eat the guy. Before that meal, he was thinking about killing Weller for what he'd done. But once he was full, he felt some of his anger toward the detective draining away. On his way, he'd decided that a guilty look and an apology were all he wanted from the man. He felt bad about killing that cop, no matter how good he tasted.

Now, as he strode stiffly along, he decided that he'd misjudged the detective. He wasn't a nice guy. Not at all. He was a bully, and he'd have to pay dearly for what he'd done. And that strange, somehow familiar voice had a plan forming. He (that voice was his, wasn't it?) wanted the detective to feel the kind of pain and hopelessness that Buck felt as he lay twisted and broken and waiting to die in that concrete dome.

It occurred to him that maybe he couldn't die. Maybe whatever had happened to him in the outskirts with the strange, blood-sucking woman and the zombie, made him immortal. Even if that was the case, it didn't change anything. He could still feel pain and he still had feelings that could be hurt. Mostly, he had a new kind of drive growing inside of him. An ambition that was somehow tied to the hunger he felt nearly all the time now, except for when he was really full. Like, just-ate-two-humans full.

He'd feed both the hunger and the drive, starting with Detective Kurt Weller.

Something darted in front of Buck and he raised eyes that had previously been counting cracks in the sidewalk. He was nearing the apartment he shared with Charlie in a part of the safe zone that was mostly low-rent housing, check-cashing businesses, and overpriced bodegas, all of which had been closed since the end of the world began.

Buck turned his head slowly. His gaze landed on a large grayish woman standing in front of a smashed storefront, staring at him. Her eyes were cloudy, her lips were missing, and she carried a severed arm in one hand. Her turquoise Muumuu was stained purple with fresh and dried blood down the front.

Buck stopped walking. The two undead anomalies stared at each other. Slowly, without so much as blinking her eyes, the woman brought the arm to her lipless mouth and crunched on bicep.

Buck's mouth began to water. He was getting hungry again.

In an uncharacteristically aggressive move, he charged the dead woman. He didn't need that arm. He didn't even want it. He could find fresh meat easily enough in the outskirts. What he wanted was a fight. He wanted to test his relatively new skills. It seemed that the weeks he had spent in unutterable pain, eating pigeons to regain his strength, had changed him somehow. Had unlocked something in him. As if a "fucks" switch had been thrown. And now, with that switch off, he gave no fucks whatsoever. Now was the time to find out what he was worth. It was practice for when he faced that asshole detective.

He moved fast, feeling like rushing water from a faulty dam bearing down on an unsuspecting village. His confidence grew with every step as the obese zombie simply stared at him, her eyes unchanged. When he was about a foot away, the zombie smacked him hard across the face with the severed arm. He stumbled and slammed into the brick wall next to a broken window. He felt a blow to the back of his head. Letting himself fall to the ground, he scrambled away, trying to ward off the meaty blows the dead woman kept heaving.

Finally, he managed to get far enough away to stand up and face his attacker. She tried to hit him again, but this time Buck snatched the arm away. The woman's thick eyebrows came together, and her nostrils flared. She made a guttural noise not unlike that of other zombies. But this was no ordinary walking dead, that much was clear to Buck.

The woman came at him, reaching for the arm.

"No!" he said, jumping back to keep the limb out of reach. The zombie stopped and looked at him with a slight tilt of the head.

What the hell? Buck thought. *Did she just respond to a command?*

She shot her bulk at him again, surprisingly fast.

"No!" Buck yelled again. She kept coming. He jumped away from her and planted his feet. When she came close, he lifted his foot and kicked her in the midsection. He foresaw her flying back onto the sidewalk with the kick, but that didn't happen. His sneaker pierced the rotting flesh underneath her gory Muumuu, his foot sinking up to the ankle in her accumulated fat.

Buck found himself hopping on one foot backward as the woman kept moving forward and reaching for the arm. He held the limb above and behind him as he hopped, unable to get enough leverage to free his foot from the zombie.

"No! No! No!" he said, to no avail. Finally, an idea occurred to Buck. He shoved the flailing arm into her face. She chomped down and stopped moving all at once. Buck wasn't ready for it, and a backward hop freed his foot from her bulk (a sensation that felt much like freeing a shoe from mud) and sent him sprawling onto his back. The arm also came with him, leaving only a small chuck in the dead woman's mouth.

Expecting her to charge him again, he got quickly to his feet and readied himself for the bulky, swaying onslaught. She stayed where she was, chewing the meat, looking at him. Buck tore a chunk from the arm with his fingers and returned his attention to the chewing woman. She stopped moving her jaw, swallowed, and then came toward him again. Buck held up the chunk, hiding the rest of the arm behind his back.

"No!" he said. The woman stopped and looked at the bloody piece of flesh in Buck's raised hand. Her eyes, those of an imperfect white marble, shifted from his face to his hand. He threw the chunk gently to the woman, who caught it in cupped hands and proceeded to gobble it up. When she was done, she returned her attention to Buck's face. She made no move.

"Good zombie," Buck said, and smiled.

CHAPTER NINE

GO WEST, YOUNG MAN

F red looked expectantly at Diirek, who gazed off into the night, thinking hard. The teenager had just finished his recounting of the werewolf spotting, and he was just waiting for Diirek to tell him to pack his things. *Get your stuff together. Bring your rifle. I'll need all the help I can get,* Diirek said in Fred's head, sounding a lot like Liam Neeson for some reason.

After a moment, Diirek turned away from Fred and walked back to the house without a word, leaving the boy crestfallen. Fred walked to the front porch and sat down, a furious mixture of rejection and sadness bubbling in his stomach. Fred stayed on the porch, listening to the bass rumble of Diirek's voice and the less-audible treble that arose when one of the women was talking. Pretty soon there was no more bass rumble but hope still crowded into Fred's thoughts.

He'll come back for me, Fred thought. But he also thought that Diirek had no reason to want his help with anything. He was just a kid, after all. A kid that hadn't even known what was happening right under his nose. Besides, Diirek probably already had a bunch of friends just like him. Friends that didn't need looking after.

After several minutes of self-talk, Fred went back inside to find Diirek. Rachel and Dena were busy cleaning the kitchen when Fred walked in.

"Where's Diirek?" he asked in a shrill voice.

"I don't know," Dena said. "But he's not here."

Rachel continued cleaning without a glance toward Fred.

Fighting the urge to cry, Fred stood there on the edge of the kitchen before gathering his ratty sleeping bag and heading outside to the porch. *Just a stupid, weak kid*, he thought. *I wouldn't want me around, either.*

Still, he felt a strong connection with the pale, mysterious man. A feeling that was clearly not reciprocated. He didn't exactly understand why this was. At seventeen, Fred didn't understand why much of anything was the way it was. But he did know a strong, capable role model when he saw one. Even if that role model happened to be very good at killing people.

Diirek was the type of guy you needed in the apocalypse. The kind of guy you needed *to be*.

Fred hadn't cried after the bomb fell on his little town and killed his dad and everyone he'd ever known, even though he'd felt like it. And he wouldn't let himself cry now, no matter how much he wanted to. He curled up in a ball on the hard planks of the porch, his sleeping bag bunched around him, and tried to sleep. At some point, he drifted off.

It was still dark when Dena came outside and shook him awake. She brought him inside and placed him on the couch. She told him he couldn't stay here past tonight, but she said it with sadness in her eyes. Half asleep, Fred nodded.

"We'll figure out what to do with you tomorrow," she said. "We just can't be around men for a while. I'm sorry Fred."

When he woke up in the early afternoon, he wasn't sure if the interaction had been a dream or not. The fact that he was on the couch was a good indication that it had been real. Either way, it didn't matter. He knew he couldn't stay. He'd known it since he saw the women chained up in the basement. It was not a place for him. It would have been the same whether the women decided to stay in the farmhouse or not.

Dena made him some food when he awoke. She gave him supplies, saw that he had bullets for his .22 rifle, water for a few days, and food for about a week. The other three women stayed in the master bedroom. Fred imagined that they were jumping on the bed in their underwear, hitting each other with pillows, like in the movies his dad used to watch. He knew this wasn't true, but he hoped they could smile and laugh and jump around sometime soon. He wanted that for himself, too.

The sun was low when Dena escorted him onto the porch, his narrow shoulders supporting a large backpack loaded with supplies.

"Thank you, Fred," Dena said to him, her short brown bangs hanging just over her pale green eyes. "And I'm sorry. From all of us . . . Be careful."

Fred nodded, unable to meet her eyes, and then stepped off the porch without a single idea where he was to go. He opened the front gate, causing a bell to ring inside the house. Otherwise, he heard no noise as he walked away. It was a house full of ghosts.

The dirt driveway was a quarter-mile long, and Fred took his time, feeling every single inch of it as a black hopelessness settled on him. The pack grew heavier with every step, and he took solace in the fact that he could end his life if it got bad enough. He at least had *that* power.

The road he came to at the end of the driveway was a slightly darker hue of dirt. Sweating, Fred swung his pack off and set it in the long grass in the armpit of the T that the intersection made. He saw no walkers anywhere, but he still held onto his rifle as he watched the sunset fade away at the dirt road's western terminus. Left or right. East or west. Left—east—was back in the direction he'd come. It was in that direction that he'd seen the werewolves. So there was really no choice at all; west it was.

Fred drank some water, ate a carrot, and swung his pack reluctantly onto his shoulder for the long trudge after the sun. The stars crept out behind him, winking at his plight, shining limited light on the dusty road. A slice of moon floated up out of the eastern horizon, adding a bit of light to help the stars.

A bright star bounced and wavered behind him. *Great, the stars are falling now*, he thought. More of the same, as far as he was concerned. The star seemed to expand, creating a long shadow in front of him. Engine noise floated on the breeze and Fred realized it was a car coming up behind him. Not a star after all.

He turned around, excited at the prospect of a person he could talk to. Then he thought he should hide. This was the way, after all, that he had come to live at the farm with God and Sicko and Dementor and Scorpion. They had come across him as he was walking down the road.

Fred knew that good people were in short supply—even shorter than before. With the bouncing headlights racing up to him, he found some tall grass at the side of the country road and crouched behind it, not sure if he wanted the vehicle to pass or stop.

It stopped.

It was an old, extended-cab 4-door truck like the kind he'd seen all his life. The kind that farmers and ranchers often drove, worked hard nearly every day of the year.

Fred raised his rifle to his shoulder but kept the barrel pointed near the ground.

"Hello? Young man?" said the darkness inside the cab. It had stopped flush with his hiding spot, brake lights illuminating the cloud of dust slowly overtaking the vehicle. The headlights turned small rocks into long black boulders in the road.

Fred couldn't tell much from the voice, over the idling engine, but it sounded almost like an old aunt he once had.

"I see you there, young man. You're hiding behind all of three weeds. I can see you just fine, and I'm about blind in the dark."

"What do you want? I have a rifle."

"Oh, dear. Aren't you a hard case?" said the darkness. Fred was sure now that it was an old woman's voice.

"Well, I live down the road apiece," the old woman continued. "But I'm awful old to be dealing with this here nonsense. The dead walking around. Some commie bastards bombing us. I tell you, my neighbor Wilfred tried to bite me! And not in a good way.

"Anyway, I saw you walkin' down the road and figured you might be looking for a place to stay. I just come from my church, where they had a bunch of non-perishables for a food drive. No one else is gonna need 'em. Matter of fact, half of them were mine to begin with. I just took 'em back, you see? And—" The woman's voice stopped. Fred waited, teetering between caution and trust.

"Well now," she said. "You've got me ramblin' like an old fool. You see, I could give you a place to stay, you'd just need to help me around the house a bit. I can't move too well anymore. My hips aren't so good. They get stiff near all time of day. I might could talk your ear off, I'll tell you that right now. But if you don't mind that, I may let you get a word in from time to time."

Fred couldn't help but smile. He squinted into the darkness, still unable to see the woman's face.

"Times like these, we got to stick together. It's a mighty lonely world. Especially where I live. My nearest neighbor is a good mile away. That's the one tried to bite me. Wilfred. But he's dead now. Not walkin' dead. Really dead."

Fred stood up, his rifle still held in both hands, but near his thighs now, instead of at his shoulder. "Where do you live?"

"Oh, just down the road apiece. But much as I'd like to, I can't stay here chatting with you all night. I'm afraid this truck noise is gonna attract walkers. Plus, it's getting to be past my bedtime. And I'd like to cook some of this macaroni n' cheese I got from the church before I fall to snorin' in my easy chair."

Fred thought about the carrot he'd eaten not long ago. He compared that taste with the thought of macaroni and cheese. His stomach rumbled. "Okay," he said, finally. "I'll come with you." He stepped out of the weeds and onto the road.

"Good! You're a smart young man. Now put your things in the back seat there."

Fred stepped up to the back passenger-side door of the old truck and opened it. A hand shot out of the dark and grabbed Fred around the neck. Before the boy could react, the powerful hand yanked, slamming his forehead into the roof above the open doorway.

The world wobbled.

The hand pushed him back and then yanked again. Fred turned his head, but the impact was just as vicious.

The world went black.

***

A bright light came on. Fred forced his eyes open. He was lying on the back seat of the truck, the dome light above him illuminating two men, who were both twisted around staring back at him from the front seats. Both men were wiry and dirty, their eyes wild and bloodshot. They were smiling at him. The one in the driver's seat had a single tooth in his mouth. The other one had a full set of teeth, but only in the sense that all the sockets were occupied. The teeth themselves were black and half-rotted. Fred wouldn't have been surprised to see one (or all) of them fall out right then.

The boy tried to move, but he couldn't. He looked down to see that he was taped to the back bench seat with silver duct tape. They must have used a whole roll of the stuff because he was covered from chest to ankles with the strong tape.

"Oh, you're a dumb motherfucker, aren't you, young man? We're gonna have lotsa fun with you, yes we are." The voice was that of an elderly woman, coming from the driver's mouth. It was clearly not his normal voice.

Fred screamed and squirmed in his silver cocoon. The men laughed as they turned around. The toothless one put the vehicle in gear, and they resumed their drive down the dusty road, their new prize secure in the back.

CHAPTER TEN

BURNING BITS

"Vampires ain't real," the single-toothed driver said. "I knew you was dumb, but sheeiiitt, man."

"I'm tellin' you," the passenger said, a blackened glass pipe in his left hand and a butane lighter in his other. "The other day at the train yard with Ricky, I saw one. I saw it come out of the dark and get Ricky. It happened true like I told you."

It sounded to Fred like the passenger was pleading his case.

He had stopped struggling after the first mile or so; it was no use. His head throbbed where it had been slammed into the truck. Every time the vehicle bumped over imperfections in the dirt road, a jolt of pain pulsed through his head. He closed his eyes, trying not to imagine what these disgusting men were going to do with him when they got wherever they were going.

"You told me this story a hundred times now, Slim. I ain't believe it the first time, and I ain't believe it now. You and I both know you'd been up for four or five days at that point, and so had Ricky. You start to see shadow people when you stay up that long."

"That's true," Slim said as he brought the glass pipe to his lips, lit the torch lighter, and applied the blue flame to the underside of the glass orb.

A chemical smell filled the cab, sickly sweet and cloying. Apparently Slim didn't correlate sleepless nights with the meth he was currently smoking.

"Whatever happened that night, it weren't no vampire," the driver said. "He probably got got by some zombies and you just thought it was a vampire. But it weren't. And I don't want to hear no more about it."

Slim blew out a cloud of chemical smoke before speaking. "But, if zombies are real, why can't vampires be real, too? They both come from the same . . . What's the word I'm lookin' for? They both in the same jean-ray. Yeah, that's the word."

"It's genre, you fuckin' idiot. And that don't mean nothin. It's not like all horror movies suddenly come real. What would be the chances of both zombies and vampires coming real? Next thing you know, there'd be werewolves running around during a full moon. And mummies walking around all stiff and dusty and . . . 'Gyptian."

"Yeah, I guess you're right, Cyrus." That seemed to settle things between the two, although Fred wasn't so sure they were right. Not that it mattered. His knowledge was useless, his situation hopeless. If only he wasn't so damn skinny and frail and weak, he could do something. If only he were like Diirek, he could kill these tweakers quicker than his grandma used to snap a chicken's neck for supper.

"You want some of this?" Slim said after taking another cloud of poison into his lungs.

"Hell yes I do," Cyrus said, hitting the brakes and slowing the vehicle quickly.

"Why don't you just keep drivin'? I'll take the wheel and steer for you while you smoke."

"Last time we did that we wrecked that Hummer and damn near kilt ourselves. This shit's rotting your brain. You can't even 'member last week and you think vampires are real. Mother Mary and Van Morrison." Cyrus shook his head as he took the glass pipe and lighter from Slim. The sound of the torch and the crackling drug filled the cab, followed again by the chemical smell. It was starting to make Fred sick.

A thump sounded from the back of the truck; the vehicle rocked slightly on its struts.

"What the hell was that?" Slim asked, fear in his voice as he spun around to look out the back window.

Cyrus looked in the rearview mirror, eyes wide. They saw nothing. Cyrus hit the gas and grabbed the steering wheel with one hand, the other holding the drug paraphernalia.

"Here." As the truck picked up speed, the driver handed the pipe and lighter back to Slim, who stuck his hand out absently, still looking out the back window. The heated glass touched his skin and he yelped, throwing the pipe back toward Cyrus. The hot glass landed between the man's legs. "Ahhh! My bits!" the driver yelled as he felt the heat through his worn jeans. He jerked the steering wheel slightly left and pushed the gas pedal to the floor as he lifted his hips off the seat to stop the burning.

Fred's eyes were wide open at this point, hoping for a crash. Surely he would have a better chance of survival than the two idiots unbuckled in the front.

Something dented the roof straight over the boy's prone body.

Still screaming about his bits (an accurate description), Cyrus couldn't find the pipe. He was distracted briefly by whatever dented the roof, and then he looked out the windshield to see that they were about to run off the road. He jerked the steering wheel clockwise, overcorrecting and causing the truck to head for the opposite side of the road.

A gloved hand punched down through the windshield and grabbed the steering wheel, righting the car. Cyrus and Slim both started screaming. Cyrus lowered his hips to the seat again and tried to yank the hand off the steering wheel. He still had the gas pedal pushed to the floor.

Slim tried to open his door, staring at the hand as he did so. The automatic locks were engaged. Screaming, he rolled down his window and climbed out, headfirst, into the night. His feet slid out the window last, and the back right wheel of the truck went over a large bump directly afterward.

Cyrus continued to scream. He punched and yanked at the hand gripping the steering wheel, but it seemed to be made of pure muscle. It didn't budge at all.

A pale face appeared upside down at the top of the splintered windshield. It glanced into the back seat and then quickly disappeared. A second later, the black-gloved hand yanked the steering wheel counterclockwise and then disappeared. The nose of the truck jerked left, the rear sliding along behind it before the momentum became too much and the vehicle went airborne, spinning through the night and landing on its roof.

It rolled three times, throwing glass, metal, plastic, and a couple of human limbs before coming to a stop.

Chapter Eleven

TOO SMALL FOR BAIT

Weller arrived at police plaza running on zero sleep once again. The sun was yelling at him with its rays, as he made his way, feeling like he was walking through a dream. Since doomsday he'd only been able to grab a handful of hours of sleep—total. And most of those hours had come when he was doped up at the hospital immediately following the ordeal in the outskirts with Merek and the zombie horde. He felt like anyone but himself, and he mostly hated other people, so it was doubly tough on him.

By the time Weller and Ricardo had stopped laughing in the street after Buck tried to flex on him, it was nearing sunrise. Wisely, the men decided to do a little bit more cocaine while Weller sang the tune that was in his head for an increasingly irritated (and irritating) Ricardo. The vampire didn't recognize the notes that Weller sang. To be fair, the detective didn't think he was doing a good job of translating what was in his head to what came out of his mouth. Ever helpful, Ricardo kept saying, "Too bad the internet's dead. We could use Kablam or whatever that app was."

Finally, it was time for the vampire to leave so he wouldn't be caught in the sunrise to cook like a marshmallow tossed into a house fire. Weller proceeded to beat himself up over his failure to do anything at all about the strangely fast zombies he'd seen. But, unlike goddamn vampires, he could operate during daylight hours.

Presently, the glassy-eyed detective sat down at his desk and thought about all he had to do. He was ninety-nine percent sure that Chief of Police William Roan had tried to have him killed a week before destruction rained down from the sky and the dead started walking the globe. So, that was something he had to deal with. Only problem was he didn't know how. He felt like he'd lost his power to think clearly since his injury and his revelation that monsters existed.

Now, he had more monsters to deal with. He just hoped that Ricardo was wrong and there wasn't a whole gang of them.

"Weller? What the hell are you doing?" A harsh voice yelled from behind him. He straightened in his chair to look over the cubicle partition, his eyes landing on the severe face of Captain Shellbourne. He was so out of it that he hadn't noticed the floor was empty. Apparently, there was an important meeting happening. He stood up, his ribs aching and his right arm a dull throb inside the white cast.

"You look like absolute shit. You planning on skipping the meeting? Because that's not a good idea."

"Mmmm," Weller replied. He had probably been wrong about Shellbourne. Not regarding the fact that she was a bad captain and a waste of good oxygen. Those things remained the same. But his assumption that she was the one who set him up was probably wrong. His guess was that she, and Weller's old partner Ray O'Shea, had simply been following orders from on high. They had no idea it was a setup when they convinced Weller to ingratiate himself with a group of dirty patrol cops.

Whatever. He didn't have the energy to think about it now. He barely had the capacity to walk to the little briefing room where the meeting was being held.

Shellbourne kept nagging at him as he walked past, but he had tuned her out already. Slogging into the briefing room, he chose the nearest seat as a dozen or so other detectives remarked on his appearance. He slouched in his seat and closed his eyes. If a bureaucratic briefing couldn't get him to sleep, nothing could. Something occurred to him and he opened his eyes and sat up. He looked to the little raised stage and the pedestal there. Shellbourne hadn't made it in yet. Weller turned to face his colleagues.

"If I fall asleep in here, the person who wakes me up will be fed to the hungry zombies I keep in my bedroom for naughty times. I hope that's clear to everyone, you goddamn savages." Without waiting for affirmation, he turned back around and slunk into his uncomfortable wooden seat.

The sounds around him started to swim and blur with fuzz as consciousness seeped from his exhausted mind. An image of his ex-wife, JayLynn, in purple lingerie floated before his mind's eye. He pushed it away with force. *Not now, brain. Sleep. Not sexy time, sleepy time.*

An image of Merek jumping out of the zombie horde materialized in its place and a frown touched the detective's face.

". . . reports of people who are dressed as zombies attacking people in the safe zone. Three people were killed last night, two attacked in the street—a man and a woman—and one inside his home. All three have been attributed to these suspects."

Weller opened his eyes and sat up as Shellbourne continued the briefing. *Fuck.* It was real. It was happening again. Only this time there was more than one of the monsters. *Maybe the department can handle this one,* he thought. *Maybe I can sit this one out. Or at least not take the whole thing upon my shoulders. JayLynn would like that.*

"What if they're real zombies?" he said, interrupting the captain.

"They're not. According to the reports, they move too fast and are too intelligent to be real zombies, *Detective Weller*." The captain spit his name out with visible disgust. "I know you're our resident deadeyes expert, but unless you know something we don't, we'll continue with the assumption that they're criminals dressing like deadeyes to rob and kill people."

Weller thought about telling the room about Ricardo's hypothesis, but that would mean telling them about the vampires and the monster Merek. And he wasn't so sure he wanted to do that. He had no idea how the police would react. They were used to being the most powerful people around. The toughest gang, so to speak. They wouldn't like to be challenged by a group of twenty or so vampires. Not at all.

"Well," he said. "What are they taking? Are the people missing anything?"

Captain Shellbourne looked down at her notes before speaking. "Not that we know of, but that doesn't necessarily mean anything. People started hiding their valuables when the world started to end."

"And what good are valuables right now, anyway? There's no economy. Food and labor are the only two commodities, and everyone has been getting rations for free and contributing what labor they can, right?"

"Aside from a very small percentage of people, yes. What's your point, Detective?"

"And how are these people being killed? Wait—don't tell me—let me guess. They're being eaten, right?"

Once again, Shellbourne looked down at her notes. She kept her eyes down as she answered. "Yes."

Murmurs filled the room as the rest of the detectives started talking.

"So, you're saying that there's fast, intelligent zombies running around in the safe zone?" a detective asked from the corner of the room.

"I'm saying we need to entertain that possibility, yes," Weller replied.

"What the fuck do you know that we don't? Huh, Weller?" This from a young hotshot detective named Bluxley. "I hear you've been into the outskirts numerous times lately. And you've been seen paling around with some shady individuals. What are you not telling us?"

"It may seem strange to you, Bluxley," Weller said. "But this is what police work looks like. I talk to people. I use my brain to think about things, then I add those things to other things I've thought about. Then, I put forth an idea that can help solve . . . wait for it . . . murder cases. It may seem hard for you, with shit for brains and all."

Some of the other detectives snickered while others outright laughed. No one liked Bluxley. He was an asshole.

"Fuck you, Weller. You shady motherfucker."

"Alright, boys," Shellbourne said. "Let's assume that Weller's correct for a minute. How do we catch these zombies? We already have makeshift police stations on nearly every other corner in the safe zone, so we can't increase manpower. Any suggestions?"

"How about we tie Weller to a light pole and wait?" Bluxley suggested.

"How about I rip Bluxley's dick off and use it as bait?" Weller countered, sure someone would do the rest.

"Because it's too small," said Detective Hardiman, an old friend of Weller's. The room erupted in laughter while Bluxley turned pink in the face. Weller had no sympathy for the man. *You play with vampires, you get bit,* he thought, then realized that he was spending too much time with Ricardo of late.

Shellbourne screamed to quiet everyone down, although Weller thought it was just for show. He'd seen a smirk there somewhere when the joke landed.

"That's enough, goddammit. Now, someone give me a suggestion before I put you all on corpse duty," she said. That got everyone's attention. Corpse duty was essentially waiting around to see if anyone died in the safe zone. A decommissioned police car was set in the middle of each block in the residential areas. When someone died in a household, one of the survivors was supposed to run out to the cop car and honk the horn until the police came running. The cars were left with the windows down for this reason. They had tried it with radios, but it didn't take long for some of them to go missing, or the channels to get switched. So now they used cop cars and horns.

Once the police got there, they essentially just finished the job before the dead person could come back as a zombie. Or, if the person had already come back, they had to eliminate the threat and make sure no one was bitten. People were encouraged to destroy the brain themselves, but not everyone had that in them. In fact, many people didn't. They still saw their husband or wife or grandfather or aunt or neighbor when they looked at the corpse. It was only when the thing got up and started walking around that people snapped out of it.

Corpse Duty was a shit detail, and it went on 24/7. There were a few scientists left in the safe zone, and they were working on a cure or an antidote to keep people from turning when they died, but that seemed to be a long way away. In the meantime, the worst job in the police department was corpse duty.

The detectives preferred that people get the police to deal with their dead because if they didn't, the police had to investigate like it was a homicide. When you encouraged people to smash their dead loved one's heads in, some people thought that they could speed up the process by doing it while the person was still alive. This wasn't a regular occasion, but it had happened a few times in the weeks since doomsday. This was the new normal. Hooray.

Presently, Weller's brain slowly began to turn as he tried to figure out a way to utilize the police force to stop these super zombies. He started to think that Bluxley had a decent idea as far as attracting them with bait.

"Fuckface shitbird is right," Weller said, gesturing at Mr. Shitbird as he spoke. "We need to have bait out in the street for these fuckers. Was there any finesse to these three murders last night? Just smash and grab? Or, smash and eat, rather?"

"A couple walking their dog were assaulted, apparently," Shellbourne said. "Someone saw it from their second-floor window. On the other side of the safe zone, about an hour later, a woman heard her husband yelling at someone from their front window. Then she heard glass breaking and she saw a zombie attacking her husband."

"What did she do? Nothing?"

"She locked her bedroom door and prayed, Weller. Not everyone is as full of testosterone as you are."

Weller ignored the jape. "Alright, here's my suggestion: we have people walking around all night, making a bit of noise, to see what happens. If they're zombies, they'll come running. If they're human, we'll have deterred them for one night. Win-win."

"Great, so what do you suggest if they're not zombies and nothing happens?" Bluxley sneered, fuming from the name-calling.

"Then we can change tactics and look for a small group of dumbass humans. That's easy. That's what some of us have been doing for years. I, for one, don't know shit about the habits of intelligent zombies, do you?"

Bluxley didn't say anything, just sat there looking like a petulant shit-bird.

"Great," Shellbourne said, laying on the sarcasm thick. "Sounds like the only plan we have. Congratulations, Weller. You won't be sleeping tonight. And I need some volunteers. We'll figure out block assignments by this afternoon."

No hands went up.

"Alright. If you're not working on a *current* investigation or up for rotation you will be out there tonight." Shellbourne decreed. "I'd suggested getting some sleep now. Report back here before sundown."

The room filled with groans. Rubber bands, balled up pieces of paper, pencils, and a couple of loose bullets rained down on Weller, who answered back with jubilant middle-fingers and pearly-whites.

***

Weller walked up his block, alternately dragging his feet, clearing his throat, stomping, and smacking light poles to make some noise. It had been dark for two hours and he hadn't seen a thing. After the meeting he had decided to head home and try for some sleep. He managed to get two hours, which was its own kind of miracle.

They didn't have a person for each block of the safe zone, so Weller rounded the corner. He was doing a figure eight around his block and the ones east and west. He had a radio clipped to his belt. All was quiet in the safe zone.

The night was warm; in a few days it would be the official start of summer. Despite the two hours of sleep, he hadn't been able to figure out the name of the song that haunted him. Still, he had managed to do a bit of thinking, but to no real benefit. He still didn't know what to do about Roan, or JayLynn, or the vampires, or these super zombies, if that's what they were. If he were to play kill, marry, fuck, he'd probably have the zombies kill Roan, marry one of the vampires, and fuck JayLynn. He'd already tried marriage with her, and it didn't work out so well. The sex had always been good, though. If only . . .

Plus, there was one Vampire who looked like African royalty, named Binta. *Meeoowww.* And being married to a woman who would never age sounded like a good idea. It would have its drawbacks, sure, like the blood drinking and the allergy to sunlight, but he was willing to entertain the notion. The world had changed, could you blame a guy for changing with—

A pattering noise like footfalls sounded from only a few feet behind Weller. An inhuman growling sound started up close. Really close. Weller whipped around, knowing he wouldn't be fast enough. Whatever it was had managed to sneak up on him. By the time he turned around he had his pistol in hand and a dumb look on his face. Ricardo stared back at him from mere inches away, barely holding in a laugh. Finally, the vampire couldn't hold it anymore and his smooth laughter filled the night air.

"You looked like you were getting ready to die!" he said, doubled over, clearly proud of his results.

Weller hit him with a left uppercut without really thinking about what he was doing. Ricardo's jaw snapped shut and his eyes went wide. Although it was a good shot, especially for Weller's non-dominant hand, it wasn't anywhere close to powerful enough to cause any real damage. Weller growled and grabbed Ricardo by the throat. The vampire's skin was cool to the touch, but otherwise, it felt like a regular human throat. Weller squeezed for a full five seconds before he came to his senses and let go, turning away from Ricardo.

"What the hell, man?" Ricardo asked, rubbing his throat. "You really don't like being surprised, do you?"

Weller shook his head, still looking away. "I—I'm sorry. I—"

"Hey, I get it, man," Ricardo said, interrupting Weller. "You're under a lot of stress lately. I mean, even some of us vamps are freaking out with this whole apocalypse thing. It's not easy for anyone to take."

Weller turned around and fixed his eyes over Ricardo's left shoulder. "It's not the stress . . . Or maybe it is. I don't fucking know, man. I don't know what's wrong with me lately. I'm just so . . . impatient. So pissed off."

"Understandable."

"It's just that, I used to be able to handle anything that came my way, you know? Not to toot my own horn here, but I was a bad motherfucker.

But now . . . Now that things like you—people like you—and things like Merek exist, I might as well be a fucking ant on the goddamn sidewalk. You know what I mean?"

"I think I do, yeah," Ricardo said.

"What would have happened just now if it wasn't you sneaking up on me? What if it had been a super zombie or another Merek? I would be dead without knowing what hit me. I don't even stand a chance. Not anymore."

"Well," Ricardo said, hesitant, "and don't get mad at me for suggesting this, but there's a way that you can level the playing field, right? I mean, I could turn you tonight. It's not hard. You could be a badass again."

Weller shook his head. "That's not even an option."

"Why not? It would solve your problem."

"No. You don't get it. It's not just me, it's everyone. Everyone in this city. Everyone left in the world. All the humans. JayLynn, Berena, my colleagues and coworkers, the people asleep in these buildings. What chance do they stand? What chance do *we* stand? Sure, if I wanted to—which I really don't—I could turn into a vampire, but it wouldn't do much good. It would be like putting a bandage on a slit throat. So what option is there? Turn everyone into a fucking vampire? That's just as bad as letting everyone die. It *is* letting everyone die, in a sense."

Ricardo seemed to consider this for a long moment before shrugging. "You want things to go back to normal, but they can't. The cat's out of Pandora's box. The Necronomicon has been opened and the incantation read. The blood of the virgin has touched the evil artifact. So, you've got two choices. You can give up, or you can fight."

"That's your advice? Give up or fight? Of course I'm going to fight, but I don't even know what I'm fighting anymore. I don't know where to go to find it. I don't even know how to begin to understand my enemy. And I'm the only human that knows what the hell is going on in the city right now. I'm the only one who knows about Merek and your people. And, no offense, but your people haven't been much help."

"Hey, we're working on it. This isn't a fucking picnic for us, either. It's all new territory."

Weller grumbled and turned to walk again. "Well, did you see any more of them tonight? I imagine you've been out looking in the two hours since dark, right?"

"That I have," Ricardo said, walking beside Weller. "But alas, I've only seen plain old run-of-the-mill zombies. This new breed is out there somewhere, though."

"What the hell? Where did you look?"

"Hey, relax, Detective. I've got some mutual friends out looking, too. If they're out and about, we'll find them. Which reminds me, I wish you'd told me about all the foot patrols out tonight. I almost ran into one on the way over here. Wouldn't have been good, that. What with the curfew and all."

"Well, devise a way to get cell phones working again or start being awake during the day, and problem solved."

It was Ricardo's turn to grumble.

"So, who is out looking? Isabelle? Binta?"

Ricardo looked at Weller as they walked. The detective kept his eyes forward, but it did no good.

"Yeah, Binta is out looking. If you want, I can tell her that you think she's pretty. Maybe you guys can meet up after school and share juice boxes."

"Hey, I didn't say anything. I just want to know who's helping so I know who to personally thank later."

"Yeah well don't try to 'personally thank' Isabelle. She may be over one hundred years old, but she's still in a fifteen-year-old's body. We won't abide that."

Weller made a face that said it all.

"Yeah, I didn't really think you were one of those guys."

"Yeah, no. That's mostly a white guy or Catholic priest thing."

The vampire and the detective walked along, keeping somewhat alert. The virgin silence between them moved slowly to pregnancy.

"So, how about we do some blow?" Ricardo asked finally. Weller turned quickly around and started walking away from the vampire.

"Where are you going?"

"To my place," Weller said. "C'mon. This way's faster."

Chapter Twelve

WHAT'S A RENFIELD?

F red's makeshift cocoon held, but he found himself hyperventilating, his chest expanding hard against the tape. Some terrible memory clawed at his subconscious and it was all he could do to keep it away as the truck rocked to a stop in the long grass of the shallow roadside ditch. Somewhere off in the dark a cow mooed as if in response to the violent noises that faded quickly into the night. The roof of the vehicle had been smashed down to within a foot of the boy's face, he realized as the world stopped spinning.

He looked around, his tunnel vision slowly fading. Some of the driver's body was pinned between the smashed roof and the center console in the front. The man's head had been split open by something and it looked like his left arm had been torn off at the elbow. Fred's stomach lurched and the carrot he'd eaten earlier came up. It was only when the vomit traveled directly out of his mouth and to the ceiling that he realized the truck was upside down. Fred began to scream and thrash feebly inside his duct tape prison.

Footsteps crunched glass outside. Fred looked down toward his feet to see the damaged back passenger door disappear in a rush of tearing metal.

He stopped screaming, but he still couldn't breathe. His chest expanded and contracted quickly. A cow mooed. A thunk sounded far off in the distance as the thrown door landed. The cow mooed again. Black-clad legs stepped up to where the door had been previously. The legs bent at the knees, slowly bringing an upside-down torso and face into view.

"You did not stay put as I instructed," Diirek said, his pale face and luminous eyes betraying no emotion.

Everything came together inside Fred in an instant, a combination of teenage rage, regular rage, deep resentment, hormones, testosterone, and whatever dark, terrible memory was clawing at his sanity. "You didn't tell me anything, you—you—you pale jerk! You said all of three words to me last night, and none of them were anything about staying put. And you didn't tell Rachel or Dena anything about it either, so they kicked me out. And then these tweakers picked me up to do who-knows-what with me. Then you almost kill me by flipping the truck!" Fred squirmed as he talked, trying to yell but unable to bring enough air into his lungs in his current position to do so. His face was bright red as he finished, staring down at Diirek.

"I apologize," Diirek said, looking down at the ground. "I have not been myself lately. I really thought I told you that I would come back for you. When the women told me you were gone, I came to find you."

"Why? Why would you come back for me anyway? What do you care about humans? You're a vampire, right?"

Diirek looked at the boy, a hardness coming into his eyes.

"I already know. You might as well just tell me."

Diirek sighed. "Yes. You are right. I am a vampire. And I need your help."

"With the werewolves?"

"No. Well, perhaps. But mostly no. I need your help with something else. I can provide protection and food for you. But I have to be able to trust you." Diirek reached into the truck as he spoke. He grabbed the top strands of duct tape up around Fred's shoulders and yanked, freeing first Fred's shoulders then his hands. "I need someone to help me during the day. Like a Renfield. A familiar."

"What's a Renfield?" Fred asked as he placed his palms against the ceiling, on either side of the orange vomit, bracing himself. "And I barely know you. You're anything but familiar."

"It's kind of like a second-in-command. A trusted partner, almost." The vampire ripped the last of the duct tape off and Fred's feet came down to meet the ceiling of the truck. He crawled backward out of the smashed vehicle and stood up to face Diirek. His rage had gone as fast as it had come. A vampire needed his help. *Freakin' sweet.*

"Okay, you got a deal," the teenager said, extending his hand. Diirek clasped it with his own. Fred could feel the cold strength within the glove the vampire wore.

"Before I can fully trust you, you will have to prove yourself," Diirek said, still grasping Fred's hand. "And there are some things you may not like. If you cannot handle it, you must tell me. I will not bear you any ill will if you cannot do the job."

"Like what things?"

"It is better if I show you. Follow me." Diirek retrieved his hand and turned to walk down the dirt road. Fred followed, glancing up at the moon to gain his bearings. They were headed the way the truck had come, going back toward the farm—east.

"Wait," Fred said, remembering. "My gun and my backpack. They put them in the bed of the truck."

Diirek stepped into the opposite ditch, bent down, and came up with Fred's backpack. He set it in the road and walked a little further down. Fred was barely able to make out the dark shape of the vampire as he jumped a barbed-wire fence. Fred inspected the bag. It looked a little scuffed up and one of the front straps was broken, but otherwise it was fine.

Diirek appeared out of the darkness holding up Fred's gun in two pieces. The stock had broken when it flew out of the truck.

"You won't need this anyway," the vampire said as he dropped the broken weapon into the grass. "You've got me now."

The tall pale creature and the not-so-tall lanky teenager headed off down the road. A cow mooed a solemn farewell behind them.

CHAPTER THIRTEEN

PROBLEMS

A nother day dawned over the city, finding Weller with no sleep, once again. And no closer to figuring out these "super zombie" douchebags. He and Ricardo had done coke and walked around the three blocks all night, talking nonsense. They attracted no zombies. They did, however, attract some angry shouts from neighbors trying to sleep. On one occasion, Weller had to pull out his badge and tell some fat asshole that he was trying to protect the safe zone. When the walrus of a man yelled back, telling Weller to protect his genitals, the detective went for his gun. Ricardo stopped him and shuffled him off down the street.

On another occasion, Weller had to hold Ricardo back when a wretched woman threw one of her cats at them from a second-floor window. It scratched the vampire's face up, causing him to get incredibly angry. He started climbing the front of the building, which scared the woman back inside. Weller grabbed Ricardo's leg and told him he could have no more drugs if he killed the woman. The vampire relented.

Oh, yeah, the cat was fine, in case you're wondering.

All in all, it was a tiring, frustrating night for the detective. He headed back to the office around 8 in the morning, preparing to eat a mile of shit for his plan but also happy that the "super zombies" were probably just slightly clever human criminals. He had convinced himself that the zombie he'd killed the other night—the one that had nearly run him over—was a one-off. The killings were a coincidence, otherwise, they would have been back last night. After all, there hadn't been a peep over the radio all night, save one Corpse Duty call. Still, he was planning to ask Shellbourne for one more night of patrols, just to be sure, because deep down he knew they weren't just humans.

But before he even got to his desk, his day took a turn into a wall of shit.

"Weller, check this out. You'll get a kick out of it." Hardiman was standing next to a patrolman and the two of them were staring down at a tablet. Weller grumbled and headed over as the two men made room for him. The patrolman dragged his finger across the screen to start the video from the beginning.

The footage had been taken at night, from an upper window or the roof of a tall building. The state of the street, with the burned-out cars, rotting corpses, and piles of trash, told Weller that it had been taken in the outskirts. The camera was focused on a pet store across the street, the large front window of which had been broken.

"Nothing's happening. Who took this?" Weller asked.

"Just wait. I took it," the patrolman said. "It was my shift on Horde Duty last night."

Horde Duty entailed sitting on top of a building near the safe zone and making sure the zombie horde didn't come close. If it did, you called in a team who would travel around to the other side of the mass of rotting humans and distract them with some sort of noise. The favorite was blowing up cars. Weller had never participated in Horde Duty, to his chagrin. He didn't want to sit and watch, but he did like the idea of blowing up cars in the middle of the outskirts. Sounded like fun.

If only his life were that simple.

"Here," the patrolman, whose name was Chilley, said as something moved on the screen. A figure appeared at the broken window of the pet shop, dragging something large behind it. As the figure stepped out of the darkened window and into the moonlight, it became clear that it was a man. A familiar man. Weller's eyes narrowed as his interest piqued.

The man looked up and down the street before turning back to the large window. He grabbed the item he had been dragging and lifted it out onto the sidewalk. It was a big white box with a colorful picture on the front.

"Is that a dog cage?" Weller asked, bringing his nose close to the tablet's screen.

"Yeah, it sure is. What the hell you think this guy has going on? He grabs like a dozen of those things," Chilley said. "But wait, the best part's coming up."

Weller watched as Buck—he was sure it was him, now—carried the boxed dog cage to a dented and broken-windowed van. He put the box in the back of the vehicle and headed for the door, but he stopped as something spooked him. He crouched slightly and raised his arms like he was about to run. His head swiveled back and forth, looking each way down the street. The camera moved swiftly left, making a blur of the street below. Then it stopped on three black-clad figures moving toward the van and the pet shop. The camera blurred again—this time the other way. Four more figures.

Buck was surrounded.

"Dog boy is so fucked," Hardiman said, laughing like he knew what was coming. Weller thought he knew, too.

The figures moved in. Buck raised his hands in a gesture of surrender and his beard scruff cracked as he spoke to the seven men surrounding him. The microphone was too far away to pick up the words, but Weller was sure he said, "I don't want any trouble." The seven laughed noiselessly at this proclamation.

Several of the aggressors had weapons in the form of baseball bats and pipes. One of them raised his beating stick. Buck ducked in and kicked the guy in the balls.

Hardiman and Chilley laughed.

The other six moved in. Buck threw a punch, knocking one of them back. Then he got hit with a bat and a pipe simultaneously. He stayed on his feet.

"You see that shit?" Hardiman asked. "Little guy has some fight in him."

Weller nodded. For the first time since he'd seen Buck alive (so to speak), he started to wonder about how exactly he lived through whatever Merek had done to him. He still remembered the sound of it. The crunching pop of bones snapping, the wet and dense sound of torn flesh. No human could have lived through that. Of course, he knew Buck wasn't human, but at the same time didn't think the guy was something to worry about, either. As he watched the action on the screen, he began to realize that he'd made a mistake. Maybe a big fucking mistake.

The guys that hit Buck looked momentarily surprised, which gave the little guy a chance to yank away their weapons, one in each hand. He moved quickly—not quite causing a blurring effect on the screen, but close. He smacked each guy in the head with his newly acquired weapons. They each crumpled to the ground, out cold.

Only three left now, one of which pulled out a gun and shot Buck square in the chest. The little man stumbled back toward the pet store, but he never dropped the bat or the pipe. Buck straightened and looked at the man who'd just shot him. His arm moved amazingly fast as he pulled it back and then shot it forward again, like a pitcher. This time his movement did cause a blur, and the guy with the gun fell back into the street, a metal pipe sticking out of his head. Only then did Weller realize that Buck had thrown it at the guy.

The two leftover thugs seemed to hesitate, then they came at Buck simultaneously. Buck took a hit from one of them while he snapped the other's left leg with the baseball bat. Even though there was no sound on the recording, Weller could tell the guy was screaming his head off.

Buck hit the last guy in the neck with the bat. As the guy fell to the ground, his head bounced wildly on his shoulders as if it were attached with a string. Even through the unreality of the recording, it was clear the guy was dead. Buck paused for a moment, looking around at the ragged circle of bodies. Then he walked to the guy whose leg he'd broken and proceeded to smash his skull in with the baseball bat.

"Christ," Weller said, under his breath.

Chilley and Hardiman became less animated as Buck continued to smash heads on the screen. Weller looked at Hardiman, who returned his gaze. The older man shrugged at Weller before returning his attention to the tablet. Chilley pressed the screen, pausing the video while Buck was finishing off the last guy. "That's it," he said, chuckling. "I bet you didn't think that guy was wearing body armor, huh? I sure as hell didn't. I thought he was a dead man when I saw it go down last night."

"Yeah," Hardiman agreed. "I thought he was a goner, too. Good for him, though. Those fuckers deserved it. He did everyone a favor."

Weller stared at his colleagues, dumbfounded. They stared back, as if waiting for a reply.

"Yeah," he said finally, after what passed in his exhausted mind as an internal debate. "I didn't see that coming. That guy is fast. What happens after that?"

"Nothing much. He loads a couple of the dead guys up into the van," Chilley said. "I taped him for maybe five more minutes, but all he did was haul pet supplies out of the store. When I came back a little later to see what he was up to, he and that van were gone. I guess he's got a bunch of dogs to take care of." Chilley shrugged. "Dog lover and gang-snubber. He's all right in my book. I hope to see him in action again sometime."

Weller nodded as Chilley and Hardiman bid him farewell. It made sense. Cops in the outskirts weren't really supposed to get involved in anything. If every cop that saw some shit go down out there intervened, they'd be fresh out of police for the safe zone. Still, Weller wished the patrolman had done something. Then again, he didn't know Buck like Weller did. *What are you up to, little man?* Weller thought.

He headed to Shellbourne's office to discuss the possibility of another patrol identical to the one last night. She shot him down before he even finished laying out his argument.

"We're doing it my way tonight, Detective," she said from behind her desk.

"And what way is that? Sit around and wait for them to come back?" Weller asked as he stood between the two visitor's chairs across from her.

"Last I checked, you were a homicide detective," Shellbourne said. "Why don't you leave the crime prevention to the patrol officers. Work on solving the murders. Find out where these creeps stay. Do your job."

"My job is to protect this fucking city," Weller said, nearly yelling.

"Watch your fucking tone, Detective. Your job is whatever I tell you it is. Now—"

"Oh, fuck you," Weller shouted, upending one of the visitor chairs into the floor as he turned to leave. He slammed the door as hard as he could and stalked away, the few people around looking at him from their cubicles.

Weller sat down at his desk and put his head in his left hand. His right arm throbbed in the cast. He breathed deeply, trying to calm down, feeling ashamed of losing his temper. Again.

He sat back in his chair and tried to focus on one problem, a test to see if he could do it for more than thirty seconds. He had plenty of problems to choose from.

The chief of police had likely put a hit out on him before the apocalypse because he thought Weller was close to uncovering his relationship with a known gangster. Problem.

There were likely still at least a few super zombies roaming around, eternally hungry, ready to kill. Problem.

Buck was alive, clearly pissed at him, and doing some funny shit. Oh, and he had somehow learned to fight—either that or to use his full power. Problem.

A vampire society lived inside the safe zone, and Weller was the only human who knew about them. The right thing to do was to tell the brass about them. Or was it? Problem.

JayLynn was nowhere near taking him back. He'd messed it up again. Problem.

His right arm was next to useless, and his ribs hurt every time he took a step or a breath. Problem.

He had done cocaine with a vampire two nights in a row. Problem.

He hadn't had more than a few hours of sleep all week. Problem.

The world was a post-apocalyptic hellscape. Problem.

He couldn't figure out the name of the goddamn song that was rattling around in his head. Big. Fucking. Problem.

No matter how hard he tried, it was impossible to focus on one single issue. Whenever he felt like he might be getting somewhere—deciding what to do—his thoughts would jump to another one. *Everything is shit,* he thought. *I need a damn vacation. A vacation from the apocalypse.*

"Fuck this," he said to no one as he got up. He looked around the room briefly and then headed toward the elevators. He needed sleep.

When he knocked on JayLynn's door twelve minutes later, he had donned his best sad puppy dog face. His ex-wife opened the door. Her eyes were hard for the briefest of seconds before they went soft and she said, "You look terrible. What's wrong?"

"I just need to sleep for a few hours. Can I do it here? I have a feeling that being close to home will help."

"This isn't your home—" she stopped, realizing what he was saying.

He hadn't planned on saying that to her, it had just slipped out. He wasn't exactly sure what her reaction would be, and he held his breath, waiting.

She settled her gaze on Weller, looking into his eyes with an attention that had been lacking from their interactions lately. He gazed back, willing her to see that he was serious. She was, and always would be, his home.

At first, her eyes were hard, but then something changed in them, morphing from dark to pale brown, the tan flecks sparkling. She smiled a half-smile and opened the door to let him in.

"Thank you," he said as she shut the door behind him.

"Hey!" Berena greeted him from the living room, jumping up from the couch and the coloring book she was working on. The small teenage girl looked much better now than she'd looked when Weller had rescued her from some bad people. It seemed as though Berena was good for JayLynn and JayLynn was good for Berena.

"Hey, kid," Weller said. "What's the haps?"

"The what?" she asked, her smooth lineless face bunching up in mock consternation.

"The haps. What's the haps? You never heard that? It means 'what's happening?'"

Berena looked at JayLynn, a delighted smile fighting her frown.

"What is it?" Weller asked, looking from girl to woman, and woman to girl. Berena broke out laughing first, followed closely by JayLynn. Weller smiled. He felt his shoulders and his facial muscles relax, not realizing until this moment that he had been carrying around his stress, his anger, in those areas. The sound of them laughing was like an elixir. A relaxation tonic. It didn't matter if they were laughing at him, he just hoped they would never stop.

"What's funny?" he asked when their laughter started dying down, hoping the question would prompt more of it.

"Jay," Berena began, catching her breath. "Jay asked me the exact same thing this morning when I woke up. She said, 'What's the haps, Berns?' Then I made fun of her for it." Berena started laughing again, hands to her stomach.

"That's not even the best part, though," JayLynn said, still chuckling, tears of joy in her eyes. "Berena said, 'I'll bet Kurt would never say that. He's too cool to say lame stuff like that.' But here you are, saying it, right on time. In fact, if I remember correctly, you're the reason I ever started saying it in the first place. Back when we were first dating."

"No, no, no," Weller said, smiling wide. "*You* were the one that would say it all the time. Not me. Berena's right, I'm much too cool for some lame stuff like that." He stuck out his hand toward Berena and received a high-five.

"Oh, I see how it is," JayLynn said. "You two are ganging up on me. Well, you, sir, can leave my house if that's how it's gonna be. And you," JayLynn turned to Berena. "You still have schoolwork to do. You can finish the coloring later."

"Boo!" Both Berena and Weller said at once, prompting another round of laughter from all three of them.

Chapter Fourteen

UNDEAD LIFE ON THE TRACKS

The silent train yard was so serene and peaceful this time of day. Fred sat in the lounge car, looking out the wide windows that commanded a view of a field stretching out to a line of trees some quarter-mile distant. The sun sank slowly behind the tall green sentinels. He would have been sitting outside, enjoying one of the last days of spring, were it not for the bugs. A walker stumbled dumbly across the field off in the distance, walking left-to-right across Fred's vision.

Behind him, through the other set of windows, sat rusting train cars and a long, low building that was the epitome of Podunk train stations the world over. On the other side of that was a one-stoplight town that had escaped the bombs of the apocalypse but not the ravages of the hellscape. Over the last two nights, Fred and Diirek had searched all of the two-dozen buildings and houses in the town proper. They saw not a soul alive. They had gathered plenty of supplies for Fred, though. Food, bottled water, a laptop and a bunch of DVDs, some old, crispy nudie magazines that had already come in handy—literally.

Fred got up as the sun did the opposite. Diirek would be up soon, and he would expect the chores to be done. To be fair, Fred only had one left, but it was the chore he hated the most. He walked out of the lounge car, through three coach cars with empty seats, through the dining car, halfway through a sleeper car, and down a narrow staircase to the lower level of the car.

At the back of the lower level of the car sat a room with four beds that folded down from the walls like hideaway bunk beds. It was a room meant to accommodate traveling families. It also had a bathroom and a shower. Fred had already turned on the head-end power system, supplying electricity to the entire train from a designated diesel engine. This was one of the first things Diirek taught him to do when they had arrived.

Fred dug the keys out of his pocket and unlocked the portal. He opened the door to the room and three sets of eyes stared at him from the gloom within. He flipped the lights to reveal three men, two of which had chains snaking from shackles on their hands and ankles. The third man only had chains attached to his ankles. The heavy metal leashes disappeared into a ragged hole in the middle of the floor, just large enough to fit all of them. The ends of the chains were fastened underneath the train, making it impossible for the captives to tamper with them. They had enough play so that the men could reach all parts of the small room, including the toilet.

"Hey, boyo," the man with free hands said. His name was Robinson, and he was the best behaved of the lot. The other two men said nothing.

"Free time," Fred said, cheerily. "Don't mess around or you'll die a slow death," he continued, without changing his tone.

"Oh no, not me, boyo," Robinson said. "I've learned me lesson, I have. I'm ready to be civilized and such. Yessiree, just let me free." He spoke with an atrocious English accent half the time, while the other half he spoke like a mid-states American. Fred guessed he was American, but it was hard to tell sometimes. He was a rangy fellow with sunken eye sockets but somehow bulging eyes. A vein constantly stood out next to his right eye, underneath his thoroughly tanned skin. That, combined with the bushy brown beard and the way he spoke, made Fred think that the man wasn't all there. Which made sense considering what Diirek had told him about Robinson.

The other two were Fuller and a man Fred and Diirek only knew as Buffalo Bob. Apparently, it was a name he donned in honor of a character from a movie called *The Silence of the Lambs*. Fred had never seen the movie and didn't have much interest in documentaries about lambs and buffalos, anyway. Buffalo Bob was always talking about lotion and baskets and eating people. He was right at home in the apocalypse, in that regard. Although the lotion thing was weird, and Fred didn't know why the guy wanted a basket. He didn't have anything to put in it. He looked like what Fred's dad would have called a "Dirty Commie Hippie," meaning he had long hair and some tattoos.

Fuller always seemed angry—at least during the 48 hours Fred had known him. He was a small, portly man with bad skin and hairy nostrils.

Fred unlocked Robinson's shackles first, having him lay face down on the bed with his arms under him as he did it. Fred backed away and then told the man he could get up. Diirek let them roam around with relatively free reign during the nighttime hours. Although after the little incident last night, the vampire had instructed Fred not to free Fuller and Buffalo Bob until he was present.

Robinson jumped around the small room for a moment, putting his butt in Fuller's face until the smaller man shoved him into the wall. It didn't seem to put a damper on the strange man's spirits. He pranced about and then headed for the door, making happy noises. Fred moved aside to let him go.

Once in the hall, Robinson stopped dead, turned around, stepped back into the room, and sat on the bunk he had previously occupied.

A shadow coalesced in the doorway and then merged with Diirek as the stoic-faced vampire all but floated into the room.

"Whose turn is it?" Diirek was looking at Robinson, but his question was directed at Fred.

"It was Bob last night—"

"*Buffalo* Bob," the hippie corrected.

"Sure," Fred said. "It was him last night, and Robinson the night before that. So that makes it Fuller's turn."

The vampire was on Fuller in an instant, his jaw unhinged and fangs sinking into the man's flesh. The other two men whimpered as they watched. Fuller's eyes rolled back in his head and his eyelids twitched manically. Fred held up his wrist, on which rested a watch Diirek had given him when they arrived at the train. He watched the second hand as it ticked out the correct amount of time, looking up at Robinson every few seconds to make sure the man stayed put.

Presently, the boy stepped up to Diirek and put a hand on the vampire's shoulder. When he got no response, he shook his shoulder slightly and said his name. Diirek detached from Fuller and stood up, his pale face somewhat less so after the intake of blood. Fuller's eyes came back to normalcy and he put a hand to his neck as he lay back on the bunk.

"You can let them out now, Fred," the satiated vampire said as he stepped into the hall.

"Make sure you eat something," Fred said to a dejected Fuller as he unlocked the portly man's shackles. "You, too," he said to the other captives. "The power will be on until an hour before sunup and there's plenty of food in the kitchen. If I have to go looking for any of you again, Diirek will hear about it. So don't mess around tonight." He paused, the sound of his still-squeaky voice fading to nothing. No matter how he tried to sound like an authority figure, it just didn't ring true to him. Not yet anyway. "Okay," he said after a moment. "Have fun, you guys!"

Fred stepped out into the hall to find Diirek waiting for him. The vampire smiled a toothless smile as they headed back upstairs. "You are getting better. Just remember what I told you. Those are bad men. I saw them do terrible things with my own eyes. They will not respect you unless you mess with them a little bit. And don't show any fear. They preyed on women and children. Fear is what they live off. But not to worry, Fred. You are getting better."

Fred smiled. He felt better. In fact, he felt better now than he could ever remember feeling in his whole life. He was still a kid, barely a month into seventeen, but he wouldn't be one forever. And maybe, eventually, he could be like Diirek. Maybe he could grow up to be a vampire.

"So what are we doing tonight?" the boy asked.

"We're going hunting," Diirek said.

"For more bad guys to bring back?"

"No. Three is enough. In fact, two would probably be enough, but I like to have a backup. Especially since humans seem to be a rare commodity these days."

"Then what are we hunting?"

Diirek smiled before he spoke, showing his brilliant white teeth this time. "Werewolves."

CHAPTER FIFTEEN

WEREWOLF VS. VAMPIRE

"But it's not a full moon," Fred said as he struggled to keep pace with Diirek.

"Was the moon full when you saw them the first time?"

"I dunno. Maybe. I suppose it was. That's how werewolves work, right?"

"Perhaps. Perhaps not. I do not know if what I saw was a werewolf or not, but the moon was not full when I saw it. And I was in the same area where you saw them. It cannot be a coincidence."

"Why didn't you go after it?"

"I was in the middle of capturing Buffalo Bob at the time. A young family would have been killed had I not intervened."

Fred nodded. He wondered if all vampires were this . . . nice. In fact, he wondered if there were other vampires at all. Maybe Diirek was the only one. Fred hadn't asked and the pale man hadn't offered any information. The boy didn't want to pry, so he decided to wait a little bit. He didn't want Diirek to get mad at him.

The vampire veered off the dirt road they had been walking on for a mile or more. Fred followed. They pushed into a large cornfield, the boy staying directly behind Diirek, grateful that the vampire was clearing a path through the spider webs that were surely there. Spiders gave him the creeps. They slowed down as they reached the other edge of the field. Then they stopped just inside the corn, peering out toward structures off in the distance.

The edge of the cornfield was on a slight rise, the ground sloping gradually down for two hundred yards or so. A stream ran parallel to the field at the bottom of the slope. Mature maple, pecan, and hackberry trees lined the water on both sides. It was pitch dark under those trees. The only reason Fred knew there was a stream down there was the faint sound of bubbling water he made out. The night was still and quiet, otherwise. The structures were visible over the tops of the trees, more than a mile away.

Fred squinted, trying to see what Diirek was seeing. All he could make out were three buildings in the middle of a stretch of flat farmland. It looked like there was a copse of trees behind the trio of buildings, but it was hard to tell from this distance. If it had been daylight, it may have been different.

One of the buildings looked to be three stories. If it was a house, which it kind of looked like, it was one of the biggest houses Fred had ever seen. The other two buildings were of similar size and structure. The buildings sat in a wide clearing, the front of which was hemmed-in by a cornfield. Or two cornfields, bisected by a road. There were other crops growing, past the dark group of trees behind the buildings.

Fred looked up at Diirek, who was still staring intently toward the mysterious structures.

"You can see that far?" he asked.

"Shhh," Diirek said.

Something moved in the dark trees bordering the stream, causing a rustling sound. Whatever it was growled. Fred's eyes went wide. He looked to Diirek, who was peering into the darkness from which the sounds had issued. More movement below—a tree shook slightly. Fred saw it out of the corner of his eye and slowly turned his head back in time to see a black shape move out of the shadows and into the weak moonlight at the edge of the trees. It looked to be about the size of a man, covered in black hair, and moving crouched on two feet. It was moving slowly, tentatively, pale reflective eyes looking to where they stood in the corn.

Without knowing it, Fred started holding his breath. Diirek stared at the hairy figure in seeming disbelief, his eyes wide and mouth slightly open.

The figure dropped down onto all fours and moved with lightning speed up the hill toward them.

"Go! Run!" Diirek commanded, giving Fred a powerful shove back into the cornfield. The boy felt dizzy as he stumbled away from the vampire, finally remembering to pull air into his burning lungs as he hit stride. The strange growling sound—almost a two-pitch sound of low and high together—grew louder behind him. His heart pounded, sweat causing his t-shirt to cling to his back. Then something crashed behind him, the sound that of corn stalks being crushed in a violent struggle. Fred ran harder, trusting that Diirek could handle himself, knowing he couldn't do anything to help but hating his weak boy's body because of it.

***

Diirek couldn't believe it. A werewolf was running at him—fast. He contemplated simply letting the thing do whatever it wanted with him. Surely this beast could kill him. Surely it could end the pain of loss that he felt every waking moment. The shame and guilt he felt for allowing Lidia to be killed. He never should have left her alone. Never.

He stood there like a scarecrow after sending the boy on his way, thinking that he would finally allow his long life to come to an end. The werewolf bounded up the hill, closer now, its strange stubby snout opening to reveal sharp, slobbery teeth. Then something happened. Diirek thought about the boy. Once this beast was done with him, it would surely go after Fred. The boy wouldn't stand a chance. *So what? He is only human*, part of him said. *Time to kick some werewolf ass*, another part said.

The beast lunged at him, and in the split second before it hit him, Diirek decided to live. At least for another night.

The beast was strong, its impact lifting Diirek off his feet and sending them both crashing through corn stalks. Diirek had managed to get his arm up, stopping the werewolf's jaws from reaching his neck. Its teeth sank deep into the flesh of his arm, the pain sending his defenses into high gear.

As they rolled to a stop, Diirek wound up on top by sheer chance, straddling the werewolf, holding it down. His right arm was still caught in the beast's jaws. He punched the side of its hairy head in an effort to free his arm, but it held fast. Claws from one of the werewolf's hand-like forepaws pierced Diirek's expensive black shirt with ease, sinking into the skin of his chest. It yanked its paw down, slicing four deep tracks into the vampire's flesh.

Diirek punched the beast in the neck, noting without interest a black leather collar with a small gray box attached to it. The beast whimpered but didn't let go of his arm. Its right paw came up again to slash him, but Diirek caught it with his left hand. The beast's free paw came up quickly, and there was nothing Diirek could do about it. He tried to turn away as the paw came up to his head, its claws piercing the skin on the right side of his face, just under his hairline. The beast dragged the paw slowly down. One of the claws cut through his eyelid and pierced his right eye, causing a bright white light to flash there before the eye went completely black.

Diirek began to panic, the pain mounting. If he lost his other eye, he would be dead shortly thereafter. He was already losing a lot of blood. And the pain . . . He hadn't thought he was capable of feeling this much pain.

The vampire yanked away from the werewolf, twisting so he could get his arm free from its jaws. As soon as he did it, he knew he had misjudged the werewolf's jaw strength. He felt the bones of his forearm snap just outside of the beast's teeth. He let out a savage yell.

Changing tactics, he quickly did the same thing again, only this time he yanked on the werewolf's paw that he still held in his left hand. He felt its shoulder joint separate with the force, and the beast howled around his now-broken arm.

He dropped the damaged right paw and caught the left one just as it came for his face again. The beast bucked under him, trying to throw him off. He tried to yank the other paw out of its socket, but the angle was all wrong. He couldn't generate enough force to do it. And he was growing weaker by the minute. He didn't know what to do. Letting go of the paw would open him up to another blow, which he couldn't take. Standing up would free the werewolf's powerful hind legs, which he couldn't do. His only option was to pull a *127 Hours* and tear his arm in two, leaving the beast with half—the good half, at that. He would simply have to go without a right arm from now on. He could salvage it if he had it. But if it was gone it wouldn't grow back, vampire or not. He yanked on the right arm, testing the waters a little bit.

No choice.

As he geared up to do it, Fred burst out of the corn. The werewolf stopped struggling for a second, moving its eyes to look at Fred. Diirek did the same, with his good eye. An awkward silence ensued. Fred's eyes were wide as he looked at Diirek and the beast. Then something in his face changed. He stepped up to the werewolf's head and began stomping the creature's collared neck with his foot.

After the third stomp, it looked as though the beast would relent. Diirek held fast, watching the limb he'd dislocated twitch as he held the other one. The werewolf bucked and fought to get the upper hand. Diirek felt the blood streaming down his face and chest. His right eye was a mess of clear-white fluid mixing with the blood pouring around it. He couldn't believe how strong the creature was. If there had been two . . .

He shook his head to clear it, to keep his consciousness intact for just a little bit longer. Fred's grunting became the only sound he could hear. That and the whimper-screams that the werewolf loosed every time the boy stomped on its throat. Then the pressure changed on his forearm and he looked down. His arm was free, although twisted and hanging at a strange angle. He lifted it out of the creature's not-quite-wolfish maw, looking at it with the detached curiosity of a man inspecting some sort of half-familiar insect he's found in his home. He turned it, noticing the bone sticking out of the black cloth of his shirtsleeve. "Huh," he said.

"Diirek!" Fred screamed, catching his attention. The vampire looked down, angling his head slightly to bring the werewolf fully into his limited line of sight. The creature's eyes were rolling as it struggled to pull breath through its smashed throat. With his right arm free, Diirek adjusted his angle and pulled the other forepaw out of its socket with his good hand. The creature didn't even whimper.

Diirek stepped up and off the werewolf. He moved to where Fred had been just moments ago and put all his energy into one final stomp to the throat, finishing the job that the boy had started. They both watched in silence as the werewolf's eyes rolled slowly in pleading misery one last time, then stilled.

Diirek looked into those still-open eyes. They reminded him of something that he couldn't quite place. Something on the edge of his mind. He moved his gaze down to the black leather collar around the neck.

Their stomping had caused the gray box to move around its neck, half-obscured from sight. A question rose in Diirek's mind, but he filed it away for a time when he wasn't bleeding to death.

"C'mon," Fred said, pulling at the vampire's good arm. "We've got to get you back. You'll be able to fix all this with a feeding, right?" Diirek looked at the boy for the first time since he'd come back to save him and noticed that the kid was near tears.

"Yes," Diirek said, smiling as best he could with half of his face sliced to hell. *If I can make it back*, he almost said, but didn't. He was trying to reassure the boy, after all.

CHAPTER SIXTEEN

HOW TO TRAIN YOUR ZOMBIE

Weller felt like an idiot as he knocked on the sealed door outside of the vampire lair, or hole, or nest, or whatever the hell they called it. The vampires' abandoned subway tunnel. Yeah, that was accurate. No editorializing there. He stood and waited what he thought was a respectful amount of time and then banged on the door again. How long does it take a vampire to answer the door of its abandoned subway tunnel, anyway? Etiquette was out the window.

Weller felt refreshed. He'd slept nearly twelve hours at JayLynn's house. He even awoke at one point to find her asleep behind him, acting as the big spoon. He had flipped over so he could face her. He studied her face for a little while, recalling all the good times and the bad.

"Are you watching me sleep, weirdo?" she said, eyes still closed.

Weller kissed her on the forehead in answer. She smiled and opened her eyes.

"Are you okay?" she asked, moving toward him, and draping a leg over his knees.

"When am I not?" Weller said.

"That's not an answer. I still know you well, Kurt. You look like you did during that one case. Back in 2012? The serial killer?"

Weller nodded. "Ray Holds."

"Right. You look like you did when you were working that case. Only worse."

"That bad, huh? So, I guess there's no chance I'll get laid in the next half hour?"

She moved her head back an inch. "You know you use jokes as a mask for stress and anger, right? It's like a defense mechanism you use so you can avoid feeling whatever it is you're feeling."

"You don't want me to feel what I'm feeling right now, trust me. It will do no one any good. I just needed some sleep, and, for whatever reason, I sleep well when you're around. So, thanks for letting me stay for a little while." Weller closed his eyes, ending the conversation.

"Just don't lose yourself in there, okay?" JayLynn whispered. "I know how you get. Don't carry the world on your shoulders. You don't have to."

He slept for a couple of hours after the short conversation. When he woke up it was nearly dark, and he had decided to pay a visit to his old friends the vamps. Whatever else was happening, he felt like seeing what they were up to these last few nights. Maybe they had a word on Buck or these crazy super zombies.

And here he was, waiting for them to answer the door.

Finally, the makeshift brick door above the actual door slid back, spilling red dust on Weller's close-cropped hair. He brushed it off, grumbling about how he needed to shave his head again. He hated having hair. Stuff was always getting stuck in it. Like brick dust. Or cocaine (don't ask).

Weller stepped back and looked up at the pale face staring back at him. It was a female vamp he had seen before, but whose name he didn't know. She looked to be around middle age, with perfectly straight blond hair, sunken cheeks, and large eyes that gazed at the detective with slack interest.

"We don't want any," she said after a moment and headed back inside, closing the brick door as she went.

"Well, you're not getting any, so we're on the same page there." The brick door continued to close. "Don't make me blow this spot up," he yelled up at the hidden vampire. The movement stopped, then reversed.

"What, you can't take a joke, Detective?" the woman said without a hint of humor. Then, "Come in."

"A little help?" Weller said, gesturing to his broken arm. The woman sighed, squatted, and reached her pale delicate-looking hand down. Weller grasped it with his left. Once again, he was reminded of how strong the vampires were, and once again it threatened to put him in a black mood. Even her bird-boned arm was stronger than Weller's whole body. And he was fairly corded with muscle. There was some fat there, but not much. It was mostly muscle, honest.

She put him down on the other side where he stood there feeling like he had as a little kid when his mom used to lift him into his high chair. Only he hadn't weighed two-hundred pounds at the time. And his mom hadn't been a creature of the night. She had been a morning person, God rest her.

"What's your name?" Weller asked, more out of a need to break the one-sided awkward silence than any real curiosity. The vampire shut the jigsaw brick door and landed noiselessly beside him before she spoke.

"Nadia," she said and continued down the carpeted hallway toward the bulk of the lair. Weller followed along, trying to remember why he had come down here in the first place.

The sun hadn't been down long, and most of the vampires were just starting their day—or night, technically. Two were playing video games on a big screen TV. They glanced over their shoulders from the couch where they sat, noted his presence, and turned back around to their game. A couple of them were reading. A few were talking, including Binta and Isabelle, who both gave him a slight smile and said hello.

Binta looked as good as ever, and he supposed she would for all eternity. Her black skin was a shade darker than his, but infinitely smoother. Her practiced posture and accent put him in mind of an old girlfriend who had been in the city on a student exchange visa from Namibia. He hadn't realized it until this moment, but it was clear to him that it was part of his attraction to her; the implied nostalgia. Logically he knew that she was probably nothing like his old fling, Sonia, but that didn't stop the feeling. And, of course, there was the fact that she was incredibly sexy. That was part of it, too.

He headed toward Binta and Isabelle to have a chat when Ricardo appeared out of nowhere and slapped Weller on the back.

"Detective," he said, smiling. "I was just getting ready to come and see you."

"What's up?" Weller asked.

"Listen," Ricardo said. "Three of us killed steroid zombies last night. There are still more out there. Gotta be."

"Well, that's good," Weller said. "That's three down out of . . . how many did you say you saw the other night? Six?"

"Yeah, I saw six, but there's more than that."

"How do you know that?"

"Because Jamie over there saw a bunch more last night," Ricardo gestured at one of the vampires playing video games.

"Last night? Why the fuck didn't you tell me?"

"What are you talking about? I was with you last night until nearly dawn, remember?"

"Oh yeah. Shit, my days are all fucked up since I slept all day. Still, this not being able to go out in the daytime shit is really hurting us. Who knows what those things have been up to today."

"Oh, yeah, sorry. I'll just use an umbrella or hope that it's cloudy and pop over to your house next time I have some news."

"You could do that the whole time?" Weller said.

"No, you idiot. That's not how it works. I was being sarcastic."

"Well, your sarcasm sucks."

"I've got a theory, though," Ricardo said, lowering his voice. "If these are the zombies that ate Merek, then maybe they can't go out during the day. You haven't had any reports of them today, have you?"

"I don't know. I've been sleeping all day, like I said. It was much needed, and I came straight here afterward."

"Great. And you're getting on my case about not being active during the day? You're the human. You won't die in the sunlight. What the fuck were you thinking?"

"I was thinking that I was useless without sleep. I couldn't even think. And I'm here now. All better. So let's get to it. Where did Jamie see these super zombies?"

***

On the northwest corner of Washington and 15th stood a restaurant supply store. It was essentially a large warehouse with a fancy brick facade. The smooth concrete floors, exposed ceiling beams, and utilitarian shelving gave the place an empty feeling. But it was far from empty. Down an aisle that still held cleaning supplies such as mops, brooms, dustpans, industrial oven cleaner, floor squeegees, and large containers of dishwashing liquid, there stood four zombies. They were all a mottled shade of dark blue and puke green interspersed with dashes of red from their various wounds that would never heal.

Each of the zombies stood straight, arms at their sides, only their eyes moving as they watched the figure walking in front of them. The zombies had leather collars on, attached to chains that were fastened to the large and sturdy metal shelving at their backs. They looked, in their ghastly state, like they wore poorly designed muscle suits. But they didn't. They had been augmented by something. The cause of the augmentation was what Buck was dwelling on as he walked in front of them, holding a large, dripping chunk of human thigh in one hand.

The small man stopped walking, absently tearing off a piece of flesh and tossing it in his mouth. He closed his eyes, savoring the sweet, coppery taste. Across his mind's eye flashed an image of Weller, running out on him. And then an image of Weller laughing at him. It seemed like every time he closed his eyes, the detective was there, haunting him.

When Buck had started gathering up these super zombies, luring them into his van with fresh human flesh, feeling like an especially deranged serial killer, he didn't have an endgame in mind. Not specifically. He had spent the last day training these four, while the six others he had caught were locked in large dog cages. He found that as long as they had flesh to eat, they were easily controlled. And the training had gone especially well. They didn't talk, but he wouldn't have been surprised if they started to, eventually.

Although Buck didn't have any evidence to support it, he figured that they were like him. Only where he had been alive when he had been turned, they had been dead already. He suspected it had something to do with the monster Merek. Nothing else made sense.

Buck looked up at the zombies who stood waiting patiently for his next command. He stepped up to the first one in line, a young woman with a thin frame who now looked like a freshly dead Olympic bodybuilder. He tore a chunk off the thigh meat and popped it into her mouth before undoing the leather collar on her neck. He let it fall to the ground and stepped back, unsure of what would happen. She stood there, eyes on him. Buck smiled.

"Come here," he said, stepping back a few paces. She came. He gave her another treat, then stepped close to whisper in her ear. "Kill him," Buck said, and extended a hand out to the next zombie in line, still chained up. She moved her head to look where he was pointing. She looked back at Buck. He thought she was about to say something, but she simply nodded her head slightly, turned, and pounced on the zombie Buck had indicated.

The fight didn't last long. The other zombie had a partially broken leg to begin with, which was torn off in short order by his attacker. Buck stood watching, slurping and chomping on sweet morsels of meat. When she was finished the zombie came up to Buck and stood, waiting. She was splattered with the other zombie's blood and rotting flesh, but she didn't seem to mind. Buck gave her the remainder of the meat. "Good, girl," he said. "That's a good little zombie."

For the first time since his death, Buck felt good about the future. He had been handed a gift, he realized. And now he had the means to utilize it properly. A plan began to form in his mind. But before he could get to the fun part, he needed information.

He thought of Weller again, balling his fists as he did so. A voice spoke up in his mind. His voice. Or was it? It sounded like him, and it had been making a lot of sense. He had gotten this far with its help, so he could go a little further.

Buck walked around the restaurant supply store, the female super zombie following behind him. His next move required two things. Or, rather, two people, if you could call them that. He needed a cop.

And a vampire.

Chapter Seventeen

IT'S IMPOSSIBLE TO FIND GOOD HELP

A nders Revak clutched his weapon and crept forward into the outskirts of the little town. A newspaper fluttered across the street in the breeze. Anders stepped forward and stomped the paper with his foot. The faded headline was still visible: GOODBYE. WE WILL MISS YOU ALL. A look of determination came across his face before he let the paper go, watching it as it tumbled in the wind, thinking it was the most beautiful thing he'd ever seen. A single tear escaped from his eye as he continued cautiously into the town. He didn't wipe it away. It fell onto his blue flannel jacket, leaving a clean streak through the dirt on his face.

One and two-story buildings lined the main street. An antique shop, a hardware store, a cafe, an insurance agency. All packed in, shoulder-to-shoulder. Some of the store's windows were broken, others were intact, giving the illusion that those stores without broken windows were ready for business. There were a few abandoned cars on the street, parked haphazardly. One small sedan was parked directly across the middle of the road, its driver's side door open. A uniform sky of gunmetal gray clouds hung above, reflected off the windshield, the sun diffused and weakened by the clouds. A single dark traffic light swung gently above the intersection in the middle of town, some hundred yards away.

Anders walked up to the sedan, looking into the impenetrable darkness of the small shops as he went. He swung his old hunting rifle—a large-caliber, bolt action piece with a scope—up onto his shoulder and placed one hand on the open door. He leaned inside the car, looking for anything useful, resigned to the fact that he would find nothing. Seeing that the vehicle was empty, Anders stepped back with a sigh and shut the door. The sound seemed to box his ears and his facial expression changed from resignation to fear. He swung the hunting rifle off his shoulder in a smooth and practiced motion. He cursed under his breath and shook his head. "How could I be so stupid?" he whispered.

He heard movement a second before he saw the zombies pouring out of nearly every shop on the previously quiet street. There were dozens of them, and they were headed right for him. He clicked the safety off next to his trigger guard, pointed the barrel at the nearest zombie, and fired. He did it again and again and again, but it was no use. They were closing in on him.

Out of bullets and with no time to reload, he used the rifle as a bludgeon, using the sturdy wood and metal weapon like it was part of him. He jammed the barrel through mushy eyes, penetrating barely-functioning brains. He snapped necks by swinging the stock, his powerful upper body creating enough force to even lop a few heads off with the blunt wooden end. In this manner, he kept them at bay for several minutes, but they kept coming.

Finally, he threw the rifle down and jumped onto the hood of the sedan. From here he found a soft spot in the gurgling and rotting crowd. He propelled himself off the car, flipping over several zombies like a gymnast to land safely behind them. But then the unthinkable happened. Several men popped up on the rooftops of the shops, wearing fearsome Halloween masks and aiming weapons at him. Bullets started piercing the air.

Anders ducked behind a streetlamp as bullets struck the sidewalk and shop fronts around him. He reached into his back waistband and pulled out a pistol, leveling it just as a masked man looked down over the roof directly above him. A single shot to the head and the man tumbled down to smack the sidewalk next to Anders.

The men firing from the shops on the other side of the street did not let up. The zombies were closing in. Anders fired off a few rounds across the road and took out a couple of zombies that had gotten close. It bought him a couple of seconds. He shoved the pistol into his jacket pocket and began to climb the streetlamp. It was easy, with his strength and agility. At the top, he twisted himself around and reached out toward the shop roof. It was out of reach. Too far out of reach. But it was his only option. Bullets were flying, striking the surfaces immediately around him.

He tensed his legs against the pole, one hand wrapped around just under the jutting metal that housed the light, the other reaching out toward the building's roof. Something stung his outstretched arm and he grunted in pain. He took a deep breath and, with all his strength, launched himself toward the roof. His chest slammed into the stone of the building, his arms hooked over the top, his legs scrambling for purchase. He braced his feet and flipped himself onto the roof, panting as he came to rest on his back. His eyes found a seemingly small floating object in the sky about ten yards above him. He smiled.

Footsteps sounded from nearby, growing closer. Anders sat up quickly, shoving a hand into his jacket pocket to retrieve his weapon. A masked man on the next roof over was running toward him. Anders yanked at the pistol, but it wouldn't come out; it was snagged on the cloth. The man stopped, bringing his automatic rifle to his shoulder.

Scrambling to his feet, Anders launched himself at the man, forgetting about the pistol. The man fired twice, point-blank range, directly at Anders's chest. Nothing happened. It didn't even slow him down. A split-second later Anders was upon him, tackling the gunman to the hard surface of the roof. Anders was much bigger and stronger than the masked man, who never stood a chance. He produced a knife and shoved it slowly through the flimsy plastic of the mask, into the gunman's left eye. The man screamed and screamed. Anders laughed until the man was no longer moving and no longer screaming.

He took the dead man's gun, ejected the clip, and replaced it with one from his own jacket pocket. He stalked to the roof's edge and peeked across the road with one eye. The firing had stopped, but the other masked men were standing on the buildings, waiting for him to pop back up. He gave them what they wanted. There were three of them, and it only took one trigger squeeze each to kill the first two. But before Anders could get the third, the man threw himself headfirst off the small building.

Anders stood up and looked down at the suicidal gunman that lay mangled on the sidewalk. His face showed momentary confusion that morphed into anger.

"Dammit! Cut!" Anders said, his brows furrowing and color rising in his cheeks. "Number One, where are you?"

"I'm in the control vehicle, Master," One said through the radio transmitter inserted in Anders' left ear.

"Gunman five just threw himself off the roof. Where are we finding these people, anyway? I expect a certain level of professionalism during these outings, and I'm not getting it. If you can't fix it, I'll find someone who can."

A long silence followed those words, as Anders knew it would.

"Yes, Master," One said, finally, his voice wavering slightly.

"Well?" Anders said as an SUV pulled up on the street below.

"I'm sorry, Master. What was the question?"

"I asked you where we are finding these people. You never answered."

"Ah, yes, of course, Master. I can get you specifics if you like, but as far as I know, we find them wherever we can. Some we lure in with the radio broadcasts, but we need to set up other outposts and more powerful transmitters because the immediate area seems to be tapped. We only get a few people a week showing up to the 'haven' now. And you tend to go through them faster than we can collect them."

"That sounds like you're blaming me. You're not blaming me, are you, One?"

"No. No. No, Master. I'm trying to answer your question as accurately and honestly as I can, Master."

Anders smiled again as he watched the wranglers push and lure the zombies back into the shops below. A cleanup crew pulled up and began to remove the zombie bodies from the street. "I know. Relax. Let's just go again. I think we got some good footage on that one. It really is getting better."

"Yes, Master. As long as you're enjoying yourself. Are you . . . enjoying yourself?"

"That I am, One. It would have been perfect if that coward hadn't killed himself." Anders watched as one of the men from the cleanup crew, a guy dressed in a full-body suit of pads and a helmet to protect from bites, approached the coward's body to remove it. The body twitched, causing the cleaner to jump back and reach for a hammer in his tool belt.

"Leave him," Anders called out to the man, who looked up, clearly surprised to have the Master address him. "Let him turn. Separate him from the others until he does, then we'll use him another time. I'll get my chance to kill him, one way or the other."

The cleaner nodded and replaced his hammer before dragging the body down the sidewalk.

"Are you happy with the same setup, Master?" One asked over the radio. "Rubber bullets for those men across the street and blanks for those on your side?"

"Yes, One. It's fine." He had initially been reluctant to use rubber bullets, thinking that they would look too fake. But when he saw them on video and heard the sounds the guns made when they fired them, he was happy. It added an air of authenticity, as well. He rolled up his sleeve and inspected the welt on his arm from a rubber bullet's impact. Small price to pay.

"Master," One said in his ear. "When can we discuss last night's issue? Someone got close enough to trip our security protocol. We—"

"And did the security protocol work?" Anders interrupted. "Did they come any closer?"

"Well, I suppose it did work. They didn't come any closer. But—"

"Then that's all that matters, isn't it, One? That's what you're here for: to deal with these issues so I don't have to. I have confidence in our system and the redundancies I designed. Unless it's a true emergency, you need to deal with it. Understood?"

"Yes, Master. Understood."

Above the little town, several drones with wireless cameras floated down as the control vehicle pulled up. It was a former police vehicle that looked like a black, tricked-out RV. Two camera operators got out of the back of the vehicle while other ones came out of the few shops that hadn't been holding zombies. They each began to clean their cameras off or replace them with fully charged ones. Another man started checking numerous cameras that had been hidden strategically throughout the town's main street to catch every angle of the carefully constructed action.

Slave One stepped out of the control vehicle and looked around the street, careful not to look directly at Anders. He limped around, double-checking details, and making sure that he looked properly hunched.

He shouted an order here and there, getting certain people to move faster, orchestrating the reset as he'd done more than a dozen times before on similar streets, in warehouses, apartment buildings, neighborhoods, and even an amusement park. He moved like his life depended on it. And, in fact, it did.

Anders took in a breath of fresh air and rolled his shoulders. He was sure to be happy with the footage they got today. Watching himself kill zombies and humans was the only thing that could bring him to climax lately, and once this one was edited together, he would get a lot of mileage out of it. Especially the bit with the tear at the beginning. His acting was coming along, that was for sure. Maybe he could even have his own TV channel, once the few earthly survivors got their infrastructure up and running. All Anders, all the time. God, how that would show his old, condescending teachers. He knew a few of them were still alive. He'd made sure of it.

Inevitably, his thoughts took a turn. The only reason he wanted to go again was to take his mind off the damn waiting. And to clear his head. Find out how to approach the vampires. Which buttons to push to get what he wanted. Now that he knew—really knew—that vampires were real, he found that he was scared. What if they didn't like him? What if they didn't let him into their little world? What if they refused to help him?

Surely not.

They would see how resourceful he was. They had to. Besides, what was there not to like? He was tall and handsome and strong, and he could flip over zombies and do things that only fictional characters could do. He could be their best friend if they would give him a chance. Like so many others had never done.

Memories and their accompanying feelings rushed into him, causing his vision to become blurry and his breathing to speed up. Even after how far he'd come, he was still haunted by his past. He put his hands on his knees and closed his eyes.

Stop. Stop it. You're getting worked up. They *should be the ones worried. What if* you *don't like* them? *Huh?* Anders smiled. He was worried about nothing. He just needed to show them the real him. They would see. If not . . . well, he would make them see.

Chapter Eighteen

BOYS WILL BE GUN-TOTING BOYS

I must be crazy, Fred thought as he moved noisily through the cornfield. Each crunching step made him wince, and he stopped every few paces to listen so hard he felt the sound blurring. He didn't know if sound could blur, but that's what it felt like. The sun sat slightly behind him in the sky, barely visible through a thick and expansive cloud cover. It was the kind of cloud cover that you could easily mistake for a clear winter sky, were it not for the covered and diffused ball of fire sitting above the world.

But it wasn't winter. It was barely summer. Not that it felt like summer today. Far from it.

Fred wore a light jacket that he had owned since before the apocalypse. It was a black and turquoise windbreaker whose ilk were seen in 80s and 90s music videos and thrift stores the world over, but rarely ever seen on any self-respecting, fashion-forward individual. Fred didn't care now, and he hadn't cared back when there had been people to judge his terminally damaged fashion sense. He liked the jacket. Mostly because it kept him warm when it was cold. And it kept the rain off his skin when it rained. His faded black canvas high-top shoes with previously white soles seemed to find with great success the loudest pieces of corn stalk and husk to crunch as he made his way toward the werewolf's resting place.

He was out here against Diirek's orders, and largely over the fright he'd experienced the previous night. Things had really sunk in as he watched Diirek's many gurgling wounds slowly heal after the vampire fed a little on each of the three captors who had been in or around the train like good little psychos. Watching that gashed eye slowly start to re-form itself had been like watching some sort of John Carpenter effect in reverse. He would never forget it.

Diirek forbade him from straying from the train and then had disappeared to wherever he went to sleep before the healing was finished, so Fred didn't get to see the whole show. But what he did see made him wonder about the werewolf. What if it had the same powers? Would it come for them? Was it really a werewolf, after all? It certainly looked *kind of* like the versions he'd seen in movies and comics and in his head since he'd been a boy. But it was also somehow *wrong*. There was something there, just under the surface, that began to nag at him until the questions finally overwhelmed his teenage mind. He'd convinced himself to go see the werewolf's body.

Now here he was, feeling somewhat safe and confident since it was daytime, but also scared shitless and unable to stop himself. *That about sums up being a teenager*, he thought in one of many increasingly regular moments of self-reflection. *Confident, yet scared shitless and unable to stop yourself.*

Something moved off in the cornfield. Fred stopped and listened. He reached behind him and pulled out a revolver that he'd taken from a dead man's hand two hours earlier. He had seen it the first time he and Diirek had explored the little town that hosted the railyard. That creepy house had been his first stop before heading to the scene of the werewolf-on-vampire crime. He didn't know if it even worked, but it was loaded. Minus the bullet that had prevented the previous owner from drawing breath again.

He felt better having it, and he felt damn cool as he pulled it out of his waistband. Although he wished he had a better place to carry it. It was damned uncomfortable back there, the cold metal barrel pressed between the tops of his insubstantial and pale asscheeks. Even before he pulled it out, he knew that some animal was to blame for the noise. The fading sound told of a small, scurrying creature much smaller than a werewolf. Still, he kept the pistol in his hand. He was getting close.

A few more careful paces brought into view an empty spot in the cornfield, and beyond that, he sensed the end of the field. He held the pistol up and walked forward one pace. Two. Three. He could see the area of flattened corn stalks now, but there was no dead werewolf. Only some blackened blood spots and vague signs of a struggle.

Fred focused on his breathing and stepped out to the edge of the cornfield, sweeping his vision and the gun around like he'd seen done on a thousand TV shows. Nothing. Green, untrimmed grass covered the distance of the sloping hill down to the tree-lined stream. Beyond the small stream, it looked as if the land sloped back up and evened out.

Over the tops of the trees, he could see the three large buildings Diirek had spotted the night before. He could see that the mansion in the center of the trio was at least four stories—five if there was a basement. The other buildings were almost as big. One looked like it could store several tractors and other large farm equipment. The other reminded him of a prison he'd seen once with his dad when they were driving to Tennessee, minus the tall fencing. It didn't seem to have any windows, or if it did, they were too small to see from this distance. It looked like a big concrete box. Not like anything he'd ever seen on a farm.

The buildings sat in the middle of a vast flat stretch of farmland with a small copse of trees behind them. There was a road through the corn, as evidenced by the gap Fred could just barely make out. One road in and one out, it looked like.

Something moved in the cornfield, behind him and to his left. Fred was inclined to ignore it, figuring it was a rabbit or birds or something. He half-listened for it to stop or get quieter but it didn't. It increased both in intensity and in proximity. Something big was coming through the corn, straight at him.

Fred looked around, muscles tensing and palms suddenly moist. Heading straight back the way he had come would be moving closer to the werewolf he was sure was loping toward him. He made a decision based solely on putting as much distance as possible between him and his attacker and sprinted to his right, along the edge of the cornfield. The sound of cornstalks being violently crushed stayed with him—grew closer even—as Fred pumped his legs, running faster than he'd ever run before.

But he wasn't fast enough.

Fred angled away from the corn too late. A hairy figure tackled him from behind. Fred went down hard, his momentum carrying him inexorably down the hill toward the meandering stream. His attacker rolled down with him, snarling and making strange noises. Fred shut his eyes and held onto the gun for dear life, knowing that it was his only chance.

They started to slow, the slope becoming less pronounced as it approached the stream. Fred ended up with his back to the ground, the figure above him. In a desperate move, his eyes still closed, he fired the pistol at where he thought the werewolf was in space. He yelled as he lay on the ground, pulling the trigger until the gun clicked empty. He waited for death to come, refusing to open his eyes. Nothing happened. His ears picked up the sound of a soft breeze ruffling tree leaves and the insistent trickle and flow of the stream. Nothing else.

There was the weight and warmth of foreign limbs on his legs but no movement. He opened his eyes, still lying on the ground, and looked at the gray sky, expecting the nightmare face he'd seen the previous night to fill his vision at any moment, expecting the figure resting on his legs to move, the muscles to bunch. He expected to feel the pain of fangs and claws entering his skin and tearing it to shreds. Instead, he felt the chilly air of the unusually cold day fill his lungs. He felt the small tremors of adrenaline begin to fade.

The minor scrapes and bruises he'd suffered on his tumble down the hill made him feel vibrant and impossibly alive. Although the injuries implied his mortality, he began to feel invincible, untouchable, immortal. With every second that passed, he felt more and more sure he had just bested a villain that would have killed any number of tough, capable men. Yet he still could not bring himself to look at it.

Fred, eyes to the sky, began to chuckle. *Wait until Diirek hears about this.* He wouldn't—couldn't be mad. He would be proud; Fred was sure of it. That notion alone got him moving. He set the pistol aside on the wild grass, placed his hands against the earth, and pushed himself up into a sitting position. For the first time, he got a decent look at his attacker. His face went slack at the sight of the figure sprawled there. That apathetic shock turned to confusion as a hundred thoughts pushed their way into his head. He looked around in a daze, thinking this some sort of weird joke.

Then it all clicked into place. The familiar eyes of the werewolf last night, the way it ran, the noises it made. It made sense but garnered more questions. Like, just what the hell was going on around here? And what, if anything, did it have to do with the trio of buildings off in the field past the stream?

Fred scrambled away from the dead figure, kicking his legs out from under it and standing up. He took a few steps back but never took his eyes from his ersatz attacker. Then he stepped back over to it and crouched down. He reached a hand out and turned its head towards him. The eyes were still open, and they seemed to verify his hypothesis.

He stood up. There was no doubt about it. Lying dead at Fred's feet was a chimpanzee. And it had a black collar around its neck with a gray box attached.

The conclusion was inevitable: Someone was turning apes into werewolves.

Chapter Nineteen

Never a Good Guy

Weller had the feeling he was being watched. And not in a cool, sexy way. In a genuinely creepy way. Like how animals in a zoo must have felt, back when there were still zoos. Or how women must feel all the time.

Having three vampires with him in the outskirts didn't put him at ease. Not surprising, seeing as the last time he was out here with vampires they left him to nearly get eaten by zombies. And then they were about to turn him into an unholy creature of the night after he got his arm and a few measly ribs broken. Goddamn vampires.

Weller looked up at the dark buildings scraping the night sky, sure that there were eyes peering from one or one hundred of those windows, watching the four of them pass below. Ricardo was on his left, unusually quiet, dressed in gray skinny jeans, a white t-shirt, and a pair of colorful Air Jordans. When Weller had first laid eyes on the vampire, he thought that his sense of style was pretty goofy for a middle-aged guy. But he'd since gotten used to it. And he had to remember that Ricardo was way past middle age. By a hundred years or so. Not that that made it any better, but vampires, in general, seemed to have either really great or truly abysmal senses of style.

On the detective's right walked Isabelle and Binta. Isabelle, the teenage vampire, wore a red and black plaid skirt and a white collared shirt over a sweater vest with a picture of a cat sewn into it. Binta wore a one-piece sleeveless yellow dress made from some sort of stretchy fabric. She moved with the grace and assurance of a lioness. Weller, aware of the creepy feeling of being watched, tried his best not to stare at her. He glanced over the top of Isabelle's dirty-blonde hair at Binta. She looked back at him, causing their eyes to meet for a moment before Weller shifted his gaze up above her and donned his best I-wasn't-looking-at-you-but-some-thing-just-over-your-head face. He just barely stopped himself from whistling nonchalantly.

For his part, Weller wore his obligatory tan suit jacket, matching slacks, and a crisp white collared dress shirt, sans tie. He had cut the right sleeve of the dress shirt away so he could fit it over his cast. Luckily, he hadn't had to damage his suit jacket, aside from a little stretching due to the snug fit of the plaster encasement. He had a police radio clipped to his belt, his Sig in his shoulder holster, and a general undercurrent of anger at his current physical ailments.

After the initial frenzied anarchy in the outskirts immediately follow-ing the uncouth arrival of the apocalypse, the city blocks they traveled seemed quiet. A little too quiet, perhaps. There was no lack of crazy shit happening outside the safe zone. But, according to most reports and the word of those individuals that still trickled into the safe zone from outside the city, it was less violent than some parts of the country.

The radio broadcasts initiated by some of the brilliant minds still alive in the safe zone gave warning to travelers heading their way. The message was twofold: We've got a little piece of safe land in which all are welcome, but you'll have to traverse a wasted city teeming with cannibalistic and downright asshole-ish assholes to get here. Good luck. (Of course, the message was much more elegant than that. I'm paraphrasing, Constant Weirdo. They had some damn good writers in the safe zone. Much better than the poor bastard who happened to record this story for posterity.)

The three vamps and one human detective were heading to where the most recent super zombie sighting had been. It was a few blocks away still, and a hush had fallen over the four of them. Weller got the feeling that it wasn't just the result of the creepy outskirts. He was sure they were all still in mourning. They had lost several of their own to the monster Merek. Lidia, Lewis, Corbin, Boris, Gretchen, and a few others would never be coming back. Weller hadn't known any of them very well, but he'd heard their names mentioned, mostly by Ricardo. He felt for them, but they couldn't just sit around doing nothing, as tempting as it might be.

Plus, with Diirek gone, it seemed that the vampires had no leader. This was in evidence back in their lair when a discussion on how to proceed in dealing with these super zombies had degraded into a shouting match. Weller had tried his best to snap them out of it, but half of the eighteen vampires wanted to go about it their own way. They appreciated what Weller had done for them with Merek, but they still felt having a human in tow would slow them down. He couldn't blame them. In his current state, he wouldn't want him around, either. Which was one reason why he needed their help. Again.

Goddamn vampires.

They walked down the middle of the street, stepping around detritus, zombie bodies with smashed heads, glass, and bullet casings. Someone had had a good old time throwing furniture and household appliances out of apartment windows far above, littering the road with the things that used to fill up people's lives but now just filled the street.

Weller's radio crackled to life at his hip, causing him to jump. He recognized the voice right away, and it caused the little hairs on the back of his neck to stand up.

"Weller. Kurt, man, come in. Come in, please." It was Hardiman, fear in his voice. Weller had never heard him this way. Ever. Hardiman was a tough old cop who would have already retired had it not been for the end of the damn world. Weller put the handheld radio to his mouth and pressed the button on the side.

"Hardiman? I'm here. Talk to me."

"He. . .he wants you to come. He's got some weird lookin' deadeyes here man, and he wants you to come. Huh? Oh, hold on. . ." Someone was speaking to Hardiman on his end of the radio, telling him what to say. The voice whispered and Weller couldn't make out what it was saying.

"Okay. Okay. Got it," Hardiman said. "I said I got it. Do you want to talk to him you little shit? Ow! Ow! Okay."

The vampires had gathered around Weller to listen, taking note of his body language and the concerned look on his face. Ricardo mouthed, '*What the fuck?*'

Weller shrugged.

"Damn. You still there Weller?" Hardiman asked.

"I'm here. What's going on? Where are you?"

"This little bastard's a pain in my butt. If it weren't for those damn deadeyes I'd whoop his ass."

Weller's eyes narrowed. Buck. The little bastard. Something growled on the other end of the line and Hardiman started yelling in pain.

"Dammit, Buck. Where do you want me to go?" Weller yelled into the radio.

"Corner of Lincoln and 9th," Buck said in a poor imitation of an action-movie announcer. Then, "Bring your friends."

Weller looked at the vamps, his eyebrows raised, but Buck wasn't done. The radio crackled again. "Where were the other drugs going?" Buck yelled in his false voice, then laughed. "Seriously, though. Come. Now. Or he dies."

"Fine. I'm coming, you little bastard."

"What other drugs is he talking about?" Ricardo asked once Weller took his thumb off the button. "The coke? What are you into with this guy, Detective?"

"Nothing. It's from a movie. The guy's an idiot. Let's go."

Weller filled the three vampires in about Buck on the way. He told them about how Diirek had saved him from Buck one night in the outskirts. And how he, Weller, had forced Buck into going on the monster hunt with him. And then the whole ordeal on top of the Paredo building.

"I remember you telling us about him that night in the alley. Saying he was a kind of half-zombie half-vampire," Binta said. "But you said he died. When did you know he was alive again?"

"Ricardo and I saw him the other night," Weller replied. "Honestly, I thought he was harmless. He was on my list of problems as soon as I knew he was alive, but it's a long list. And Buck didn't seem like much of a threat. But now I think he has something to do with the super zombies."

"Why do you think that?" Isabelle asked.

"I saw a video of him getting a bunch of dog cages and other supplies out of a pet store in the outskirts. A gang swooped in on him while he was at it, but he didn't seem to have any problems taking them out. There was something different about him on that video, too. He didn't carry himself the same as when I first met him. It's not good."

"And now he has a pal of yours. He must want payback, Detective," Ricardo said.

"Yeah, well, he can get in line," Weller said. "I need to know if you guys will help me with this. He's not smart, but he might be able to use his special abilities to his advantage. So we need to catch him. Or, if it comes down to it, eliminate him. But only on my say so."

"I got your back. You know that, Detective," Ricardo said, slapping Weller on the back.

"I'll help," Isabelle said.

"Me too," Binta agreed.

Weller nodded, unwilling to voice his concerns about them leaving him high and dry like they did last time. He hoped that horde wasn't nearby this time.

The four of them turned the corner at Lincoln and 8th to find a strange scene arrayed before them a city block away at 9th. There were four metal barrels at the intersection, one placed on each corner. Flames sprouted and jumped out of the metal drums, casting light on several figures standing there between the barrels, as if blocking off either side of 9th street. Or making a corridor down Lincoln. In the middle of the intersection stood a lone man, small in stature. Buck.

Weller looked around for Hardiman but didn't see him. There were seven figures total. Three on each side of the street and Buck in the middle. The detective really hoped that the other six weren't super zombies. It was his one wish right now. An even higher priority than the song of which he still couldn't remember the name. But, as the four of them approached, Weller realized that the figures *were* super zombies. And the fact that they were standing there, staring at him and the vamps, was terrible indeed.

The four of them stopped about fifteen yards away. "Where's Hardiman?" Weller called out.

"He's . . . around," Buck said, tenting his fingers and smiling. The flames from the barrels gave him the look of a crazed, evil idiot. The worst kind of evil, and idiot, for that matter.

"All right," Weller said. "No Hardiman, no reason for me to be here. Bye, Buck." Weller turned around and started walking away. The vampires did the same.

"Wait," Buck shouted. "Okay fine. He's here. Can't blame a guy for building suspense. Sheesh, dude." The small undead man gestured to the three super zombies to his left as Weller and company turned back around. Two of the zombies marched off into the darkness beyond the firelight and came back with a bloodied, bound, and gagged Hardiman.

Weller glanced quickly at the man, fighting the urge to show his fury. He put his eyes back on Buck. "What do you want?"

"I want you to acknowledge what you did to me," Buck said. "People like you—cops like you—are always leaving a trail of collateral damage behind them. Even now, in a world where the greatest threat is the undead, you still manage to get people hurt and killed. And you can't even apologize for it? That's fucked up, dude. And it has been happening since . . . forever. So, I just want you to apologize. To me. In front of your friends. And I'll let Hardiman go."

"Buck," Weller said, unable to stop himself from shaking, "I am sorry. I never meant for that to happen. And I wasn't laughing at you the other night. I was laughing in relief. And because of drugs . . . But mostly relief that it wasn't some monster coming to kill me. It was—"

"Only me? Only little old Buck. The butt of everyone's jokes. Nothing to fear from him. He's a fuck-up and he's too short to be taken seriously."

"That's not what—"

"Shut the fuck up, Detective," Buck yelled, and his voice seemed to change. Like it went down an octave or suddenly belonged to someone else. "What you don't know is that I *am* something to fear. And I'm not an enemy you want."

"No. You're not my enemy. At least I hope you're not. You're one of the good guys, right?"

"That's right," Buck said. "I am. Unfortunately, you think you're one, too. But you're not. You never were. Never."

Weller had no response to that. Not only because he hadn't expected any of this from Buck, but because during dark times in his life, he had been plagued by thoughts much like those the strange little undead man expressed. Things weren't going the way he had hoped, and he was beginning to see why Buck was pissed. It made sense when he put himself in the smaller man's much smaller shoes.

But it didn't mean he would forgive and forget what Buck had done to Hardiman. You don't just kidnap a cop and get away with it. Not even during the end of the goddamn world. And the fact that these super zombies were listening to Buck was even more disconcerting.

The detective sensed a change next to him, noticing that the three vampires were backing slowly away from him.

"Stop moving," Buck said. The vampires stopped.

"I'm sorry, all right Buck? Now, can you please let Hardiman go? If you can't keep your word, you can't really call yourself a good guy, right?"

Buck smiled. "I was always going to let him go. That's the difference between us. I really am a good guy. Only I never thought I was." The small undead man walked a few steps to Hardiman and the obedient zombies. He pulled a bloody plastic bag out of his pocket, dug around in it, and tossed a piece to each of the zombies. Once the two zombies had their treats, they stepped away from Hardiman.

"Is that human flesh?" Weller whispered to Ricardo.

"I believe it is. I can smell it from here."

Buck used a key to unlock one of Hardiman's own handcuff clasps, leaving the metal bracelet dangling from the man's right arm. Then he leaned down and ripped what looked to be bunched-up plastic wrap from around Hardiman's ankles. Buck shoved the man toward Weller, leaving the tape over his mouth, which had been wrapped around his head.

Hardiman stumbled quickly towards Weller, trying to speak but having trouble ripping the tape from around his mouth. His eyes were wide, and his hands were shaking. Weller stepped forward to help his old friend and mentor.

All at once the vampires started shouting, calling out warnings to Weller. The sound of running footsteps filled the air around them, seeming to close in from the darkness on all sides. Weller reached Hardiman and put his hands on his shoulders just as he heard the yelling from the three vampires intensify. He looked back over his shoulder to see a small stampede of super zombies approaching from behind them. Binta, Ricardo, and Isabelle attacked without hesitation.

Weller turned back to Hardiman, who was still struggling with the tape around his mouth and stuck to his bushy mustache. Something warm and wet splattered Weller's face, causing him to snap his eyes shut. He opened them a half-second later to see a bloody hand sticking out of Hardiman's chest. The old detective's eyes were wide with pain and unfathomed horror. He groaned into the adhesive blocking his mouth. The hand shot forward and grabbed at Weller, who moved his head back just in time. The bloody hand grasped his shirt collar instead of his neck.

The sounds of fighting and bones snapping from behind Weller increased steadily and grew closer. Buck's head poked over Hardiman's shoulder to stare at the detective. Hardiman, hands still at the tape, seemed to rally his strength and rip it down, taking much of his mustache with it. Then he took the open handcuff bracelet that hung from his right hand and clicked it around Buck's hand protruding from his chest.

"What the fuck?" Buck said, standing on his tiptoes to see what had just happened.

"I'm sorry," Hardiman gasped, looking at Weller. "I told him—"

Buck let go of Weller's shirt and yanked his hand out of Hardiman's chest, but it was connected to the older detective's wrist. The resulting action looked much like Hardiman was slapping himself very hard in the chest. The two intertwined men lurched away from Weller. Hardiman started to speak again, tears rolling down his cheeks, while Weller looked on in blank terror. "Get to J—" Buck yanked again, only this time he put enough power on it to snap Hardiman's wrist with the handcuff. Weller's old friend screamed, his hand now canted up at a vicious angle, pinned to his chest.

Weller pulled his pistol and aimed it at Buck through Hardiman. The detective could hear with some faraway part of his mind that Binta and Isabelle were screaming in fury.

Buck yanked a third time, and Hardiman's wrecked hand folded back on itself and his arm was swallowed by his own chest up to the elbow. Weller moved around to get a better angle on Buck.

Hardiman convulsed, gasped, and looked up at Weller. Slowly, the old detective pulled his right arm out of his chest. It came out without a hand. Only a bloody, broken nub that dripped blood continuously. He held it up to Weller as if in evidence. His mouth opened, his chin pushing the bunched tape down on his neck. No sound escaped his mouth. He fell forward, his dead weight smacking the blacktop, fragile facial bones crunching with the impact.

Hardiman's fall revealed Buck, who retrieved Hardiman's severed hand from the handcuff hanging off his wrist and threw it away with a smile.

Weller yelled and emptied his gun into the small man, savoring the slowing of time and each twitch of Buck's body as bullets tore through his flesh and bone. He reloaded and kept firing, ignoring the pain shooting up his broken arm with every shot. Halfway through the new clip something slammed into him from behind, knocking him forward. He instinctively put both hands out to cushion his fall. His cast shattered and his healing arm broke again as he hit the ground.

For a few long seconds, his fury was replaced by pain. Only pain.

He tried to get up, to finish emptying his new clip into Buck, but something smacked into his head as he moved. His world was once again pain. And darkness.

Then someone was laughing. And Weller had the sensation that he was moving. Things were quiet. He had a vague hope that he was dead.

But he was far from it.

CHAPTER TWENTY

SOME THINGS CAN'T BE UNSEEN

D iirek stood in the cornfield, gazing through binoculars at the three large structures in the distance. He stood back, semi-hidden by some intact cornstalks. His eyes were binoculars of sorts, and like binoculars, they were limited in how far and how well they would allow him to see. The binoculars he had found were slightly better.

Fred was back at the train, on Diirek's orders. He had been furious at the kid for coming back to the spot without him, daytime or not. His anger even surprised himself. He was coming to like the kid. Which was exactly what he didn't want to do. He wasn't ready to like anyone again. Especially one so fragile as a human.

Lidia's loss was still fresh in his mind, and she had been more capable than most vampires, let alone even the most badass of humans. The likes of Chuck Norris, Bear Grylls, and any number of Navy Seals would cower in her presence like frightened kittens. And that wasn't an exaggeration. She had gone through a phase in which she enjoyed frightening supposedly tough grown men. Diirek had been there. It was hilarious.

A half-moon hung over the world far to Diirek's right, its light was dulled, blocked by thin but persistent cloud cover that stretched to every horizon. He brought the binoculars away from his eyes and looked down at the area in which Fred claimed to have killed the ape. There was no body there. No evidence, aside from the dark spots that may have been dried blood.

Diirek believed the kid, though. He had no reason not to. And the fact that the werewolf's body was gone indicated that there was something more to this picture. Something that had to do with the buildings off in the distance. And maybe even something to do with the bombings and the zombies. It was a hunch, but one he intended to investigate.

Not for the first time, Diirek thought it would be useful to have Weller here with him. Detective work had never really interested Diirek, and as a result, he hadn't spent much time developing those skills. He'd never needed them. Now that he did, he was seriously thinking about some more backup. If not Weller, then maybe Isabelle or Binta. After all, they and several others had volunteered to go with him, but he had refused their company. He had wanted to mourn alone. He still wanted to, but things were getting a little more complicated. The existence of werewolves—whether human- or ape-based—was not something to take lightly.

If someone could so easily create werewolves, he thought, *what would stop them from creating zombies? And to what end?* He had seen movement at the buildings in the form of a few vehicles coming in on the single road and electric lights turning on in two of the three structures. The third didn't look like it had any windows to emit any light. Fred was right, it looked like a prison, without the fences.

The vampire started to bring the binoculars back up when a tree on the other side of the small creek shook. Diirek crouched and peered out from between the cornstalks. A werewolf lumbered along the stream. Diirek caught glimpses of it as it passed between the trees blocking his view. As he watched, it stopped and seemed to sniff the air. It canted its nose upward and swung it back and forth, snorting at the air.

Looking at the beast, Diirek knew that Fred was right. It was an ape underneath. The way it moved and the slightly simian look to it was affirmation enough. It was what had looked so familiar to him the previous night. He'd simply been unable to place it.

The werewolf swung its nose in Diirek's direction and then stopped. It lowered its snout and seemed to look right at him across the considerable distance that separated them. Diirek made no move, staring back, waiting.

The beast propelled itself forward, leaping the small stream easily, and bounding up the hill toward Diirek. It began to growl and yap as it came, moving incredibly fast. Diirek started to move when a crashing sound erupted from the cornfield almost directly behind him. He froze.

That same strange yapping sound filled the air, now from the other direction. The dry cacophony of snapping cornstalks grew closer. Diirek couldn't see the beast, but he knew it was a werewolf. They were coming from both directions. The vampire flexed his leg muscles, ready to pounce at whichever one got to him first.

The yapping noises were ear-splittingly loud. The sound from the corn told Diirek that the werewolf was almost upon him. He didn't think he could survive two of them, but he'd try. The thought of giving up was far from his mind tonight. Why this was, he wasn't exactly sure.

A werewolf flashed by the vampire some five feet away in the corn. Diirek moved his head, watching in confusion as the beast burst out of the vegetable field to slam directly into the other werewolf. The two beasts continued yapping as they rolled down the hill in a flurry of black limbs and snapping jaws.

Diirek watched, amazed that he wasn't being torn apart. The tumbling werewolves came to a stop near the bottom of a hill and the yapping changed somewhat, growing more frantic. They were struggling errat- ically at first, then a rhythm became apparent to Diirek as he watched them fight. Only, he realized slowly, they weren't fighting. Just the op- posite, in fact.

After a moment of disbelief, Diirek came to terms with the fact that he was watching two werewolves have strange, violent, hairy, werewolf sex. He found it hard to look away for a long moment, his eyes narrowing in a confused and curious disgust, bordering on outright nausea. Then something strange happened. Not quite as strange as two werewolves having sex, but still strange, nonetheless.

When it looked like the furry frenzy was coming into its own, both the werewolves convulsed. Their yapping and humping stopped, and they began to howl. The convulsing and howling looked and sounded like pain and frustration, but Diirek wasn't sure. He'd never seen werewolves mate before. *Maybe that's just how they finish*, he thought, confused. The two werewolves moved away from each other, and they each seemed to claw at their collars. Then one of the creatures ran away to the left and out of sight.

The howling stopped. So did the neck-scratching.

The lone remaining werewolf loped off into the darkness under the trees bordering the stream. It slurped some water out of the brook and then sat there, doing nothing. Diirek wasn't sure, but he thought that the creature was lamenting the loss of its mate. Or, more likely, the fact that it had been interrupted before it had finished. Diirek felt for the beast. He'd been there before, and he wouldn't wish it upon anyone.

CHAPTER TWENTY-ONE

A DARK AGREEMENT

Weller came to in a small room. A painting of a quaint blue house in a field of wildflowers came into focus slowly. At first, he thought he was in a motel room, judging by the quality of the painting, but he quickly realized that it was worse: he was in the hospital.

Daylight slashed through the gaps in the curtains over the window to his right. He looked at his surroundings, wincing at the pain in his head and neck. His twice-broken arm had been reset and re-casted. There was a note scrawled on it, marring the pristine whiteness. "Break it again and you're on your own." It was barely legible and signed with a swooping series of letters that looked like hieroglyphs. Some doctor he had.

The pieces of the night before began to fall into place, but they seemed far away and dreamlike. He kept coming back to Buck shoving his hand through Hardiman's chest. Like a goddamn Xenomorph. Had that really happened? He recalled Hardiman trying desperately to tell him something. Something vitally important. What was it? He remembered emptying one or two clips into Buck, making himself feel better momentarily. But if the monster Merek couldn't kill the little bastard, a few measly bullets weren't going to do it, either. But he could always hope.

As sleep fell away from him like walls from a house fire, the realization that it had all really happened came crashing down on him. Hardiman was dead. Buck had a small army of trained super zombies. All because of Weller and Diirek's actions one day three weeks ago. Weller had made an enemy of Buck by forcing him to help hunt Merek. Diirek had formulated the plan that killed Merek—but that had the unwanted effect of creating these freakish, semi-intelligent zombies. He needed Diirek back. If for no other reason than this was *his* mess too.

He should be here to clean it up. And maybe to help keep me from getting killed, Weller thought as he started getting out of bed.

He found his clothes in the small wardrobe. They were covered in Hardiman's dried blood and caked with dirt. Just as he was pulling his pants on, the door to the small room opened. Weller was beyond modesty. He didn't protest as Shellbourne came in with a strange look on her face.

"Captain," Weller mumbled, as he shook his stained white shirt out, wincing as he did so.

"Detective," Shellbourne said, staring at him. She held the look for too long, which was the first clue that something was seriously wrong. On reflex, Weller looked down and noticed that his uniform dark brown skin was a mottled mess of nasty purple bruises, mostly where his ribs had been broken, although there were new ones forming from the previous night.

"What's up, Captain?" Weller said, gingerly sliding his right arm into his dirty shirt.

This seemed to break the severe woman's daze. She looked up at him and took a sighing breath. "First off, I need to say something to you. And I need you to know that I'm only saying this now because I have to. Because in a few moments you won't be capable of listening to me."

"What the hell are you—"

"Let me finish, Weller," she interrupted. "We are going to have to talk about whatever the hell is going on with you. About what happened to you last night. How you got those bruises and how you broke your arm again."

Weller opened his mouth to talk but the look on Shellbourne's face kept the words in his throat.

"But," she continued, "now is not the time. I know that, and you'll know it in a second. You are going to tell me the truth the first chance we get. I have a feeling you will want to."

Weller stared at her, dumbfounded. He'd never heard her speak this way. To him or anyone. She sounded so . . . human. It freaked him out. Whatever was coming next wasn't going to be good. He felt sick with anticipation.

Shellbourne sighed again, looking like she would rather be anywhere else, but resigned to saying whatever she was about to say to him. "It's JayLynn," she said. "Someone broke into her apartment last night. We don't know where she is. She's missing."

Weller felt an impossible blackness open inside of him. The quiet room suddenly got very loud with the sound of blood rushing through his ears. His hands, which had been fumbling with a button on his shirt, fell to his sides then curled into fists. Bile rose in his throat and one word floated in his mind, repeated insanely fast and with growing intensity: *No*.

Weller opened his mouth to speak once again. His throat clicked. He swallowed savagely before speaking. "What about Berena?"

"Who's that?" Shellbourne said.

"The girl. Was there a girl there? She was staying with my—with JayLynn." He'd almost said wife, but that wasn't right. She wasn't his wife. Not anymore. But that made no difference now.

"That explains the clothes and the made-up room," Shellbourne said. "I'm sorry, Weller. We didn't know that anyone else was supposed to be there. There was no girl."

Weller grabbed his shoes from the wardrobe cabinet and bent over to put them on. "Maybe she was staying with a friend," he said. "She has a friend in the apartment building. Maybe she was there. Maybe they were both there. Maybe—"

"Weller. There was some blood—"

"What!? How much? Why didn't you tell me?"

"Not enough to mean anything. I'll tell you everything if you just sit down."

"No. I need to go there and check for Berena. She may be with the friend. Then we can talk."

"Weller. What is this all about? Do you know? Is this someone trying to get at you?"

Weller looked at her steadily. "You're right, captain. I'll tell you the truth. Just not right now."

***

It was clear to Weller as he surveyed the wreckage of JayLynn's apartment that it was Buck's doing. The detective had played Hardiman's words—his half-choked sentences—over and over in his mind as he made his way to his ex-wife's apartment. He had been trying to apologize for giving up JayLynn's address. He'd been trying to warn Weller.

The detective's first stop had been Berena's friend's apartment. The family who lived there, two women and their daughter, had not seen the teenage girl in several days.

Buck had taken them both.

There were signs of a struggle. Broken lamps. Smashed furniture. A small but worrisome amount of dried blood dribbled over the carpet.

The void grew inside Weller as his eyes took in the scene. And as that void grew, so did a sickness he felt to his core. A furious notion took hold as he stood transfixed by the strings of dark crimson staining the carpet. He felt something twitch in his right eye, noting it in a barely conscious manner. His teeth groaned as he clenched his jaw. Something wet and warm touched his lips.

There was movement behind him—the sound of a foot scuffing carpet. Weller turned around to see JayLynn's elderly neighbor Rick Grimes standing there. The man, well into his seventies, stood two paces inside the apartment. He was dressed in striped pajamas under a light robe. Worn house slippers covered his feet. He held a cane in his left hand. His right hand was missing. The guy had never told Weller how he'd lost the hand, and Weller had never asked.

"Detective," Grimes said, without even an inkling of pity in his eyes. Weller thanked him silently for that. The old man seemed to radiate the strength that Weller felt was so severely lacking in his own resolve. Not for the first time, Weller wondered what the old man had been through in his life.

"Grimes," the detective said. "She's gone." It was all he could think to say.

The old man nodded, then looked over his shoulder. Shellbourne was out in the hall. She had insisted on coming with him. He hadn't had a vehicle at the hospital, so Weller had taken a ride from her. She knew enough to wait in the hall for him.

"What is it?" Weller asked. Grimes stepped stiffly back to the open door and swung it shut with the end of his right forearm. He locked the deadbolt. Shellbourne immediately started banging on the door, shouting halfheartedly for them to open up. Weller stepped over to Grimes. The old man had something. He had seen something.

"You're bleeding," Grimes said, gesturing at Weller's face.

Weller stepped to the wall between the kitchen and living room to a small decorative mirror. His nose was bleeding and a few blood vessels had burst in his right eye, turning much of the white sclera blood-red. He wiped the blood away with his hand as he stepped back to Grimes.

"Listen," Grimes said. "I know you don't want to hear any sort of advice from an old man like me. Especially now. But I have to tell you this." He paused, his eyes moving in surety of thought. "You do whatever you have to do," Grimes said, bringing his eyes up to meet Weller's and hold them steady. "There's no sense telling you not to. But you can't expect to win. Not outright. You'll lose something. You can count on that." The old man's gaze strayed toward his right arm as he spoke, but he seemed to catch himself. With some effort, he returned his gaze to Weller's face.

"But you'll likely lose everything if you go after these guys expecting complete success," Grimes continued. "You need to get your mind around the fact that you will experience more pain than you ever have. There's no getting past that, now. I don't know exactly what's happening here. But I do know how the world works. And it has only gotten worse since my day. So, you go into this thing knowing that you'll lose something, and you may just come out ahead. It will allow you to think clearly. That's your greatest weapon."

Grimes took a deliberate breath and placed the stub at the end of his right forearm on Weller's left shoulder. "Do you understand what I'm saying to you? What I mean when I say pain?"

Weller looked down at Grimes. He said nothing.

"Good," Grimes said, bringing his arm back to his side. "Good."

Shellbourne abruptly stopped banging on the door. Neither man seemed to notice.

"Now," Grimes continued. "Here's what I saw: There was five of them. And I'll be damned if they weren't dressed up as zombies. Hell, maybe they were zombies, although I hope to God that's not the case. A little guy seemed to be calling the shots. He was the only one that talked, anyway. And he looked a little worse for wear. Almost like he'd been shot, and the wounds were still healing.

"When they took them, both of the girls were still alive. From what I could see through my cracked door, JayLynn had a cut on her head. It was bleeding like a sonofabitch, but that's how head wounds do. It didn't look too bad otherwise." Grimes broke eye contact with Weller again, this time looking down at the floor before he spoke. "I . . . I thought about doing something. I still have my revolver. But I haven't fired it in a while. I was afraid I'd wind up killing JayLynn or Berena."

Weller put a hand on the old man's shoulder and squeezed. "Thanks, Rick," he said.

The detective stepped around the old man and unlocked the door. He opened it and looked over his shoulder at Grimes, seeing the man clearly for the first time since he'd known him. Seeing a piece of who he'd been. His advice was sound, Weller thought. And he'd do his best to follow it.

As he stepped into the hallway Weller made an agreement with that complete darkness he now found filling himself. An agreement that he would give himself over to it if he could only get JayLynn and Berena to safety. He'd give himself up to whatever awaited him. And he would do it happily. Willingly.

With a fucking dead man's grin on his face.

CHAPTER TWENTY-TWO

MEDIUM-RARE ZOMBIE

"Hardiman's dead," Weller said to Shellbourne as they walked out of the apartment building. They stopped on the stairs and she looked at Weller, shock on her face. A warm wind stirred her frizzled, crinkled hair. Her eyes were a bright gray in the sunlight of the afternoon, her slender and rodent-like face momentarily took on a more human countenance as she absorbed this information.

"How?" she said after a moment.

"That's where it gets complicated, and I don't have time for all the questions that will inevitably come from the answer to that one. I need to find my wife and Berena. I just needed you to know that Hardiman is dead. I'll tell his wife and kids as soon as I can if you want me to."

Weller started walking down the stairs to the sidewalk. His car was parked about a mile away. He could get there quickly if he ran.

"It's the zombies, isn't it?" Shellbourne said behind him. "They're real. Not humans playing dress-up, right?"

He turned to her, a combination of annoyance and surprise on his face. "That's part of it, yeah."

She nodded once, a small, reluctant motion.

"Where the hell are you going, anyway Weller? Do you know where they are? Because if you do, you need to tell me right now so we can get a plan together. You have the police department at your back for this."

His plan was to head back to Lincoln and 9th to see if he could find anything useful to find JayLynn and Berena. Once it got dark, he would head to his old friends the vampires. With enough of them, they could put up a decent fight. But he wasn't about to tell Shellbourne any of that.

He realized that he would prefer the help of the vamps over the help of the cops. Less chance of hostages getting killed by friendly fire that way. "The police can't help. Not with this," he said. "Things have changed. It's a different world now, Captain. Our way of doing things is no longer the right way. If it ever was. We're outgunned but the other side doesn't even use guns. . ." He trailed off, his thoughts turning to how exactly he would get JayLynn and Berena back safely. Thinking about what Grimes said, and all the city had been through since the apocalypse shattered reality.

"What do they use?" Shellbourne asked, genuinely concerned.

"Immortality," he said. "Or close to it."

"You're serious? This is worse than zombies? Worse than the world exploding?"

"Much worse. Everything is shit. More so than ever. But don't worry about me. I've got some. . .friends that I think can help sort this out. Get everything back to normal levels of shit. Status quo shit."

"Are these friends immortal, too?"

Weller looked at her hard, surprised by the question. Maybe he never gave her the benefit of the doubt. Maybe she was good police, after all.

"I gotta go, Cap. I'll let you know how things turn out. Or not. If you don't hear from me in a couple of days, I'm dead. You'll have to tell Hardiman's family."

"I'll tell them," she said.

Weller looked at her hard then said, "Thanks, Captain," before starting off again.

"Wait," Shellbourne said, running down the steps to her car parked at
the curb. Weller watched as she opened the door and grabbed a handheld
radio out.

"Just in case," she said, tossing it to him. He caught it left-handed and
looked at it like it was about as useless as his broken right arm. Which,
for what was coming, it was. But, then again, Buck had a police radio, so
perhaps it would come in handy. Weller raised the radio slightly in thanks
and then turned to run. Shellbourne watched him go.

***

Weller arrived at Lincoln and 9th twenty-three minutes later. By now
the National Guard troops that manned the one legit safe zone entrance
knew him well. They simply moved their blockade vehicles and waved
him through.

He pulled over at the curb and got out. The afternoon sun shone
down 9th street, making the intersection seem innocuous.

The barrels in which the fires had been burning the night before were
still there. There were a couple of super zombie bodies lying around. It
was kind of hard to tell exactly how many since they were in pieces, but
it looked like three total. The vamps had put up a fight while Weller had
been dealing with Buck. Of that he was sure.

He looked around for Hardiman's body but couldn't find it. He
guessed that his old friend was now wandering around with cloudy eyes
and an insatiable appetite for human flesh. The thought both chilled him
and made him furious.

Something glinted in the sunlight, catching his attention. He went
over to the nearest barrel on the right. Snagged at the bottom of it was a
bunched-up piece of plastic, moving slightly in the soft wind. He picked

it up, remembering that it had been used to bind Hardiman's feet. Buck had ripped it off so the man could walk over to Weller.

There was nothing special about it at first glance. It was clear plastic wrap. He had a roll of the stuff in one of his kitchen drawers. Used it to cover leftovers on occasion. But as he pulled it apart, stretching it out to take a closer look, he realized that it was much wider than the roll he had at home. Almost twice as wide. And maybe just slightly thicker. A millimeter or two. Not the kind of thing you could see with your eyes, but the kind that you knew by the feel and strength of the plastic. It was industrial grade. Like the kind people used in restaurants. Back when there were restaurants in operation.

Weller held the dirty plastic in his hand as he traversed a map of the city in his head. He came up with damn near ten restaurants close by. Any one of which Buck could be hiding in.

He looked back at the ground and walked around, looking for another clue. Something with a restaurant's name on it would be preferable. Buck was definitely that dumb. Or, he had been. Maybe not so much anymore. The small man had changed. A change wrought by Weller—at least partially.

His search of the area around the barrels brought no results, so he widened the area. He spent the better part of an hour searching each side of the intersection to a depth of fifteen yards. But he had to keep going back over the same ground again. He couldn't focus, couldn't concentrate. His mind wasn't working.

When he finally finished his search, he'd found nothing useful. Nothing. No blown napkins. No to-go boxes. No menus. No pens with the name on them. Nothing.

Weller dropped the plastic wrap into the roadway and kicked one of the metal barrels down. He stalked to the next barrel and kicked it down, grunting with the pain that seemed to permeate his entire body with each movement.

"Fuck!" he screamed into the waning afternoon, collapsing to his knees in the middle of the intersection. "Just give me something, God-damnit. Let me think clearly for five fucking minutes."

Something moved down 9th street about a block away. It was a pair of zombies turning the corner, headed toward him. Weller jumped up and ran to the zombies, picking up a broken bottle from the gutter as he went. He jammed the jagged glass of the bottle into one zombie's eye socket. The other one he hit with the curved elbow of his cast, causing him to cry out in pain as he jarred his broken arm. The first zombie stopped moving with the bottle to the brain, but the second was still writhing on the ground. Weller stomped its head in, a joyless smile on his face.

He headed back to the intersection breathing hard, shaking the brains and skull fragments off his shoe as he went. He walked around in a circle, taking everything in, trying to see it with fresh eyes. He noticed the super-zombie pieces again and decided to give them one last look, for good measure. He brought the errant limbs together, recreating the bodies. The only items missing were the heads. But, judging by the small piles of gore around, the heads had been smashed.

There were a couple of limbs that didn't belong to the bodies lying there, but he managed to partially re-assemble two men and a woman. It was the woman's right leg that caught his attention. He went to pick it up to complete the zombie puzzle when he noticed that the left knee was wrapped in plastic. And there was something bright pink poking out of the skin around her knee joint.

Weller unwound the plastic wrap to get a closer look. As the plastic came away, it was clear to Weller that the knee had been severely damaged. There was a jagged wound that almost completely circled the leg just under the kneecap. When he had removed the plastic wrap, the wound opened slightly, revealing colored plastic stuck through the muscle around the knee. He widened the wound and pulled out the pink plastic piece. It was about three and a half inches long, with one end pointed and the other rounded. It had embossed letters on it. Weller used his thumb to wipe away the gore obscuring them.

M - RARE, it read. It was a steak marker. Restaurants used them to keep track of which steak was cooking in which way. He set it aside and looked back at the knee. There was another wedged in there. He pulled it out. This one was white, and it said MEDIUM. He turned the leg, inspecting the outside of the knee, pulling the knee joint apart, looking past the rotting meat for more markers. He found a third, but it was a different style than the other ones. It was made from wood instead of plastic. He dug into the flesh and pulled it out. It was slightly longer and sharper than the other ones. This one read WELL DONE.

He arranged all three of them on the sidewalk and stared down at them. It was clear that they had been a shitty attempt to hold the knee together. They had been shoved through the wound, pinning the knee back together. And then the whole thing had been wrapped in the food-grade plastic. It told him that Buck didn't have an endless supply of these super zombies. Otherwise, why would he go to the trouble of trying to repair one? But another, more pertinent question came to mind: *Why would a restaurant order two different types of steak markers?*

They wouldn't. Weller jumped up and ran back to his car. It was late in the evening. By the time he got back to the vampires, it would be dark. He could get them together and formulate a plan. Then they could go save JayLynn and Berena. Because he knew where they were.

CHAPTER TWENTY-THREE

THE ORIGIN OF ZOMBIES

T he tablet had one video on it. It had a bunch of apps that were useless without the internet. It had no passcode, no pin, no fingerprint protection. And it belonged to some guy named Britton Delarange.

Val, a vampire who looked like the shadow of a Russian model—the very same vamp who had accidentally helped turn Buck into what he now was—looked at the tablet with furrowed brows. It had just been sitting there, propped against a column. It was almost as if the tablet had been waiting for her. Val's pale blue eyes glanced around the abandoned subway station, questing for signs of life. She found none, save a couple of rats the size of guinea pigs and a variety of crawling and scuttling insects. She was alone.

She navigated back to the sole video on the flat computer and re-read the name. *Vampires - Watch Me*! It read. So she did. She clicked on the button with one slender and ageless finger. And she watched. At first, she chuckled. But as the video went on, she began to feel like this was bad news. Or some sort of joke. A very elaborate joke. Several minutes later, when the video was over, she looked around again. Seeing no one, she headed further down into the abandoned subway tunnel. She needed to show this to the others. Now.

***

The screen went black momentarily, then a smiling face appeared. A white guy, early thirties, smooth-shaven cheeks. The top half of his head somehow didn't match the bottom half. If you were to see him with some sort of lower face covering, you would assume that he had a strong jaw. Maybe even a dimple in his chin. His thick hairline, slight widow's peak, smooth forehead, prominent cheekbones, and the divots of his temples all screamed "leading man," but his nose was a little too wide and his chin nearly non-existent. His lips were thin and frail-looking, and his jaw looked not only punchable, but glass to boot.

He smiled wider, revealing a row of perfectly white and orderly teeth. It was a stretch to think that they were his original teeth. Probably all brand new. His neck was visible on the screen, his Adam's apple half-hidden beneath his weak chin. The tendons and width of his neck bespoke a fit but thinly framed body.

"Hello," he said in a high voice, still smiling wide. "My name is Anders Revak. Welcome to my crib!" The camera pulled out to reveal that Anders was standing in front of large wooden doors outside of a house. It cut to a drone shot in double speed as it circled around the house, then it returned to the front of the house and moved in on Anders on the large stone porch, his arms stretched out in welcome.

The house was massive. A mixture of a medieval castle and the White House. It had nearly a dozen windows in the front, all of them with Juliet balconies. There were parapets on top, bordering the sloping roof, which accounted for much of the European castle look. In the middle of the top floor there was a covered balcony projecting from the facade, and it wasn't a stretch to see this man orating to his subjects from there. If he had any subjects.

The drone camera pulled out further in fast motion, revealing a large circular driveway bordered by cornfields. There were two other buildings in the background, partially hidden by the bulk of the house.

The screen cut back to Anders on the ground. "Come on in," he said to the camera, winking as he turned to open his front door. The inside of the house was an interior designer's nightmare. It continued the mishmash of architectural stylings so evident from the exterior. He showed off the impressive entryway and the sitting rooms to either side. Next was the giant kitchen, complete with a large brick oven in the middle.

"This is where I like to watch my human flesh cook," he said, smiling mischievously at the camera. Then he laughed, doubling over, and slapping his knee. He wore a cream-colored silk shirt, the top two buttons unfastened, revealing a glimpse of his thick and hairless upper chest. His black slacks and dress shoes looked expensive and immaculate. "But seriously. This is my favorite room in the house. I mean, who doesn't love a nice big kitchen? All the sharp instruments. Plenty of places to drain blood out of dead meat. Just wonderful . . . Okay, let's keep the tour going. I hope you guys are enjoying my crib!"

Anders walked out of the kitchen and into a long hallway. He walked through various rooms filled with uncomfortable-looking furniture, famous pieces of artwork, and musical instruments. He showed off a large, circular library on the second floor. The space was in the middle of the house, and the camera tilted up to reveal stained glass skylights far above. When the camera did this, it also became apparent that the library had three levels. It extended all the way up to the fourth floor. Each level had a staircase to the next, and all the shelves were filled with books. Hundreds of thousands of them.

"My second favorite room. I read books. A lot. I've read all the books in this room. Swear to God I have. No foolin'." When he said this last sentence, it had the ring of a doomed politician catering to a crowd of country bumpkins. Even a child could see through this man's bullshit.

Next up was the home theater, which took a full two minutes as Anders listed all his favorite movies. Many of them were vampire films. Adjacent to the theater was a room dedicated entirely to vampires. Here, Anders became serious. Almost somber.

"This is my shrine," he said, picking up a small stone statue of a cloaked and hunched man. The walls were black and nearly covered with images from vampire lore and pop culture. There were books on vampires, stacks of Blu-ray discs, artwork, graphic novels, action figures, and even a refrigerator filled with packets of blood. "I come in here when I need to think, or I need to remember why I do what I do. I can't let myself become sidetracked. This is how I remind myself."

The next five minutes of footage entailed more of the same. Different rooms of the house filled up with convenience and luxury and cutting-edge technology. He had an editing suite, a music studio, a study with a bat-shaped fireplace, and even a bowling alley.

It all seemed innocuous until Anders guided the camera out to one of the other buildings on the property. The first shot of the video had been in daylight, but it was now nighttime as Anders led the way outside and to another nearby building. He stopped and turned at the smooth metal door, almost dancing back and forth in excitement. "You're going to love this," he said, smiling wider than ever. He turned around and punched in six numbers, each accompanied by a beep, on the keypad above the knob, using his body to block the camera's view. The door opened automatically, swinging slowly out, revealing its sturdy construction. It was eight inches thick and had three cylindrical bars recessed in the door that would slide into place when the door locked. They were each three inches in diameter.

There was another identical door inside, about six feet into the building. The interim contained sensors and cameras that stared down. Red lights swept up and down on the other side of the frosted glass that made up the small room between the two doors. Anders paid them no mind, but the camera took it all in, even turning around to watch the exterior door close. After it did, Anders bent down and bit a piece of soft plastic extending from the wall next to the interior door. He let go of it and removed his mouth, licking his lips. The plastic held the shape of his teeth as it retracted into a panel on a thin metal arm. A screen above the panel turned from red to green. The words "Welcome, Master!" appeared on the screen just before the door opened.

Anders walked through into a wide room with tall ceilings. Everything was sleek and modern. The floors were made of a dark and shiny material that could have been marble. The room looked to be about thirty yards wide and sixty deep. There were cages bordering the room almost the entire sixty yards. Instead of bars, the cages were made of glass or thick, clear plastic. Each cage, save one at the end, was bordered on the top and sides with wide, bright lighting, illuminating the subjects trapped inside.

The camera followed as Anders strutted over to the first cage on the left. He looked inside at the gruesome figure for a long moment before turning to face the camera. His eyes were bright and his smile genuine. "This was my earliest attempt at perfection," he said. "I've come a long way since then. Each one of these specimens represents a leap forward in my experiments." He gestured at the line of cages, then turned his attention back to the one at hand.

The figure inside was lying on a hospital bed. It was the only furniture in the room. Tubes snaked from the figure's arms and mouth and into the wall behind it. One of the tubes had a red substance inside. The figure itself was covered in what looked like dark scales from afar. As the camera zoomed in, it became clear that the scales were in fact scabs, black on top and tinged with red underneath, like the crust that forms on top of cooling lava.

It was impossible to tell if the figure had been a man or woman. The eyes were the only thing that looked unchanged. But the fact that they stared out from wide, unblinking eyelids added to the unreality of the figure.

"I keep him as a reminder of the early days. In fact, that's why I keep all of them. They are markers of progress." Anders walked across the room to the cage opposite as he spoke. "This one, my second attempt, is a little different. I tried something new with her."

The figure in this cage had been pinned to a padded wall that covered the back of the cell. Tubes snaked from her arms back into a hole in the wall. It wasn't possible to tell gender here, either. Only Anders' words gave any hint to that. The woman was covered in mottled black and gray fur from head to toe. Her ears were twisted and elongated to points. Her nose looked as if half of it had been chopped off, making the protrusion look more like a snout. Her arms were spread out to the sides, held there by straps at the wrists. Just below the left wrist started a tattered, leathery wing that hung limp like a cape. It looked to be attached all down the inside of her arm, through her armpit, and down her ribcage. It ended just above her hips. The right side of her body was the same. A thick strap encircled her waist.

Her lips were peeled back in a permanent sneer, due to the mess of thin, sharp teeth crowding out of her mouth. Her legs were much shorter than those of any adult human. They ended in strange, twisted talons right about where her kneecaps would have been.

Like the other subject, her eyes still looked human. Unlike the other one, hers were not still. They darted back and forth, clearly seeing Anders and whoever was behind the camera. It looked like she was trying to open her mouth to speak, but she was only able to separate the teeth a few centimeters. After a few moments of this, she started banging her head against the padded wall behind her. The camera panned from her to Anders.

"Oh, she'll tire herself out soon. The wall is made of padding for a reason, you see," he said, waving his hand dismissively. "Yes, I tried something quite different with her. But, again, I was in the early stages. The hardest part back then was finding people that no one would miss. Well, it wasn't *that* hard. Still, I hadn't refined my processes yet. And just so you know, I wasn't trying to make a bat-man. Or bat-woman in this case. I'm sure you're not so imbecilic to suggest that. Alas, I did have someone close to me ask me that once, and I . . . Well, let's just say I had a temper problem back then and leave it at that."

As they moved further into the room, stopping briefly at each cage, the subjects grew more recognizable as humans, although most of them were immobile and drugged. There was a total of six cages on each side. All of them but one was clearly occupied.

Inside the eighth cage, there crouched an anomaly. Anders stopped and allowed a moment for the camera to zoom in on the hairy beast within. It was slightly smaller than an average-size man. It snarled at the camera, long canine teeth and a lolling tongue in a stubby snout. Yellow eyes held fast to the two people outside the cage.

"I'm rather proud of this creation, although it was the result of frustration on my part," Anders spoke off-screen. "I had hit a wall again and decided to try something different. So, I created a real-life werewolf. Lots of them, actually. In fact, I'm training a brood of them now. Well, not me, exactly, but my employees. I don't have time for such nonsense.

"I initially started on humans," he continued, "but it became clear that I didn't have enough of them. After losing the first five, I switched to chimps. That's what this one is, a chimp werewolf."

The camera panned from the werewolf in the cage to Anders outside.

"They're dumb beasts, but they should make great guard dogs. They're not werewolves like you see in the movies, though. They don't just turn with a full moon. After all, what use would that be? No, these werewolves turn when the sun goes down. After all, although this was a detour of sorts, I hadn't given up on creating a vampire. I thought that if I could make a werewolf that turned when the sun went down, I would be closer to creating a vampire that only hunts at night." He turned and walked, passing quickly by two glass cages, the contents of which he apparently deemed unimportant.

Anders stopped at the eleventh cage and took a deep breath. "This is where my breakthrough happened. Although it wasn't so much a breakthrough of science as it was an epiphany." The camera moved off of Anders and onto the figure inside. This one was loose. It was a man, naked, his skin colored green and yellow as if he were covered in bruises. He walked stiffly up to the partition and slapped his hands on it, looking at Anders with cloudy eyes. He made a strange groaning sound and bumped his head gently into the cage, leaving an oily smudge.

"At first I was disappointed. I was so close, yet so far away. Then I realized what I had created. A zombie. It's funny, because when I failed so badly the first several times, I set my standards a little bit lower. If I could create a humanoid being that could survive indefinitely on human flesh alone, it would be only a small step to surviving on blood. So that became my goal: immortality fueled by human flesh alone. But—and here's the funny part—I never thought of that as a zombie. It seems so obvious now. But back then, it was only a stepping stone to cracking the code of the vampire.

"So, when I created a zombie, I didn't realize that that was what I had done. But it was a win. I was getting closer. A zombie is closer to a vampire than a human is, for instance. Or a werewolf. Sure, there are some crucial factors there, like sentience. Pretty important, considering. But when I started thinking about it, it hit me! I could use the zombies and kill two birds with one stone. I could turn the world into a zombie wasteland, which, I mean, who doesn't fantasize about that? It wasn't high on my priority list, but still. Better than the shitty world we had, right? And, in doing so, I could create a world in which vampires didn't have to hide anymore. With zombies roaming around and the human population cut down, vampires could take charge of this world.

"You see, I didn't have any hard, concrete evidence that vampires existed. But I *knew* they did. I knew it in my heart and my soul. And I knew that they were tired of living underground, hidden away like freaks. I knew I could give them the world on a silver platter—I'm sorry." Anders stopped, smiled wanly, and shook his head. "I keep saying 'them' when I should be saying 'you.' I'm still wrapping my mind around the fact that I've found you. Even though I knew the day would come, I still have a hard time believing it. It's the culmination of a lifetime of extremely hard and lonely work. But I'm getting ahead of myself. I still have much to show you."

The camera panned quickly over the back of the room. There were several stainless-steel tables, rows of clean and shiny instruments on the back wall, a glass-fronted fridge with all kinds of drugs and pouches of blood. There were canisters chained together in the corner—presumably filled with volatile anesthetics. There was another metal door to a stairwell, although it wasn't clear how many floors were in the place.

Finally, the camera swept past the twelfth and final cage in the long room. It was the only dark cage in the room, and, as the camera's movement blurred it, one could just make out a large, dark figure in the corner. No more than a vague shape that could have been a trick of shadows. The camera slowed, settling on Anders' back as he walked toward the front door. The screen went black.

When an image came back up a moment later, Anders and the camera operator were in a different building. It looked exactly like the wing of a small prison. Where the cages in the previous room were clean, sleek, and made from thick plastic, the cages in this room were made from square metal bars. Anders walked into the middle of the concrete floor and held his arms up. The camera took him in and then moved up to reveal the railings of three more floors above. Although it was impossible to see the cages from this angle, it was clear that the entire building was a prison or a barracks. The utilitarian construction left no possibility for anything else.

The camera came smoothly down and paused on Anders again, who said, "This is the best part. You're going to love it." He headed to his right and the camera followed. There were two adults and two children in the cell that Anders approached. The two adults, a man and a woman of similar age, pulled the two little girls nearer. The four of them, grimy and dirty in cream-colored prison jumpsuits, glared out with frightened eyes. The girls were no older than ten, the man and woman in their early thirties.

"See?" Anders asked the camera. "Plenty of food here. I've been preparing for this for some time now. And the apocalypse has made everything so much easier. No more dealing with nosy police or paying off judges and politicians. Now, we just go out and get the people we need. Or they come to one of our little traps." Anders looked at the family in the cell with a little pout before turning back and smiling at the camera. "Now you can see why the zombie was such a critical invention. It made all this possible with little hassle. Which is good because I had INTERPOL creeping around. They never would have caught me, but still, every snooping cop takes energy and time to deal with." The man sighed contentedly and then headed to a stairwell in the middle of the rectangular room.

On the second floor, Anders stepped to a guard shack in which two burly white men in blue collared shirts sat. It was about the size of a large walk-in closet, bordered with thick glass. The men's faces shone with light from computer monitors on the desks before them.

The bulk of the rectangular floor was identical to the ground level except that the cells to either side were separated by a large gap in the middle, protected by waist-high concrete walls. The two floors above were constructed the same, meaning you could look all the way down to the ground floor from the top level.

"Open twenty-one through thirty," Anders said to the guards. They nodded and one of them turned his attention to a computer monitor. After a few keystrokes, all the cells on the right side clanged open, sliding back on tracks. Anders yelled a command in another language, his high voice ringing throughout the four floors of cells. Men in yellow jumpsuits stepped a pace out, one from each cell. They stared straight ahead like soldiers waiting for inspection. There remained a few feet of space between where the men stood and a concrete wall overlooking the floor below. Enough room for a man to walk down and inspect the prisoners.

Anders strode up to the nearest man, whose name tag identified him as number Twenty-One. He laid a hand on the back of Twenty-One's neck and then turned to the camera. The man hadn't moved at all. He hadn't even blinked.

"Okay, so I lied. *This* is the best part. I have a small army of men, ready to be turned. Ready to do whatever it takes to help us make the perfect world. And I'm confident that when I can take a look at your blood or your tissue, I'll be able to change these men quickly. They will be ready days—perhaps even hours—after I look at what makes vampires tick, so to speak. Just a sample of blood. Maybe skin and saliva. And we can have an army of vampires. We can do whatever we want.

"But first, I'll ask that you turn me. That's kind of the point of this whole video. I wanted you to get to know me first before I come to you. I didn't want to just barge in without you knowing who I was and what I've already done for you. I've watched some video of you at work, and it's the most beautiful thing I've ever seen. I can't wait to share it with you. And, of course, I don't expect to be in charge or anything. We can be equals. The world is definitely big enough for us to all get what we want. I just hope you'll be able to show some gratitude for the sacrifices I have made for you all." He paused and rolled his eyes, embarrassed. "God, I feel like such a fanboy right now," he said, laughing nervously. "Anyway, I'll be coming to the city tomorrow night. Twenty-four hours from the time you get his video. And don't worry, I know where to find you. I can't wait to meet you all. But first, before I sign off, a little demonstration to show you how serious I am. And what I can share with you."

Anders' face was that of a child's on Christmas morning. His grin reached past his eyes and, even through the video, his energy was palpable. He turned his head to Twenty-One, who looked to be in his 40s. His brown hair was trimmed close, his green eyes staring at nothing, his plump face covered in a thin sheen of oily sweat. Anders whispered something in the man's ear and then stepped away. Twenty-One took two steps forward and launched himself headfirst over the concrete railing. The sound of his body impacting the concrete below was clear, even though the camera operator wasn't quick enough to watch the man's body hit the floor. Some of the people in the cages below started screaming. The camera zoomed down on the man's cracked skull and disfigured body. A pool of blood was expanding slowly out on the concrete floor below him.

The camera moved back to Anders' smiling face. "Pretty awesome, right?" he said.

CHAPTER TWENTY-FOUR

A BASEBALL BAT, A TORCH, AND A CLEAVER

"What the fuck did we just watch?" Binta said. She kept thinking that the video was some sort of joke. Hoping. The rest of the vampires were crowded around their makeshift living room, staring at the now-blank TV to which they had hooked up the tablet. They were down to seventeen, not including Diirek.

"So, did that guy just admit to us that he caused the zombie apocalypse?" asked Nadia.

"It has to be joke," Val said in her heavy Russian accent. "How could one man cause entire world to collapse?"

"What would be the point of a joke like that?" Jamie, a young, red-headed vampire asked. "If that was all fake—which, I can't see how—it would be an expensive joke. I think he's serious."

"But why would he show such cruelty? It was like he wanted us to see how ruthless he was—like that would endear us to him." This came from Isabelle, who was probably the sweetest vampire to ever live. Or die. Whichever.

"We're not like that," Jamie said in answer. "But some vampires are. I don't know if people are like that before they turn, or if turning does that to them. I know I had some dark times for a while after I first turned."

The rest of the vampires nodded slowly in agreement, caught in remembering.

"This guy, Anders, probably thinks that all vampires are cruel and evil," Binta said. "I mean, if you believe most of the lore, it's not hard to guess that. He doesn't know us. Which is good. Because we can't let him become one of us. In fact, if he created the zombies, maybe there's a cure or an antidote or something. So we let him come. We make nice and then—what's that?" There was a banging sound coming from the entrance. Val and Nadia headed out to see what it was. The rest of the vamps listened carefully and then relaxed when they heard Weller's voice.

The detective came in quickly, his face drawn. "I need your help," he said to the group of vamps. "Where's Ricardo?"

"They got him," Isabelle said, with not a little anger in her voice.

"What?" Weller asked. "Who? Who got him?"

"Last night. When they attacked us, and you were dealing with Buck? They took him away. We couldn't stop them. There were too many."

Weller's face darkened and Binta half expected him to explode. She noticed he was just barely shaking. Like an overworked engine. Just little vibrations. "Well," the detective said, after a moment, "they have my ex-wife and daughter now, too. But I know where they are. I need your help. Hopefully they have Ricardo there, too."

"You have a daughter?" Binta asked.

"No. Yes. It's a long story. As far as anyone is concerned, Berena is my daughter. We need to go. Now."

"Detective," Binta said, sighing, "I'm sure we're all willing to help you, but you need to watch this video first. For the sake of your ex-wife and daughter. And everyone you know. Then we can formulate a plan."

Weller looked like he hadn't heard her, although his eyes seemed to see nothing else but Binta. Finally, he said, "What video could be more important than this? I tell you my wife and daughter—"

"Ex-wife and not-daughter," Nadia corrected.

Weller glared at her. "What fucking difference does that make?" he asked.

"Just making sure everyone's clear on the details. We don't need exaggerations muddying the waters."

Weller looked like he wanted to hit Nadia, who seemed to sense this and backed out of his immediate reach.

Before Weller could resume his train of thought, Binta spoke up again. "This video, it's about the end of the world."

"Who's exaggerating now?" Weller yelled, throwing up his good hand.

"Seriously," Isabelle said. "We think we know who did it. He told us because . . . he wants to be our friend."

"What the fu—"

"Just watch the video, Weller," Binta said. "Goddamn humans." This last part Binta said under her breath, heading over to the tablet.

"Fine. But if my ex-wife and not-daughter die in the next ten minutes, I'll do . . . something to you. Something you won't like."

"Scary," Nadia said.

Anders Revak's face came on screen.

No one talked until the video was over.

Weller, who had watched the whole thing standing up, sat down hard on the couch next to Jamie. "Christ in a sidecar," the detective said. "That's the worst episode of *Cribs* I've ever seen. And I accidentally watched an episode of *Teen Cribs*."

"Yeah," Jamie agreed. "That was like *Cribs: Psychopathic Killer Edition*. But maybe this guy's lying, too. Half the original *Cribs* episodes were fake."

"He's not lying," Weller said. "He fucking did it. He killed millions—maybe even billions—of people. All because he wanted to become a fucking vampire? This is the craziest shit I've ever heard."

"How do you know? Maybe he didn't have anything to do with it. You sound so certain, but you don't know." This came from Nadia. *Always the devil's advocate*, Binta thought.

"After eighteen years as a cop, I know when people are lying. And, even if this Anders guy is making this all up, if I am wildly off base in my judgment—and that's a big if—that family in the cage was definitely not acting. And the guy who killed himself looked pretty fucking real to me. No, I think this is real. Everything is a big pile of shit."

There were murmurs of assent to Weller's declaration. It did seem that everything was pretty shitty.

"It's too bad Diirek's not here," Weller continued, slumping down on the couch and closing his eyes. "We could use his help with this."

"Let me see if I can reach him," Isabelle said.

Weller's eyes shot open. "Reach him? You're in contact with him?"

Isabelle looked at him like he was an imbecile. "Yes, of course. We're practically family. And we know how to use a radio."

"Why didn't you tell me?"

"You never asked. I've never even heard you mention his name since he's been gone."

"Fair enough."

Isabelle headed off down the tunnel, presumably to where they kept the radio.

"Okay," Binta said. "Now, tell us where Buck is and what you think we should do."

Weller sat up straight and began to talk. The vampires listened.

They talked until Isabelle came back twenty minutes later.

***

While Weller talked and the vampires listened, a drone sat on the edge of the roof of a building that housed an apothecary, a tax specialist, and five floors of apartments. The building overlooked the subway entrance the vampires used. A camera on the front of the drone transmitted video via radio signal to the drone's controller. Between the drone's landing pads sat four miniature tactical munitions and a machine gun with a sixty-round clip.

The drone itself was ten feet in diameter. The munitions, machine gun, and camera maxed out its weight load. The miniature tactical munitions were five pounds each. They could be fired one at a time or all at once by remote. What they lacked in accuracy they made up for in sheer explosive power. One of these five-pound missiles was roughly the equivalent of two and a half grenades.

This drone was not the one that had been keeping an eye on the vampires since Anders had discovered their location. It wasn't much for stealth, although it could fly high enough to go unnoticed by the casual observer. It could at night, anyway, which was the only time it was needed.

What Anders saw of the confrontation the night before had rattled him. His drone had captured the fight at the intersection of Lincoln and 9th. The vampires were at war with—well, he didn't know exactly what. The foot soldiers looked like zombies, whereas their leader looked like he could be a vampire, but he didn't move or act like one. He had none of the grace that the others did.

The fact that the vampires seemed to be helping a human gave him hope. If they were already willing to help the black policeman, he was sure they would be willing to help him, too. He cursed the problem of audio transmission. The small drones he was using had microphones on the cameras, but he couldn't risk getting in close enough for them to be effective. As a result, he only had the video to go on.

Although the zombies and their leader were interesting, they paled in comparison to the vampires. He already knew how to make zombies. A little experimentation would surely allow him to create these smart zombies. The real prize was, and always had been, the vampires. And that was why he'd ordered the armed drone in. He wasn't about to risk having the vampires killed by the little ginger zombie wrangler. They had managed to kidnap one of the vampires—the Hispanic-looking one—while Anders watched, helpless. No, he wouldn't risk it. It had taken him too long to get to this point. Too much work and too many sacrifices had been made.

There was no telling what he'd be able to do once he cracked the vampire code. He could make something new. Something the earth had never seen. Something beautiful and terrifying. And he would have all the time in the world to do it.

But . . . one thing at a time.

Anders hoped that by this time tomorrow the conflict would be over. He didn't want it to take away from their first meeting. He didn't want the vampires to be distracted. He wanted their full attention when he presented himself. Even now his palms were sweaty and his heart fluttering. Surely the video had done the trick. Surely they could see how handsome and successful he was. And what he had done to give them the world. Surely.

For now, Anders sat in a small room with One. They were surrounded by electronics and screens. One was at the drone controls, but there was nothing happening. They were still waiting for the vampires to come out of the subway. And it seemed to Anders like they had been waiting for hours already. He sat back and tried to control his breathing. *Just wait,* he thought. *The time will come. Don't rush them. Let them get used to the*

*idea. Tomorrow will be great. It will be the best day of your life. You'll be
immortal. You'll be a vampire! Oh my God, it's so exciting!*

***

Buck couldn't meet the woman's eyes. Every time he went into the little
back office of the restaurant supply warehouse, she seemed to be waiting
to pounce on him. Of course, she was tied up so she couldn't physically
pounce on him. But still, her tan-colored eyes assaulted him every time
he went into the room. That little voice inside him that had grown so
big since the run-in with Merek seemed to disappear when he was there,
with her. But he couldn't stop checking on her and the teenage girl.

He was giddy with excitement and could barely hold back using the
radio to call Weller. If the detective was worth a shit, he'd find out where
Buck was. And if not, well, Buck would just have to tell him. It wouldn't
be as fun, and Weller might suspect something, but he'd come. For the
woman, he'd come. Everything was ready. The plan would work, and he
could feed his rage first, then his hunger.

Instead of looking at the woman, Buck looked at the teenage girl. They
were tied to two metal office chairs, back-to-back. Like that scene from
that one Indiana Jones movie. Only there was no lighter to burn the rope
with. No gang of Nazis behind a trick fireplace. Well, Buck supposed that
some of the zombies out in the warehouse could have been Nazis in a past
life, so that was a possibility. But there definitely wasn't a trick fireplace.
Of that, he was sure.

Buck ignored the woman's muffled shouting and looked the girl
up and down. She wasn't squirming, wasn't gasping, or trying to yell
through the gag in her mouth. She just kind of sat there. Like she'd done
this before. It was starting to creep him out. He hoped Weller would get
here soon.

In truth, he hadn't started this with a plan to kill the woman and the girl. He just wanted to see firsthand the sick desperation on the cop's face. Buck wanted him to know that he wasn't a man that could be laughed off. He wasn't a man that could be left to die at the hands of a monster only to forgive and forget. He wanted to hear Weller beg for the lives of the women. And once he'd heard that, he would kill Weller and capture any friends that he'd brought. Then he'd let the women go. If he felt like it. They were a means to an end. An end to Detective Kurt Weller.

Once Weller was gone, then the real work could begin. The things he had discovered during the last day were eye-opening, to say the least. The vampire—Ricardo—had been more helpful than Buck had ever even imagined. It took a little while for the implications to sink in, but when they did there seemed to be no end to the possibilities.

Buck smiled to himself and left the room. He would make one more round. The troops were probably getting hungry, anyway. They got rowdy when he didn't feed them. One more round and if Weller hadn't shown up after that, he'd have to get him on the radio.

Buck headed out of the office, into the main room of the supply store, and turned right. He had six people shackled to one of the big metal shelves. Three men, two women, and a little boy. As he walked toward them, all but one began to squirm and shout through their gags. The odd man out simply stared at Buck, apparently unwilling to show his fear and respect.

Just as something akin to empathy began to sprout in Buck's mind, that now-familiar voice spoke up. He listened to the words that weren't really words. He let the feeling—one that seemed to come from the deepest darkness of his mind—take hold. The bit of empathy there stood no chance. It was snuffed out by the voice and the emptiness and the swirling blackness blossoming like a fireball inside Buck.

He picked the captive who was staring at him. He was a big guy. Over six feet tall, for sure. Probably a touch under three hundred pounds. He'd go far.

Buck grabbed a baseball bat off the nearby shelf where it sat between industrial meat slicers. It was sticky with blood and hair.

He walked up to the man, who finally started to squirm. Buck smiled, feeling a warmth spread through his stomach and chest. A single bash to the head put the man down, at which point Buck put the bat back in its place and grabbed the meat cleaver he'd pilfered from another part of the store, which was also sticky with blood and hair.

It was quick work to remove the man's left leg at the knee. Then he cauterized the wound with a miniature torch. All the while, the other four captives tried to scream, yanked at their shackles, and were a general nuisance. The nearest man even tried to kick Buck, but he was too far away. He should have known that by now. This was the third person they'd seen it done to.

Three already? Buck smiled down at the still-warm lower leg in his hand. *They sure do eat a lot, don't they?* He thought. *My dudes are hungry.*

***

"Diirek wants to talk to you," Isabelle said to Weller.

"Alright," the detective said, standing up from the couch. They had just finished hashing out the plan for getting JayLynn and Berena and Ricardo back. The group of vampires watched him go, their eyes glazed in undead deliberation.

Isabelle led Weller down a concrete platform skirting the wall of the disused subway tunnel. There was an open steel door at the end, leading into what had once been a large storage room. There was a table in the near corner with a spongy office chair in front of it. On the desk sat a ham radio next to a cup of pens and a yellow legal pad, the top sheet of which was blank.

Weller sat at the chair and grabbed the mic, which looked like the ones in police patrol cars. He depressed the button with his thumb and spoke a greeting, then removed his thumb and waited.

"Hello, Detective," Diirek said through the machine and only a little bit of static. "I know you are in a hurry, so I will make this quick. Isabelle has filled me in on the video you received tonight. Can you describe to me the grounds? What did it look like? Please, use as much detail as possible."

"Can't this wait, Diirek? I'm in the middle of something. I need to go save a couple of my loved ones. And Ricardo."

"No, Detective, it cannot wait. If you and the others die during your rescue attempt, I need to know this. I think I may know where this Anders man lives. So please, tell me."

"I think the odds of you knowing where this psycho lives are a billion to one, but okay. His house was kind of a rectangle, as far as I could tell. It was boxy, but not at the top. It had a couple of . . . what are those things on top of castles called?" Weller looked at Isabelle, his finger still holding down the transmit button on the mic.

"Parapets," she said.

"Right. Parapets. It had a couple of those. And a central balcony on the top floor. Like Evita. That movie with Madonna? Anyway. It was an off-white color. And it was big. Four floors, from the outside. Then there were at least two more buildings. Both of them kind of behind and to either side of the house. They were nearly as big. One of them may have been bigger. We didn't get a good glimpse of the one behind and to the right of the house. The one to the left was the lab and it was protected by a thick, steel door. With some weird security measures. That building was big and boxy, too. A similar color, as well. Like sandstone."

"Good," Diirek said. "What about the surrounding area? Was there anything else visible? Greenery? Fields of crops?"

"Yeah. It looked like it may have been in the middle of a field of something green. Could have been corn or maybe something smaller. It was hard to tell. We only really got a glimpse of the surrounding area as the drone camera went around the house at the beginning. And even then, it was sped up so the background was blurry. Does it sound like what you've seen?"

"Yes. It does. It is too similar to be a coincidence."

"So, you just happened upon it? That seems unlikely. If this were a movie, I'd call that lazy writing."

"If this were a movie, Detective, I would find the people who wrote it and kill them slowly. But, no, I did not just happen upon it. I never planned on staying in this area long but then I saw something that changed all that. Something that had to have been done in a lab. By a very strange individual indeed. And it sounds like Anders Revak fits the bill."

"What was it that you saw?" Weller asked.

Diirek sighed, a sound that made it clearly across the intervening miles. It was the sigh of a man who suspects he might be going insane but knows deep down that he's not. "It was a werewolf. Three of them, total, actually. Only it was not a man underneath. It was a chimp. I think they are being used as guard dogs for an estate with three large, sandstone-colored, boxy buildings. In the middle of a field of corn."

"Wow," Weller said. "Everything really *is* shit. I need a vacation."

"Yes. We are in agreement, Detective. Everything is shit and we all deserve a vacation someplace with long, zombie-free nights. Now, go save your loved ones. Don't get killed. I will be waiting by the radio all night. If I don't hear from anyone by this time tomorrow night, I will assume you're all dead. At which point myself and Fred will have to make a move."

"Sounds great. When we talk again, you'll have to tell me all about this Fred character. I don't like the sound of him."

"You sound jealous, Detective."

"Not a chance, buddy."

Weller smiled thinly and stood up. Isabelle looked up at him. Her teenage spunk had gone from her face and demeanor. Weller glimpsed her true age as he looked into her eyes for a long moment. It struck him that she was much tougher than she looked. It was a good thing. Every passing day made it apparent that the world required toughness more now than ever. Even from vampires. *Especially* from vampires. They were turning out to be humanity's best hope.

Weller smiled a half-smile at her. She mirrored the gesture and they both headed back to the others.

CHAPTER TWENTY-FIVE

THE SNAPPING OF BONES

"**M**aster, there's movement," Slave One said.

Anders Revak jerked upright. He had been dozing in his command chair in front of the wall of electronics, waiting for the vampires to emerge. He hadn't been asleep, by any means, but he had drifted off in his mind. Thinking about how much fun being a vampire would be, and how cool it would be to have best friends forever. Literally. Although he wouldn't use the abbreviation "BFF" no matter how much he wanted to. Vampires didn't use silly abbreviations like BFF or LOL or TTYL. At least, he didn't think they did. He'd find out soon enough.

Then One had spoken up and startled Anders out of it. His heart began to thump loudly, and his Adam's apple bobbed uncertainly under his chin as he repeatedly swallowed the saliva his mouth was generating at a rapid rate. He looked at the screen and, sure enough, figures were emerging from the subway access. There had to be nearly twenty of them, he noted with glee.

"Okay," Anders said, trying to control his wavering voice. "I don't want to spook them. You use the stealth drone and follow them. I'll hang back with the tactical drone just in case they run into trouble."

One nodded and picked up the drone controls. The image on the screen showing the footage from the stealth drone camera wobbled as the drone lifted off. It steadied momentarily as One flew it to optimal height. He lost the large group of vampires for a second, causing panic to flood Anders' veins, but then they came back on the screen. Anders breathed out, thinking how crazy it was that this would make him nervous. It was the uncertainty that did it to him. Everything would be fine tomorrow, he told himself.

Anders waited for the group to move a few blocks before he grabbed the controls for the tactical drone and got it airborne. He followed behind One's drone from two city blocks back, half watching his screen and half the other. They also had a GPS map of the city with two dots representing the drones, but he hoped he wouldn't need that one.

For now, they just had to observe. Stay with the vampires.

Protect them at all costs.

***

Weller split from the vampires and went to get his car, which he had parked two blocks away. He didn't think anyone was following him, but he wouldn't put it past Captain Shellbourne to try and track his movements. When he had parked it, he had walked around the block to make sure no one was tailing him and then headed over to the subway entrance. Presently, he headed to the sole official exit from the safe zone while the vampires went over one of the unmanned barriers. The last time the detective had tried to keep up with the vampires on foot, he'd been left behind. Twice. He wasn't about to make that mistake again.

The National Guard soldiers waved him through without so much as a questioning glance. They had grown used to him leaving and coming back at all hours. One of the privileges of being a police.

It took him ten minutes to get to the meeting spot. He pulled up cursing because he didn't see a single vampire around. He didn't see *anyone* around. But as soon as he got out of his car they seemed to materialize from all around. It looked like they were all present and accounted for. And they were being cautious. Taking this seriously. Which was good.

Weller rehashed the plan again, making sure everyone knew their roles. Six vampires, including Jamie, Val, and Nadia, took off toward the target, only three city blocks away. They would circle around and come in from the back, if possible. Jamie had the handheld radio but was under orders to maintain radio silence until they had reconnoitered the place.

Weller and the others waited five minutes and then headed to the target. Half of them would hang back and wait for the word from Jamie while the others would present themselves at the front of the building. The plan was to trade Weller for JayLynn and Berena. Everything else was just too risky. Even with vampires, getting the upper hand in a hostage situation was nearly impossible by force. If invading the building and neutralizing the threat could be done quietly from the back, all the better. But only if Buck refused the trade or tried something. Weller was ready to die if it meant allowing JayLynn and Berena to live. Grimes' words kept repeating in his head, and he'd made peace with the fact. It wasn't hard to do, and it took him all of a minute to come to that conclusion. His life for theirs. The vampires would be his insurance if Buck tried to kill Weller and the women. And even then, nothing was guaranteed.

The restaurant supply store was in the middle of the block, set back behind a parking lot and between two three-story buildings that had housed a random assortment of shops and professional services before the apocalypse. The store itself was only two stories tall, but there was no second floor inside the place. It was just a fancy, air-conditioned warehouse with high ceilings. The parking lot was fifty yards deep and about eighty yards wide. There were a few cars still in the lot, all of which had broken windows, scorch marks, and flat tires. Large flat metal carts like those at hardware stores were scattered about, along with a smattering of regular steel shopping carts.

Weller stopped on the sidewalk with Isabelle to his right, Binta to his left, and two more vampires, whose names he hadn't bothered to learn yet, behind them. One was a man of Asian descent that looked to be about Weller's age. He hadn't said a word since they'd left the subway station. The other was a plain-looking white guy in his twenties. They surveyed the place, seeing nothing at first. Then, figures began to pop up from the darkness, much like the vampires had at the meeting place.

Silhouettes loomed, two each on the three-story buildings to the right and left of the supply store. More figures walked slowly from the smashed-out automatic doors at the front of the restaurant supply store. All these shadowy figures stopped in what Weller assumed were predetermined positions and stared out at the parking lot. No one moved.

***

"Shit, shit, shit," Anders whined. "Why did they have to split up? What the hell are they doing, anyway? Goddamnit, why can't we get some decent microphones on these things?" His breathing was erratic. He felt hot and cold all at once as his entire plan seemed to evaporate in front of his eyes. He would have been pacing had it not been for the drone controller in his hand.

"Maybe it's nothing, Master," One said. "Some sort of uneasy truce?"

"It doesn't look like nothing, One. It looks like a goddamn standoff, is what it looks like. I bet it's that same guy from last night. The little one who kidnapped one of the vampires. He's starting to piss me off.

And why are they even listening to the human anyway? He doesn't look special. Why the hell are they helping him? This doesn't make any sense."

"I don't know, Master," One said after a moment. "I don't know."

***

The radio clipped to Weller's waist crackled. It was Jamie. Weller snagged it up and listened.

"There's no way in back here," the vampire said. "Not quietly, anyway. We could break in if it comes to that, but they've got the place buttoned up good and tight."

"Copy," Weller said. *Shit.* He stepped forward, crossing the threshold from the sidewalk to the parking lot. It was too dark to see the faces of any of the figures that stood as still as statues around the store. The only light was a faint electric glow emanating from deep inside the store. Weller turned back around and asked Isabelle if she could see their faces. The teenage vampire nodded. "They're zombies, from what I can tell. They all have that super zombie look. And . . . something else." She shook her head in dismissal.

"What? What something else?" Weller prompted.

"I don't know. They look," she paused, choosing her words, "more aware somehow. Only it's not so much a look as it is a feeling. I don't know. Does it change anything?"

"No," Weller said. "It doesn't." He looked up at Binta, who gave him a nod. Weller smiled. "Stay here," he told them. Then he turned around and walked toward the store.

"Buck!" he yelled. "Buck, I'm here. Now please, let JayLynn and Berena go. They don't have anything to do with this. You know that."

Weller kept walking as he spoke. He was about twenty yards from the store when Buck answered.

"Stop there, Detective!" His voice rang out from inside the store, but Weller couldn't see him, although he could hear footsteps coming toward him. None of the super zombies had moved. They just stared. Weller stopped walking.

"So, you got my clues?" Buck said. "You really are some detective, aren't—"

"I'm sorry," Weller cut him off. "This is weird. I can't see you, Buck. Can we at least talk face to face?"

There was a pregnant pause before Buck answered. When he did, his voice was sharp with anger. "I'm right here."

"Where?" In truth, Weller could see the top of the man's head from where he was in the parking lot. There was a burned-out car in the way.

"Just—Just move to your right, dude," Buck said.

"You told me to stop moving. Are you sure your super zombies aren't going to—"

"You're an asshole, you know that?" Buck said as he stepped to his left and came into Weller's line of sight.

"I'm not trying to be one, honest. I just thought you'd like to talk man to man. Was I wrong?"

"No. You weren't wrong. And it doesn't seem like you're sorry, either. If you're not sorry now, you will be soon."

"That's where you're wrong, Buck," Weller said. "I am sorry. I am truly sorry. I told you that the other night, but you still killed Hardiman. So, I don't know how else I can put it. Just tell me what you want from me. I'll do it. Just let them go. Please. Take me. Feed me to your pets. I don't care. Just let them go."

"I want you to beg me," Buck said, moving forward, closing the distance between them. "On your knees. I want to see the sorrow in your eyes."

Weller dropped to his knees. At that moment he felt no anger. Only a sick and sharp pleading that left a terrible taste in his throat. He almost preferred anger over that feeling. "I'm sorry, Buck. And not just because you have the love of my life in there. Honestly. On the night I took you up to the top of that building, when I thought you were dead, when I thought that I'd gotten you killed, I felt terrible about it. You can even ask—" Weller gestured at the vampires behind him, then stopped. "Oh, no. Diirek's gone and Lidia's dead. Shit. Well, you can't ask anyone. Not right now, anyway. But please, take my word for it. I'm sorry."

"That's better," Buck said, now five yards away. "Do you remember when we first met?" he asked Weller. "That night that I attacked you and tried to eat you?"

"Yeah. Of course I do, Buck."

"Of course. Well, I remember that night, too. I didn't at the time, but I do now. It was strange, back when I first was coming to terms with what I am now. It was like I couldn't handle it. Like a switch was flipped and something else took over when I got hungry enough. Then I'd wake up, covered in some poor dude's blood and guts, my stomach full to the brim." Buck moved closer to Weller, who was still on his knees on the asphalt.

"But then something changed," Buck continued. "When I was up in that dome, after you'd left me for dead, something happened. I couldn't hardly even crawl. Everything was broken. The pain was huge. I was just lying there, hoping I would die so the pain would stop, when I realized that I could control this. Whatever it is. Because I wasn't just in pain. I was hungry, too. I was hungry like you've never known it. Like no human has ever known it. Because humans die when they starve, but not me. Not while I was up there. And that's when I learned that I had the power to control myself. Do you know what changed? What my secret is to controlling the thing that I have become?"

"What?" Weller thought he knew what was coming, but he tried to sound as interested as possible.

"I'm always hungry."

"Oh, you've got to be kidding me. You can't be serious with that shit."

Buck laughed. "You know," he said. "I had a lot of time to think while I was up there, in that dome, hoping for death. About what happened to me. And about what Merek was. I developed a few theories of my own once I had a few pigeons in my stomach. Then, when I finally got the strength to make my way down, I discovered these . . . special zombies." Buck gestured at the nearest stoic super zombie. "I didn't know what had caused them. Not until last night. Your friend Ricardo told me all about how you guys got rid of Merek. Not that he'd wanted to tell me. But turns out vampires succumb to torture just like humans do. Anyway, he told me his theory about how these zombies ate some of Merek's flesh. And that got me to thinking about what would happen if they ate a regular vampire's flesh. Luckily, I had a vampire there to test it out."

Weller's eyes went wide.

He turned, looking at one of the super zombies nearby, implacable dread scratching at his insides.

The zombie looked at Weller.

And smiled.

"Oh fuck," Weller said.

Buck gestured, raising both his hands above his head, palms wide, and the super zombies all moved quickly. But they didn't move toward Weller. They headed out, toward the vampires at the edge of the parking lot.

Buck grabbed Weller by the shirt just as the radio on the detective's belt crackled. Weller only made out the words, "they're coming for us," before Buck yanked the unit away.

Buck moved fast, jerking Weller up to his feet, discarding the radio, and then snapping Weller's left wrist like it was a twig. Pain flared, bright and sharp. Weller felt like he should scream but couldn't. He looked down to see that his hand was on backward and hanging at an odd angle. Then Buck kicked him in the right shin with savage force. He felt the splintered bone puncture the skin of his calf. He crumpled to the ground. Looking down at his leg, it appeared that he had two knee joints, only the bottom one was going the wrong way.

He pulled air into his lungs and screamed.

Buck laughed.

Something that looked like a small rocket screeched through the air over Buck's head. The small man stopped laughing and looked at the projectile in confusion as it hit the building. The front of the restaurant supply store exploded. Bits of flying glass, metal, and wood impacted the area. Weller was dimly aware that JayLynn and Berena were probably still in there, and he yelled in agony, willing them to get out. To get clear.

Another small rocket flashed into the wall of fire that the first had made. Another explosion rocked the building, this one coming from deeper inside, shooting burning shrapnel out on an inferno of scorched air.

Buck was no longer in evidence. All was fire and chaos and bits of raining death.

A machine gun was firing somewhere.

Weller pulled acrid smoke into his lungs to yell again, JayLynn's face in his mind's eye, when a third explosion erupted, this one from behind him. Before he could let the sound loose, a large flat sheet of metal slammed into him and threw him toward the burning building.

CHAPTER TWENTY-SIX

ASSIMILATION

A car horn honked. Weller yelled an obscenity at the driver while simultaneously and instinctively jumping up over the front of the hood as the driver slammed the brakes. He pulled his legs out in front of him, knowing he wouldn't make it all the way over. He landed on his butt then slid off the hood, no doubt leaving an ass-shaped dent behind. It was a minor concern. Within two steps he had regained his momentum and equilibrium. His legs pumped, arms pistoned, lungs burned, and his eyes were zeroed in on the man running away some fifty yards ahead.

It was a serial killer case. His first as a lead detective. He'd been working it for months. He and his partner, Ray O'Shea, who was somewhere in the maze of streets, trying to cut the guy off with the car. Only, shortly after Weller had started the chase on foot, he'd rounded a corner and slammed into a slowly moving bike messenger. The radio he'd been holding in his hand went flying under a parked car. There was no time. It was the radio or the suspect. Weller had jumped up and took off after the man. The next corner he'd rounded almost got him hit by a car. Corners were dangerous.

Presently, the suspect, a fast white guy in his late twenties, rounded a corner of his own and slammed into a hot dog cart. This happened out of Weller's view, but when he rounded the corner himself (slowing a bit, this time), he saw the dented cart, its irate operator, and the suspect, now only twenty yards away, limping slightly. Weller smiled and kept running.

The street they were on was busy with weekend traffic and pedestrians. People were out in droves, enjoying the last of summer. This helped Weller and hindered the suspect. The guy had to dodge through people, who were then on alert and out of the way as Weller passed. Civilians were all right, sometimes.

Weller gained on him. Only ten yards away now. The guy started looking around wildly, looking for anything to help him get away. He took a sharp right, running up a short flight of stairs to a greystone building that had a sign for a therapist and a dog groomer. There were probably apartments above the businesses. It was that kind of neighborhood. That kind of building. Weller couldn't let him get loose in there.

The guy pulled the wooden door shut behind him and started to fiddle with the lock, looking up through the large glass pane, sweating, nervous. Weller reached the door a half-second later and kicked it in stride, deforming the frame but not actually knocking it open. The guy took off into the building. Weller kicked the door again. It swung open.

There was a staircase to the right in the entryway and a long hallway to the left. The suspect was at the back of the hallway at a pair of closed wooden double-doors. Weller went for his gun but thought better of it. There were civilians in this building, no doubt. He couldn't risk shooting through a wall or a door and killing someone. So he ran.

The guy was trapped. He was slamming his shoulder into the double doors. Weller could hear a woman yelling from behind those doors. His legs pumped, arms pistoned, lungs burned.

Closer now. Closer.

Weller slammed into the guy. The double doors burst open as the two men collided with the wood. Weller landed on top of the guy on a fancy area rug. Suddenly, there was a hand on his throat. The guy was quick. Weller jabbed him twice in the face, bloodying his nose before he got his hand up to block another blow. The grip tightened on his throat. Strange lights started flashing in his vision.

A women's tennis shoe came into the fray, attached to a foot, crashing into the guy's head once, twice, three times. Lights out. Both the suspect's hands went limp, and Weller sat back, sucking in breath.

As his vision cleared, he looked up at his savior, and his breathing shallowed again. There stood a woman about his age, looking into his eyes with concern and a little bit of satisfaction on her face. She wore low-cut jeans and a sweater with an ivy league college's name in crimson across the front. Her springy hair was tied back into a fluffy ponytail, and her smooth skin was a dark chestnut brown.

Just as Weller was finding his bearings, a scream sounded from behind him and to his right. He jerked around to see a pale, middle-aged woman convulsing with terror in a comfortable-looking chair. Weller recognized the look on her face. She was a Karen.

"Calm down ma'am," he said while pulling out his handcuffs and flipping the unconscious suspect over. "The situation is under control. Your friend here just helped apprehend what I believe to be a very dangerous suspect."

The Karen was only whimpering now, the fact that Weller was a cop was dawning on her slowly, it seemed.

"Oh, we're not friends," the beautiful head-kicking woman said. "She's my patient." Then, she seemed to realize the impact of her words. Her face darkened slightly. "I mean. We haven't known each other long. That's all."

Weller got the handcuffs fastened and tried not to smile when he saw the hurt look on the Karen's face. Then he took notice of the surroundings. It all clicked into place. The two comfortable-looking chairs not quite facing each other, the tasteful coffee table over the nice but not extravagant rug, the shelves of books, and a couch that looked brand new. It was a psychiatrist's office.

Weller looked back at the woman. "Whatever you are, you saved my ass. Thank you. I'm Detective Kurt Weller. You are?"

"Doctor JayLynn Whittaker," she said, smiling.

***

Something was very wrong. Weller couldn't breathe. He couldn't see Doctor JayLynn Whittaker. Even the Karen was gone. He tried to move, but pain flared and scorched his rational mind. His eyes refused to focus, and his breath was ragged, unsteady. His heartbeat was arrhythmic in his chest, sounding to him like Morse code. A final SOS.

Something was very wrong. His body was failing. He felt like he was dying.

Weller brushed JayLynn's thigh through her skintight jeans with his pinky. She squirmed in the movie theater seat next to him, a harsh intake of breath accompanying the movement. He'd chosen the perfect time to do it; right when the music pulsed, and the possessed mother appeared behind her son in the dark.

JayLynn looked at him in surprised shock for a moment. There was just enough anger there that Weller decided he'd misjudged her. That this would be their first and last date. That he'd made a mistake in scaring her. Then she smiled at him and grabbed his shirt, pulling him toward her in the dark theater, the movie momentarily forgotten. Weller realized with excitement that they were about to kiss. He thought it was a fine idea. Making out in a movie theater was always a favorite pastime for him. But the kiss never came. Instead, JayLynn shoved a handful of popcorn down his shirt, pushed him away, and then returned her attention to the movie.

He let the popcorn sit between his skin and shirt until later, after they had walked around for two hours. They were on her front stoop, about to kiss—for real this time—when Weller stopped, untucked his shirt, and let the popcorn fall at their feet. He was grinning like an idiot the whole time. Without a word, he walked down the steps and away, making it about ten feet before JayLynn burst into laughter behind him. It was the sweetest sound of his adult life and he joined it with his own laughter.

She grabbed up a small handful of the well-traveled popcorn and chased Weller around the dark streets of her neighborhood with it, trying to force it into his mouth. It wasn't long after that he knew he wanted to marry her.

***

Someone was yelling Weller's name. A cold, hard weight was lifted from him and a familiar face looked down.

"JayLynn?" he asked, his eyes blurry with pain and smoke and blood.

"No," the woman said. "She's gone."

"Berena?"

The woman shook her head.

She grabbed him under the shoulders and pulled him from the smoldering mass of metal and rubble he'd been trapped under. The restaurant supply store was a smoking shell. The parking lot looked like a warzone. Weller looked down at his broken left wrist and his wrecked right leg. He noticed a jagged piece of metal sticking out of his abdomen, just to the left of his belly button. His heart and lungs struggled. He could feel them failing. He'd lost too much blood.

"Please," he said to the woman. "Please." Tears streamed down his cheeks.

She spoke to him, but the words seemed to disappear once they reached his ears. He tried to say more, to have a conversation with her, but he wasn't sure if he was speaking out loud or just in his mind.

As she put him down on the sidewalk, away from the parking lot, consciousness slipped from him once again.

***

He was in an empty room. It was both dark and bright. JayLynn sat across from him, suddenly there in her comfortable chair, staring at him, speaking.

"Don't you do this, Kurt. Don't let this happen. Don't you dare." She spoke solemnly and without force. It was a tone he'd heard her use only when she was really, truly hurt. There was no anger in that tone, just disappointment and longing. She spoke as if she knew Weller better than he knew himself.

Maybe she did.

"Dammit, Kurt. I love you. Come back to me. Please, just come back to me. It can be good again. It can, I promise you. Just come. Don't let them do it."

Weller spoke, but no sounds came out. The light fluctuated and the distance wobbled. Berena was there, sitting in JayLynn's lap. She, too, began to plead with Weller.

Fine, he wanted to say. Fine, I'll do whatever you want. I only ever want to be with you. I'll stop this and we can be together again.

But he didn't know what he was supposed to stop. And he couldn't speak. Couldn't breathe. Couldn't think.

The distance stretched again, like a rubber band being pulled too tight. JayLynn was yanked away from him, off to the other side of the dim darkness that suffused the nowhere. Weller felt something sharp prick him. He raised his hand to the spot on his neck. It came away bloody. He opened his mouth to yell, to tell JayLynn he was coming, and blood poured out. His eyes went wide, and he clamped his teeth together. They began to hurt. A sweet-sour taste filled his mouth and kept filling. So much blood.

So much blood but he couldn't spit it out.

He needed it.

He swallowed. And swallowed again. And again. The blood kept filling his mouth. It was so fast he thought he might drown. All he could do was gulp it down, letting it fill his belly, letting it flow into his veins, letting it plug his wounds. Letting it fix him.

Suddenly there was no more blood in his mouth. He opened his jaw and inhaled a breath of stale air. Something shifted inside him like a frightened animal. There was a coiling, a tension ready to give.

JayLynn screamed, off in the nothingness. She screamed his name. And then she was gone. Like a popped bubble, there was nothing left. He was alone now. Alone with the pain. But it was dulled somehow. His pain had changed. He didn't think it was possible.

His pain had changed.

And so had he.

***

Weller sat upright on the sidewalk. Binta was kneeling next to him. Next to her was a man's body. "What?" Weller said, looking down at his body, remembering so clearly the feeling of his limbs breaking. His wounds were gone but there was something else in their place. A deeper injury. In a place he never knew he had.

"What did you do to me?"

CHAPTER TWENTY-SEVEN

THE WEREWOLF EXPRESS

"Diirek! They're outside! Oh my gosh, they're right outside!" Fred said, looking like he was about to pee his pants.

"Calm down, Fred," Diirek said, licking blood from the corner of his mouth. "Who are 'they' and where outside are they?" The boy and the vampire were in the small hallway outside of the family room at the back of a train car. Diirek was feeling good, having just finished feeding on Buffalo Bob, who was lying down, eating a cookie on one of the bunks. The other two men in the room listened closely to the conversation outside.

"Them," Fred said in a not-so-quiet whisper. "The werewolves. I just saw two of them sneaking around outside."

Diirek tried not to show his concern in front of the boy. But he was concerned. He had feared this would happen. Between him and Fred, they had killed two of the werewolves in as many days. Granted, one of those hadn't been in its werewolf form, but still. It was bound to be noticed by whomever lived in that giant house. Which was why, after Diirek had talked to Weller on the radio, they turned the train around using a wye junction in the train yard. They then moved the train ten miles back toward the city and stopped at another small train yard on the outskirts of another small, deserted town.

Diirek had given Fred a crash course on how to operate the train. To Diirek's surprise, the boy had handled it well. Not at all like he was now handling the appearance of werewolves outside the train.

"It will be fine, Fred. Lock the men inside and stay here. I'll be right back."

Fred nodded and Diirek headed up the stairs to look out the window. He moved swiftly to the upper level and kept low as he ducked into one of the small sleeper rooms that occupied the top level of the car. He stared out a window overlooking a small field. He saw nothing. No movement save for a rabbit near an old barn and a few birds passing overhead.

He was about to move to the other side of the train when he saw them come out from behind the barn. They were about a hundred and fifty yards away, sniffing around. The rabbit sensed the werewolves and bounded away from them. One of the three werewolves pounced on the poor creature and snapped its head off like it was eating a carrot.

Diirek watched them as they went, hoping they would keep going, that they wouldn't come any closer to the train. He couldn't take three of them. It wouldn't be possible. One had been hard enough, and he almost lost his arm at that.

The rabbit eater scarfed down the rest of the body and then got back into a ragged line with the other two, walking on all fours, noses to the ground. The werewolf in the middle lifted its nose from the ground and placed it firmly into another's ass, appearing to take a rather large sniff. The harassed werewolf snarled a warning over its shoulder, which the sniffer seemed to ignore. After another deep inhale, the werewolf apparently liked what it smelled because it mounted its growling companion and began humping away. But it didn't get very far. After the fourth or fifth thrust, it convulsed violently and was thrown back into the dirt by some unseen force. It began clawing at its neck, tearing out wiry black hair and drawing a bit of blood.

Diirek looked closer, using his camera-like vision, remembering the collar on the werewolf that had almost taken his right arm off and the collars on the ones he had seen next to the stream. Sure enough, there was some sort of collar around this werewolf's neck with a small gray box attached. Some sort of remote electrocution device like those that had been used on unfortunate dogs back before the world ended. It was one way to keep them on task, he supposed.

Presently, the werewolf sprung off its back and rejoined its companions in sniffing around. Lesson learned, apparently. For now, anyway. Diirek confirmed that the other two werewolves had identical collars. Which meant that they were being monitored somehow. Perhaps there were proximity sensors in them that produced an electric shock when they got too close for too long.

He ducked out of the roomette and moved quietly to the next car down, keeping pace with the werewolves. The power was off to the entire train. This was a call Diirek had made as soon as they had turned the train around and moved away from their old spot. Leaving it on would telegraph their location to anyone looking for them. But it was a risk. It took nearly twenty minutes to start the train's diesel engine. There was no such thing as a quick getaway. And Diirek wasn't about to give up the train. It was his best possible means of transportation. The roads were clogged with abandoned vehicles and roadblocks erected by surviving psychos. He had seen at least two major highway cloverleaf interchanges that had been destroyed by the explosives that had rained down on Z-Day. Yet the track he was on remained unscathed—at least between here and the city.

Traveling in anything other than a train would limit his safety options. He needed a fresh supply of human blood, which he had. He also needed a place to sleep where he wouldn't be disturbed. Which he also had.

Traveling in a car, or even an RV, would not give him either option to his liking.

If it came down to him or the train, he would ditch the cumbersome locomotive. But not if he could help it. He'd put too much work into getting it in working order for his needs. Not to mention the work he'd had to do to clear the tracks on his way out of the city. It had taken him the better part of a week to travel here, which was only a little over one hundred miles outside of the city. Giving up the train meant giving up his best chance for survival.

Diirek went over his options as he slowly followed the werewolves all the way to the end of the train. He watched as they rooted around for a while, stopping occasionally to loose strange, yipping howls at the moon. The werewolves had traveled what Diirek approximated as nine miles from the cluster of buildings they were tasked with protecting. Again, he wondered how many there were. After his conversation with Weller, Diirek was sure that the compound belonged to Anders Revak. Which meant they needed to kill Revak and free his prisoners. And they needed to do it soon.

Diirek waited for half an hour to make sure the werewolves had gone before he grabbed Fred. "We are going to start the train, Fred. We need to go meet some friends of mine and we need to get there quickly. I think we can get there a couple of hours before dawn."

"Okay," Fred said in a small voice. "Are we running from the were-wolves? Are they still out there?"

"They are gone. For now. Do you remember how to start the train?"

"Maybe? There were a lot of switches."

"I will show you again. It is easy once you know how to do it."

The two of them stepped outside and went to start the train. Twenty minutes later, Diirek got it moving while explaining everything to Fred again, who looked over his shoulder.

"I just followed the track from the city. I did not have a particular destination in mind so I did not care where it took me. So, unless someone has messed with the railroad switches, we should have no problems finding our way back."

"What about intersections with cars on them? Or other trains on the track?" Fred asked.

Diirek shook his head. "I do not think we will have any issues. I had to clear a few intersections on the way down. The way back will be clear."

"How did you learn to drive this?"

"I was a train engineer in a previous life," Diirek said.

"Wow, really?"

"No," Diirek said flatly. "I read this." He reached down and pulled out a thick employee manual.

"You read the whole thing?" Fred said, astonished.

"Most of it, yes. I read very quickly. And I retain knowledge. Stopping is the hardest part of driving the train. You have to stop miles ahead of your destination when you're going fast. This is why I went very slow on my way down here. On the way back, we can go a bit faster. Perhaps you can—" Diirek stopped mid-sentence and canted his head toward the window.

"What? What is it?" Fred asked.

"Open the door and look back. Tell me what you see."

Fred nodded and walked over to the door. They weren't moving fast, so there was little wind resistance as he swung it open. He put his right hand on the yellow safety bar outside the door and leaned out, looking back down the length of the train.

"What do you see?" Diirek asked.

"Nothing. Just train and darkness."

"Come here. Take over."

Fred did as he was told, sitting in the leather seat Diirek had just vacated.

"Remember, you do not have to worry about anything but the brakes and this button. An alarm will go off every fifty seconds. Push this button to turn it off. Otherwise, the train will stop. If you see something big on the track use this to apply the brakes. If it is something small, just keep going."

Fred looked down at the controls, his face growing long as if finally grasping the enormity of his responsibility. He looked back up to see Diirek's feet disappearing from the top of the door frame. The door swung shut a moment later.

The train wasn't moving fast but it still took Diirek a bit of concentration to walk along the top of it. He made himself simultaneously light and heavy, moving with a swiftness unmatchable by any human, yet able to keep himself centered so a gust of wind wouldn't blow him off his footing.

He gazed to the back of the eight-car train as he moved, seeing no sign of werewolves. But he had heard something. It was a faint thump that caught his attention, and it had come from the back of the train.

He looked into the sky, seeing a few dim clouds, a waxing moon, and about a million stars. He looked over his shoulder, making sure the coast was clear ahead. It wouldn't do to have his head ripped off by a tunnel entrance or a telephone wire. He remembered going through one short tunnel on the way down here, but they wouldn't hit that stretch for sixty miles or so. There were a few small towns on the way. But even going as slow as they were, those towns would flash by in an instant.

Nothing to worry about, aside from the possibility of a rather dramatic fight on the top of a moving train.

As he reached the fifth car down, a furry black shape crawled out onto the train in front of him on the last car. As a result, he didn't notice the second furry shape slide onto the top of the train behind him. Diirek stood his ground, waiting for the werewolf at the back of the train to make its way toward him, which it did. Slowly.

The beast was still one car length away from Diirek when he heard the scratch of nails on metal from behind him. Instead of trying to turn around, he launched himself backward, operating on instinct. He caught the werewolf in the snout with the crown of his head, feeling some of its teeth shatter on impact. Claws sank into the flesh of his upper back as the two of them hit the metal roof, Diirek landing awkwardly on the werewolf. The beast started fighting wildly to get him off.

The vampire was trying to get up when he noticed the second werewolf lunging at him. He rocked backward, feeling the claws sink deeper into his back, and shot his feet up just as the second beast reached him. He used the werewolf's momentum to toss the beast back over his head, managing to flip away from the other one as he did so. The werewolf he'd thrown hit the side and bounced, but Diirek wasn't sure if it had fallen off the train.

He landed on his hands and knees and lunged at the beast whose claws he had just escaped. The werewolf was getting to its feet, back to Diirek, when he made contact. They went sprawling but Diirek managed to hang on, pinning the werewolf face down on the top of the train car.

He wrapped his hands around the beast's muscular neck just under the collar and brought the head up about a foot off the ridged metal surface of the train. He slammed it back down, snout-first, into the metal. He could feel the muscles move underneath the beast's hide like writhing snakes as the werewolf tried to gather its limbs under it. Diirek slammed the beast's face into the metal, again and again, leaving behind a gory deposit of flesh, blood, and teeth.

Diirek looked over his shoulder and saw that the werewolf he'd thrown was scrabbling back up onto the roof. It would be on him in moments. He took one hand off the werewolf's neck, leaned back, then snapped forward, slamming his elbow into the back of the beast's head. He felt its skull give from both the front and the back at once.

He stood up and nudged the twitching body toward the side, watching it fall to the slowly passing ground as its weight pulled it off the train.

The other werewolf was picking its way along the top of the roof toward Diirek, who looked past it and saw four gouges in the metal of the train roof from the beast's claws. He was losing blood from the wounds in his upper back. His black satin shirt was soaked. He'd been lucky so far. It was the kind of luck that wouldn't hold.

As soon as he thought this, he heard something behind him in the darkness. He looked over his shoulder, past the two and a half car lengths of train. Shit, he thought, turning his head back to face the werewolf. A sick feeling took hold in his stomach and he looked back into the darkness again, quickly, as if to confirm what he'd seen. I knew my luck would not hold, but this is ridiculous, he thought. His fears had been confirmed.

More werewolves were coming.

Diirek backed up quickly, putting two car lengths distance between him and the werewolf, who was crawling on all fours, its head down, yellow eyes staring at him. Its hackles were raised, its powerful muscles bunching under the thin hair and mottled gray skin of its hide.

Diirek ran toward the beast at a dead sprint, noting the momentary look of confusion on its face before it, too, started running toward him. When they were a pace apart, Diirek launched himself into the air as high as he could. The werewolf reached up with its claws, managing to rake them along Diirek's favorite pair of shoes, ruining the shoes and gouging his feet to the bone. But it wasn't enough to stop the vampire's forward motion. He flipped through the air and landed on his back on the third car. He rolled up quickly and sprinted to the front of the train.

"Go as fast as you can, Fred," he yelled down at the boy driving the train. "Now. Do it now! They're after us."

A moment later he felt the train lurch under him. The wind quickened around him as they slowly gained speed. The odd farmhouse passed by in the night, the rest of the landscape lush, wild early summer greenery and neat lines of crops.

This isn't fast enough, Diirek realized. The werewolf was coming at him from the back of the train. Diirek ran toward it again. He gained speed quickly. When he was a pace away from the werewolf, he made it look like he was about to jump again but instead planted his left foot down hard, turned his shoulders, and propelled himself forward. The werewolf took the bait, jumping as if to meet the vampire in the air, all sharp claws and dripping fangs. Diirek timed it perfectly, driving his shoulder into the lunging werewolf right above the hips.

The werewolf somersaulted in the air twice before landing on its back at the edge of a train car and then falling to the passing dirt below. Diirek watched it sweep past him until it was past the end of the train. But then his eyes found more werewolves, a dozen or more of them, bounding after the train. The locomotive was moving fast, but not faster than the werewolves. But it was still gaining speed. He could feel it. The wind rushed past him, cooling the lukewarm blood seeping out of his wounds.

One wolf, the closest to the train, jumped with some effort onto the small metal platform at the rear of the train. Diirek stood above it, looking down at the beast, weighing his options. He had the high ground, and he would keep it. He just prayed that nothing had been moved onto the tracks that would cause a derailment. He would probably survive the crash, but not the fifteen werewolves that would be upon him shortly thereafter. Fred, no doubt, would be killed by such an accident.

A few more werewolves were gaining on the train, running on all fours with their legs pumping, tongues lolling. But there wasn't enough room on the small platform. The beast there now seemed to realize this as it looked around frantically. There was a door there, but it was locked. The werewolf made no indication that it knew how to open doors, anyway. There was a window in the door, but it was too small for any one of the beasts to fit through.

Suddenly, Diirek had an idea. He looked at the few werewolves who were close enough to get on the platform. He looked at the one currently on it. And he stepped back, out of view. He had to do this quickly and he had to do it right. Otherwise, he would end up on the ground with the werewolves.

He crouched down and moved closer to the end of the train, waiting. The werewolf jumped up a moment later. Diirek leaped out of his crouch and shot his right foot forward in a savage kick that caught the werewolf at the base of the neck. It tumbled backward, slamming into the two closest werewolves. They ended up in a hairy tangle of limbs which quickly receded from view as the train continued its course. The rest of the werewolves followed for a few hundred yards, but they were no longer gaining. One by one, they stopped running and stood up on their hind legs, staring after the train with their sickly yellow eyes.

Diirek smiled and headed to the front of the train.

He was three cars away when a great smashing sound erupted from ahead and Diirek was thrown from his feet.

Chapter Twenty-Eight

UN-LIFE

Weller looked down at his left arm, his right leg. They looked normal. There was no pain there, but he remembered the immensity of the sensation as Buck had broken his wrist. Then his leg. *Is this a dream?*

His right arm was still in the cast, although the cast was now cracked, discolored, and dirty. He moved his right arm inside the plaster, testing it. He knew right away that it was no longer broken.

"Where is she?" Weller asked Binta as he stood up. "Where are they?" He looked around. He was in front of the three-story building just north of what used to be the restaurant supply store. He had no idea what time it was but had the feeling that several hours had passed since his encounter with Buck.

"Where is she, Binta?" Weller asked, looking down and noting the severely burned dead man at his feet. Weller knew instinctively that the man had provided the blood to heal him. He didn't remember being turned, nor drinking the dying man's blood, but he did. Surely he did.

Binta stood up and Weller noticed the look on her face. "Weller..." she said, but he had already turned toward the building. He walked quickly, ignoring the few vampires milling around in the street looking drained and defeated. He ripped the cast off his right arm as he stumbled through the rubble and into the shell of the building. He made his way over the small mountains of wrecked ovens and dishwashers. He crunched over plastic kitchen implements and industrial cleaners. He skirted the skeletal shelves that had once held the implements of a booming industry. He hoped against hope that Binta was wrong. That the impossible was possible.

When he saw JayLynn his stomach cramped, and his legs froze. "Oh, no."

She was crawling on the rubble, groaning, and dragging her broken legs behind her. Despite her cloudy eyes, scorched skin, and the blood coating much of her body, Weller had no trouble recognizing JayLynn.

"Oh, Christ no," he said, falling to his knees in front of her. She looked at him with all the interest of an insect, discounting him as a food source and then moving her eyes past him. She continued to crawl, adjusting slightly for his presence.

Everything else left Weller but the wish to be human. He knew logically that the woman he loved was nowhere in there. That she had died and something else had taken over. But that didn't stop him from wishing with all the impossibility of his new un-life that he could be human again. So she could look at him, even with those cloudy eyes, and see something she wanted. He would gladly take her in his arms and let her devour him. It would be a mercy. It would end his pain, his hate, his sorrow. His anger.

Weller was vaguely aware of something inside him. Something dark that swelled and shifted dryly like a snake in a crumbling terrarium. He turned and punched a half-broken industrial microwave that lay in the rubble next to him, putting his fist through the cracked glass door.

He reached for his Sig in his shoulder holster but found the leather pouch empty. He paused, looking down at the groaning, deformed, and broken corpse of his ex-wife. The love of his life. He grabbed a two-pronged carving fork from the rubble and, without hesitation, stabbed it into the back of JayLynn's head. She stopped moving.

Weller gathered her body and held her to his chest. Her scorched and mangled body seemed to relax. His eyes fixed on her legs, both of which had been crushed below the knees by large chunks of debris.

He looked further back into the wrecked store and spotted Berena's charred body. The girl was lying on her side, still tied to the office chair in which she died. Her skull had been smashed by a large chunk of office wall. She hadn't come back as a zombie. It was a small mercy.

The scent of JayLynn's blood assaulted Weller's sense of smell, causing his stomach to cramp violently. It was unmistakably the smell of blood, but it was more complex and richer than it had ever been before.

He pressed JayLynn tight against his chest as he retched and vomited the meager contents of his stomach. When he was done vomiting, he cried. He screamed and rocked and kissed the torn and burnt flesh of his ex-wife's face.

With every cry, every spasm of pain that moved through his mind, whatever it was that had been awakened in him moved impatiently. It was now more than just an inkling. More than a psychological imperative. It was as if he could feel it rustling behind his ribcage, in his skull, spreading through his arms and legs. Pain, hate, bloodlust, and a thirst for revenge made manifest. And he fed it happily. With images of JayLynn as a zombie. With memories of her love. With remembrances of Berena, the innocent teenager who had already been through so much, only to be crushed and burned in the shitty office of a restaurant supply store. And with fantasies of what he and that darkness would do to Buck and to whoever else was responsible for this. He had a good idea who that was.

He put JayLynn's body down gently, taking one last look at her, searing the image in his head. As he stood up, he heard movement behind him.

"Do you want to bury them?" Binta asked in a small voice.

Weller shook his head. "We need to end this," he said. "Did Buck survive? Did anyone see who was lobbing explosives at us?"

"I don't know. We haven't found Buck's body."

"Gather everyone here. I need to hear what everyone saw while it's still fresh. How long was I out?"

"No more than two hours," Binta said as they both turned to walk back out to the rubble-strewn parking lot.

Weller nodded, turning his attention to the task at hand. He promised that darkness inside him release when the time was right. When he found Buck.

Buck had been surprised when the store blew up. Weller was sure of it. That wasn't his doing. Still, it didn't mean he was innocent. He had tried to kill Weller, after all. And he was the one who had brought JayLynn and Berena there in the first place. If Buck was still alive, he would have to pay dearly. And, by all accounts, he was still out there somewhere.

Weller counted heads as everyone gathered. He couldn't remember exactly how many they had started off with, but it looked to him like their numbers had almost been halved. Jamie, Val, and Nadia were missing. Along with five others. With the addition of Weller to their ranks, they were a total of eleven. If Diirek ever came back, he would make twelve. When Weller had first met the vampires, they had been near thirty in number. The apocalypse had even been hard on the immortal, it seemed.

"So," Weller said as all the surviving vampires gathered, all looking a little worse for wear. "What the fuck happened?"

"There was a fucking drone, man," a vampire by the name of Johannes said.

"A drone?" Weller asked.

"It was targeting the super zombies," Isabelle said, brushing ash and soot off her blue jeans. "Like the thing was trying to protect us. Honestly, whoever it was probably saved our asses. There were at least as many of those super zombies as there were of us. And they seemed different somehow. Less like automatons and more like . . . us."

"Wait, back up," Weller said. "You're saying a drone launched the explosives? What about the machine gun?"

The vampires nodded.

"It has to be that Anders guy that did it. I'm guessing he was following us from the subway station," Binta said. "Protecting us because he needs us to turn him."

"I don't really give a shit if he saved your asses," Weller said quietly. "He killed my family. I swear if any of you turn him, I'll kill you as creatively as I possibly can." Weller looked at the remaining vamps for confirmation.

"Of course we're not going to turn him," Isabelle said. "He's a monster."

The rest of the vampires voiced their assent.

"Uh, guys?" one of the vampires said, his head turned away from the rest of the group. Weller didn't know the vampire's name, but he was of Asian descent. It was the first time Weller had heard him speak. "We're about to have company," he continued, looking out at the dark city. "I hear the horde coming."

"I don't hear anything," Weller said.

"It doesn't come all at once. It takes time," the Asian guy said.

"What's your name?" Weller asked.

"Jules," the guy said.

"Well, Jules, never mind the horde. We need to figure out what the plan is. Anders said he's going to be here tomorrow night. I'm guessing he's already in the city, what with the drone and the killing of my family and all. I'm guessing he'll come expecting gratitude for what he did, but he doesn't strike me as the kind of guy who will come without fail-safes and protection in place. We need to be ready.

"And you all need to know what Buck told me just before everything went to shit. He said that he had fed Ricardo to the super zombies and that it made them smarter somehow." Weller paused. "Well, he didn't come out and say it, but one of the zombies looked at me and smiled right on cue."

"Smiled? Are you sure?" Binta asked.

"I may not smile much, but I know one when I see one. Yes, I'm sure. It's not good."

"They did seem faster and stronger. More intelligent, too. Not by much, but still," Isabelle said. "If Anders engineered them like he said, it would make sense," she continued. "If he was trying to make vampires, but made zombies instead, he wasn't too far off. We know that zombies crave human flesh to live. They absorb energy from the blood and meat of humans, but not in the traditional way. Not in the way calories work for humans and other animals. So, it follows that zombies can absorb some of our energy, too."

"That's like no science I've ever heard. But, then again, there's nothing that explains you guys," Weller said.

"That also explains how the super zombies came to be. By eating Merek, like we thought."

"But they wouldn't have if we hadn't coated him in human blood. And the zombies don't pay any attention to us. So how would Buck get them to eat vampire?" Binta asked.

"Same as we did," Isabelle said. "Mix it with some human meat."

"But, if they're intelligent enough now to know how important vampires are, they'll seek you—us—out themselves," Weller said. "Everything is a bunch of bullshit," he murmured.

"Let's hope they're not. Let's hope they were acting on orders last night when they tried to capture us," Binta said.

"Yeah. Because that's so much better," Weller replied.

"I say we move," Jules said, looking around. A large group of zombies had appeared idiot-walking toward them from two blocks away. "All the noise we made is bound to attract more attention. And who knows if we're still under surveillance from that Anders guy."

"We need to find Buck," Weller said.

"Fine. But we won't find him standing here," Jules said, and started walking. The rest of the group followed. Weller looked over his shoulder into the restaurant supply store. He stared for a long moment before running to catch up with the others. Just as he did, one of the other vampires fell in line beside him and started speaking to him.

"Um, yeah hi." He spoke in a light, breezy voice with a Western European accent. He was a tall, skinny man with a shaved head and a stubble beard on his pale cheeks. Weller had never learned his name, but he had seen him hanging around in the Underground.

"Detective," he nodded at Weller. "My name is Bram. No relation. I think I may have seen something you may be interested to know. The more I think about it, the more important I think it is. Shall I tell you now?"

"Yes. Yes, Bram. Tell me."

"Okay. Very good. One of the super zombies grabbed a dear friend of mine, Nadia, and ran off with her. Nadia had apparently suffered an injury in one of the explosions because she came out of the building very badly burned. Her left arm was missing, too. She looked weak and I was running to help her when one of the big zombies ran past and picked her up." Bram paused as if to ensure that Weller was following the story as they walked back toward the safe zone.

"Yes. Get on with it, Bram."

"Okay. Very good. So, I ran after the zombie. He ran down the street and away, carrying Nadia, who clearly didn't know what was happening. So, I was following, trying to catch up—this zombie was fast—when a big truck came out of the side street and ran right into them." Bram paused again and looked around. It was now clear that all the vampires were listening to his tale.

"I was about two blocks away and I kept running," he continued. "But then two men got out of this strange truck. One of them shot the zombie with a shotgun in the face. I was happy about that. But the other one grabbed Nadia and shined a light in her face. It must have been a UV light because I had to look away and Nadia began moaning in pain. Believe me, I know her moans of pain and pleasure very well. And this was pain."

"Gross," Weller said. "So they loaded her up and drove off?"

"Yes, Detective. They turned off the light and the two of them dragged her around the side. I couldn't see what exactly they did, but they drove off and she was gone. They must have taken her. I had almost reached them when I was tackled by a super zombie from behind. By the time I finished destroying him, the truck was long gone."

"What did the truck look like? Was it like an eighteen-wheeler? An extended cab? What?"

"It looked like one of your mobile command center vehicles. Or a mobile crime unit. Only it was painted black and had no police markings."

"You watched the video with us tonight, right? Was one of the men Anders Revak?"

Bram shook his head. "I don't know. They wore masks and suits like black-ops guys. Many things of electronic and protective equipment on them."

"It has to be Revak. Now he has one of you. And soon he'll be one of you. Then he can turn as many people as he likes. He can build a fucking army of vampires." Weller was still getting used to the idea that he was a vampire. He wasn't ready to say "one of us." No one corrected him.

"You don't know it was Revak," Isabelle said, without conviction.

"The guy's obviously filthy rich," Weller said. "I'm sure he has his ways. He couldn't have put all his hopes on that stupid video of his. You said he was watching us. Maybe he wasn't trying to protect us with the bombs and machine gun. Maybe he saw his chance to take one of us by creating a little chaos."

"If he doesn't come to us tomorrow, or contact us, it was definitely him," Isabelle said.

"Shit," Weller said. "We can't wait until tomorrow night. We have to find him. Luckily, I think Diirek already did." Weller paused, thinking. "You told them all what Diirek said, right?" He asked Isabelle, who nodded.

"On the way to the outskirts," she said.

"We shouldn't wait," Binta said. "We need to be out looking for him. Or at least for Buck."

"There's no way Anders would have stayed in the city if he could help it," Weller said. "Not if he got what he was looking for. But we've got a leg up on him. We know where he hangs his hat. After all, how many compounds like that can there be?" Weller's initial skepticism had waned over the course of the night. Unless more than one psycho was experimenting with turning people and animals into monsters, the compound Diirek found had to be Anders'.

"As for Buck," he continued, "you're right. We need to go find him." Weller paused, closing his eyes. He remembered how it felt as the two-prong fork slid into JayLynn's skull. That gloom inside him seemed to rattle and squirm, making him momentarily lightheaded. "Did anyone see him take off when the chaos started? Was he injured at all?"

"Maybe?" This came from a stocky woman vampire with short black hair and the physique of a bodybuilder. Weller had never interacted with her directly.

"Go ahead . . ." Weller trailed off, hoping someone would fill in the blank.

"Luana," the woman said. "I'm Luana. I was with the group you told to hang back. We came up after the first explosion. I was far back, but I think I saw Buck get hit with the third explosion. The one that slammed the metal cart into you. I thought you were dead for sure."

I was—I am, Weller thought. Weller studied the woman as she paused, her eyes wide in remembrance.

"Anyway," she continued, shaking her head. "I could swear I saw Buck get thrown by that explosion in the parking lot. Then he got up and limped away. But he looked bad. Like the whole right side of his body was a mess of burned and bleeding flesh. His arm hung limp at his side. But then the smoke got in the way and when it cleared, he was gone."

"Okay," Weller said. "If Buck was injured, he couldn't have gotten too far. His priority would have been finding a human to heal himself. Does anyone know where there are any humans nearby in the outskirts?"

Everyone looked at each other, shrugging.

Weller thought for a moment, then turned his attention to Isabelle, Luana, and Jules. "You three see if you can locate Anders' truck. Only spend two hours searching, though. We'll need you if we need to go meet with Diirek. If you find Anders, take him out any way you can. I wouldn't bet on it, though."

They nodded their assent.

"The rest of you, with me. We're going after Buck."

"Okay. Very good," Bram said cheerily to no one in particular. "Let's fuck this shit up."

Man after my own heart, Weller thought.

CHAPTER TWENTY-NINE

A CRASH COURSE IN VAMPIRISM

Weller, Binta, Bram, and five other vampires moved out into the night, as the other three vampires stood in a circle, formulating a plan. Bram moved ahead to take point while the rest of them traveled in a small group, Binta and Weller bringing up the rear.

"Can I fly?" Weller asked as they walked. He wanted to know what he was dealing with. What kind of powers came with being an unholy creature of the night. Mostly he wanted to know that he could rip Buck apart if they met—when they met.

"Have you seen any of us fly?"

"Not exactly. I saw Diirek kind of float once. And I heard something about Merek being able to turn to smoke. Can you do that?"

"Diirek is very old. He can do some things that most of us can't. The same could be said for Merek. He was on a whole different level, what with the steady diet of vampire blood he consumed. Plus, he may have been the original vampire. Or one of them, anyway."

"Okay. What about turning into a bat?"

The look Binta gave him said everything.

"I had to ask."

"No, you didn't. What is the expression? One I've heard you say a few times . . . Oh, yes, 'Such bullshit.'"

"What if I am caught in the sunlight? Do I burst into flames and then disintegrate into ashes? If so I hope it looks cooler than what I've seen in every single vampire movie ever made."

"If you're caught in the sunlight you will experience the most pain you have ever felt in your life. And now that you're a vampire, your body won't go into shock. You will continue to feel the pain until it stops. But, no, you won't burst into flames the instant sunlight touches you. It takes a while to burn down. And, when it happens, it doesn't leave behind ashes. Just a disgusting blob of scorched and melted flesh."

"Great. And about pain. Don't I have a higher tolerance now?"

"Somewhat, yes. But that doesn't mean to go running toward danger. Getting shot still sucks. You can still lose a limb if you're not careful. And if you lose your head, it's over."

"Yeah. I'm definitely clear on that one." Weller paused, going over what he'd learned about vampires from movies and TV shows over the years. "How about the mindfucking thing? Does that work?"

"Mindfucking? What are you talking about?" Binta said, looking at him like was a vampervert.

"Maybe that's not the scientific name for it . . . hypnosis. That's it. Can I look a human in the eyes and convince her to do anything I want?"

"Ugh. Men," Binta said, shaking her head. "If that were the case, we'd have it easy. Diirek could have just hypnotized you to go find Merek instead of asking you for help. Can't enhanced strength, super speed, better senses, and immortality be enough?"

"Well, I feel different, but I don't feel any stronger or faster or anything. When does it kick in?"

"How do you mean 'different'? Explain it to me."

Weller began to speak but thought better of it. He looked off into the trashed outskirts, noticing that his vision did seem better. He could see further and clearer than before. He thought about telling Binta about the thing inside him that flared up whenever he thought of Buck and, to a lesser degree, Anders. That coiled, pitch-black animal that wanted so badly to be let loose. But it seemed like that had always been with him. It had simply grown more powerful after he had been turned. He wasn't sure if it was a result of the turning or of JayLynn and Berena's deaths. He knew instinctively that it was dangerous. *But it's a danger I can control*, he told himself as they walked.

"I can't explain it," he said, finally. "I just feel . . . lighter and heavier at the same time. Does that make sense?"

Binta looked closely at him. For a moment, Weller thought she was going to challenge his answer, but she didn't.

"It's a little different for everyone," she said. "Who you are as a vampire is more about who you were as a human and what you choose to do with the power. Which is why we must stop Anders. It's clear he will cause tremendous harm to many people if he gets what he wants. With enough vampires, he could enslave what's left of humanity. It wouldn't be hard. Not as the world is now."

Weller grunted, thinking about who he had been as a human. He liked to think he had done some good.

Binta grabbed him by the arm and they both stopped walking. She looked at him closely again. "You have some darkness in you, Detective. Maybe more now than ever. But you'll have to use it as a tool. Not as a drug. Do you know what I mean?"

"Sure. I've been a cop for most of my life. It's—"

"No," Binta said, cutting him off. "It's not the same. The power you have as a policeman is great in human terms, but your power now is incomparable. You'll have to make a thousand decisions. A million. For as long as you're alive, you'll have to decide what to do with that darkness inside you. And the decisions are not equal. One good choice is not the equal and opposite of a bad choice. Not even close. One bad choice can send you spiraling down. Can turn you into a monster. Can cause you to lose the rest of who you are—who you were—as a human. Which is why you have to keep making the good ones. Over and over again. For people like you—people like us—it never ends."

"Christ. No pressure or anything."

"I'm only trying to be honest with you, Kurt."

"What about Isabelle back there? And Diirek? Are they the same as us?"

Binta smiled. "For Isabelle, it's much easier. Her darkness is . . . in permanent hibernation. The same was true for Lidia when she was still alive. But Diirek. He's very much like you. He has to keep that darkness at bay constantly. Especially after losing Lidia. I think it is part of the reason why he left the city. To make things easier on himself. To get himself back under control."

Weller nodded. It made sense to him.

Binta nodded back and then took off after the others. Weller followed. They were moving fast now. Weller managed to catch up to them as they slowed at an intersection.

"What's happening?" Weller asked as they all gathered.

"The horde is close," Bram said. "What should we do? Spread out?" Everyone looked to Weller for directions.

"There's eight of us," Weller said. "Bram, you and I will go north. The rest of you, pair up and pick a direction and search for five blocks. Look for anything out of the ordinary. If you see anything, come find me. If not, we'll meet back here as soon as we're done searching the five blocks from this intersection."

Binta gave Weller a worried look as he walked away. Weller saw the look and ignored it, grabbing a clearly delighted Bram by the arm and heading toward the intersection. Once they were headed north, Bram attempted conversation.

"I'm sorry about your wife and daughter, Detective."

Weller said nothing. His eyes moved constantly, taking in the apocalyptic detritus that littered the dark streets, the concrete and glass cliffs of the valley in which they walked, and the limited swath of sky above. Several blocks ahead a single zombie stumbled slowly away from them. Weller reached under his left arm for his pistol, which still wasn't there. It was among the rubble of the restaurant supply store, no doubt.

"Shit," he said, under his breath.

"How do you like being a vampire, Detective?"

Weller said nothing, made no indication that he heard Bram.

"Do you smell that?" Bram asked. Weller did. It was the pungent and noxious smell of rotting flesh. And it was getting stronger. They came to the first cross street and looked left and right. Four blocks to the left a thick crowd of zombies milled about dumbly, filling the entire intersection. It looked like they were traveling south.

"The horde," Weller said in a whisper. He squinted, seeing if he could enhance his vision. It worked for a second, enlarging the horde clearly in his sight. Then everything went blurry, like an out-of-focus camera. He blinked and relaxed his eyes, allowing his sight to return to normal.

"See anything strange?" Weller asked.

"No. Just a bunch of zombies being zombies."

"Let's keep going."

They continued north for two blocks, seeing nothing of importance. Weller began to grow impatient. The outskirts were already so fucked up, he had a hard time imagining what Buck and the super zombies could have done to alert him to their presence. Aside from a light on in a building or running across a super zombie out for a jaunt, there was little hope. He started to feel sick with anger as the minutes ticked by and nothing came of their search. Then Bram stopped. "You hear that, Detective?" he said.

"No. What is it?" Weller said, stopping too and turning slightly.

Bram turned around and looked directly south. Weller followed his gaze and saw a figure running toward them, three blocks away. He tried to focus in, but his vision grew blurry again.

"Come," Bram said. "It's Silvan. They must have found something."

The two of them ran toward Silvan, who was one of the vampires Weller hadn't officially met. He looked to be in his late thirties with strong Greek features. When they were close, Silvan waved at them, turned around, and headed back the way he'd come. Bram and Weller followed, the early summer night quiet around them. Only their feet made noise as they moved. Silvan turned right, heading west, and slowed to a stop two blocks later, crouching behind a burned-out car. A block away, the intersection was crowded with zombies.

"What is it?" Weller said as he and Bram joined Silvan.

"Look in the crowd," Silvan said, gesturing to the horde, which apparently stretched back several blocks north. It had to be thousands strong now.

"Where did your partner go?" Weller asked.

"To alert the others. Just look."

Weller lifted his head and looked at the crowd. He saw nothing at first and was about to tell Silvan as much when he saw a figure moving through the mess of zombies, cutting a lane like a stick through sand. The figure stopped suddenly, then ducked into the crowd. For a moment, Weller thought he'd been spotted, but the figure came back up, another zombie slung over its shoulder in a fireman's carry.

"What the fuck?" Weller whispered. Bram raised up beside him to look. The figure moved through the crowd again, only this time it headed in Weller's direction, parting the slow-moving corpse river. Weller grabbed Bram's shoulder and pulled him down just before the figure emerged from the horde. It was a burly super zombie that had once been a man. Its skin was blue-black, and its muscles bulged. Weller watched through the windowless car as the super zombie walked to the sidewalk away from the crowd and set the zombie it had been carrying down. Were it not for the slash across the zombie's neck, it could have passed for a regular person. It was a young man, maybe late teens, or early twenties.

The super zombie reached back and pulled a large plastic fastener out of its back pocket. It crouched down and pulled the thick black fastener around the zombie's legs then went to work trying to secure it. Weller, Bram, and Silvan watched as the super zombie struggled to get the two ends of the fastener together. It grunted in anger, apparently unable to perform the delicate task of inserting one end of the fastener to the plastic tab on the other end. The regular zombie kept trying to walk back to the horde, compounding the burly super-z's problems.

Finally, when the zombie tried to walk away for a third time, the big zombie lost his temper and punched the other zombie in the kneecap. The crunch of the joint breaking echoed off the brick buildings. The zombie collapsed, unable to stand on its newly broken leg. Realizing what it had done, the super zombie stood up, grunting in anger, and put its hands to its head. Then it began to utter little frustrated yells as it stomped the broken zombie's head to slush, which took the better part of a minute.

Shoulders slumped, the super zombie turned back to the horde and walked toward it. Something sounded from down the street. A clattering of metal. The super zombie, and several regular zombies from the horde, looked that way. Weller, Bram, and Silvan dropped down.

"Shit, he saw us," Silvan said.

Weller ignored him, looking down the street to where the noise had come from. He saw the rest of the vampires crouching behind another car down the road. They were visible from his vantage point, but not from the super zombie's. He signaled for them to stay put. "Don't move," he said to Bram and Silvan before raising his head back up very slowly. The burly zombie had turned around and was wading through the horde again. They hadn't been spotted.

Weller watched the super zombie amble around in the slowly moving horde. It ducked down again and came up with another zombie over its shoulder. Only this time it didn't come back out of the crowd. Instead, it turned south and started walking with the flow of the horde.

Weller turned and signaled to the other vampires down the street, indicating that they should come, but quietly.

"What's happening?" Bram asked.

"We need to follow it. It'll lead us back to Buck," Weller replied.

"How do you know that?" Silvan asked as Binta and the other four vampires arrived.

"Isn't it obvious? Buck's soldiers were depleted. He needs new ones. That super-z has been sent out to collect likely candidates."

"I'll follow him," Bram said, standing up to head to the horde.

Weller looked up at him, fire in his eyes. "No fucking way. I will."

"Not a good idea, Detective. I've been sneaking up on people for longer than you've been alive. I got this," Bram said.

"He's right," Binta said. "This isn't the time to learn."

"Fine," Weller said. "Don't lose him. And don't get caught, for shit's sake."

Bram nodded and took off.

Silvan shook his head. "So it's safe to assume that he got away with several of us last night. Who knows how many more super zombies he can make? I wonder if any of the others are still alive. Val, Jamie, Louis . . ." he trailed off.

Weller looked at the others, all of whom had their heads down in solemn remembrance. It was the first time he'd really noticed that he wasn't the only one hurting. And that he'd held the vampires aloft in his mind as somehow emotionless. Since they were vampires, they were already dead, so it didn't matter much if they died for real. Or they were somehow numb to death after having lived for so long. Then he remembered how hard Lidia's death had been on Diirek. And the feeling in his own chest told him that he would never get used to losing those close to him. Ever.

"We know they're definitely gaining intelligence, if not sentience exactly," he said finally, trying to keep their eyes on the prize.

"If they're out here alone, making choices, then yeah," Binta said. "I wonder how much of them is left . . . inside. Could we bring all these people back to their former selves with our blood or our flesh?" she asked, gesturing at the horde.

"No," Weller said, simply. It was nothing more than a gut feeling, but he was sure it was true. "They've been dead too long. They're gone. Whatever comes back isn't them. It can't be."

"If it can for us, why can't it be the same for them?" she asked.

Weller shook his head in answer, looking at the horde as the zombies passed with small, shuffling steps. Flesh hung off bone, eyeballs swung like pendulums, tongues lolled between pale blue and pink lips, cloudy white eyes stared blankly ahead in utter idiocy. Braindead. Undead. Walking dead.

Where the fuck is Bram? Weller thought, his impatience swelling again.

As if on cue, Bram seemed to materialize from out of the horde. He gestured at the rest of the vampires and whispered, "Got 'em."

CHAPTER THIRTY

THERE'S NO CRYING IN THE APOCALYPSE

F red had no way of knowing it, but the maroon SUV had been parked across the tracks by a pair of lizard-brained brothers two days ago. The brothers, who shared the last name Haggard, were known as Earl and Merle (no relation). Their father, whether by happenstance or by subconscious suggestion, was a fan of the famous country singer.

Earl and Merle had seen the train pass through their little one-horse town when Diirek had just started his journey. Since the end of the world, the brothers had been making their living robbing, looting, and beating anyone who got in their way. So, when they saw the train pass by, they got to thinking. All they could come up with was to put an SUV across the tracks to make the next train stop.

When they heard a train coming back through, they hustled from their new home a quarter mile away (taken by force from the previous owners). On their way they heard the impact of the train hitting the SUV and thought of all the goodies they would have in their possession soon.

Train goodies. When they arrived at the spot, they saw the remnants of the SUV, which had been smashed in half, and saw the back of the train disappearing into the dark distance.

The impact had been enough to throw Diirek off his feet as he made his way back to the front of the train, but it hadn't been enough to throw him completely off the moving locomotive.

Fred, on the other hand, didn't get away so clean. Although he came away from the impact unscathed, it had jarred something loose in his mind. It was a terrible memory, and it came bursting into his conscious mind just as train met SUV. As glass shattered and metal screamed and sparks flew, Fred couldn't help but remember the worst day of his life. A day he had managed to suppress for the bulk of his time on earth.

He must have been four or five at the time. He remembered being in the front seat of an old pickup truck. It was a bench seat. The kind that could fit three adults if the one in the middle straddled the center hump. It was an automatic transmission, making it slightly more comfortable than a manual, where the gear shift would've been in the middle of that center hump. But there were only two people in the truck in Fred's memory. Himself and a woman.

Fred was strapped in on the passenger side of the truck, with what seemed like a great distance between him and the woman. He remembered wanting to be closer to her. He remembered her sandy blond hair, her ready smile, and her hazel eyes as they squinted at him in the sun. *Mom.*

"You ready, Freddie?" she asked, smiling at him after twisting the key and starting the truck. She wore a sleeveless floral shirt with large pink buttons down the front and pink flowers on a white background. Her worn blue jeans had a small hole at the right knee. She had on an old pair of athletic shoes which she called her rock kickers.

Fred giggled and laughed and nodded. He liked it when she called him Freddie. His father only ever called him Fred or Frederick.

His sneaker-clad feet barely reached the end of the bench seat, and his head was just tall enough to look out the passenger window and the windshield. He wore overalls that were shorts at the bottom. Under that, he had a white shirt with a purple duck on the front. The duck's cartoon eyes and head poked out from between the overall straps. The frayed blue and white cloth of the old pickup's seat was coarse and itchy on his bare lower legs, but he paid it little mind. He was going on an adventure with his mom. Nothing else mattered. Everything was new and exciting. The weather was perfect, and the sun shining down through the old oak tree in their front yard sprinkled him with shifting sunlight as the breeze stirred the brilliant green leaves.

His mom put the truck in reverse and turned in her seat to look behind her as she backed out of the driveway. Their nearest neighbor was about a mile away along the dirt county road on which they lived. Fred looked out the window, watching first their farmland and then the neighbor's stream by. He knew all the names for the different crops that were growing, and he said them aloud as they went, his mom confirming happily as she drove.

They came to another county road and stopped behind the ragged stop sign. His mother looked left, right, then left again. Fred did the same, although he couldn't see past his mom to the left very far. He couldn't have believed then that anything bad would ever happen. Not while his mom was around, anyway. His absolute faith in her ability to protect him was not even something he ever contemplated. It just *was*. A normal part of growing up with loving parents, where all of life's tragedies were so far in the future as to be nonentities or impossibilities.

She took her foot off the brake and put it on the gas, turning left onto the road that led to town. The road was paved at the town limits, but until then it was hard-packed dirt. There were no speed limit signs along the stretch, either. At the town border, right where the dirt gave way to dried tar, there was a sign noting the speed limit at twenty-five miles per hour. Fred's father often referred to the seven-mile stretch of road as America's Autobahn. Fred didn't know what an autobahn was, but he thought the word sounded funny whenever his dad said it. A few farmers liked to go sixty miles an hour in their big produce trucks down the seven-mile stretch that was as straight as a road could get. Fred's mother, a cautious driver by nature, liked to go no more than forty miles per hour. Thirty-five when she had Fred with her.

So, as she turned the old truck left toward town, she proceeded to apply steady pressure to the gas pedal until the speedometer hovered at thirty-five miles per hour. She checked her mirrors, seeing nothing behind her but empty road. Nothing ahead, either. It wasn't a road with a lot of traffic, but she continued to check her mirrors like good drivers do.

"What're those, Fred?" she asked, pointing to buzzards circling in the bright blue cloudless sky ahead.

Fred looked at where she was pointing and squinted his fleshy eyes. A look of furious concentration altered his normally smooth and chubby face into a series of graceful cracks and unmarred crevasses. His mother smiled at him.

Fred's face suddenly returned to normal, then shifted to a knowing smile that seemed to move past his eyes in its completeness. "They're buzz—"

A loud pop sounded from under the truck and the wheel twisted in his mother's hands. She reacted immediately, taking her foot off the gas and fighting the truck's urge to pull them right and off the road into the ditch. The road was raised about three feet off the surrounding farmland, meaning there was no shoulder to pull off onto, just soft and steeply sloping dirt. She got as far over to the right as she could without driving off the road.

The truck slowed quickly as she fought the flat tire. Fred's face distorted into a grimace. He sucked in an impossibly long breath of air which he then let out in a piercing cry. Tears started flowing down his cheeks as the truck came to a stop. His mother levered the gear shift up and left into park, then turned to face her screaming son.

"Oh, baby, it's okay. It's just a flat tire," she said, reaching over to wipe tears away from Fred's plump face. But Fred was having none of it. His cries came out in racking, slobbery sobs interspersed with nonsensical words.

"Freddie," she continued. "It's okay. It's okay."

Fred looked at her through his tears and reached his hands out toward her, the gesture used by children everywhere when they want to be held.

"Okay, I'm coming, Freddie," she said, over his unceasing cries. Fred was too big for her to hold comfortably in the cab of the truck, so she unclipped her seatbelt and opened the door to walk around to his door, even if it meant standing on the slope at the side of the road.

She held the door open with her left hand and stepped halfway out of the truck when a large, speeding vehicle sideswiped the driver's side. One moment Fred was watching his mother step out of the truck, crying his head off, and the next she was gone. The truck rocked violently as the other vehicle grazed it, removing the open door and the woman holding it. The sound of smashing metal and shattering glass was the loudest thing Fred had ever heard. Bits of blood and flying debris pelted him.

The impact knocked the truck's nose down into the ditch so that when the local sheriff came upon it later it was canted at an angle, the back tires still on the dirt road. The sheriff came from town after an anonymous call about a hit and run. Since he arrived from town, he came upon the accident from the front. He stopped his cruiser, radioed for an ambulance, and got out well away from the scene. The only noise was the soft ticking of the old pickup's engine. He walked forward slowly.

The first thing Sheriff Brendan Hess came across was a crushed and severed arm. The second was a mangled and severed leg. The third was the woman to which the limbs clearly belonged. The fourth was a young boy, about four or five, sitting a foot from the woman's body, staring with red and empty eyes at the scene before him.

"Fred?" someone said, causing Fred to jump in his seat at the controls of the train. It was Diirek, looking a little beat up and bloody but alive.

"Are you all right?" Diirek asked.

Fred nodded and wiped his eyes at the same time.

"I will drive now," the vampire said. "You did well."

Fred got up and moved to the assistant's seat as Diirek sat behind the controls.

Fred stared blankly at the twin lines of track and the monotonous ties as the train rolled on. And replayed the terrible memory over and over in his mind. It was as if he couldn't believe that it was real. That it had really happened. But a part of him knew it was true, no matter how much the rest of him wanted it to be a product of his imagination.

It was a flood that refused to stop. Tears spilled down his cheeks again, but this time he wasn't bawling. He was silent in his misery. After all, if he hadn't been crying, his mom would have been able to hear the truck approaching. If he hadn't been crying, she wouldn't have even gotten out of the truck at that moment. They still would have been sideswiped, he guessed, but his mom would have lived. She might have suffered minor injuries, but nothing more.

He didn't understand how he had locked the incident away so completely. Or, for that matter, how every memory of his mom had been locked away with it. But those memories—those happy memories—were somehow back, and for that, he was grateful.

What he couldn't recall, although he desperately wanted to, was whether they had found the driver who had killed his mom. It was probably a moot point, now, but he wanted to know anyway. He wanted to know that there had been some sort of justice in the old world. He looked over at Diirek and decided that there could be justice in this new, changed world. He and the vampire would see to it.

He remembered how he'd felt when Diirek had rescued him by flipping the truck with the tweakers inside, how the dead methhead looked all crushed and bloodied and destroyed. He remembered how he couldn't breathe in the duct tape cocoon. And how the memory had tried to surface then, but he wouldn't let it. He realized now why he only saw his mother in his nightmares. And why he could never remember them when he awoke, only that his mother had been there and that something terrible had happened.

He realized that there was some sort of relief in unburying that memory. A strange mixture of shame, guilt, and relief.

"Look," Diirek said, pointing out the windshield. Fred looked. In the distance, he could see the dark shapes of buildings against the night sky. They were close. It was Fred's first trip to a city. He felt excited and scared all at once.

Chapter Thirty-One

MASSACRE

"He headed straight into the museum," Bram said to the group of seven vampires.

Weller thought for a second, picturing the layout of the streets in his mind. "The history museum?" he asked.

Bram nodded.

"What a cliché," Weller said, rolling his eyes.

"Maybe he's been eating vampire, too," Binta said. "It's smart. There's only one way in. Well, two if you count the rear doors, but those are big, heavy, and would be hard for even us to get through. Plus, the place is kind of a maze. Three floors of exhibitions and plenty of places to hide."

"Sounds like you know the place well, Binta."

"I do, Detective. I've spent many hours there. I like museums."

"No surprise there. Well, you can give us the layout, then."

"Fine. But I haven't been there in several months. They may have changed some exhibitions around. They do that sometimes."

"Fine. Let's just go."

They made their way into the horde one at a time, Bram and Weller in the lead. The nearby zombies swiveled their rotting heads toward the newcomers, giving them each a brief once-over. Dull acceptance settled over the sagging flesh of their putrefying faces and one by one, without fail, the zombies realized that there was nothing in the vampires that they wanted. Whatever inherent instinct on which the zombies operated protected the vampires as they made their way to the museum. The zombies were after human flesh.

As Weller moved through them, he realized the feeling of indifference was mutual. Whatever instinct that had been thrust upon him when he joined the ranks of the undead told him that these post-humans were not for feeding. He figured that had something to do with the stench, which was almost unbearable. Worse than he remembered it being when he'd almost been devoured by members of the horde in a dank alley nearly a month ago.

Of course, that month had not been kind to the zombies. They continued to rot, whereas the vampires were forever fixed in their bodies as they were, ageless and full of empty vitality. The only rotting they would do would not be so easily discernible. The soul would decay where the flesh would remain intact. Perhaps the sanity would slip away slowly, like the erosion of a hillside that eventually tumbles a neighborhood into the maw of the earth.

"Are you okay, Detective?" Bram asked as they broke away from the horde to approach the museum.

Weller ignored the question, looking around instead. The other vampires were looking at him strangely as they, too, exited the mass of brain-dead roamers.

"What? What is it?" he hissed. "Why are you all looking at me like that?"

"No reason," Binta said. "Just . . . ready for you to tell us the plan."

Weller knew it was a lie. Something was up, but he didn't have time to worry about a bunch of overly sensitive vampires now. Buck was close. He could smell the little bastard. "Give us the layout and I'll give you a plan," he told Binta. The eight of them gathered in an alley between the horde and the museum.

Binta gave them the layout as she remembered it. The exhibitions and their locations, floor by floor. She had a hell of a memory, Weller had to give her that, but it was taking too long. He felt as if he was vibrating. He could imagine his dark skin cracking as something black as night freed itself from the cage that was his body. "Okay, I think that's good enough," he said, interrupting Binta as she got to the third floor. "Here's what we're going to do. I'll go in first and take the main floor with Bram. Silvan, Binta, and Cuba Gooding over here will take the third." This last was directed at a vampire whose name Weller didn't know but who did, in fact, possess a passing resemblance to the famous actor. "You other three, take the lower level. First priority is to locate Buck. Second is to rescue any survivors. Third is to eliminate any super zombies you see. You find Buck, give a shout. I need to have words with him. Got it?"

"Shouldn't the *first* priority be to rescue any survivors?" Silvan asked.

"No. Any other questions? Good, let's go."

They approached the museum from the west. The main entrance faced south but there were windows lining every side of it. There was nothing they could do about that. If Buck still had enough soldiers to place lookouts on every side, he would know they were coming.

The structure took up half of a city block and was made entirely of white Georgia marble. To Weller, it looked like every big city museum he'd ever seen. Large, imposing, and designed to be grandiose without looking like it was. Its architecture was a throwback to that favored by European cities in centuries past. Seeing as how it was a museum, he figured that was appropriate. The building itself was a glimpse into the past.

As he approached the museum, Bram by his side, Weller thought about what little good museums had done to fend off the end of the world. It was a confirmation of his disregard for the lessons contained within the building ahead. He had been more concerned with the history of policing, forensic science, and criminal psychology than the rise and fall of ancient civilizations. Yet even that had done him no good in the end. All it had taken to end the world was one rich psycho possessed by an unhealthy obsession with vampires. And the vampires themselves—their very existence—seemed to fly in the face of his entire life as a law enforcement officer. And as a human. And a man.

He thought of all the times he had been so sure about the immutable laws of the world. All the times he had told himself that the playing field was level because, after all, everyone was just as human as he. All the times he had warmed himself in the basking glow of a life dedicated to a cause. It was all bullshit. The existence of vampires proved it.

The years he felt stretching out before him, toward an unfathomable eternity, reminded him of a recurring nightmare he had as a child. There were no monsters in that nightmare. No evil coming to snatch him from his bed. In the nightmare, everything was *massive*. His room, his bed, his dresser, the walls of his room, and everything beyond those walls was gigantic, looming, intimidating. Yet he remained the same size. Like everything but him had changed, leaving him behind to be driven insane by the impossibility of it all. The sheer scale of that nightmare world was enough to wake him from his slumber on countless occasions, sweating and crying for his mother. It had been the worst nightmare, and the most recurrent.

Now he couldn't escape that feeling. The feeling that everything had changed but him. Never mind the fact that he was now changed, too. Reality as he knew it kept slipping further and further away with every passing day, the scale of the universe expanding inexorably in every conceivable way while he himself was unable to match that speed, no matter how hard he tried. As if his mind simply wasn't equipped to handle such a drastic shift in the status quo.

It scared him to his core. And, with that fear came a wave of deep, unrelenting anger. Looking back with sudden clarity, it was now apparent that his two defense mechanisms had always been anger and irreverence. But really, his wry comedic outlook only served to mask the anger building inside of him. It had always been that way. He responded to fear, to any threat, with semi-controlled anger and a defensive wall of snappy comebacks and put-downs.

It was something he had never realized until this moment, the museum now looming, filling his vision in the dark early-summer night. It all came clear as he searched inside himself, trying to get a feel for this dark anger that pulsed and grew with each step. That anger seemed to talk to him in a voice not quite his own. And not even a voice at all. More like a white noise from which realizations seemed to bubble up, like whispers in the howling wind.

Those realizations didn't seem to come with any sort of power, any sort of control. He felt on the verge of giving himself over to the darkness inside him. No matter the consequences. He knew there would be no controlling it if he did let it loose. He knew that instinctively. In fact, attempting to control it would be a mistake that his sanity could not survive, that darkness seemed to say. And he believed it.

Weller circled around to the front of the building at a dead run and started taking the stone steps three at a time. He was no longer making any attempt at surprise.

"Weller? What are you doing?" Bram hissed from far behind him.

Weller ignored him. Reaching the doors, he was surprised to find that all but two of the glass portals were intact. He pushed through a set of doors and then another to enter the lobby. The place was miraculously untouched. It appeared looters and outskirts gangs had passed on the museum for more enticing targets like jewelry, grocery, and electronics stores.

Past the ticket booths and stanchions, through the darkness, he could see the preserved skeletons of a couple of well-known dinosaurs and a wooly mammoth with long, curved horns. The third-floor railings were visible on either side of the dead creatures' skulls. Between him and the extinct giants, there were two sets of stairs, one on either side. Leading down to the bottom floor and up to the third. He saw no sign of super zombies or of Buck. But he could feel them. They were here, somewhere.

He stepped further into the lobby. Movement stirred from the darkness surrounding the skeletal exhibits. Buck's soldiers moved toward him. Six of them at first glance. Burly super zombies, their skin tinged blue, and their eyes a mixture of yellow and white.

Weller felt the darkness move dryly. It shifted impatiently inside of him, itching for release. It was time to make a decision. He pushed the fear down, causing his anger to swell. He could hear the other vampires coming up the steps toward the front doors.

Weller grimaced, set his jaw, clenched his fists.

And gave in.

***

As Binta made her way up the steps to the museum entrance she could not shake the feeling that had seized her. In truth, it had been with her since she had turned Weller not long before. But it had been masked by the sorrow and anger she felt at losing so many of her friends—her family. It had grown steadily stronger, a sixth sense that she had had to develop as a vampire.

Then, as they had been moving through the horde toward the museum, surrounded by putrescent bodies and their special, eerie kind of death, it had hit her like a hammer blow. She began to watch Weller closely. When they moved out of the crowd of shuffling zombies, she knew that the others felt the same thing. A palpable sense of dread surrounding the detective. But she could think of nothing to do. In truth, she didn't *know* what to do. It was only a feeling. A strong one, but still, just a feeling. As much as she would have liked to, she could not see into the future. Not hers, nor Wellers, nor anyone else's. So she pushed forward. Tried to buy time, explaining every single detail of the museum that she could recall. Hoping that some brilliant flash of insight would come to her or one of the other vampires. But none did.

Then Weller spewed a plan that couldn't even be considered a plan and turned around to go. She realized that the possibility of losing more of her family was very real as she watched the detective head toward the museum, moving fast. And losing Weller felt like a certainty to her, then. She felt as if she'd made a terrible mistake in turning him. She should have let him die.

As Weller suddenly moved even faster, pulling away from Bram and the rest of them, she'd had a hard time believing what was happening. *She* couldn't even move that fast. He was up the stairs and in the museum before the rest of them had even rounded the corner.

Now, as she came to the line of outer doors, instinct told her to duck as the top half of a super zombie came smashing through the glass doors right in front of her. She dropped to all fours and the half-zombie soared over her head. She turned her head against the splash of glass shards that pelted her face and arms. She was able to see the zombie land face-first on the stone steps, arms flailing and entrails dragging as it tumbled down the steps and came to rest with a gash in its head from the impact with the stairs. It didn't move.

She stood up and looked to her left at the other vampires, all of whom stood outside the first set of doors, staring inside with shocked faces. She pushed through the smashed doors, crunching on broken glass, and stepped into the lobby. Her face soon reflected those of her comrades.

There was a super zombie head blinking dumbly on the tile floor nearby. Its armless body was draped across the ticket counter like a too-realistic Halloween decoration. She saw one of its arms lying on the other side of the lobby. It was only when she looked back at the body that she saw the other arm. It was sticking out of the zombie's rear end, partially obscured by the bulk of the zombie's body. The hand sticking down between its legs seemed to be waiting for an awkward high-five.

Another zombie was standing straight up, arms out, chest against a wall by the stairs. Only its head had been smashed into the wall, leaving behind a stain that looked like old lasagna mixed with pulverized squid.

There was no sign of Weller. She stepped further into the lobby, hearing the other vampires finally make their way inside, tentatively. The skull of the tyrannosaurus rex had been knocked down and used to decapitate another super zombie. Its body still lay by the side of the extinct beast's jaw, gripped at the flesh of the neck by the large, polished teeth. The dinosaur seemed to be grinning at its good fortune.

The sound of breaking glass broke the silence. Binta glanced up toward the third-floor railings overlooking the skeletons. There was a grunt, sounds of a struggle, and then the clopping of shoes on marble tiles. From the darkness of the third floor, a super zombie came wheeling over the railing, headed straight for the wooly mammoth. It hit chest-first on one of the huge, curved tusks attached to the skull. The dull point gouged through the zombie's chest cavity and came out its back to the left of the spine. As the zombie slid slowly down the tusk, the weight became too much for the metal armature holding the skull in place. The mammoth's head, tusks and all, came crashing down to the museum floor, ripping a larger hole in the zombie on impact.

Binta watched as the super zombie tried to stand up, to work its way off the tusk, only to slide back down, coating the bone in gore. A few vital organs spilled out onto the floor at the zombie's feet. The next time it tried to stand up, it slipped on a kidney and slid back down the tusk.

Everything went quiet again, which seemed to snap Binta out of her daze.

"Okay. Let's go," she said, turning to face the other six vampires. "Find the others, if they're still alive, and get them out of here. Bram, you come with us."

The rest of the vamps shook their heads as if to clear them and nodded, splitting up and heading off into the museum.

***

Weller moved through the darkness of a third-floor bird exhibition with a purpose and a blank clarity that could only be compared to an out-of-body experience. The stuffed birds in the wide glass cabinets stared at him with fake, unseeing eyes, reflecting the static state of his own. He seemed to glide across the thin, blue-gray commercial carpeting. Instinct in the form of a voiceless, black urge compelled him forth.

He paid no attention to the blood, bone, and brain coating his fists and forearms. He stalked out of the bird exhibition, down a short hallway, and into a vast room characterized by a sign that read *Inside Ancient Egypt*. He paid no attention to the sign. Words were of little concern to the part of him that was in control, whether spoken or written.

The exhibition was shaped like a large dome inside the high-ceiling room. Glass cases of various shapes and sizes curved away from him along the walls. In the center of a room sat a large pillar of exhibits displaying various recreations or artifacts of the ancient culture. He moved into the room without stopping, going right, following the curve of the glass display cases.

Footsteps sounded from behind him. He reacted too late. He turned to see a super zombie a pace away. The zombie tackled him and they both went smashing into the glass cases along the outer wall. A jagged shard slid into the back of Weller's left thigh. He felt it sever some important tendons or muscles as pain flared and function was immediately impaired. He rolled out of the shattered glass, wrestling with the zombie. Weller found himself on top, but it was not to his advantage.

When it had been alive, the super zombie must have been a giant man. Its arms were long and muscular, and the hands at the end of them were clamped around Weller's throat. He heard and felt his windpipe collapsing as the zombie squeezed, its white-yellow eyes staring up at him, a rotting smile on its face. Weller tried to reach down and grab the zombie by the neck, or to gouge its eyes, but his arms were too short. Its arms were locked at the elbows, keeping Weller out of reach.

He swung his arms out, hitting the inside of the zombie's elbows with his forearms, both at once. The zombie's arms unlocked, and Weller dropped a few inches. In one smooth motion, he grabbed the zombie by the shoulders and jackhammered his head down, smashing the curve of his forehead into the zombie's face. He felt bone give under the blow. He whipped his head back up and slammed it back down again, feeling one of the zombie's eye sockets collapse. The zombie's hands loosened around his neck.

Weller used all his newfound vampire strength to headbutt the zombie again. The other eye socket collapsed.

And again. The forehead domed inward.

And again. The nose and cheekbones shattered to pieces. The zombie's hands fell away.

And again. Bone fragments were forced into the frontal lobe. The face no longer resembled a face at all, but a bloody mess of shredded skin and jagged bone. The mouth was a twisted mess. The upper jaw was distorted and collapsed while the lower jaw remained untouched. Weller stuck the four fingers of his right hand into the zombie's mouth, securing his grip with a thumb under the chin. He pulled back in a savage yank, removing the lower jaw. It came away with a wet and roaring rip as the sinew, tendons, and muscles stretched and then snapped with the force.

Using his right leg to hold his weight, Weller stood up and limped to the back of the room, transferring the dripping jawbone to his left hand, and slinging off some bits of skin as he did so. There was a double doorway lined with recreated stones designed to resemble the entrance to an ancient chamber room. The sign above the doorway read *Mummifi-*

cation and Burial. His left leg dragged along behind him, only serving to hold his weight on the locked knee joint as he moved his right leg ahead for another step. He held the jaw down by his left leg as if he'd forgotten about it.

Buck was in the room. At first, Weller sensed his presence, more than saw him. He let his eyes scrape around the chamber slowly before letting them come to rest on Buck. The small man stood with a humorless grin behind a lidless stone coffin located in the middle of the chamber room. The coffin was surrounded by shiny metal stanchions with red velvet ropes. A beat-up super zombie stood to Buck's right. It was clearly intelligent enough to hesitate as it eyed Weller but made no move to come toward him.

Buck no longer looked like himself. He'd been burned on one side of his body, but he didn't seem to notice the scorched skin. It was clear to the part of Weller still somewhat coherent that Buck had changed. Whatever humanity that had been left in Buck's eyes had long since fled. Or been forcibly removed.

There was a pile of fresh bones cluttering the corner, leaning against two walls lined with cracking hieroglyphs and representations of people who had been dead for millennia. If there had been any light in the room the wet gristle still clinging to those bones would have sparkled like gruesome diamonds. But all was darkness. Still, the three parties had no trouble seeing each other.

Behind Weller, protected by a glass case, sat those well-known tools used by the ancient Egyptians for mummification. They were lined up on what was effectively a stone workbench for the embalmers of old. There was a chisel, a wooden spoon, and a hook used for removing brains. There was a well-preserved obsidian blade, used for removing organs from the abdomen. Two bundles of incense sat further down in the display. Canopic jars, linen, and natron powder all had their place, and each had a little placard denoting their use in the process.

"How did I know it was you?" Buck asked in a rasping croak.

Weller said nothing.

"How does it feel to be undead? Is it worth it?"

Weller said nothing. His insides sizzled with anticipation. The pain in his leg faded away to nothing. He was aware only of Buck and, to a much lesser extent, the other zombie. He was hyper-aware of the jawbone in his left hand. JayLynn and Berena had become more than memories. He had to do nothing to hold them in his mind. They were simply there with him. And they had been since they had died. Before that, even. Since he'd met them. JayLynn especially. Her presence was there, inside of him. With him.

His darkness coiled, getting ready for action. He no longer felt it. He *was* it.

"I guess they died," Buck said slowly, without a hint of remorse in his voice. "I never wanted that."

As Buck spoke, the super zombie turned its head slightly and looked at Buck out of the corner of its eye. Buck did the same, turning his seemingly frozen face just a fraction, moving his eyes to convey a message.

The zombie moved. Fast.

When it was a step away, Weller brought the jawbone up in his left hand. He had his fingers around the teeth at the middle of the bone, using the two hinge-points that connected under the ears as prongs of sorts. A quick jab to the face was all it took to sink one of those prongs into the zombie's left eye, popping it out as he yanked the jawbone back. The move caused the optic nerve, connected near the back of the brain, to become yanked loose and then snagged in gray matter. The zombie swung wildly, disoriented as its eye swung around and bounced off its cheek and nose.

Buck, seeing how the super zombie was faring, had moved toward them.

Weller jabbed again, sinking the jawbone deep into the zombie's right eye socket. He yanked it out, stepped clumsily behind the zombie, and jammed the jawbone into the soft spot at the base of its skull, where the spine meets the head. Weller followed through, sending the zombie smashing face-first into the glass over the antique workbench. Before the zombie was sprawled on the ground, Weller had snagged two tools from the workbench and turned around to see Buck charging at him.

Weller swiped at Buck with one of the mummification tools. The obsidian blade passed through the cartilage of Buck's throat easily. It opened a gash in his neck, exposing the inside of his windpipe. Buck didn't seem to notice, aside from the fact that it threw off his trajectory. He corrected, grabbing at Weller's left arm to keep from passing the detective and running into the stone workbench. His grip strengthened around Weller's forearm. When Weller made no move, Buck smiled up at him and yanked, looking to remove the limb. When Weller's arm barely moved, Buck's smile collapsed. Then it was Weller's turn to smile. He swung the obsidian blade down on Buck's left elbow. The first swipe separated the forearm almost entirely, save for a thin piece of muscle on the outside. Weller swiped again, cutting through the thread of meat. Buck's forearm and hand fell from Weller's to land with a faint thump on the floor.

Weller wasted no time. He swung the blade up, stabbing it into the soft flesh under Buck's chin. He left the blade there and grabbed Buck's right hand with his own. He snapped the wrist with a quick twist. Then he kicked Buck's left knee, snapping the leg and causing it to fold the wrong way. Buck collapsed, wide-eyed. The detective crouched over Buck on the floor and brought the chisel up from his left hand. He shoved it up Buck's nose and pulled it back out, twice. He stood and limped over to the workbench and grabbed the hook from amid the shards of broken glass. Buck was sitting up when he turned around, so Weller grabbed the back of his head in one hand and shoved the hook up his nostril with the other. Then he went about pulling Buck's brains out, his one hand clasped gently at the curve of Buck's skull while the other worked furiously with the hook.

Buck's eyes stayed open the whole time. But sometime during the session, any passing semblance of life or intelligence left them.

Weller kept working.

***

Binta went searching for Weller after securing the two remaining vampires, Val and Jamie. There had been two super zombies tasked with holding them, presumably for later feeding, on the other side of the museum, and they had put up a hell of a fight. But Binta and the others managed to put them down without too much trouble. Had there been any more of them, it would have been touch and go.

Presently, she crossed through the bird exhibition and into the Ancient Egyptian room. She saw the jawless zombie with the smashed head and wondered again how it was that Weller was so powerful. As much as she wanted to believe it was a good thing, her instincts told her otherwise.

She padded on light feet into the recreated burial chamber and saw the zombie with the mandible shoved into its skull, face down on the stone workbench. Then she noticed that there were body parts scattered all around the room. A foot here, a calf there, a finger here. The parts that weren't covered in blood were white, so she knew they didn't belong to Weller, but the detective was nowhere to be seen. "Damn," she said. She looked around for a minute, checking inside the stone coffin and noting the bones piled in the corner of the room. Then she left, heading back to the Underground with the others.

CHAPTER THIRTY-TWO

A MURDEROUS REUNION

Diirek tried to stop the train right about where he'd found it, which was just past a wye track a half mile from the massive train station that had served the city before the apocalypse. They ended up a little further past the turnaround track than Diirek intended, but it would do. Diirek considered it a success, for how fast they had been going.

They left the train running and headed back to the three psychos chained up in the sixth car back. Robinson was blubbering on distractedly, whereas Fuller and Buffalo Bob started asking questions immediately. They had heard Diirek and the werewolves fighting it out on top of their train car and had felt the impact with the SUV. They wanted to know what had happened.

"It is none of your concern," Diirek said to them. "Now shut up so I can drink your blood."

It was Buffalo Bob's turn. When Diirek was done, he and Fred walked back to the upper level of the train car.

"I think Bob is enjoying my feeding sessions more and more," Diirek said.

"Yeah. The look on his face gives me the creeps. He definitely likes it."

"Well, it is not all so surprising," Diirek replied, absently. "Feed them and then eat something yourself," the vampire directed. "Then come to the front and find me. I am going to change clothes now that my wounds are healing."

The two of them parted ways. Fred brought the men some cold soup in plastic bowls with no spoons while Diirek changed out of his shredded and blood-soaked shirt. Fred scarfed down some cold soup, with the help of a spoon. Then he went to meet Diirek and found him talking on the radio in the engine car.

"See you soon," Diirek said into the radio, indicating that Fred had caught only the end of the conversation.

"Who was that?"

"One of my friends that we are going to see," Diirek said. "We should get going. The sun comes up in a few hours."

The sound of the train had attracted several walkers that were milling about near the front of the locomotive. Diirek dispatched them quickly with a crowbar while Fred waited inside the train. Once the coast was clear, the boy and the vampire headed up the tracks, toward the station located directly between the edge of the city and the sprawling suburbs.

"So we're going to find your friends?" Fred asked as they walked. Everything was dark. The vast city loomed ahead. None of the buildings had lights on, and it was very quiet.

"Yes. They will help us go back and deal with the werewolves."

"What?! Why? Why can't we just stay here with your friends or find another safe place? We don't need to deal with them. We can just leave them alone."

Diirek shook his head. "I do not think so, Fred. There is a man that those werewolves are protecting. We think he is responsible for all this." The vampire gestured at their dark and desolate surroundings.

"For what? Everything? The walkers and the bombs and everything?" Diirek nodded.

"Well, how do you know that? And how could one man have caused all of this? He'd have to be like an evil genius or something."

"He sent a video to my friends wherein he admitted that he did all of it. My friends believe the video. And I believe my friends. That is how I know. As for how he could have caused all this by himself, I plan on asking him that very question." Diirek hesitated for a moment, unsure he wanted to say what he was thinking about saying. "And I do not think that the term evil genius is all that far off."

"No way," Fred said, incredulous. "That kind of stuff only happens in movies . . . right?"

"Yes. Along with zombies and vampires and werewolves."

"Good point."

"I have seen some very strange things during my lifetime," Diirek said as they left the tracks and headed into an employee parking lot, skirting the station itself. "And I spent many years searching for answers to those strange things. I spent years searching for answers to the mystery of my existence—the existence of vampires—and I have yet to find any satisfactory answers." Diirek paused, thinking. "And it seems that this man, this Anders Revak, who claims to have spawned the apocalypse, has done it all in hopes that it would unearth vampires. He has dedicated his life to becoming immortal and powerful. And it seems that he may be achieving that goal as we speak."

What Isabelle had told Diirek on the radio was more than a little disturbing. It sounded as if more of the vampires, some of whom he'd known for centuries, were now dead. He felt an old anger building in him, but he kept his face and voice impassive. Not only for Fred's sake but for his own, as well.

"Woah. That's insane. He torched the whole world so he could become a vampire? That's messed up."

"I agree. But it seems that he didn't actually torch the world. Not completely. He was very strategic about it. Which is why there is no radiation. At least not around here. Maybe in other parts of the world, there is. A nuclear holocaust would have killed everyone, even vampires, if I had to venture a guess. He knows that vampires can only survive on human blood, and he acted accordingly with his plans. There is probably a sizable population of humans still left out there. But with no means to communicate and chaos reigning supreme, they will be easy to control. To harvest, so to speak."

Fred shook his head. "What the hell . . . But aren't you, like, happy about it? Doesn't that mean that you and your friends can come out of hiding?"

"The fact that you have to ask that offends me, Fred. I have no wish to harvest humans or to rule the world. I liked the world as it was. And I liked the people I shared it with . . ."

"But isn't holding Buffalo Bob and the other guys the same thing? What if this Andrews guy only wants to capture bad people and use them for blood? Would you join him then?"

"His actions killed hundreds of millions of people. If not billions. If he is willing to do that, I do not foresee him having any qualms about enslaving any and all humans he can get his hands on. And then there are the vampires who will no doubt stand against him. He will have us destroyed, as well. This is not a man that you join. This is a man that gives you two choices: serve or die."

"I see what you mean," Fred said, nodding. They had made their way past the station and were walking down the middle of the street, heading east. The buildings were two or three stories high here, but they got gradually bigger in fits and starts toward the city center. The street was covered with trash and debris. Torched and smashed cars lined the road at random intervals, some half on the sidewalk, others upside down, while still others looked like they had been expertly parked before they were destroyed. There were a few figures walking dumbly in the far distance.

"I am glad you do," Diirek said. "What are your thoughts on him? Do you think we should give him a chance, or should we stop him?"

"Well, I guess I understand about him wanting to be a vampire." Fred spoke with his eyes on his feet and his hands in his pockets.

"Do you?" Diirek asked in an amused voice.

"Yeah. I think it would be pretty cool. Being strong and fast and stuff. I've always been weak and slow. Not good at anything. So being a vampire would be cool. But all the other stuff isn't cool. I mean, my dad wasn't the best. He drank a lot after my mom died and he used to hit me sometimes, but I still loved him, I guess. And this guy killed him. And everyone I ever knew. So, he sounds like a bad guy. He went about getting what he wanted the wrong way."

"Oh? And how would you have gone about it?"

"Easy. I would have just asked."

Diirek smiled. "Would you have? Then, if you want to be a vampire so bad, why haven't you—" Diirek stopped mid-sentence and looked around, eyes wide. The crack of a rifle pierced the air and a bullet hit the street about a foot in front of them. The bullet whined crazily as it ricocheted off into the night, sending small chunks of asphalt toward the two.

Fred yelled in pain, reaching down to grip his left shin. Diirek yanked him by the collar and dragged him behind a blackened sedan. The rifle fired again, a sharp sound that echoed off the buildings. The thump of a bullet striking the sedan was almost instantaneous. The shooter or shooters were close.

Fred yanked his left pant leg up to reveal a bloody shin. "Oh god. I'm shot," Fred said, his breath hitching and his eyes impossibly wide.

"No," Diirek said, clearing blood away from the wound with one hand. With the other, he quickly dug out a piece of asphalt that had been lodged in the skin. Fred winced and sucked in breath. The vampire held up the bloody piece of black rock to show Fred, then discarded it.

"Put pressure on it," Diirek said, pulling Fred's sock up to cover the small wound.

While Fred gripped his shin with one hand, Diirek stuck his head up and tried to spot the shooter. Another gunshot sounded and a bullet punched through Diirek's upper back, slamming him into the sedan.

"Behind us," Fred said just as Diirek realized what was happening.

"Don't you fucking move," said a man's voice from behind. Diirek looked over at Fred, whose eyes were fixed on whoever was behind them. He made a snap judgment not to move. Instead, he gasped and moaned, leaning heavily against the car. He focused his hearing and listened to the footsteps. There were three distinct sets. And they were too far away. If he made a move now, Fred would surely take a bullet.

One of the group whistled loudly and a moment later Diirek could see two people about two hundred yards away, walking toward them from where the first two shots had come. They were both holding rifles.

"Get up, kid," the same voice said. Fred looked at Diirek, the fear in his eyes complete. "Get the fuck up or I shoot him again," the guy said. Fred stood up shakily, using the burned sedan to help.

Their footsteps were closer now, but not close enough. Diirek turned around in a clumsy, slumping effort, sitting with his back resting against the car's fender. He held one hand up to the exit wound on his right pectoral muscle. There were two men and a woman, walking in a line. The woman was sandwiched between the men, about three feet separating each of them. Under their dirt and grime, they looked like they could've been suburbanites. The two men wore dark green cargo pants and black jackets over nondescript t-shirts. The woman wore blue jeans and a shiny olive-colored jacket with a bunch of pockets. All three of them were armed. The man on Diirek's right held a short and stocky submachine gun pointed at Fred's chest.

"How old are you?" the guy asked Fred. He was the only one who had said anything. The presumed leader.

"Seventeen," Fred said.

"Told you," the guy said, although it wasn't clear which of the other two he was speaking to. Maybe both.

"He'll do nicely," the woman said.

"For what?" Diirek said in a gasp. All three of the others looked at him like he had just taken a shit in their cereal.

"You're not dead yet?" the leader asked, never moving his gun from Fred's chest. They were about fifteen feet away now. Diirek was starting to think that he wouldn't be able to get Fred out of this alive. He was fast, but he couldn't get up off the ground and reach the guy before he had a chance to twitch his trigger finger. Of that, Diirek was sure.

"Look at that sweet piece of ass," another man said from behind the sedan. It was one of the two snipers. They rounded the sedan and joined their companions. Two more men. Both wore similar garb and looked like they could've been related to the leader.

When they saw Diirek up against the sedan, one of them spoke. "He's not dead yet? Why are you wasting time? The horde isn't far from here. There will be about a thousand zombies on us in five minutes. Let's go."

"Look at how pale he is," leader man said. "He doesn't have long. Maybe we just leave him for the roamers."

"Whatever. Let's just—" The guy made a choking sound and reached up to his throat. There was a dark spot there, right under his Adam's apple, that hadn't been there a moment ago.

"You okay?" the other sniper asked. The guy made no answer. He was busy pulling a piece of jagged metal out of his throat. Blood was now leaving his body in earnest through the hole in his neck. He placed one hand on his throat and held up the piece of metal with the other, looking at it like it was a trinket he'd just found on the sidewalk. It was about two inches long, about a half-inch thick, and ended at a jagged point.

"What the fuck?" the leader said. Something moved in the darkness behind the guy and his head suddenly whipped forward like he'd taken a baseball bat to the back of the skull. His chin hit his chest as vertebrae separated with a popping sound. When his head snapped back up it was no longer securely attached—it bobbed and lolled crazily. His momentum caused him to stumble toward Diirek, who decided it was time to move.

As Diirek got to his feet and stepped a pace toward the severely injured leader, he caught movement in the corner of his eye. The other sniper, who had been standing in dumb disbelief next to his dying comrade, was struck in the back by something. Hard. He went flying into the torched sedan like he'd been launched out of a cannon. His legs struck the hood at the upper thighs, sending his face and chest slamming down on the top of the hood in a splatter of teeth, blood, and spit. One look told Diirek that the guy's face was shattered.

Diirek turned and kicked the dead-on-his-feet leader in the chest, sending him slamming into the woman, who fired her weapon wildly in a last-ditch effort to kill Diirek. But her reflexes were slow compared to his and she wound up firing into the leader's back just a fraction of a second before the two collided. The woman went down like a ragdoll with the dead leader on top of her. The sound of her skull cracking as it hit asphalt reverberated off the buildings.

Diirek turned toward the remaining man to find a dark, blood-coated figure standing with his back to Diirek, his face buried in the last guy's neck. Miniature geysers of blood arced into the air while the guy twitched and tried to scream and grew impossibly pale as his blood left him. Diirek's eyes narrowed as he watched the bloody scene play out.

"Detective?" he asked, unbelieving. "Is that you?"

The guy twitched one last time before his eyes wrenched closed in peaceless death. The bloody figure let the guy's body fall to the ground and straightened up, then slowly turned around. He looked at Diirek for a long time before speaking.

"Do you know the name of this song?" Weller asked, before singing the tune to a song Diirek had never heard and hoped to never hear again.

When Diirek didn't answer after several moments of shocked silence, Weller spoke again.

"So," he said, a bit awkwardly. "This must be Fred."

Diirek snapped out of it then, looking to his left to find the boy standing next to him, a look on his face much like he assumed was on his own. Diirek turned back to Weller, searching for words. "How—What—What happened to you?" he asked, finally. "Did you know we were coming?"

"Man, I was starving. I've never been so hungry in my life," Weller said, looking down at the man whose blood he'd just ingested. "I didn't know you were coming. I was just out looking for a meal when I heard gunshots. Then I saw you and the kid. But I'm glad you're back, buddy. Maybe you can help me with this whole thing. I don't know if you could tell, but I'm a vampire now. As for what happened, that's a bit of a story."

"Only hours ago, you were going to save your wife and stepdaughter, yes? Did you?"

Weller shook his head. "They're dead," he said, looking past Diirek. "I would have been dead, too, if not for Binta. She turned me."

"My condolences, Detective. I am truly sorry for your loss."

"Yeah, sorry, Detective," Fred said.

"Buck did this?" Diirek asked.

"Yes, he did. And that Anders guy I was telling you about over the radio. They're both responsible. But Buck has been taken care of."

"How is that? You?"

"I'm pretty sure I found him. It all seems kind of strange. Like a dream, almost. But I'm almost positive I tore him apart."

Diirek looked hard at Weller. "Good." He paused. "So, Binta turned you tonight?"

Weller nodded. Something caught Diirek's attention, and he looked down the street. "The horde," he said, pointing. "Let's go. They'll be after Fred if we stay here."

Weller looked over his shoulder at the crowd of zombies meandering down the street several blocks away. "So let's go," he said. The trio started off down the street, heading toward the safe zone.

"Tell me everything," Diirek said. "Everything from when I last talked to you."

Weller nodded, the look on his face one of pure dread. They walked on in silence. After a few steps, he spoke again. "So, neither of you recognized that song? It's driving me nuts. I can sing it for you again if you want."

"No!" Diirek and Fred said at once.

Weller shrugged and proceeded to tell Diirek about the night's events.

CHAPTER THIRTY-THREE

THE BIRTH OF A GOD

Fred thought about how wild and scary and insane the city and its inhabitants were. But he also continued to replay the newly-surfaced memory of his mother's death—a death that he had caused. If anyone had asked him before the apocalypse, back a lifetime ago when he was sixteen, if his feelings could get any more complex, he would have laughed. No way, he would have said, as his hormones swamped his emotions while he tried to figure out his place in the world. But now, as he and two vampires walked down a subway tunnel, he looked back on sixteen as a much simpler time.

He felt like he didn't belong—didn't deserve—to be hanging out with these two badass vampires. Although one of them (he only knew him as 'the detective') had only been a vampire for a short time. Still, before he had been a vampire, the detective had been a badass human. Fred couldn't say the same. His shin hurt like hell where the little bit of asphalt had struck him, which made him limp a little bit, which made him feel like even more of a little wussy wuss. A panzyass puss in boots, like his dad used to say. Although, at the moment, he was wearing sneakers, not boots. Fred thought back on the little encounter with the five people who had been dispatched so viciously and got down even more on himself. He had been so scared he could do nothing but sit on the ground and shake.

He was useless.

No reason for him to exist at all. And soon these vampires would realize it, if they hadn't already. But maybe not. After all, Diirek had seemed preoccupied ever since they came into the city. He kept staring at the detective with a strange look on his face. Like he was mad at him for turning into a vampire or something. And the detective seemed preoccupied, too. He was mumbling to himself and looking around wildly before they went down into the subway tunnels. It was starting to freak Fred out.

They came to a brick wall with a steel door in it and Fred thought they were going to go through the door, although it looked sealed pretty tight. Then Diirek jumped up on a little brick outcropping above the door and pushed a secret door aside. The detective grabbed Fred around the waist and tossed him up to Diirek, who caught him easily and dropped him down into a short hallway with thick carpeting on the other side. Fake candles lined the wall, their fake flames flickering with battery-powered light.

Fred stood there until the two vampires joined him, then they all walked down the hallway and through a steel door that actually opened. The first person Fred saw was a teenage girl about his age. Her smooth white skin glowed, her face framed with dirty blond hair. She wore blue jeans, strappy but sturdy sandals, and a pink V-neck t-shirt with short sleeves. She was in the middle of a large subway platform that had been turned into a living area of sorts, and she was talking to a man with black hair and tanned skin whose face Fred could not see. He was immediately jealous of the faceless man.

There were about a dozen other people in a loose group around the couches and chairs off to the right. The girl and the black-haired man were standing behind the couch when Fred, Diirek, and the detective entered. All eyes turned to them as they stepped inside. The girl's green eyes landed on Fred for a moment, and he felt himself blush with a ferocity unparalleled in the world—at least in Fred's mind.

"Weller!" A gorgeous and tall black woman said as she stood up from the couch. "Diirek? And some strange kid?" she said, clearly perplexed.

"Hello, everyone," Diirek said. Then everyone started talking at once. Fred thrust his hands in his pockets and floated back toward the wall. He watched as the beautiful teenager seemed to fly through the air to wrap Diirek in a hug. He listened hard and caught Diirek saying, "Hello, Isabelle. I've missed you."

Isabelle, Fred thought with an inward sigh. *Jeezly crow.*

After a few long moments of verbal chaos, things died down a bit.

"This is Fred," Diirek said to the room. "He has been helping me. No one kill him, please."

Suddenly everyone was looking at Fred. Sizing him up or thinking about how good his blood would taste. *Are they all vampires? Wow.* "Hello," he said. "I'm Fred and I would prefer not to be eaten. Thank you."

The guy Isabelle had been talking to laughed at that, along with a few others. The guy had turned around and Fred could see that he was Asian. Fred decided that he didn't like the guy. Not because he was Asian, but because he and the others laughed at him when he'd been completely serious. He *did* prefer not to be eaten.

"You brought home a stray?" Isabelle asked Diirek in French-tinged English. He had only just met her, and she was already breaking Fred's heart. "I'm only kidding," she said, stepping forward and putting out her hand. "I'm Isabelle. Welcome, Fred."

"Uh, yeah, um, thanks I guess," Fred replied, shaking her cold hand with his hot and sweaty one. Isabelle looked him up and down, seemed to come to some sort of decision, then released his hand and stepped aside. Fred's heart pounded in his skull.

"Where'd you go?" the gorgeous black woman asked the detective, whose name was apparently Weller.

"I had to eat, Binta," Weller said. "Something happened and I got injured. I was very hungry."

"And you did?"

"Oh, yes. He ate," Diirek answered for him.

"Wait, you said 'something happened.' You don't know what?" Binta asked.

Weller hesitated. "It's all a bit of a blur," he said, placing a hand on his brow and massaging his temples.

"So you don't remember killing five or six super zombies in the span of a minute? You don't remember using a jawbone to poke out another one's eyes? You don't remember tearing Buck to pieces?"

"I remember the last part . . . mostly."

"Wait, what did he do?" Diirek asked, looking back and forth between Binta and Weller. The rest of the vampires were staring at Weller as if trying to see inside him.

"You left that little detail out of your story," Diirek said, staring at Weller.

"So I went a little crazy. I was—I am—upset. I tore a bunch of bad guys apart. Is that bad?" Weller asked.

"I don't know," Binta said, then paused. "It's unprecedented."

"Yeah, well, my whole life has been unprecedented. Why should death be any different?"

"You saw him do this?" Diirek asked Binta.

"Most of it, yeah. Kind of. It was definitely him."

Diirek turned to look at Weller, who stood there in his tattered and bloodied clothing. No one spoke.

"I know kung fu," Weller said, doing his best Keanu Reeves imitation.

"There's something seriously wrong with you," Binta said.

"This may be a good thing," Diirek said.

"What? Diirek, you know—"

"Not now, Binta," Diirek said. "We have to deal with Anders. Isabelle, Luana, Jules, I'm told you were tasked with finding him. I'm guessing you didn't have any luck?"

"Not a trace," Isabelle said. Jules shook his head, looking ashamed. Luana shrugged.

"We must find him,' Diirek said. "And we must do it soon. I need all of you to come with me. If we go now, we can get back to the train before sunrise. I know where Anders lives."

"Wait, what is Binta talking about, Diirek?" Weller asked, serious again. "Is there something wrong with me? Something I should know? Binta?"

"We will discuss it on the way," Diirek said. "Let's go."

***

"You're not one of those weird train guys, are you?" Weller asked when they were underway. They had made it to the train without incident, all fifteen of them. They had turned it around in about twenty minutes. The sun would be coming up soon, and there had been a big debate about keeping the train where it was until nightfall came again. Diirek would have nothing of it. He told them that Fred knew how to drive the train. That they would be in good hands. That they didn't have time to wait twelve hours. And that he had blacked out an entire sleeper car, which wasn't all that hard since all the rooms had dark curtains, anyway. He had simply duct-taped them shut.

"What do you mean a weird train guy?" Diirek asked. He, Weller, and Fred were in the engine car. Fred was at the controls. The train was moving slowly. Thirty-five miles per hour, tops. Which was fine with

Weller. He didn't want to crash and get torched by the sun because the kid was a speed demon.

"I knew it," Weller said. "We good?"

"Yes," Diirek said. "I already told—"

"I'm not asking you. I'm asking him," Weller said, gesturing at Fred. The kid turned slightly to look Weller in the eyes. He nodded once and then turned back to the controls. Weller could sense the kid's fear. He could smell it. And he didn't like it. But he trusted Diirek.

"Remember," Diirek told the kid. "Go for a mile or two after the SUV wreckage and then stop. Get some rest. We will be okay during the day."

"Okay," Fred said.

Diirek nodded and then walked with Weller through the power car toward the blacked-out sleeper car.

"So what's the plan?" Weller asked. "You know how we're going to do this?"

"The hard part will be getting past the werewolves. Once we've done that, we shouldn't have much of a problem."

"And how many did you say there were? Dozens?"

"At least a dozen. Probably more."

"Great. As many of them as there are of us. You said one nearly got you? So how the fuck are we going to get past them? Most of the others don't have the skills you have. And I don't know what the hell is going on with me. You can't expect me to do whatever crazy shit I did to Buck and his soldiers."

"No, you will not be involved. You will be hanging back."

"What? No way. No fucking way. I can be of some use. And you never know, I may just go crazy again. Kill 'em all."

Diirek shook his head, his pale face grave. "You need to be able to control yourself. If not . . ."

"If not then what? What are you not telling me?" They had made it into the business-class car directly behind the engine car. Diirek bent slightly to look out the window toward the faintly glowing horizon.

"There is something you need to know about vampires, Detective. They are not all like us. In fact, many of them are not."

"What does that mean 'like us'? What, they're actually forthcoming with their information? They aren't all as racially diverse as your little group? What is it?"

"Something happens to people when they become vampires. It is as if they have two choices to make. They can give themselves over to the . . . urges that come with vampirism. When they do that, they seem to lose whatever humanity is left inside. Or they can hold onto that bit of humanity and make the choice to stay true to who they were as a human."

"Oh, Christ. The dark side of the force and all that nonsense? Nothing is that straightforward. There are gray areas everywhere."

"That is comical coming from you. I have not known you long, but I doubt you have ever seen a gray area in your life. Besides, I used to think that, too. But I have seen too many vampires make the wrong decision and . . . lose themselves. For some, it is a gradual process. But for others, it is a decision they are faced with almost immediately. Before they have a chance to get a handle on their powers. And those vampires often are unique in their abilities. Like you seem to be."

"So? I'm still me. Don't you see that?"

"I see you trying to be your old self. Trying to forget about the tragedy you have just suffered. And I can see that it is not working."

Weller blinked, staring back at Diirek.

"The thing is, Detective, every time I have seen a vampire that had powers like yours from the beginning, it does not end well. There is some sort of fury that seems to drive them away from their humanity."

"So you're saying that I'm destined to turn evil or something? C'mon man. This is such bullshit."

"All I am saying is that every time I have seen a vampire with immense power and abilities born, they have turned destructive and, if not truly evil, they've turned . . . apathetic. Without fail. And I do not want that to happen to you." Diirek paused, choosing his next words carefully. "I do not want to have to kill you, Kurt."

***

Anders Revak reveled in his accomplishment. It had all worked out, after all. He had been foolish to send them the recording. He realized that now. But it didn't matter anymore. All that mattered was this feeling, this sensation that gave him chills. He had done it, by God.

No . . . not by God. By Anders.

He had done it. God had nothing at all to do with it. God's pitiful creations were nothing compared to what Anders was now. Men before him had dreamed of ruling the world. They had dreamed of immortality and the true power of life and death. But not one of them had even come close.

Alexander the Great? Attila the Hun? Caesar? Morons!

Weak, pitiful, inept, impotent morons, the lot of them.

All he needed to do now was figure out how to avoid catching fire in sunlight. That was his main concern. He'd spent the ride back to his compound getting information out of the vampire. At first, she'd been unwilling to help him in his endeavor, but she no longer had a choice in the matter. She would be of great use to him now that he had her on his side. His first request as soon as she'd come around was for her to turn him. And she did. And it was glorious.

But his work wasn't done. He still needed to be able to move around during the daytime. And he didn't trust anyone else with that truly important work. Not even Slave One. But he would figure it out soon enough. Having a vampire to experiment on would make it only a matter of time. And if she died during his experiments, so be it. He could simply make more vampires.

Soon enough he would have a whole army of vampires that could roam the earth, day or night. And they would only answer to him. Soon after that, all the humans left in the world would come to know his name. He would be their God. Revak, the ruler. The God. The all-powerful.

Anders liked the sound of that.

He grew drowsy in his large, uber-secure room. He was curled up on his silk sheets as the sun came up outside, its light unable to penetrate the steel window shutters that had slid solidly into place ten minutes before sunrise.

Thoughts of world domination danced through the sociopath's head as he stuck his thumb in his mouth and fell fast asleep.

CHAPTER THIRTY-FOUR

THE (TERRIBLE) PLAN

"I only have three humans on board," Diirek said to the gathered vampires. They were all in the dining car. Including Weller and Diirek, there were a total of fourteen vampires on board. Weller, Diirek, Binta, and Isabelle sat at one table with the rest of the vampires arranged around them. Some were sitting, some standing, and some looking out the windows at the newly formed night. Fred was a wallflower in the shadows. "We'll need to find more. Three isn't enough for all of us." Diirek scythed a glance at Weller as he said this last.

Weller had already met the three humans, just after sunset. It seemed that Diirek was giving him priority feeding rights because he was a new vampire who hadn't learned to control his hunger yet. Weller was fine with it. He woke up out of his dead sleep incredibly hungry. Famished, even. Diirek had been there waiting, which was a good thing. Otherwise, Weller might have gone after the boy.

This wasn't a fact that he shared with Diirek. And it wasn't something he had even thought about consciously when he'd awoken. But once he'd fed (on Robinson), he started thinking clearly again. It was only then that he realized he would have gone after Fred. It was simply a matter of the nearest human. And Weller had been able to smell him. He had also been able to smell the other three humans on the train, but Fred was closer.

Diirek had been in the middle of explaining the feeding process when Weller lunged at Robinson. When all was said and done, it was a miracle that Robinson had survived the ordeal. Weller had cut up the human's neck pretty bad in his frenzy, but the man would live. Weller hadn't cared too much about it. He had some sort of instinctual knowledge that the three captives were bad men. Whether from his experience as a police officer, his trust in Diirek's judgement, his heightened instincts, or all three, it didn't really matter. He was right to think that, as Diirek explained afterwards.

Presently, Weller listened as Diirek explained the plan for the night.

"Bram, Silvan, and Luana, I want you to spend tonight finding at least three more humans we can use. There are plenty of small farmhouses and tiny towns around here. I trust your judgement when it comes to picking them out. I am sure it will not be too hard. If my trek through this area initially was any indication, you will have plenty to choose from."

"Are the roads clear enough to use cars down here?" Luana asked.

"For the most part, yes. In fact, that may be the best way to draw our kind of people out. If you drive around for an hour, you are sure to lure some unsavory characters to you. Make sure to search out their supplies, too. We're going to need all the help we can get."

"Yes, very good," Bram said, rubbing his hands together and looking incredibly vampiric.

"The rest of us will test the compound's defenses. Carefully," Diirek said. "But I need one person to stay here with Fred and the train."

"I can't come with you?" Fred asked.

"No. You are too important. You are the only one of us who can operate the train during the daytime."

Fred's face flushed and he crossed his arms and mumbled something under his breath.

"What was that?" Weller asked, propping his hand behind an ear.

"Nothing," Fred said, pouting.

"I think he said, 'bunchafuckinbullshit,'" Weller exclaimed, laughing.

"Whatever. You're a mean jerk," Fred said, leveling a finger at Weller. When the boy realized everyone was staring at him, he stormed out of the dining car.

"This is not helpful," Diirek said to Weller.

"What? I'm just messing with the kid. He's gotta toughen up."

"Isabelle," Diirek said. "It's clear that Fred likes you. Would you mind staying tonight?"

"Sure. He's très mignon," Isabelle said, slipping into her native French. "I'll cheer him up."

"Thank you. Just . . . don't scare him."

"Who, moi?" Isabelle said with a smile.

Diirek proceeded to sketch the layout of the compound on a piece of notebook paper. He had a map of the area which showed the stream running parallel to the property, but otherwise only showed empty space. Not even a line indicating the driveway. He laid out the plan that wasn't really a plan at all. Not to Weller's mind.

In the detective's opinion, it was the same tactic hapless campers use when they find a bear lying in the woods. They poke it with a stick to see if it gets up and rips their faces off. If it doesn't, they get to live (at least until the next idiotic calamity) and claim that they poked a bear with a stick and walked away with their faces intact. If it does, then they die by bear face-ripping.

For all any of the vampires knew, their entire crew would be eaten by werewolves this night. Which would leave Isabelle, Fred, and the three human-hunting vampires to get eaten by werewolves at a time and date yet to be determined.

Diirek had already told Weller he was to stay with the train, but that was a joke. No way he was staying with the train. In fact, Weller had a feeling that the whole thing about asking Isabelle to stay with Fred was really a ploy to stick Weller with a babysitter. Fat freakin' chance. Unless, of course, she could tell him the name of the tune he had stuck in his head . . .

Essentially, Diirek and the other vampires would surround the compound at a safe distance and then work their way toward it cautiously to see what popped out at them. Brilliant. But, to be fair, Weller didn't have a better idea. He'd never seen the place except for the little flashes of it during Anders' episode of *Cribs: Sociopathic Mass-Murderer Edition*. Which was one of the main reasons he wouldn't be sticking around the train. He wanted to get eyes on the place. He also wanted to be the one to rip Anders to pieces. No, he didn't just want that. He *needed* it. He felt that new but somehow familiar dark impatience inside. And he wanted to let it loose again. But he needed to point it at Anders first, which meant getting through the compound's defenses.

As Diirek finished up, Weller slipped out of the seat and stretched like he'd been sitting for hours instead of thirty minutes. He wandered away from the group, trying to be nonchalant about it. No one said anything as he stepped out of the dining car and found an exit.

The night sky was clear, the stars brilliant and unfathomable. Fred had stopped the train in the middle of a gently rolling stretch of land. Weller looked around and then half jumped and half clambered onto the top of the train. It was graceless, but more than he could have done as a human. So there was that.

It was mostly wild grass in all directions but one, south. Perhaps a mile down the train tracks there were a few small buildings. Weller tried to focus his sight on them and succeeded for a few seconds before they blurred, and he had to shut his eyes. The buildings looked to have been abandoned long before the apocalypse. The train was in a wide, shallow valley out of which he could not see. It had been a long time since he'd been out of the city. It was a melancholy feeling, all that space and emptiness.

His mind drifted to JayLynn and Berena, and a chorus of pain accompanied the flash of memories in his mind's eye. That powerful . . . thing inside him twisted and rattled, seeming to say, '*I haven't gone anywhere. I still have work to do.*'

He heard footsteps and looked down at the ground. Binta was there, looking up at him with her bright and lively eyes. Without so much as a telltale twitch, Binta jumped onto the train, landing without a sound next to Weller, who pushed his pain back down, letting it and his darkness get to know each other a little better, to feed each other, for better or for worse.

"You need to stay here," she said.

"Bullshit. Why? Some nonsense about going over to the dark side?"

"It's not nonsense. I was trying to tell you that back in the city. Before you and Diirek had that conversation. It's easier than you think to give yourself over to it."

Weller said nothing. He thought about how it felt to get suspended, back before the end of the world. How he slid down the spiral so easily. The sex, the drugs, the feeling of hopelessness. The feeling he had now was similar. He knew it. Binta knew it. Diirek knew it. But Weller felt he was stronger now. Stronger than whatever darkness was threatening to overtake him.

"I'm stronger," he said, quietly.

"Famous last words. Like, 'I can quit whenever I want,' or 'this time will be different.' But you don't know that. You haven't had any time to figure out how you have or haven't changed. Don't mistake a power you've inherited for one you've earned."

Weller looked out at the deep wild grass. There was a rabbit out there, hopping along. He could hear it.

"Just stay here tonight. It's a recon mission anyway," Binta said. "Get to know the new you—"

"Ugh. What the fuck does that mean?"

"It means work on your hearing, your vision. See if you can get up on the train like I did, instead of like a dog in socks on a polished floor. Hell, see if you can jump over the train. Think of it as the academy. Vampire academy."

"Oh, boy. Can there be drama and gossip and more white people?"

"You know what I mean."

"Fine. I'll stay. On one condition,"

"What?" Binta asked. "That I stay with you?"

"Damn, you're good."

"You're too predictable, Kurt," she said, smiling.

For a second, Weller felt pretty good.

Below them, the train emptied. Diirek led that large group east and south while the human-hunters headed southwest. Isabelle and Fred stood outside the train, watching, much like Binta and Weller were doing on top of the train.

"You didn't tell him you weren't going," Weller said to the beautiful undead woman standing close to him.

She turned her head to look at him, smiling again. "You probably thought that Isabelle was supposed to babysit you, right?"

"It was going to be you all along," he said with a small shake of the head.

"You and the kid are similar in many ways. Very easy to see through. Perhaps because you're both men. Or, close to it, anyway."

Weller shrugged. "Give a man a gorgeous woman to talk to, he'll do just about anything."

"Less talking, more training," Binta said, backflipping off the train car and landing in the grass. On the other side of the train, Fred shot Weller an impetuous look before getting back on the train. Isabelle followed him.

Over the next four hours, Binta did her best to teach Weller the vampire basics. To his credit, he was a fast learner. He could do the binocular thing with his vision for about fifteen seconds by the time the large group returned. With a running start he could jump onto the top of the train somewhat gracefully, although Binta insisted that he didn't need a running start. He told her that old habits die hard. "I guess I'm still a slave to physics."

He hunted rabbits in the field, catching them and then letting them go, watching them hop in terror away from him. He practiced his hearing, which was how he located the rabbits in the first place. The furthest one he heard was about a hundred and fifty yards away.

But he didn't feel much different at the end of the session. Binta told him it would take time. And time he did not have.

Weller was telling Binta the story of how he and JayLynn met when Diirek's group came back. They were spaced out and none of them were talking. It was easy to tell by their body language that things didn't go well. Weller and Binta went out into the field to greet them.

"What happened?" Weller asked the first person he came to, which happened to be Jules.

"They have the place locked up tight. There must be twenty or more of those freaky fucking werewolves. They're each patrolling a small section, from what we could tell. It's going to be impossible to get in there. We'll have to bomb the place or something."

"There are a bunch of captives in there," Binta said as other vampires walked by, dejected.

"There were," Jules said. "We don't know if they're even still alive. They may all be vampires by now, for all we know."

"You didn't see any movement? Besides the werewolves?" Weller asked.

"I didn't. I haven't talked to everyone else, but the few people I did talk to said they didn't see anything of use."

"Shit. Where's Diirek?"

"Bringing up the rear. I'm starving. Did the others get back with any humans yet?"

"Not yet."

"Well, they better soon. Or those three humans on board are going to be sucked dry." Jules pushed past them, headed for the train.

"Any ideas?" Binta asked.

"We need another meeting. We'll figure something out. I just need all the information I can get." Weller paused. "Goddammit this is why I should have gone. We're losing time." Weller stalked back to the train, fists balled and shoulders bunched.

"So much for progress," Binta said to herself before starting after him.

Twenty minutes later they were all in the dining car again. There were numerous conversations happening. Weller heard two vampires talking themselves into heading back to the city. They were questioning Diirek's leadership and the need for intervention at all. The other vampires were talking about how to get in and stop Anders and his evil plan for world domination.

The detective was trying to listen to Diirek give the lay of the land, but all the other conversations started getting into his head.

"Fuck!" Weller screamed and slammed his hand down into the table at which he sat. A third of the table snapped off, sending little pieces of particleboard in the air. Everyone went silent.

"What do you think is going to happen if we don't stop this guy?" Weller asked the two vamps who had been talking about leaving. They said nothing.

"Seriously, it's not a rhetorical question. What do you think would happen? Huh?"

One of the two men, a blond man who looked Swiss or Swedish, looked down at his feet. The other, a guy with short black hair, cargo shorts, and a Phish T-shirt, spoke.

"What's the big deal, man? The world is fucked anyway. Is this guy really going to make it any worse? I mean, so what if he takes over the world? If he's a vampire, he'll have to keep some humans around to feed off, right? I'm sure we could work out some kind of barter system or something. Things will change, sure, but we'll survive. We always have."

"That's a very good point—what's your name?" Weller asked.

"Johannes," the guy said.

"That's a very good point, Johannes. Except for the fact that everything you just said, and your whole way of looking at the world, is dog shit."

"Hey, man—"

"What fucking idiot made you a vampire? I thought there was some sort of I.Q. requirement to get into this undead club of yours. Seriously, who turned this idiot?"

The other vampires looked at each other guiltily. Johannes was clearly getting pissed. Fred was in the corner near Isabelle, shaking his head as if to allay any blame that might splash on him from this shitshow.

"It was Elena," Bram said finally. "Johannes is her brother."

Johannes shot him a hurt look.

"You mean, the little brat that I shot in the face?" Weller asked. "She was your *sister*? And you didn't do anything when we killed her?"

"Yeah—No—I mean yeah, she was my sister, but she was a bad leader. She deserved what she got. Besides, she turned Bruno, too. He was one of her servants," Johannes said, pointing to the blond man across from him.

"Woah, hey, I—" Bruno began in a thick German accent, but Weller cut him off.

"Wow. If you two want to go back to the city, get the fuck out and go now."

"No way," Johannes said, his voice changing in anger. "The sun will be up before we can get there."

"You'll just have to get creative. Because I will not have two inept douchebags getting in the way of what needs to be done here. It's bad enough that the guy has killed hundreds of millions of people, but you just want to let him finish the fucking job. Does anyone else agree with these two shitbirds?"

Before anyone could answer, Johannes was out of his seat, pointing his finger at Weller, stepping closer with each sentence. "*You* will not have!? *You* have no say in what the fuck we do. *You* are not the leader of this group. In fact, since you killed my sister, we haven't *had* a leader. I went along with your shit because everyone else seemed willing, but *you* don't get to tell *us* what to do."

Weller waited until Johannes was right in front of him. In a blur of motion, he brought his leg up and kicked the vampire in the chest from his sideways position in the booth. Johannes smashed through the window behind him and landed outside the train with a thud. Weller rocketed out of his seat and went head-first out the window, slamming into Johannes just as he was getting up off the ground.

"Shit," Diirek said before getting up and diving through the window.

By the time Diirek reached them, Weller had broken nearly every bone in Johannes' face. Weller showed no signs of stopping. His fists pistoned repeatedly, smashing into face and body with dull crunching sounds. Diirek slammed into Weller and the two went tumbling off into the grass. Weller threw Diirek off and started back for Johannes, who was lying there, pulverized. Diirek tackled the detective again, and this time Weller swung at him, punching him in the ear. Once again, Weller got free and ran back to Johannes. Weller got one punch in before a strange, incredibly loud noise caused him to look up.

Diirek was rushing at him, eyes fiery and fangs out. The pale vampire slammed into Weller and carried him backward to the train. Weller's back struck the side of the metal car enough to dent it and rock it on the tracks.

"You're going to kill him," Diirek hissed.

"Fuck him," Weller said, although his heart wasn't in it. He hadn't meant to let it go so far.

"Listen, goddammit. This is not helping. I have a plan, but it is a long shot. I need your advice. Are you done?"

Weller nodded, pressing his anger down. "What about him?" he asked, gesturing over Diirek's shoulder.

"Fuck him," the vampire said, letting go of Weller.

Johannes groaned and exhaled blood and broken teeth from his spot in the grass.

On their way back into the train—through the door instead of the window—Weller and Diirek passed Bruno on the way out to collect his friend. Weller stared him down.

"Can I at least get him healed?" Bruno asked Diirek.

"He has made his decision," Diirek said. "If he refuses to contribute, he's on his own. Both of you are. You can ask the others when they return if they are willing to share their humans to heal him."

Bruno, who had avoided eye contact with Weller, turned from them in a huff and started toward his buddy.

"So what's this plan of yours?" Weller asked as they rejoined the others in the dining car. The detective ignored the accusatory stares many of the vampires levied at him. If the tension in the room had been able to hold moisture, no one could have seen their own hand in front of their face.

"I approached from the back of the property," Diirek explained, sitting down. "And I saw a large empty cage under the gathering of trees back there. The kind of cage that could hold a large group of werewolves . . . or chimpanzees."

"So?" Weller asked. "If they're not in the cage, how does that help us?"

"Because," Fred said, stepping forward with his hands deep in his pockets. "I went there during the daytime and saw a monkey—or chimp, I guess—out next to the stream. It attacked me and I shot it."

"So, what? They're chimps during the day and werewolves at night?"

"That is the theory," Diirek said.

"So," Weller began, "your assumption is that they'll be in chimp form during the day. Then we can sneak onto the property and do . . . something before they turn to werewolves?"

"We can drug them, kill them, or just sabotage the cage so they can't get out to buy us some time," Diirek said.

"But none of us can go out there during the day. Except for Fred. Or the three psychos you have locked up."

"Letting one of them go is out of the question," Diirek said, shaking his head. "It has to be Fred."

Weller looked over at the boy, who gulped audibly and tried to shove his hands even deeper into his pockets. "Okay . . ." the detective said. "You sure about that, Diirek?"

"I can do it," Fred said in a wavering voice.

"How long did it take you to come up with this plan?" Weller asked. "All of two minutes?"

"I talked it through with some of the others on the way back. It is the only way."

"What do you think, Fred?" Weller asked. "Last time, one of the chimps attacked you. How are you going to deal with a whole group of them without getting killed? And how do you know they don't have the cage under surveillance? If they see you, the whole thing is over."

"I have a plan for that, too," Diirek said, glancing at his watch. "Which is why Fred and I need to get going. Where is that tablet? The one Revak gave us?"

"Get going? Where?" Weller asked.

"To get help."

CHAPTER THIRTY-FIVE

HELP

F red did as he was told, waiting about two hundred yards from the farmhouse on the dirt driveway. As he stood there, waiting, he relived the whole ordeal with the two tweakers that had kidnapped him. He started to feel nauseous as he recalled the car accident, interspersed with hazy flashes of his mother getting killed. *My fault*, he thought. *But the enslavement of humanity will not be my fault. No freaking way.* His determination did nothing to not make him shit scared. So scared that he nearly messed his trousers when a gunshot rang out from the dark shape of the farmhouse. He jumped onto his belly in the grass next to the driveway.

A woman yelled something incoherent. A gunshot followed shortly after. Then there was the unmistakable sound of polite knocking and Diirek saying, "It is me, Diirek. Please do not try to shoot me again."

Silence. The squeaking of a door opening.

"Okay, Fred. Come forward."

Fred stood up and brushed his jeans and T-shirt off, checked to make sure that he didn't literally mess his trousers. He made his way through the gate and saw the four women that had been held captive and abused right under his nose for nearly two weeks. Of course, it hadn't even been that long since he'd left the place, but it seemed like a lifetime. Time moved differently in the apocalypse.

"Hey, Fred," Dena said. She was holding a candle and standing next to the other three on the porch. Diirek stood slightly apart from them.

"Hi," Fred said to all four of them. Rachel stood next to Dena with an automatic rifle in her hand. Sharon and Shirley stood to the right, each holding a weapon. They looked much better than when he'd last seen them. He was glad for that.

"So, Diirek says it's time we return a favor," Rachel said. "Why don't y'all come in and tell us about it."

Just under an hour later, Diirek left the house by the front door. Fred watched him go and hoped that they would see each other again. He would sleep on the couch again. The next day they would head off to help save the world.

***

The plan was simple. At least that's what Fred kept telling himself as he, Rachel, and Dena warily approached the property. It was a brilliant early-summer afternoon. The air smelled like clean dirt and foliage. On a day just like it, Fred and his only real friend from childhood, Zach, had experienced true fear and pain for the first time in their lives.

Fred had been seven years old and Zach eight. They had been wandering the woods, swinging sticks that were imaginary swords, throwing rocks that were hand grenades, and climbing trees that were mountains higher than Everest. They soon came upon a hornet's nest and, as is the habit of young boys everywhere, they decided to see what happened when they hit it with a hand grenade. They returned home defeated, out of breath, and in great pain—but alive, nonetheless.

Now Fred was no longer seven, he was seventeen. Those ten years and the events contained therein had changed his life. He was basically a man now, and men could die. As a kid, he had been somehow invincible, as evidenced by his feet on the ground, the air in his lungs, and the incessant and disruptive banging of his heart.

He wasn't going to harass a hornet's nest—no, nothing so juvenile. He was going to sabotage a nest of werewolves and God-knows-what-else. If he returned home covered in stings and in immense pain, he would be lucky.

He thought that the women were crazy for joining him. It was something he *had* to do because he wouldn't—couldn't—let Diirek down. But the women, they didn't have to do it. Sure, they had Diirek to thank for saving them, but anyone would have done that, right? And the favor the vampire was asking seemed over and above the saving.

And, although Diirek and Fred had been entirely truthful with the women, the boy didn't think that they fully grasped the situation. How could they? They hadn't seen the werewolves up close. They hadn't seen Diirek snap his own arm while trying to free himself from those vise-like jaws. Hadn't seen how utterly ripped-to-shreds Diirek had been after that encounter. No, they hadn't seen anything.

But maybe, just maybe, they wouldn't be in werewolf form. Maybe they would be in monkey form, lazing around in a big cage among the trees and away from the house.

Maybe.

They had no real evidence that this would be the case, aside from Fred's encounter with one. And that may have been a fluke. Rachel and Dena knew as much. They had been told the night before. Fred had expected them to respond with disbelief and hostility to such a claim as werewolves, but they didn't. They didn't so much as blink an eye when Diirek had explained his supernatural existence. In fact, Dena had nodded like she had suspected as much. Then, when they all watched the video on Anders' tablet, everything hit home for them. They realized what was at stake.

These were not the same women Fred had seen just after their release from bondage. And, he realized after their intense conversation, they had sent him away because they needed time to adjust. To transform into the people they were now. It was a change that shouldn't have happened, but also one that *needed* to happen, in a sad and disturbing kind of way. They were citizens of this new, changed world. They knew the rules had been changed, the rug yanked out from under their feet. And, Fred supposed, it had been a painful and traumatizing realization. Much more so than his own experiences during the apocalypse.

So while the boy was scared shitless, he was also very happy to have company. Looking into their somehow dull and bright eyes gave him a modicum of comfort. It was much better than attempting it alone. Of that he was sure.

They slowed down as they came to the edge of the field. They stayed in the shadows provided by the trees and looked out over the flat land toward the copse of trees at the rear of the property. They were directly behind it so that it was blocking the entirety of the main house. They could see about half of each of the buildings flanking the house, but none of the house itself. Between them and the trees there stood neat rows of various vegetables. But none of them as tall as the corn that grew on the other side of the property, in front of the house. At their current position, it was three hundred yards from tree line to tree line. Too far to run without being spotted, if they had sentries or cameras out.

Down to their left, the stream and its line of trees merged with the woods. It looked to be the best bet. They could stay in those trees and work their way up close to the house, then break away to the objective. Minimize their exposure. Provided there were no werewolves or killer chimps in the trees. The three of them conferred quietly and agreed that it was the best way, as Diirek had suggested the night before. They stayed in the trees and worked their way down toward the stream, keeping their eyes peeled.

They made their way upstream slowly. The plant life was thick enough to provide adequate cover but too thick in some spots to get by. As a result, they had to wade in the small stream several times. By the time they reached an ideal spot, their shoes and pant legs were soaked. They communicated wordlessly when they reached a good spot closer to their target, swinging off their backpacks and hunkering down to check that their contents hadn't shifted too much.

Fred swung his backpack back on and looked over his shoulder, back toward the field in which he and Diirek had first encountered a werewolf. Sharon and Shirley were supposed to be there somewhere, watching. They each had hunting rifles with scopes adequate to watch the progress. But neither of them were good enough shots to intervene should something happen. None of them were. Sharon and Shirley were there to watch and alert the vampires come sundown—a couple of hours away yet—if things didn't go according to plan.

"Do you see them?" Rachel asked in a whisper.

"No," Fred replied, facing the compound.

"Good," Rachel said. "That means *they* can't see them, either."

Fred and Dena nodded. They all looked up the shallow but steady incline between them and the trees at the back of the compound. Less than seventy-five yards. Better than three hundred, but still. Wide open space. A lot could happen in seventy-five yards.

Time to sack up and go, Fred thought, using a term he'd heard Weller say the previous night. The women looked at him as if he'd said it out loud. They each nodded once, then turned and bolted away from the stream, running as fast as they could. Fred followed.

He kept expecting a gunshot to echo in his ears. To feel the punch of metal through his skin. It would feel worse than the bit of rock he caught two nights previous, an injury that wasn't bothering him much at the moment. Perhaps because of the adrenaline in his veins. Or maybe because he was tougher than he thought.

Dena made it to the trees first, followed closely by Rachel and then Fred a half-second later. They sat in the shade, sweat rolling slowly down their faces, breath rasping in and out of unaccustomed lungs. They listened. For what, none of them knew. For anything, really. Anything but what they heard, which was the enduring sound of soft wind through tree branches and the consequent movement of leaves. Birds chirped nearby. Something small rustled under decaying organic matter.

After a long minute, Fred stood up and began maneuvering through the trees.

"I think I see it. A cage. But I don't see any monkeys." He spoke in a whisper.

The women joined him. He pointed through the random and haphazard placement of tree branches and trunks at the small section of dull silver cage.

"I see it, too," Dena whispered, her compact face glowing with sweat and determination. "But I don't hear them. Shouldn't we hear something? Aren't chimps loud?"

"Let's work our way toward it. Now or never," Rachel said, starting forward.

The three of them worked their way slowly through the trees, each new step bringing more of the metal structure into view. It was a large rectangle, covered in chain-link metal fencing, about twenty feet tall and sixty feet long. It was hard to tell how deep it was from their vantage point, but it looked to be no more than twenty feet wide. Twenty-five at maximum. And there did look to be brown shapes in there, amongst the trees and netting and wooden structures like treehouses. But none of them moved. They were either dead or asleep, Fred decided as he got closer.

They looked for cameras in the trees, attached to the cage, inside the cage, and every other conceivable place. They found none, but any halfway decent hiding place would be nearly impossible for them to see.

They moved closer. It was a risk. The whole thing was a risk. And the closer they got to the cage, the worse their plan seemed to Fred.

Not a creature stirred within the cage as the trio arrived just outside the metal diamond fencing. They were all asleep. Had to be twenty-five or thirty of the primates. Their bodies moved with their breathing, which was the only way to tell that they were alive. The three humans were along the back side of the cage. They began to work their way around to the front of the cage, where there was a gate. The trees thinned out toward the front, and they could see the back of the large house, about two hundred feet away. A dozen windows stared down at them, the sun reflecting off the glass, making it impossible to see inside.

Fred's skin began to crawl. He hated being this close to the house. At least the chimps were asleep. That was something. Maybe this would be easy after all. Maybe they could just place the drugged food inside the cage and be on their way, hoping the chimps would eat the cookies, fruit, and other assorted snacks into which sleeping pills and opiates had been inserted. The pills came thanks to the vampires who had gone human hunting the night before. They'd returned a few hours before sunrise with all kinds of goodies, including four humans.

The original plan had been to drug the chimps first, then sneak into the cage and remove their collars. They had discussed killing them outright, but there was some consternation about that among the women. Personally, Fred had been all for it, although now that he was looking at the peacefully sleeping primates, cold-blooded murder didn't seem like such a good idea.

There was a keypad lock on the gate. The kind that apartments have on gates to swimming pools or common areas, requiring a four-digit code for entry.

"Shit," Dena said. "We should use the bolt cutters. We'll never guess the code."

Fred had his back turned to them, watching the house.

"We don't know if the fence is electrified. It could kill us," Rachel said.

"It's not," Dena said, after a moment.

Fred thought he saw some movement in the house, at one of the windows. He stared.

Nothing.

"How do you know it's not?"

"See how all the metal is connected here? There's no way to keep electricity from going to the gate. Anyone who touched the keypad would be shocked. There's no barrier. Plus, there's no wires or electrical boxes around."

"Okay," Rachel said. Fred heard her swing her bag down and unzip it. He still hadn't looked back at them. Something was wrong. He could feel it. *We need to get out of here.*

The first loud snapping of thick chain-link made Fred flinch. He turned around and saw that Rachel and Dena were both frozen. Rachel with the bolt cutters in her hands, Dena crouching next to her. All three of them stared into the cage at the sleeping chimps. One chimp stirred, flipping over in its nest in a tree branch. The chimp settled back down, apparently still asleep.

"Do chimps sleep during the day?" Dena asked.

"These ones do. They're up all night being werewolves. Gotta sleep sometime," Rachel said.

"Remember," Fred said, his eyes darting around, "we don't need to take all their collars off. Just as many as we can safely. Then we can rig the fence back and get the hell out of here. Even five of them should be enough for a distraction tonight." He spun back around to face the giant house, his uneasy feeling intensifying with every passing moment.

"I still don't think removing the collars is the best way to go," Rachel said. "Who says that will create enough of a distraction? We don't even know what the collars are for. They could just be for tracking. We only have anecdotal evidence that they keep each other from . . . humping."

Rachel pulled a handgun with an attached silencer out of her bag. "We should take as many of them out as we can."

"We do that," Dena said, "we will definitely be caught. Even with a silencer, they'll hear that gun. Plus, that takes away the element of surprise Diirek was hoping to use tonight."

"For all we know, Anders already knows they're here. We need to be aggressive, and you—"

"Shhh!" Fred said, still staring toward the house. He'd heard something.

Something moved—something big. Fred whipped his head left, looking in the trees where he'd seen the movement out of the corner of his eye. Nothing.

A branch cracked to his right. Fred crouched, looking in that direction.

"What was that?" Dena asked.

Fred opened his mouth to shush her when he felt something puncture his chest. In the same instant, he heard the dull thunk of a silenced weapon. He stumbled back, trying to stand up straight, to turn around and run. He felt sick. Something hard hit him in the face. He felt the ground come up to meet his back, forcing the air out of his lungs with savage violence.

Before he lost consciousness, Fred heard Dena and Rachel scrambling around, yelling.

Then he heard what could only be chimps screaming in excitement.

CHAPTER THIRTY-SIX

THE SCREW-DRAGGER

Some great fucking plan, Weller thought. He was having a hard time keeping his thoughts in order as his mind drifted to the smell of blood wafting from the two women. Sarah and Shelly, or something like that. Diirek had introduced them to the group of vampires that had been awake for all of two minutes.

The women clearly didn't care about meeting all the bloodsuckers. They were freaking out. They had watched the kid and their two friends get captured or killed—they weren't sure which. All they knew was that some people outside of the massive house had dragged the trio's limp bodies through a back door. If they were alive, the two women said, they must be rescued.

Everyone was outside the train, standing in the dirt and the grass because the two women, Susan and Serena (or something), refused to come into the dining car. They had apparently arrived about half an hour before sunset and had been running around the train banging on windows, trying to wake the sleeping dead. Not the brightest candles in the candelabra. But, then again, the whole undead thing was hard to get your head around, so Weller cut them a little slack.

Still, it didn't stop him from wanting to drink their blood.

"This was your shitty plan," one of the women said in a Southern drawl, leveling a finger at Diirek. "And, Lord help us, we went along with it. So what are you going to do to get our friends back?"

"I suppose we will have to . . . try the direct approach, Sharon," Diirek said, thoughtful.

"We don't have much of a choice, now," Binta said. The other vampires nodded and voiced their half-assed assent. Weller realized their numbers were down a bit.

"Hey," he said. "Where did fuckhead and dipshit go?"

"You mean Bruno and Johannes?" Diirek said, looking around. "I saw them when we woke up. Isabelle, could you please go check on our captives?"

Isabelle nodded and climbed into the train.

"I'll go with," Weller said, tonguing his extended fangs.

They now had seven captives. Bram, Silvan, and Luana had returned just before sunrise with all kinds of goodies. They had managed to capture two men and two women who had all been working together to run the vampires' car off the road and steal any supplies aboard. Of course, it was a rude awakening for the four when they realized they weren't dealing with some hapless travelers. And, turned out, their nearby camp had been full of all kinds of awesome stuff.

Among other things, the vampires had returned with a serious collection of guns and ammo, a couple of hand grenades, bulletproof vests, an M60 machine gun, flashbangs, and pretty much any prescription drug you could think of. They had been ambushing people on the road for a while, it seemed. And they had been good at it, until they came across the vampires.

Isabelle and Weller checked on the newcomers first. They were hog-tied and each put into a separate room since there had been no time the previous night to create proper accommodations. All four of them were still there, and all of them were awake and angry, if their muffled curses were any indication.

Weller managed to follow Isabelle down to check on Diirek's three captives, who were all present and accounted for. Then, unable to help himself, he latched onto Buffalo Bob and drank deeply. Isabelle had to slap him to get him off, but at least this time he didn't take a chunk out of the guy's neck. Progress.

"My turn," Isabelle said and went to work on Fuller's neck. She didn't need any help to stop. "Self-control," she said, licking blood off her lips as they left the room. "Work on it."

"Yes, master," Weller said with as much sarcasm as he could muster with a belly full of blood. He felt his mind calming down again, his thoughts falling in line like a troop of drunken boy scouts. "So, what do you think our chances are?" he asked the old-young vampire walking in front of him as they went up the stairs to the top level of the car.

"I guess it depends on how many vampires he has already. If he has a small army, we're probably screwed."

"What about the werewolves? It sounds like we'll have a hard time even getting to the compound. We'll wind up ripped to shreds by genetically mutated chimp-wolves. Maybe we can use some of those goodies Bram and the others brought back."

Isabelle said nothing as they moved into the next car in line, and then down the stairs and into the newly formed night, joining the others. Something occurred to Weller, then.

"Can any of you guys shoot?" he asked the group.

"We have not had a need for firearms," Diirek said. "We were, until recently, the baddest beings on the block. Would that we had known about the apocalypse, we could have practiced our shooting."

"None of you?" Weller asked. "No one was a sniper before they became a vampire? Or a soldier?"

"I was a soldier," Silvan said. "In the Revolutionary War."

"Oh, Jesus. Don't tell me what side you fought for. I can already guess," Weller replied. "So, when was the last time you shot a rifle?"

Silvan thought for a moment, his hand to his chin. "Almost two hundred years ago," he said, finally.

"Well shit. So what the hell are we going to do?"

"You can shoot, right?" Diirek asked.

"I'm better with a handgun, but yeah, I'm a decent shot with a rifle," Weller said. "And for our purposes, I think we can do some damage with that M60. Unless anyone has a better idea than an all-out assault?"

"Whatever we do, we need to do it soon," Sharon said. "Before our friends get killed."

The vampires agreed with that notion. They gathered supplies and crowded around the map while Diirek and Weller spelled out a plan.

Some great fucking plan, Weller thought. *But it's all we've got.*

***

Fred woke in a sweaty delirium, thinking he was dead. His surroundings gave credence to the idea, but the pain in his head and chest told him otherwise. He sat up from the stone on which he had been laying. He was in an honest-to-goodness dungeon. There were flickering torches on stone walls that seemed to leak water at a slow trickle. There were shackles attached to chains attached to the walls. There were authentic torture devices placed around the dank and moist space, some of them with old, dried blood hardened to a gory sheen.

His right ankle was shackled to the wall, giving him about two feet of give. He tested the chain. It was fastened tight. His backpack was gone, but at least he still had his own shoes and clothes.

Fred looked around for Rachel and Dena, but to no avail. It seemed there was only one other occupant of the cruel-and-unusual-punishment playground. An emaciated, bearded man was slumped against the wall on the other side of the dungeon, his shackled arms held up in a Y and his head lolling to the side. His feet were tucked under him, as it was clear he couldn't sit on the ground—the shackles didn't provide enough slack. His eyes were closed, and he seemed to be unconscious. Or dead.

"Psst. Hey, you alive?"

The bearded man stirred, his tattered gray clothing shifting slightly on his too-skinny frame. His eyes didn't open.

"Hey!" Fred said, louder. "Wake up. Where am I? Where the heck am I?" Fred felt a crushing anxiety press down on his shoulders and chest. He felt the hysterical bubbling of tears getting ready to flow, and he pushed them down. He refused to cry. Not now. Not ever again. His mother's worried face came into his mind, threatening his tenuous hold on his emotions. The scene began to play out again—her death—his fault. A small sound escaped his throat, the beginnings of a sob.

"Are you real?" the bearded man said.

Fred cut off the sob, looking across the room at the man, clearing his throat. "Yes. I'm real," he said. "What is this place?"

"What the heck does it look like, child? It's a damn torture chamber." The bearded man spoke with a slight southern twang. He seemed unable to keep his eyes from roving all over. They were dark eyes that made Fred uneasy whenever they landed on his face.

"Is this . . . Anders' place? Are we in his house? Or one of the other buildings."

"I don't have any idea what you're talking about, boy. All I know is that I've been down here for years. And she—"

The clanking of an old-fashioned lock reverberated through the dungeon, cutting off the bearded man. The loud squeak of a rusty hinge followed soon after. A bar of light spilled along the stone wall to Fred's left as a heavy old oak door swung open at the top of a flight of stone steps. Fred looked back at the old man, who had resumed the position he'd held moments before: eyes closed, head lolling.

A shadow moved along the bar of light. Someone was coming down the stairs. Fred watched the slow progress. It was a man dressed in some sort of uniform, yellow and black. His hair was cut short, and he held a blank stare on his plain features. He ignored the old man altogether and made his way to Fred.

"What's happening. What did you do to Rachel and Dena?" Fred asked.

"Come with me," the man said in a monotone voice, reaching down to unlock Fred's shackle. Once Fred's leg was freed, the man stood back and gestured toward the stairs. Fred started toward them, walking as casually as possible while getting his mind ready for a berserker attack. He sensed the guard close behind him, so when he reached the stairs he put one foot up on the stone step and used it to launch himself backward, twisting in midair and leading with his elbow. The guard turned and raised his shoulder, which took the brunt of the blow.

"Ouch! What the hell, man?" the guy asked, his voice barely a notch above monotone. Fred stood there with a throbbing elbow, staring at the guy, who outweighed him by a good seventy pounds, wondering why his berserker attack didn't work. "Just go up the stairs, you jerk," the guard said, rubbing his shoulder. Fred did as he was told. This time the guard stayed a few steps back.

"Just because it's the end of the world doesn't mean you have to get all nasty about everything. *You* were sneaking onto our property, after all. Trying to have sex with our chimps. Disgusting."

"What?!" Fred asked, incredulous. "That's not what we were doing."

"Oh, no. Don't tell me you're one of those bread groups that set animals free. Bagel or pita or ciabatta? That's even worse."

Fred stepped out of the dungeon and into a lavish, wood-paneled hallway. He had expected the inside of the house to resemble a medieval castle, but it was far from it. The carpet underfoot was lush, the recessed lighting and artwork gave the hallway a comforting museum feel.

"Left," the guard said, giving Fred a little shove that way. Fred walked down the hall, turned right at the end, and headed down another, more utilitarian hallway. He took a left into a room at the guard's direction after passing several closed doors on both sides of the hallway. Dena and Rachel sat, each bound to sturdy-looking wooden chairs with colorful climbing rope. They were in the middle of a large room, facing a wall of flatscreen monitors. Under the monitors sat three computers, with three keyboards in front of three chairs. One of the chairs was occupied with another normal-looking middle-aged white man, dressed in the same yellow and black uniform shirt. There was a colorful patch on the shirt above the left breast pocket, but Fred couldn't make out what it said.

On the other side of the room was a couch facing a TV, with every video game console known to man on the shelves of the large entertainment center. Beyond that, there was an old white fridge, a sink set in a long countertop, and cabinets. The room was one third break room, one-third lounge, and one-third security control center.

"Fred!" both women said at once. They looked a little haggard and dirty, but otherwise they seemed fine.

"What's going on? What have they done to you?" Fred asked.

"What's with the third degree?" the guard said wearily, grabbing a wooden chair from the wall next to the door and setting it between Rachel and Dina. "Sit down," he said, gesturing at the seat. Fred sat and had a whispered conversation with the bound women. They were okay, they said. They were in the main house, they thought. The others would save them, they said. Fred wanted to think so, but he couldn't imagine how.

The guard came back over with some more of the colorful climbing rope and started tying Fred's legs to the wooden chair. As the guy knelt in front of him, Fred glimpsed the patch on his uniform shirt. The patch was round and about the size of a badge. In fact, it was a badge, of sorts, Fred figured. The bottom half of the patch held a discolored earth as seen from space—the blue was too light and the green too dark. A name floated in the blackness of space above the planet. Monsteranto, it said in bright turquoise letters.

"Monsteranto?" Fred said to no one in particular. "Where have I heard that name before?"

"It's pronounced mon-strant-oh. Not monster-rant-oh," the guard said without looking up.

"Yeah," the other guard said from his seat at the large desk. "Get it right!"

"Then why is it spelled that way?" Rachel said. "And you guys do make monsters here, right? So the name fits."

"You don't know what you're talking about," Fred's guard said. "We help people. We help feed the world—or at least we did before the world ended. But without us there's no way civilization will ever form again. What we do is important."

"You're that chemical company," Dena said as if she was calling out a trivia answer in a bar. "You helped create herbicides and pesticides that cause birth defects and cancer. And now you're altering chimps? Turning them into monsters? Doesn't sound so great."

"Hey, we have nothing to do with that," Fred's guard said, now working on binding his hands. "That's all done off of company property with private money and scientists."

"Why are you arguing with them, Reggie?" the other guard asked. "They don't know shit about shit. They don't know that Monsteranto's crops allow people in desolate regions to grow food. They don't know that we bought a medical technology company. Ever heard of nanotechnology? It's designed to help people. Or we *were* into medical technology. Before someone had to go and blow up the world. We're here, making sure people will have food and advanced medical products whenever we get some kind of order back in the world. And you people are sneaking around trying to do God-knows-what. Why? What were you hoping to accomplish?"

"Your boss is going to rule the world," Fred yelled, losing his temper. "He's going to become a vampire and create an army to take over humanity. How do you not know that?"

The guy at the desk laughed. "You realize how crazy you sound right now, kid? Vampires? You were probably one of those people who believe Pizzagate was real or that QAnon was JFK or Elvis or whatever. You don't know what the fuck you're talking about. You don't know anything about us or our boss. Nothing."

"Hey, Pizzagate was real," Fred's guard—Reggie—said. "Not that it matters now. Democrats probably have their fill of children. Wouldn't be surprised if they started this zombie apocalypse."

"Oh, Jesus man, don't start."

"Then tell me," Fred said, "what do you have in the other buildings? You ever go inside them? Or are they off-limits?"

"Bob goes inside them," Reggie said, gesturing at the other guard. "The rest of us aren't allowed."

"Stop talking, Reggie," Bob said, a note of warning in his voice.

"What's in the buildings, Bob?" Fred asked as Reggie finished tying him to the chair.

"Yeah, what's in the buildings, Bob?" Rachel asked.

"Yeah, Bob. What?" Dena put in.

"See? Look what you did, Reggie. She'll be here any minute and you've gotten them all riled up. Now we'll have to beat them to calm them down."

"Sorry, Bob," Reggie said, walking around to the back of the chairs. Fred turned his head just in time to see Reggie punch Dena in the back of the head, snapping her skull forward as she cried out.

"Hey!" Fred yelled. "Don't—" Reggie punched Fred in the ear, hard. His right ear was ringing and burning but he still heard the thump of fist on skull as the guy punched Rachel next.

They each gritted their teeth and made little groans of pain, but otherwise were silent.

"That's better," Bob said. "She'll be here soon. Sit tight and behave yourselves."

Fred blinked tears out of his eyes. Reggie still stood behind the three of them, waiting. Bob hit keys on the keyboard in front of him, cycling the screens through images. Live CCTV footage from cameras all around the compound. Mostly they showed farmland, the stream, the fields of corn, the crops behind the copse of trees. And the chimp cage. Fred groaned inwardly. Of course they had the chimp cage under surveillance. *Of course.* Why hadn't Diirek and the others guessed that?

It was a wide view of the cage, with a couple of small branches blocking an entirely clear view, but it was good enough. Judging from the view, the camera was high up in one of the trees, pointed down at a steep angle. Nearly all of the images were different shades of white and black since it was now dark outside. In fact, some of the images were hard to make out. Fred guessed they were using some sort of night-vision technology like that used in many home security systems. He'd seen cell phone video with similar technology. But it required enough light to work, and the night was dark. Fred felt a bit of hope blossom in his chest.

Then things started going bad.

A woman walked through the doorway. She looked to be in her late forties or early fifties. Her dark hair was piled atop her head and held there with a shocking number of hairpins, chopsticks, and clips. Her face was angular and serious with a hint of mischief. She wore a brown pantsuit and held her hands down by her sides, her fingers bent as if ready to claw a face or two off. She glared at the three captives and then quickly moved her head to the monitors.

"What's happening? Have there been any more *tres*passers?" she asked in an anxious tone, spitting the first syllable of the last word.

"No, ma'am," Bob said, his back suddenly straight and his voice all-business.

"What have they said? Anything?" This question was directed at Reggie.

"Nothing of value, ma'am," the guard said.

"Well?" she said, looking at Fred expectantly. She was high-strung, that much was clear. It made Fred nervous. He stumbled over his words, not sure what he was even trying to say.

"We came to free your poor chimps," Dena said, suddenly and very loudly. The woman jumped.

"They're mine. You don't have any say in what I do with them. And besides, they're not chimps. Not really," the woman said. "Are they still in the cage, Robert?"

"Yes, ma'am."

"Show them."

Robert punched a few buttons and all the screens changed to the view of the cage. The chimps were writhing and squirming in the cage. Their jaws were elongating, their limbs bubbling with muscle, their fingers growing longer as claws sprouted from their digits, their hair changing from brown to black, and they seemed to be screaming at the sky. There was no audio, but if there had been Fred was sure it would have been ear-piercingly horrific. It looked painful, and Fred could barely watch.

The woman looked at her watch. "Right on time. The sun is now down." She smiled like an extinct reptile. "But you've seen our little group of wolves before, no? You didn't come to free them. You came to kill them. Or to try and use them as a distraction. Isn't that right?"

"No," Rachel said simply. Fred's eyes were still fixed on the screen. Bob hit another series of keys and the door to the cage popped open. The werewolves started pouring out, going their different directions.

The woman followed his eyes, still smiling her carnivorous smile. "They're learning by the day. It's a tough love. It has to be. There is no other way," she said. She let her gaze linger on Fred, Rachel, and Dina in turn before speaking again. "I'm afraid it's going to be tough love for you three, as well." She smiled sadly. "Bring me the screw-dragger."

Reggie left the room, presumably to get whatever the hell the screw-dragger was. Whatever it was, Fred doubted it would be pleasant.

"Maybe one of you wants to tell me what you were really doing here?" the woman asked. "Otherwise, it will be very unpleasant for all of you."

The trio exchanged looks, as if gauging each other's resolve, then set their jaws in a physical sign of silence.

"If he gets back with the device before you answer, you'll all get the special treatment. And make no mistake, one of you will tell me what you were hoping to accomplish by coming here. And what your little gang of miscreants is up to."

Fred's eyes went wide at that comment. Afraid he'd given her information just with that look, he blurted out the question at the front of his mind, "What's a screw-dragger?"

"Trying to change the subject?" she asked, amused. "Well, the screw-dragger is a device that . . . drags screws. It's a very succinct name. And here it is now."

Reggie walked through the doorway holding a small, spiky metal item attached to a wire or string. The spiky ball, Fred realized, was a collection of small silver screws, all pointing outward, creating a sphere shape. It was about as big as an oversized ball of bubblegum, like the kind often found in grocery store vending machines. A thick string about a foot and a half in length was attached to the device. At the end of the string was a plastic handle of sorts about the size and shape of a roll of quarters.

Reggie swung it like a pendulum as he entered. Rachel, Fred, and Dena all stared at it in shocked horror.

"Beautiful," the woman said. "Hand it over." Reggie did. Fred was sweating suddenly. He tested his bonds and found them to be holding tightly. His left hand had a little bit of give, but not much. Not enough. The rope itself was a little stretchy, but again, not enough.

"We have vampires outside," Dena shouted. "We were coming here to take the collars off your . . . chimps, or wherever they are. Your boss is planning to take over the world. If he's not a vampire already, he will be."

The woman, screw-dragger in hand, looked shocked. She glanced at Reggie, who had taken position behind the captives again. Then she turned and looked at Bob. She mumbled something that Fred couldn't quite make out. Something that sounded like, "The bastard was right." Then her eyes changed. The wonder went out of them and she walked up to stand in front of Fred, smiling her dead smile again.

"Well," she said, "even if you're being serious, which I doubt, it doesn't change anything. I told you the terms and you chose to ignore them. Everyone gets chatty when the screw-dragger comes out." She reached out and grabbed Fred under the jaw. "Open up, young man," she said, opening her mouth as if to show him how it was done.

Fred glared at the gleaming screws and kept his teeth firmly together.

"Oh, don't be like that," she said, pouting. "Reggie?"

Strong hands gripped Fred from behind. Rachel and Dena began yelling and screaming for them to stop. One of the hands clamped onto his cheekbones and the other on his jaw. Reggie pulled Fred's head back, so he was staring straight up at the man. Reggie's muscles bunched and flexed as he pried Fred's jaw open. Fred resisted, his jaw muscles beginning to burn. After several long seconds, Fred's mouth opened a half-inch.

The woman dropped the screw-dragger down.

Reggie's right hand slipped off, allowing Fred to snap his jaw shut—but not before a tip of one of the screws got between his teeth. Fred felt his tooth break. Pain shot up into his palate and he tried to force the screw tip out of his mouth. As he was doing so, Reggie took advantage, yanking his jaw wide open. Suddenly, the screw-dragger was in his mouth. The sharp tips and razorlike ridges prodded his tongue, cheeks, and the roof of his mouth. His eyes immediately began to water, and a trickle of blood and saliva traveled down his throat.

Fred held his mouth wide open, trying to not to move his tongue even as all he wanted to do was jerk his head forward and spit the thing out. But he couldn't. Although Reggie had let go of Fred's jaw, he still had his head jerked back with a handful of hair. Fred swallowed involuntarily, moving his tongue, shifting the sharp device around in his mouth.

"Shut your mouth, my dear," the woman said.

Fred refused. Tears were pouring down his temples, his head still looking at Reggie's too-normal face and the ceiling beyond.

"Fine," she said. Fred heard the click of a button and then the screw-dragger was vibrating in his mouth, jumping around, banging into his teeth, and piercing his soft flesh again and again. He clamped his mouth shut to stop the thing from moving. The sharp screws sunk deep into his tongue, the roof of his mouth, and his gums—but that didn't stop it from vibrating. The screws clashed against his teeth as the device shook. Blood filled his mouth. He coughed through his nose, spraying blood out of his nostrils. His stomach heaved, sending digestive fluids, blood, and half-digested fruit up his throat. He opened his mouth, the vomit spewing past the vibrating torture device.

"Nasty," Reggie cried, letting go and stepping back, his hands coated in blood and vomit. Fred snapped his head forward as his stomach convulsed again and he proceeded to vomit the screw-dragger and the contents of his stomach onto his lap and the woman's shoes. The woman stared down in anger and disbelief.

Rachel and Dena were screaming and whipping around in their chairs, trying to get free.

Fred screamed, too, as soon as he was done vomiting. It was a sharp, short, breathless scream. Then he saw something move on one of the security monitors—just a glance. The fact that he happened to be looking near that monitor at that moment seemed fortuitous. What he saw made him smile a knowing, bloody, cracked-tooth smile.

CHAPTER THIRTY-SEVEN

SIEGE

The loud *thunk-thunk-thunk-thunk* sound was like music to Fred's ears.

"What the hell is that?" the woman yelled, still holding her hand out away from her body because it was spotted with Fred's slowly drying blood. She had dropped the handle of the screw-dragger, presumably in response to Fred's first bout of regurgitation. So when he vomited it out, the whole thing had landed in his lap. Presently the device vibrated off Fred's lap and continued its schizophrenic dance on the floor.

"I believe that's gunshots, ma'am. Hitting the house. North side, it sounds like." Bob spoke while cycling through the different cameras, trying to get a read on the gun. His voice held an unmistakable note of fear.

"Well, where are the goddamn werewolves? Why aren't they taking care of it?" she asked, starting to lose her cool. Rachel, Dena, and Fred were all silent, looking at each other. The *thunk-thunk-thunk* of gunshots stopped then, and the room went quiet as six pairs of ears perked up.

On one of the screens Bob had an interactive GPS map pulled up. On the map were little red dots—the werewolves, presumably. "I think they're trying to take care of it, ma'am," Bob said, pointing at the screen. His finger indicated a small grouping of several dots, five or six. Everyone in the room leaned toward the screen. The screw-dragger bounced back and forth on the ground at Fred's feet, buzzing like a particularly loud phone on vibrate. Fred swallowed a mouthful of blood and noted with dismay that his mouth began to fill back up again with the copper-tasting liquid.

"What the fuck am I looking at, Robert?" the woman asked.

"Well, that's a grouping of werewolves. But they aren't moving."

"So? So what? Why aren't they moving?"

"Because . . . I think they're dead. Which means that the machine gun is—"

"Machine gun?!" the woman cried, sending spittle onto the computer screen and Bob's right cheek. "That's a machine gun?"

"Well, yes. That's what it sounds like to me. Just about all it could be, I think. Well, I suppose it could be more than one person firing semi-autos at us, but the spacing is a little too neat for that. What did you think it was?"

"I don't know. I don't hear gunfire often, like you apparently do."

"War movies," Bob said, as explanation.

Reggie snorted from behind the others. "Well, I served, and he's right ma'am. That's a machine—"

The gunfire started again, this time the sound of the bullets hitting the house was closer.

"Where are they? Can they get in?" the woman asked, a high, hitching tone to her voice. Movement on one of the monitors caught her attention and she looked up. Fred followed her gaze. Two figures had rolled into frame—a woman and a werewolf. They were caught in a struggle in which neither of them seemed to have the upper hand. Bob was busy doing something on one of the other screens—trying to figure out where the machine-gun fire was coming from.

"Orders, ma'am?" Reggie asked. The woman put out her hand without taking her eyes off the struggle on the screen. It was an absent "wait one" gesture. The sound of gunfire stopped again.

A third figure converged on the woman and the werewolf. It was hard to tell what it was at first, whether it was man or beast, since it was moving so fast. But it slowed as it approached the other two. It was a man. He came upon the werewolf from behind, holding something in his hand. The resolution of the image was too poor to see what the item was. But when he pulled the werewolf's head back and began the violent movement of his arm, it was clear enough what it was. The grainy man on the screen stabbed the werewolf in each eye, twice. The beast convulsed and swung a clawed hand, which missed the man but struck the woman across the chest, leaving visible gouges behind. He stabbed the blade into the beast's neck and began sawing back and forth across its throat, his hand disappearing in a torrent of blood that showed black on the screen. The beast went limp. The man threw it down and then helped the woman up. They both ran out of frame.

"What the fuck? How is that bitch still alive?" the woman, who Fred now thought of simply as Ma'am, said. No one answered her.

"Lock the place down," she said, turning to Reggie. "Get everyone in the building behind a gun and positioned for defense. Give everyone radios. Robert, I want updates as quickly as you can give them to me. I've got an idea." As Ma'am spoke, she opened a small metal cabinet set on the wall beside the security station. She took out a radio with a headset and began to put it on. "How many do we have left?" she asked Bob.

"There are . . . eighteen still moving . . . Look here," Bob said. He had switched to a shot of the wide area in front of the house where there was a circular driveway. A man with only one arm and one leg was dragging himself toward the corn, leaving a trail of blood and his severed limbs behind him. Nearby, there was a decapitated body—that of a woman—lying sprawled on the concrete. Fred thought he recognized both vampires, but the resolution was too poor to tell exactly who they were. Neither was Diirek, of that he was sure.

Shit. They're getting killed. For us, Fred thought, tears coming to his eyes. His mouth was full of blood again. He felt that swallowing it would make him sick, so he simply parted his lips and let the blood drain down his chin.

Ma'am smiled at the sight on the screen. "They're tough sons of whores," she said. She went quiet and turned to look at Fred, Dena, and Rachel as if something had occurred to her. The gunfire started again, the noise seeming to return her focus to the matter at hand.

"How long to sunrise?" she asked. Fred's eyes went wide.

"Ma'am?" Reggie said.

"How long to sunrise. It's not a hard question. What time does the sun come up?"

Reggie looked at his watch. "Um . . . about nine hours yet."

She nodded at this. "Reggie, remind me to kill Revak when this is over," she said. "That son of a bitch was right. And he doesn't want to share . . . I'll be damned."

"Uh, yes ma'am," Reggie said.

"Let's go. I've got a surprise for these fuckers. You get entrances covered and lock the place down."

"Yes, ma'am," Reggie said and walked out.

"Remember, Robert," Ma'am said, "I want updates as quickly as you can give them, got it?"

"Yes, ma'am," Bob said.

Ma'am looked over the captors one last time, smiled, and walked out of the room.

***

Weller picked up the M60, adjusted his backpack with the ammo inside, and proceeded to move through the corn. It hadn't taken long for everything to go to shit once the werewolves were let out. He had seen at least two vampires get ripped apart by those fuckers. He wanted to throw down the machine gun, leap through one of the hundred windows on the main house, and find him some assholes to kill, Diirek's orders be damned. That was the plan, after all—to get into the house. But it seemed as though the werewolves had a prime directive of protecting the house at all costs. Any time vamps got near the house, they were beset by multiple werewolves.

The first vamp he saw killed was Luana. She'd almost made it to the house—was in the driveway—when two wolves came down on her and ripped off her head like she was a stuffed doll. She didn't get so much as a love tap in. Weller himself had been moving positions at the time and had fired from the hip, but he didn't think he hit either of the beasts before they bounded off around the house.

The second vamp, a guy whose name he'd never learned, had been even closer than Luana when the werewolves came down on him. They tore off an arm and a leg before Weller heard the guy screaming and ran over to help. He held the machine gun in one hand and grabbed the guy's remaining hand and dragged him backward into the cornfield.

Snarling and the snapping of jaws seemed to fill the air. Screams and yells of anger, frustration, and hate birthed occasionally, only to die just as quickly, swallowed up by the night sky. Weller let go of the guy's hand and bent down to speak to him when a thrashing sound erupted behind him.

"Look out!" The deformed vampire yelled. Instinct took over. Instead of turning around, Weller jumped straight ahead—away from the sound bearing down on him. He landed outside the edge of the cornfield, about fifty yards from the house, and turned around. The werewolf bounded out of the corn a split second later. Weller backpedaled and got his finger inside the machine gun's trigger guard. He waited for the werewolf to land. Just as it touched the ground, about ten feet from him, he squeezed the trigger. Bullets punched into the hairy beast at a rate of over eight per second. The supersonic lead tore through the beast's chest, smashing major organs, bone, and viscera. A quick twitch of Weller's wrist sent the deadly spray upward, tearing the beast's head apart in a moment.

Weller realized that he was smiling as the gun went empty. Smiling as he killed something. No, not smiling, grinning. *What the fuck is happening to me?* He had time to think before two werewolves smashed into him from behind.

***

"Copy that," Bob said into his radio. "Opening doors R-1 through R-6 now. I can open the rest in sequence, to lead them out, ma'am."

Fred's eyes were fixed on the screen. He'd just seen the detective, Weller, attacked by two werewolves. They had gone off-screen shortly after he had been attacked, and Fred knew, he just knew, that Weller was dead. They were losing. And whatever Bob was releasing would seal the deal. The bad guys would win. It wasn't supposed to be like this. Not like this.

He wanted to cry. More than anything he wanted to cry. The pain in his mouth was horrendous and it kept filling with blood, which he let drain out, soaking his shirt and the lap of his pants. He felt sick to his stomach and was getting lightheaded. He felt the strength draining out of him. The rope holding him to the chair seemed to be getting tighter. He was useless. But he wouldn't cry. He would not let himself do that again.

He looked down at the screw-dragger, still buzzing around on the floor. It had moved to his left a bit and was now about halfway between his seat and Rachel's. Rachel looked down at it and then back up, into

Fred's eyes. He couldn't hold her gaze for long. There was something in her eyes. Something he couldn't place but assumed it was a different version of hopelessness.

Suddenly, Rachel started bawling. It was almost theatrical in that it seemed oversized compared to what little Fred knew of her personality. He looked over at her. So did Dena. Bob turned around to see what was going on.

"Oh, Christ in a game of spades," Bob said. "Shut the hell up." He turned back around and continued tapping keys on his keyboard. Rachel continued bawling, although not as loud.

"Rachel?" Dena asked, leaning forward and looking past Fred. Rachel looked over and did something with her eyes. She inclined her head as if to say, "go ahead."

Fred furrowed his brows and turned his head to look at Dena. He watched recognition come into her eyes. Then she, too, started crying noisily.

"Shut up. Don't make me get up and deal with you," Bob said, without turning around. Both Rachel and Dena lowered the volume a little bit, but they didn't stop. *This must be some sort of girl thing*, Fred thought, marveling.

"Now you," Rachel whispered between sobs.

"What? Me?" Fred asked.

"Just do it," she said, while Dena provided the white noise to conceal their whispers. "Be convincing," she said. Fred didn't think that would be a problem.

He hung his head and tried to cry. Nothing came. Only moments before he had been on the verge of a total breakdown but now, nothing. He scrunched up his eyes and twisted his mouth down and tried to forget about the promise he'd made to himself the day his mother died.

"Come on," Rachel whispered. "It's alright, Fred. Just, let it out."

"I—I can't."

"Yes, you can. Do it, *now*."

Fred looked away. His mother's face filled his mind. How worried she looked just before she went to step out of the car. Just before the vehicle sideswiped their truck and took his mom away forever. He remembered sitting in the road, looking at her mangled body until the sheriff showed up. And then something funny happened. He knew instinctively that it was a memory that floated up out of the haze and played in his mind like a too-real movie.

He remembered that his mom had still been alive when he got out of the truck and went over to her in the road. He remembered that she grabbed him with her good arm and smiled at him. She told him everything was going to be alright. And, as Fred sat bound to the chair, his mouth bleeding, he remembered the last words his mother ever said to him, and he began to cry in earnest.

"I love you, Freddie," she had said to him. "Now get out of the road. I don't want you getting hurt on account of me." It seemed to Fred that she had waited for him to get to the side of the road before she died. Maybe that was wishful thinking.

Fred cried hard at first. A whole childhood of tears held back and let out all in one brilliant moment. Bob only looked back in disgust.

"Scoot that way," Rachel said to Fred. Using his hips and his feet on the ground, Fred moved his chair toward Dena, who was also crying.

Rachel nodded, signaling Fred that he could stop moving. She looked down at the screw-dragger, vibrating on the floor next to her chair. Suddenly Fred realized what she was planning.

Rachel still made sobbing noises, but they were half-hearted. She was concentrating on positioning herself correctly, moving in little jumps and slides like Fred had done to vacate the area. When she was confident she was in position, she nodded to Fred and Dena, who nodded back.

Rachel rocked right in her chair as Fred and Dena raised the volume of their cries to cover the sound of her chair legs hitting the floor. She rocked left, gaining momentum, then went back right again. Her chair paused briefly at the tipping point, then smashed to the ground, her right arm—and the rope binding it to the chair—landed right on the screw-dragger. Fred and Dena both cried out as loud as they could to cover the noise.

"When I'm done, I'm going to kill one of you," Bob screamed without turning around. "Unless you shut the fuck up!"

Rachel was gritting her teeth on the floor, clearly in immense pain. A couple of the screws had pierced her arm as well as the rope, but otherwise, it looked promising. Blood spread out in a small pool as she moved her arm up and down, loosening the rope. Then she yanked her bloody arm out of the binds. But the screws were deeply embedded in the flesh of her forearm, so the screw-dragger stayed stuck in her bloody arm. She peered at the still-vibrating device for a long moment as if she couldn't believe it was there. Then her face changed, and she started to shake her arm, trying to get the screw-dragger out of it.

The look on her face, the sheer terror there, stopped Fred's sobbing. He stared at her, speechless and struck with empathy. He was willing the screws out of her arm. Willing the three of them out of this situation. Willing Bob's eyes to stay glued to the screens.

Dena seemed to be taken aback by the sight of her bleeding and panicking girlfriend, as well. She was still making crying noises, but they were fading fast.

Blood flew in little droplets as Rachel shook her arm, lying on her side on the floor, her other arm and both legs still bound. Finally, the screw-dragger came out and clattered to the floor near Fred's chair. It suddenly seemed incredibly quiet in the room and the clattering of the screws on the floor seemed to echo throughout the space.

Fred sensed movement from Bob, causing him to tear his eyes from Rachel and place them with dread and foreboding on Bob's back. Slowly, as if this were all a dream, the man at the computer turned in his chair to look at the captives. When his eyes finally took note of the partially-freed woman, they went wide. He jumped up from his chair and darted toward them, fear and anger in his too-wide eyes.

Fred flexed and rocked and twisted in his chair, a kind of growl erupting from his still-changing voice. It was no use. He couldn't break free. Bob was almost upon Rachel. Three steps away now. It was all over. They would die here, only after watching their friends die outside.

Fred looked down at Rachel as if to say he was sorry. Sorry he couldn't keep crying to cover up the sound. Sorry he even got them into this mess in the first place. Sorry for the end of the fucking world, while he was at it. But what he saw Rachel doing changed his attitude in an instant.

She reached out with her free hand and grabbed hold of the plastic handle to the screw-dragger. She snatched it up and swung it around awkwardly once as if it were a small mace, which it kind of was. Then, from her position on the floor, she threw it at Bob's face.

It seemed to cover the distance faster than Fred thought possible. As if Rachel had been a professional pitcher before the end of the world. As if something were guiding it along, sending it to hit Bob's unassuming face.

Which it did. Hard.

It struck him in the left eye, a couple of sharp screw-tips puncturing his eyelid and momentarily sinking through his cornea and into the iris underneath. Other tips pierced the skin around his eye before the thing bounced off and landed, once again, within grabbing distance of Rachel's free hand.

Bob screamed and clutched his damaged eye as much as one can clutch an eye. He fell to his knees, essentially holding his hands in a protective shield over the profusely bleeding eye. Too little, too late.

Rachel grabbed the screw-dragger again and yanked it across the ropes wrapped around her other arm even as she wiggled and loosened the ropes around her body. While she did this, Bob stood up, sobbing, and stumbled back to the computer, making small hurt noises. He kept one hand over his eye and used the other to punch several keys on the keyboard. One of the screens changed and Fred watched, trying to figure out what Bob was doing.

Then he saw them on the screen. More werewolves. Only these weren't the same ones he had seen before. They were bigger. They walked more upright than the other ones, and with less grace. It was almost as if they walked like . . . humans.

The image on the screen was of a hallway outside a door. Six of these new werewolves gathered outside the door and tried to open it, but there was no knob. It was a heavy metal door with a keypad next to it. One of them tried the keypad, but it did no good. Bob looked up at the monitor with his one good eye. Then he looked back down at the keyboard and hit a few more keys.

The door opened. The large werewolves ran out into the night.

Rachel stood up right as Bob was finished releasing the beasts. She walked over to the man and, without a word, elbowed him in the side of the head. Bob hadn't seen it coming. He'd been doing something else on the computer. He fell, hit his head on the desk, then collapsed to the ground, unconscious.

Rachel came over to free Dena and Fred. She was still bleeding, but she had a smile on her face. Fred smiled back, but he couldn't hold it for long. Those werewolves looked mean. They had to do something to help their friends outside. But what?

***

Weller felt his flesh separate as claws tore away his ammo-laden pack and sliced down his back. The pain was bright and real and sickening. And yet, even as he was feeling his skin torn like cheesecloth, something was happening to that feeling. It was a transmutation of some kind.

At first, it was bright and overwhelming but then something inside of him—something new—took hold of it and turned it into a dark pillar of power. A monolith that grew with the pain. And underneath that monolith was that coiled animal of revenge and hate and vengeance and rage. It sat, ready to add its energy to that pillar and turn it into . . . into what?

Was he evolving or devolving? He couldn't tell. And at the moment he didn't have the patience or the wherewithal or the inclination to philosophize about it.

A werewolf paw came around the front of him, sinking its claws into the flesh of his chest. *Bad idea.* Until that moment, the werewolves had been concentrating on his back. He was face down in the cornfield and their weight was pinning him to the ground. But it was clear they were getting greedy. They wanted to turn him over and tear his front apart, too.

Weller reached his right hand up, grabbed one of the werewolf's fingers, and snapped it. The werewolf howled and tried to pull its paw back, but Weller grabbed two more of its fingers and snapped those, too. The beast yanked its hand away, and Weller used the moment to turn around. He flipped his hips and sent the other beast sprawling on its back nearby while the injured one cradled its broken fingers for a moment.

Weller was up in an instant. The uninjured werewolf faced him in a low crouch, ready to spring. The other one was to his left, either genuinely scared of him or pretending to be. Weller jumped forward. A tenth of a second too late, the werewolf jumped. But by then it was a foregone conclusion. Weller had the upper hand. He met the beast in mid-air, leading with his right knee, smashing it up under the werewolf's slightly elongated jaw. Fangs shattered as its jaw snapped up and its head cracked backward. Weller came down on his feet in the corn while the werewolf came down in a heap.

The sound of bone and cartilage snapping caught Weller's attention and he turned to the injured werewolf. Diirek was there, leaning over the beast, pulling his bloody hand out of its collapsed rib cage. The two looked at each other and nodded.

"Get the gun. We will need it," Diirek said, picking up the backpack Weller had been wearing moments before.

Weller took a step toward where he'd dropped the gun—toward the mansion—and stopped. "What the fuck?"

Diirek followed his gaze. "Those are different," he said.

Standing in the clearing in front of the mansion were six huge werewolves. Double the size of the ones they had been fighting. Their fur was more of a mottled gray than the mixture of black and brown of the other ones. And they looked more cognizant of their surroundings. There was an animal gleam in their eyes as they walked around, slightly stooped, but there was also some form of self-awareness there, too.

They stood in a semicircle, facing out toward the corn and the surrounding emptiness, sniffing the air and noting their surroundings. It seemed that their presence had some effect on the other werewolves because the sounds of fighting died away. Rustling sounds erupted and then faded as the other beasts ran away.

Something in the air, Weller thought. He could smell them, too. They smelled like a dead fish stuffed with a gangrenous skunk.

Diirek crouched and whispered for Weller to do the same—they hadn't been spotted yet. The detective looked down at his companion, shook his head, then returned his eyes to the six werewolves. He felt that now familiar swelling inside and, without any cognition that he recognized, he walked out of the corn to face the beasts.

All six of them heard him coming. They turned their heads to face him but made no movement otherwise. Weller stepped into the clearing and stopped, his eyes never leaving these new werewolves. They each stood a foot taller than him, and probably fifty pounds heavier. Bulging, oversized muscles sat like armor on each beast, clearly visible under their fur. Their yellow eyes shone in the half-dark. They were like the super zombies back in the city, only, it seemed on inspection, more dangerous. Their lips seemed in a perpetual growl—pulled up and back over sharp teeth.

Weller had a moment to think about how dumb Little Red Riding Hood must have been to mistake a wolf for her dear grandmother. There was no mistaking these beasts for anything but semi-intelligent killing machines.

Weller heard the crunching of foliage behind him and a moment later saw Diirek join him in the clearing. Other battered, bleeding, and bruised vampires emerged from the darkness, stepping up to form a wide half-circle around the werewolves. Binta was there, and Isabelle. Silvan stumbled up to join them, gravely injured and barely able to walk. Bram emerged to stand a dozen yards to Weller's right. Jules and Jamie came from either side of the mansion and stood at the edge of the half-circle.

The werewolves showed no fear. Their faces didn't change at all, not even when it was clear that they were outnumbered.

Weller felt his body thrumming, his mind going a bright blank yellow, like staring at a nuclear explosion. Whatever unconscious part of himself that had taken over at the museum crawled its way into his mind, treading on images of JayLynn as a zombie. The pain from his gashes faded to background noise.

The two groups stared at each other. No one moved for a minute. Then one of the werewolves twitched. And the fight began.

CHAPTER THIRTY-EIGHT

BOOM

"I don't know how this stuff works," Fred said, sitting in Bob's chair at the computer. Bob was still unconscious, on the floor. "Just because I'm younger than you two doesn't mean I'm a computer whiz." He punched a couple of keys, trying to get the screens to cycle, but nothing happened. The monitors showed no movement, but the front of the mansion was no longer on any of the screens. In its place was a shot of the hallway through which the new breed of werewolves had gone. They hadn't seen them again since.

"Let me try," Dena said, gently pushing Fred out of the seat. Rachel had located a first aid kit in one of the cabinets on the other side of the room, and Dena had just finished bandaging her up. Fred got up and stood next to Rachel. They watched Dena and the screens intently. She used the mouse to click out of the current window and then opened another one.

Fred glanced at the closed and locked door to the hallway. It was the first thing he'd done after Rachel freed him. But it wouldn't do much good if someone really wanted to get in. Even if they didn't have a key, which they surely would, it wouldn't be hard to knock the door down. They didn't have long.

"We should just get out of here," he said, still looking at the door. The wounds in his mouth were still bleeding, although not as bad as before. Whenever he talked his mouth hurt even more, and he had to spit out blood and saliva every minute or so.

"We don't know what's happening out there," Rachel said. "Or where those other werewolves went. We could just step out the door and get ripped apart—" she stopped, a faraway look in her eyes. "Wow, those were two sentences I thought I would never utter."

Fred thought for a long moment. "That's true," he said. "But we're fish in a barrel in here. Sitting ducks. A deer in headlights."

"Yeah, we get it," Dena said. "We need weapons. That lady talked about arming everyone. There has to be some nearby."

"Let's go, then, Fred," Rachel said. "We'll search the surrounding rooms and see if we find anything. If not, we'll come back."

"What if Bob wakes up?" Fred asked, gesturing at the unconscious man sprawled on the floor to the left of Dena's chair.

"I'll kick his ass," Dena said.

Fred didn't think that she could kick the large man's ass. But, then again, he didn't think Rachel could've either, but she put him down. And the tone of Dena's voice reassured him. He was learning a lot about women with these two.

"Okay," he said after a moment of deliberation. "Let's do it. But first . . ." his voice trailed off as he walked to the other side of the room. He opened several drawers and found a couple of kitchen knives. Under the sink, he found a small fire extinguisher. Rachel took one of the knives in her right hand. In the other, she picked up the screw-dragger and clicked the button on the side of the handle, stopping it from vibrating. Fred kept the other knife in one hand and the fire extinguisher in the other.

"Baby," Rachel said to Dena, "I love you. I'll be back."

Dena turned around in the chair and looked at Rachel. "You better be, my love."

Fred blushed. Dirty images involving the two women and many, many more created a kaleidoscope of naughty in his head for one moment, before he shut it down. *I think something's wrong with me*, he thought, appalled at his imagination. It was only a half-serious thought. Currently, his teenage libido was the least of his worries.

He unlocked the door and opened it a crack to peer out with one eye. The hallway looked clear right . . . and clear left. He stepped out. Behind him, Rachel told Dena to lock the door.

"Which way?" Fred said as the soft click of the door locking sounded behind them. The hallway stretched for about eighty feet to the right, and fifty to the left. There were doors at regular intervals along it, some open and some closed.

"Right, first," Rachel said. "I think that's the way Reggie went when he left the room."

The first door to the right was locked. It had a keypad and a place for a swipe card. The door across from it was a large supply closet. Mops, brooms, vacuums, giant packages of toilet paper, and other necessities lined the shelves. It seemed they were in the part of the mansion that housed the help. Which was probably why the hallway wasn't as nice as the rest of the place.

"This must be it," Rachel said after glancing at the other nearby doors. "I mean, it makes sense, right? Right next door to the security room. Protected by a keypad. None of the other doors in the hallway have keypads. It must be the armory."

"Probably," Fred said. "But how do we get in? You think Bob has the code written down somewhere? Maybe in his wallet or something?"

"Doubtful. But maybe we can wake him up and ask."

***

One of the werewolves went straight for Silvan, who was the most vulnerable due to his injuries. Silvan put his good arm up in defense, but it only delayed the inevitable. The giant werewolf caught Silvan's arm in its maw, pinning it to the vampire's head as its jaws closed around his skull. The beast's jaws snapped shut, crushing Silvan's head in a rush of skull fragments, blood, and brain matter. In the same instance, it chomped through Silvan's arm like it was a piece of kindling. The vampire's body came to rest on the ground, his severed hand caught under his shoulder blade in a gruesome parody of a gesture of consolation.

Weller was aware of Silvan's death as it happened, in a target-tracking sort of way. He jammed his left foot into a werewolf's crotch and yanked on the beast's left leg by the ankle. He felt the knee joint separate just a second before the leg came apart and Weller flew backward, the werewolf's hairy lower leg and foot still held in his hands. He looked at the bleeding limb, then at the howling and scrambling werewolf from which he'd just taken it.

He was standing over the beast in an instant. Around him, the vampires were fighting the other werewolves but struggling. Weller upended the leg and jammed the shin bone into the beast's chest right above the heart.

He rushed over to the one that had killed Silvan, not a conscious or discernable thought in his head. The werewolf tried the same thing with Weller, opening its jaws wide as he approached. Weller caught the beast's upper and lower jaws, one in each hand. He yanked them apart, ripping the lower jaw from its head and then using the sharp teeth there to slit the beast's throat.

He turned around and saw Isabelle was having a hard time fending off one of the giant werewolves. She was coated in blood from a gash on her forehead, and her hand was being chewed up by the beast. Weller moved fast, causing the sound of rushing air as he moved. He spotted the empty machine gun in his path and picked it up.

When the beast spotted him, it dropped Isabelle and squared off, crouching on powerful haunches. Weller moved forward and jammed the barrel into the beast's right eye, reaching the gun up above his head to do it. Then he slapped the stock forward, feeling the barrel bounce off the inside of the beast's skull. He pulled the gun out as the large werewolf fell back into a heap of mottled fur. He turned around, the empty machine gun still in his hand, and looked for something else to kill.

Binta and Jules were working on one of the other werewolves about fifteen yards away. The beast had its back to him, its attention on the two vampires in front of it. Weller ran up behind the beast and swung the machine gun like a baseball bat, snapping the werewolf's neck as the stock connected. It fell to the ground, dead. There were only two werewolves left, and the others had them surrounded.

Weller turned and looked at the house. His jaw clamped and his muscles clenched as he thought about Revak. *I know you're in there somewhere. I can't wait to tear you apart*, he thought with an inner voice that was not quite his own. Without a backward glance, Weller ran to the front door of the mansion and smashed through it.

Behind him, Diirek yelled something about more people coming. About hearing engines in the distance. Weller ignored him.

***

Bob screamed. "Okay, okay," he said, sobbing, staring at the knife that had just been stabbed into his leg. "I'll tell you. The passkey is in my right hip pocket."

"You mean this one?" Rachel said, holding up the keycard.

"Yes, yes. That one."

"The code. What's the code?" Dena asked.

"One, three, five, eight, nine," Bob said, tears streaming down his face.

"Let's go," Fred said. He and Rachel headed toward the door once again. As Fred put his hand on the doorknob, someone banged on the other side of the door. Fred jumped back.

"Who's in there?" a male voice asked. "Bob, is that you screaming? What the hell is going on in there?"

Fred and Rachel's heads both snapped over to Bob. Dena was whispering in his ear, a knife to his throat. He made not a sound.

"Do you have a key?" the guy outside the door asked, obviously talking to someone else with him. Then, after a moment, "Well, find one, goddamnit."

Fred breathed a sigh of relief. He stepped over to the couch. Rachel followed his lead, and they began to drag the furniture against the door.

"You're going to tell me how to release the captives," Dena said to Bob. "Now."

Bob started punching keys on the keyboard while Dena held the knife against his neck. "Okay," he said. "It's done."

"Prove it," Dena said. Bob cycled through the cameras and found the one he wanted. It was a feed from inside one of the other buildings. People were stepping tentatively out of cells, looking around, doubting their luck.

"I want to see them get outside," Dena said. "What were all these people for, anyway?" she asked, her voice terse and heavy.

Bob sniffled, his voice barely above a sob. "For the experiments," he said.

"Who are they? Where did they come from?"

"I don't know . . . From all over. Most of them were wandering around after the bombs dropped. We gave them safety and food. We were helping them."

Dena pressed on the knife, drawing blood from Bob's neck. "Don't you even fucking pretend you were helping these people. You were the ones that caused the bombs to drop in the first place."

Bob started to shake his head but thought better of it. "No. No, we didn't do that. We wouldn't. I don't know anything about that."

"Bullshit. I saw the video of your boss. He all but admitted to it."

"My boss is a woman. You met her. I've never even met the guy you're talking about."

Dena ignored this. "How many people have you killed or changed with your experiments? Those . . . things that you released, were those people you captured? Against their will?"

Bob didn't answer. His cheeks were running with sweat and tears.

"That's what I thought," Dena said. "I bet you've been experimenting on people even before the apocalypse. Not just those chimps, which is bad enough already. How long has this been going on?"

Someone started banging on the door again. Dena looked over and saw that Rachel and Fred had stacked up all the moveable furniture in the room against the door. Fred and Rachel backed away from the door, which sounded like it would break open at any moment.

Dena returned her attention to Bob. "How long has this been going on? How *fucking* long?"

"Years," Bob sobbed. "Decades probably. I don't know exactly. I swear I don't know. And I was never involved with that stuff. I just work security."

"You're disgusting," Dena said.

On the screen in front of her, people were making their way into the night, walking through the door of the building that looked like a prison. She saw Diirek approach them with his hands held out. He was talking, but she couldn't make out what he was saying. There was no sound. Some of the people ran away while others were clearly hearing him out.

An explosion issued from the door. Chunks of wood flew like shrapnel into the room, causing Dena to yank her knife away from Bob as she reacted. Someone had used a shotgun to blow a hole in the door just above the stacked furniture, at about head height. Dena looked at Rachel, who was looking back at her from the floor next to Fred. They looked okay.

A man's face appeared at the hole in the door, then disappeared again. Dena looked over at where Bob had been to find him out of his chair and on the floor once again. He held a hand to his throat, but it wasn't doing much to stop the fountain of blood from flowing out.

"Shit," Dena said.

Fred got into a crouch and grabbed the fire extinguisher that stood nearby—the one he'd been wielding in the empty hallway minutes earlier. He scrambled over next to the door, to the left of the hole, and waited. Rachel and Dena both stepped quickly over Bob, trying to avoid the growing puddle of blood there. They huddled against the wall between the desk and the door, waiting for whatever came next.

Another hole punched through the door, the spray of splinters harmlessly assailed the floor and the opposite wall. The sour smell of burning gunpowder and the sweet smell of scorched treated wood filled the dwindling refuge.

Fred looked up to see that the second hole had served to make the first one larger. A hand reached through that hole and sent two insubstantial office chairs clattering to the floor. Fred thought briefly about his knife, which was currently in Bob's leg. The other one was in Dena's hand. But she wasn't close enough to use it.

The man's hand reached further in, down toward the knob, to unlock it. Fred stood up and smashed the guy's hand between the fire extinguisher and doorknob, as hard as he could. The guy yelled and cursed and pulled his mangled hand back out the hole. The black bore of a shotgun took its place, pointed at a shallow angle toward Fred, who dropped to his knees as the gun fired. Two of the kitchen cabinets exploded with the shot.

Fred looked up at the hole, expecting to see the shotgun still there. Instead, what he saw was the crown of a man's skull emerging through the ragged hole in the door. Fred scrambled up just as the guy got his head into the hole up to the neck. The insane look on his face spoke to how angry he was and explained why he could have made such a stupid mistake. His eyes burned with a hatred that surprised Fred, and his mouth was frozen in a sneer. Nostrils pulsed quickly as the man's breathing escalated. Then his eyes went wide as he saw Fred and realized his error.

Fred smacked him with the bottom of the fire extinguisher, right between the eyes. The bridge of his nose collapsed with a resounding crunch. A half-second later blood began to cascade out of his nostrils and from the two gashes the cylinder put in his eyebrows. His head slumped as he lost consciousness, but his chin caught on the bottom of the hole, keeping his bleeding head there, at least for the moment.

Someone screamed just outside the door. Gunfire ensued, then stopped abruptly. Fred heard what he thought was a whimper but couldn't be sure.

Suddenly the unconscious man's head spasmed, then, impossibly, it fell off.

Fred watched in horror as the guy's head fell a foot or so down to the furniture stacked against the door. His forehead smacked the edge of the small dining table which Fred had placed sideways on the couch. Then it rolled down the back of the couch and came to rest on one of the cushions, leaving a trail of incredibly dark blood behind it.

"Shit," Fred said, echoing Dena's sentiment from about two minutes earlier. He held up the fire extinguisher and looked at its bottom. *How the hell?*

The thump of a body hitting the floor sounded from just outside the door. Fred thought about looking out the hole but thought better of it, noting the severed head barely a foot away from him.

Something shifted on the other side of the door. Then the door exploded—actually exploded this time—or that's what Fred thought in the moment. The furniture he and Rachel had stacked up flew across the room in an arc, followed closely by bits of the door, and smashed against the far wall. Fred dropped the extinguisher and fell back, trying to shield his face from the airborne debris. He felt a presence next to him before he saw a figure there. And in that instant before he opened his eyes, he knew he was dead. And that whatever was about to kill him would do it in the most gruesome manner imaginable.

But when he opened his eyes Weller stood over him, gazing down with a confused and unfriendly look on his face. His body was coated in blood. Impossible to tell whose it was. But judging by the blood smeared around his mouth, most of it wasn't his. "Weller?" Fred asked. It looked like Weller, but . . .

"Fred?" Whatever Fred had seen in Weller's face was suddenly gone as he spoke. "I found a sword. Can you believe that?" Weller said, raising a true-to-life sword in his right hand. The kind favored by medieval knights. "There was two of them. Just on the wall in the front hallway." Weller shook his head. "White people, right?"

"Uh . . . yeah," Fred said, because he didn't know what else to say.

Weller put his left hand out and helped Fred up.

"Rachel, Dena," Fred said. "It's alright. He's . . . here to help."

Weller turned around and looked at the women as they stood up and stepped around Bob, who was clearly dead now. "Have you seen Revak?" Weller asked them. They shook their heads, unsure what to think of this blood-coated and crazed-looking figure.

"I don't think he's here," Fred said, quietly.

"What? Why do you think that? This is his place, right?"

"I mean, it looks like it, but I'm not so sure. We met a woman who seems to be in charge."

"Fine. Maybe she knows. Which way did she go? Wait, what did she look like?"

"Late middle age," Rachel said. "Five-foot-ten. Graying."

Weller looked at her for a moment. Then he walked out the door without a word. Fred and the women looked at each other, shrugging. Then Weller came back in. With a body.

"This her?" he asked, holding up a dead woman with one hand. Her torso had a wide diagonal slice from shoulder to hip. Presumably from the sword Weller held in his other hand. Some of her insides were hanging out.

"Yeah," Rachel said, putting a hand to her mouth. "That's her."

"Fuck!" Weller screamed. He threw the woman's body savagely into the corner, then looked at Fred. That strange and unfriendly look was in his eyes again. But it wasn't just his eyes or his face that changed, Fred realized. It was more of a complete change that made Weller look unbelievably menacing, although Fred couldn't put his finger on why, exactly. An image flashed into his mind as he looked at Weller, and Fred suddenly realized the impression he got. It was that of a deadly kind of cosmic emptiness. Like a black hole in human form. Or, rather, vampire form. Barely contained rage contorted Weller's face as he turned and moved toward the door without a word.

As Weller reached the doorway, the ground shook with an explosion.

"What the fuck is this?" Weller screamed, running off into the house.

Fred thought back to how the ground shook when his little town exploded on the night of the apocalypse. He looked at Rachel and Dena, and the look on their faces told him they were all thinking the same thing: escape. Fred made it out the door first, almost tripping over three bodies in the hallway. He turned left as the ground shook again, the women following, but then stopped when he realized he didn't know where the hell he was going. Rachel and Dena nearly ran into him.

"Which way is the exit?" Fred asked as the ground continued to rumble. Cracks spread crazily up the walls. Plaster dust fell from the ceiling.

"Fred!" A voice yelled from behind the trio. Fred recognized it instantly. It was Diirek.

"This way," Diirek yelled from the other end of the hallway as Fred turned around. Rachel started running hand-in-hand with Dena. Fred ran after them.

As he reached the end of the hallway, he heard Weller—or whatever was inside him—scream from somewhere deep in the house. It was a wail of pain, anger, and unstoppable determination. The hairs on Fred's neck raised as some part of his brain told him to run as fast as he could away from that sound. And he did. He caught up with Rachel and Dena as they slowed to take the corner. Both the women spared a frightened glance over their shoulders, as if to make sure whatever made that sound wasn't following them.

The ground began to undulate as Fred and the two women reached a rear service door, which Diirek was holding open. A roar filled the air, but it was not a sound made by human or machine or explosion. It was the sound of tons of earth and rock moving. The three of them burst into the night and kept running, Diirek bringing up the rear. Fred could see people up ahead, running to the trees where the chimp cage was located. As they got further away from the mansion, the shaking of the ground turned to vibrations.

Fred chanced a backward glance and watched as the top two stories of the farthest building—what Fred thought of as the research building—collapsed down into the ground. It was as if a hole had opened under the building and swallowed it. Then the ground shook again, causing Fred to trip and sprawl in the dirt.

As he looked back at where the building had been, a flower of fire shot out of the hole in the ground, reaching twice as high as the building had stood. A piece of concrete about the size of Fred's head thunked into the ground nearby, followed by smaller pieces of the building, blown clear of its grave by the explosion. Diirek grabbed Fred from the ground and pushed him ahead with a hand on his back. Rachel and Dena were just reaching the trees, turning around to watch. Fred and Diirek ran the last thirty yards with small and large pieces of concrete and stone raining down around them, Diirek nearly carrying Fred as they went. The ground stilled as they reached the trees.

"You okay?" Dena asked when Fred joined them, doubled over and panting. He nodded. There were some other people hiding in the trees, eyeing them warily. Fred didn't pay them much mind.

Diirek grabbed him and pulled him into a hug. Fred smiled.

"Where is Weller? Did you see him?" Diirek asked, releasing Fred.

"Last we saw he was still in the big house," Fred said.

"Did he find Anders Revak?"

"I don't think so," Fred said. "I don't think he's here."

Diirek nodded. "I was afraid of that. Things look slightly different than they did in the video. I don't think this is the same place we saw on that tablet."

"Dammit," Fred said. "He's still out there."

A third-floor window broke at the back of the mansion as a man flew out, screaming until he hit the ground. Then all was quiet again.

"It looks like Weller is still in there. I will be back," Diirek said. He moved toward the house at a jog, but it was about three times faster than Fred could run at a full sprint.

When Diirek was just over halfway to the house, the bottom left of the structure exploded.

The windows on that side of the house shattered outward on a wave of superheated air, pieces of wall, burning furniture, and bits of random household items. The sound was deafening. Diirek stumbled and fell to the right, then he was lost from sight in a ball of gray smoke. Fred felt the aftershock as a strong wind. Little pieces of shrapnel landed well away from him. Some of the people in the woods around him screamed and ran. Although Fred, Rachel, and Dena had all instinctively turned from the explosion, they stayed put, enraptured, mouths hanging open.

The right side of the house rocked from another explosion. Fred took a step back this time, his eyes wide, looking in vain for Diirek. Then some movement caught his eye. Some of the billowing smoke was twisted and dispersed by something flying near the height of the house. A drone. It had come around from the front of the house and now moved in a smooth curve around to the back.

It hovered for a second before launching a small projectile at one of the back windows. As soon as it let it go, the drone shot up into the sky far above the house to get clear of the explosion, which erupted two seconds later, sending yet more debris out into the night, and destroying more of the huge house.

The drone came back down again, lined up on the left side of the house, and sent another explosive in one of the bottom windows. With the fourth explosion, the house fell in on itself. The roof crumbled, falling almost straight down into the heart of the large house. The walls encompassing the top stories fell inward as if in resignation. Dust and smoke billowed out as the structure began to settle as a pile of rubble.

The drone lifted again and flew over the destroyed house and out of sight. Fred ran to where he last saw Diirek.

"Diirek," he called as he entered the perimeter of smoke and dust that now surrounded the pile of stone.

"I am here," Diirek said from nearby. Fred walked to him and helped him out, although the vampire seemed to be moving all right, just limping slightly. As they walked back toward the woods, Dena and Rachel came near. The rest of the vampires—those that were still alive—started coming from all directions. The sound of engines permeated the deep silence that had settled over the area after the explosions and the house collapsing.

"What's that?" Fred asked, looking around. "Trucks?"

"He is coming to finish the job," Diirek said. "Many trucks coming. From the road through the corn."

Binta and Isabelle came around the smoldering pile of stone from the front of the house.

"We need to go. Now," Binta said.

"It is him, isn't it?" Diirek asked.

"It must be," she said. "Who else? He's making sure we don't have access to any of his research. Destroying everything."

"He must have more of these," Fred said. "It's the only thing that makes sense. More of these facilities, more of these people. Around the country. Maybe around the world. What the hell do we do?"

"Weller?" Diirek asked, looking around. "Did you see him come out before the explosions?"

Binta shook her head.

The engine noise was closer now. They were coming.

"It has begun," Diirek said. "The world is about to change for the worse. Again."

"We can fight, right?" Fred asked. "We have to."

"There's too many of them," Isabelle said. "Even if they're only humans, I doubt we could take them. Not the state we're in. Plus, those other werewolves could come back any time."

Diirek looked around. The remaining vampires were gathering. There were only eight left, including himself. Most of them were injured. Some seriously. Most of the humans, freed from the prison building, had already run off. There were a few stragglers, apparently waiting to see what was going to happen next. Or hoping that the people coming in the trucks were saviors.

"What do we do?" Fred asked.

"We must run. We cannot win. Not today." After Diirek spoke, he looked over his shoulder at the pile of stone, as if willing Weller to appear. He did not.

Although Diirek was injured, he told Fred to get on his back. Rachel got on Binta's back and Dena on Jules'. Then they ran.

When they reached the edge of the forest they stopped to look back. The grounds were crawling with figures.

"Look out!" Isabelle yelled just before a piece of stone smashed into the woods nearby.

"What the hell was that?" Rachel asked.

"That," Diirek said, "was Anders Revak. He knows we're here. It seems that was his way of saying hello. He threw that rock all the way over here."

Fred looked across the field and saw a figure standing in the distance, looking their way. "He's a vampire now," Fred said, a note of despair in his voice.

"He's smiling," Binta said. "Why doesn't he come after us?"

"Because he knows he won this round," Diirek said. "He is not done with us. Not while we are still alive." Diirek paused, keeping his eyes on the distant figure. "Let's hope that him leaving us alive tonight is a mistake on his part."

"We're not done with him," Binta said. "Not while we're still alive. Not while *he's* still alive."

"Let's go," Isabelle said, clutching her mangled hand.

Only eight vampires were present, along with Fred, Dena, and Rachel. The other two women had waited back at the train. The undead among them were Diirek, Bram, Binta, Isabelle, Jules, Val, Jamie, and a vampire named Ekon who had given just as well as he'd taken. Bruno and Johannes had left the group as soon as the sun had gone down. And, of course, Weller had been inside the mansion when it had come crashing down.

The group moved off through the woods, clutching their wounds and avoiding eye contact. They had enough time to make it back to the train—if it was still there.

Fred stopped and turned back to look for Weller, thinking he would pop up somewhere like the wraith he seemed to be. The teenager only paused for a moment, knowing that Weller was important somehow. He wasn't sure how, but he felt that his loss was a debilitating one.

He turned and moved off after the others, thinking about the coming dawn. He couldn't help but feel despair, knowing that when the sun came up in a couple of hours it would be the dawn of a new and terrible world.

Chapter Thirty-Nine

MISTER
WORLD-ENDER

Weller snapped awake in a bright room, screaming. His pain bounced off the solid walls of his prison and came back to him distorted, unearthly, and inhuman. With more effort than he thought he possessed, Weller managed to swallow the pain enough to stop screaming. Instead, whimpering grunts bounced back to him, even more foreign to his ears than his own screams were.

There was no bed in the room—no furniture to speak of. He was lying on cold concrete, bright recessed lights blaring at him from the other side of the room. A glance down revealed his shattered and scorched body. Bones stuck out of his skin in dozens of places. His arms and legs were smashed nearly beyond recognition. Most of his skin was burned the black of an overcooked marshmallow. Some patches of skin had fallen away, along with most of his clothes, to rest on the floor next to him, revealing pink and white swaths of muscle pebbled with blood. He could not move any of his limbs—he could barely lift his head—but he could feel the savage pain signals that his undead body was clearly still capable of sending to his brain. He swallowed his agony as he looked around the room.

The place was somehow familiar to him. Looking past his feet he could see a wide rectangular window which was, presumably, the front of the holding cell. Not so much a window, in fact, but a wall made of some kind of thick glass. The recessed lighting surrounded this wall, illuminating both the inside and, to some extent, the outside of the cell. Across from his cage there sat another, but it was dark. He could not see inside.

Something moved above and behind Weller. If he had been able, he would have jumped at the sound. But, as it was, he tilted his head right, clenching his teeth against the anguish of the movement. A naked and discolored male figure staggered forward and stopped in line with Weller, who looked up and into a pair of cloudy, lifeless eyes.

Everything came together then. It all came crashing down on him much like the mansion—the one he thought had been Anders'—had come crashing down on him as it exploded. He was looking into the eyes of the zombie from the video Anders Revak sent to the vampires. He was a captive in Revak's laboratory of horrors. Fred had been right. They had chosen the wrong place.

The zombie stared down at him for several long moments, then stumbled stupidly to the front of the cell and stood there, looking out at nothing.

Weller put the crown of his head against the floor, looking back at the rear wall of the cage. It was a blank white wall, smooth aside from the greasy handprints that had clearly been left by the zombie. He looked around again, feeling somehow less pain as he did so. Anger was beginning to take its place.

No fucking door? How did I get in here? He asked himself. His mind turned to the others, wondering what had happened to them after he'd run into the mansion. He remembered the first explosions rocking the house, but for some reason he'd decided to ignore them. No, it wasn't hard to know why he'd ignored them. Why he'd stayed in the building, tearing it apart, searching for Anders. It was pure rage that drove him to it, that clouded his judgment and led him to this place. This cage. It was a rage that was building within him again now, rattling and squirming in him like a nest of vipers trying to escape from a forest fire. The fact that he could barely move only added fuel to the fire.

If anger got you here, what good was it? A small voice asked, almost hesitantly. The snakes didn't like that, and his mind clouded with swirling thoughts of JayLynn and Berena. Weller yelled and tried to move, causing pain to flare everywhere.

Ignoring it, he only grew angrier and tried to move again, but his shattered body made it impossible. The pain grew more insistent, and he thought he could feel the grating of each snapped bone as the pieces rubbed against each other. He could feel the blistered flesh of each burn open up as his few working muscles contracted. He felt every fissure, every cut, every laceration, every compound fracture.

And with the immense pain—pain that would have been enough to kill a human—a frayed sense of clarity came to him. *Look*, that same small voice said. *Fuck you*, another voice screamed back.

You can't even look? What are you afraid to see? The small voice whispered.

Before the other, louder voice could scream again, Weller looked.

He was seeing himself, as if from above. And what he saw was barely recognizable as him. His jaw and fists were clenched, the muscles of his neck stood out, and his eyes were dark slits of hate, staring back at him.

What good is this? The voice asked.

It's everything, the other voice grated.

Clearly not, the small voice said. *You know it's not everything. But you've made it into everything. Why? What good is it? What good does it do?*

"None," Weller answered, suddenly aware of himself, suddenly able to see through the screaming haze of hate and rage and anger that had been controlling him.

"None," he yelled. He was suddenly back inside himself, looking up at the blank ceiling, feeling his entire body relax, the pain receding.

"None," he whispered and sighed at once, feeling a sense of freedom, despite the cage around him.

He could feel the dark cloud, the vipers, the fire within him. They hadn't gone anywhere, but they had calmed.

For now.

A sound issued from above and behind him. It was the sound of metal sliding against metal. Weller raised his chin again and looked back at the rear wall. Anders Revak was there, standing in a doorway that hadn't been there before, upside down in Weller's vision. Revak stepped inside, smiling at Weller, his hands clasped behind his back. The door closed behind him, and it blended seamlessly into the blank white wall. There was nothing on this side to indicate there was a door there at all.

"Mr. Weller, isn't it?" Revak asked as he circled around to stand at Weller's feet. The zombie turned to look at Revak, then turned back around and resumed its imbecilic vigil.

"*Detective* Weller," Weller croaked in response.

Revak laughed at this. He stepped forward and brought his hands out from behind his back. He held an opaque sports bottle in his right hand. "You must be in tremendous pain," Revak said, extending the bottle toward Weller's mouth. "Drink some of this. It'll help."

"What is it?" Weller asked.

Revak looked at him quizzically. "What's the only liquid that can help a vampire? For a supposed detective, you're not very good at deductions."

"I'll deduct your head from your fucking neck," Weller said and smiled.

"Yes!" Revak exclaimed in apparent joy. "But not before you drink this. You'll need your strength to decapitate me."

Weller searched Revak's eyes before gesturing with his chin for the bottle. Revak upended it and squeezed gently. The sweetest liquid Weller had ever tasted flooded his mouth. It was blood all right. And he could feel it go to work healing him immediately—but he could also feel that he would need much more than what was in this measly bottle. His stomach spasmed and lurched in delight and his eyelids fluttered involuntarily.

Revak pulled the bottle away what seemed like only seconds after he'd put it between Weller's lips.

"I'm not done," Weller said, trying hard to keep the pleading tone out of his voice.

"You are, actually," Revak said, and pointed the bottle at the ground. He squeezed and a single drop came out. "All done."

Weller's skin and some of his broken bones had begun to heal, but he was nowhere near a hundred percent. He found that he could move his arms now. He propped himself on his elbows and looked at Revak.

"They'll come for me. They'll come looking. And if not for me, they'll come to kill you," he said.

"Oh, yes. I know. One of your human friends watched from afar as my men pulled you out of the wreckage this morning. Apologies for the burns, by the way. Couldn't be helped. But it looks like you're already healing up nicely. Besides, it's nice to have some hard evidence of what happens to us in the sun." Revak smiled. "And how much damage we can take."

"You did it?" Weller asked. "You turned yourself?"

"You sound surprised. Last I checked, you were a human not even two days ago. You can enjoy immortality, but I can't? How is that fair?"

Something moved in the dark cage across the way, catching Weller's eye. It was only a large, dark blur moving around beyond the thick glass of the other cage. Then the blur came forward and slammed into the glass, causing faint vibrations that Weller felt through the floor.

Small, red eyes stared across at him from a furry, angular head. Long claws scraped at the glass as Weller watched, transfixed. The claws came out of the top of a large, leathery wing. Immediately Weller remembered the poor woman from the video who looked like she'd been sloppily deformed into a bat-thing. But this thing didn't look like her. For one thing, it was much, much bigger. Seven or eight feet, easily. And the wings looked genuine, like they could fly. Where the woman had looked more human than bat, this thing looked more bat than human. Essentially, it looked like a giant nightmare bat.

Revak turned, following Weller's gaze. As soon as the bat-thing saw Revak looking its way, it screeched and disappeared back into the darkness of the cell.

"What the fuck?" Weller whispered.

"Oh, yes. You saw my earlier attempt at that in the video, I suppose. That one is much better. But still, it's no vampire. It's just as mortal as all the desperate humans still scrambling for food and water on this pitiful little world. I imagine it will come in handy one of these days. We'll see. Not a top priority right now."

"That used to be a . . . person?" Weller asked.

"That's debatable. It was a murderer. A remorseless sicko who was going to die from lethal injection. Some would say that what I did was a mercy."

"How many of these places do you have?" Weller asked, thinking of the compound they'd raided.

"Enough of them that blowing up the one last night was relatively painless," Revak said, pulling his shoulders back in pride. "And all my labs are rigged to blow, just like the one last night. So nothing can fall into the wrong hands. You see, Mr. Weller, I've thought of everything. I've been working on this—or some version of it—all my life."

"How long has that been? Thirty-five years?"

Revak laughed. "I appreciate the compliment, but no. Looks can be deceptive. I've been working on immortality in one way or another since I was a teenager. Now that I have it, I'll change the world forever. Everyone will thank me for it." Revak paused. "Well, *almost* everyone."

Weller shook his head. "They'll come. For me. For you. They'll come," he said. "This shit . . . you can't get away with this forever. They'll come stop you."

Revak's smile grew wider. "Yes. I'm counting on it. But when they get here, they'll have to contend with you and me."

"What? What does that mean? You're going to brainwash me like you did that guy who killed himself?"

"Brainwash?" Revak said, mock outrage on his face. "What is this, some sixties B-movie? I don't need to brainwash anyone."

"Fine," Weller said. "What's your secret? Your magnetic personality?"

"Nanobots, Mr. Weller. You've just ingested a few thousand nanobots along with the blood. They'll slowly work their way into your brain over the next few days. Then I won't need to brainwash you. I can control you with an AI program I designed myself." Revak waved a hand and Weller heard the hidden door open once again. Revak walked toward it.

"You will be the first commander in my vampire army," he said, barely able to keep the high-pitched excitement out of his voice. "And I'll use you to both lure your troublemaker friends here, and to kill them. It's going to make quite the movie."

Weller was at a loss. Anders walked out and the door closed before Weller said, "Sounds like a great evil masterplan, but I don't buy it."

Once again, Weller found himself alone with the naked zombie. He looked around, taking stock of his surroundings, wondering if the story about the nanobots was true.

"Well," he said to himself, "looks like I have nothing to do but wait and see." He paused, feeling the dull and insistent pain that permeated his body. The blood had helped. A lot. But he still wanted more. His legs were still mangled, and he couldn't move them. He laid back down on the cold concrete, putting his hands behind his head, concentrating on keeping his calm. "Not the vacation I would have chosen, but it'll do. This thing is out of my hands, for now. Unless you know a way out," he said to the zombie.

The zombie turned to look at Weller. It stared at him as if waiting for words of wisdom.

"Well, shit. I've got nothing either, pal. We're pretty well fucked . . . Wait," Weller said, his eyes brightening. The zombie seemed to stand up a little straighter. "Do you know the name of this song?" Weller asked, and began to sing.

EPILOGUE

"What the fuck was that?" Matt said to Sheila as he swung his M27 rifle up, pointing the barrel at the pile of rubble that was once a mansion.

"What?" Sheila said, tensing and bringing her own M27 up to her shoulder, glaring into the dark.

"You didn't hear that?" Matt asked, his voice shaky. "Something moved over there. I swear I heard something."

"Where? In the rubble? It's probably a raccoon or something. We definitely killed all the walkers in this area today." Sheila paused, thinking. "They're nocturnal, you know."

"No, they're not," Matt said. "You just said yourself that we killed a bunch of them today."

"Not zombies, you idiot. Raccoons."

"No shit, Miss Trivia. Everyone knows that raccoons are nocturnal. And that they have opposable thumbs."

"What?" Sheila said. "Seriously?"

"You're fuckin' ridiculous."

"I'm not the one jumping at shadows."

"Whatever," Matt said. "This place gives me the creeps. It looks exactly like HQ—or at least it did before we blew it up. Did you notice that?

When they showed us the pictures of the place during prep, I had to do a double-take."

"Apparently the big boss has places like this set up all around the country. All around the world, even. They do all kinds of off-the-books shit at them. He even keeps slaves at some of them. That's what I heard, anyway."

"That's what you heard? From who? You fucking an officer or somethin'?"

"It's just what I heard. And who I fuck is none of your business. Sounds like you're jealous." Sheila smiled and elbowed Matt in the ribs as she said this last.

"Ugh. In your dreams," Matt said. "I just don't understand why we have to stay here. There's nothing left. We trashed everything but the holding cells. Why can't we get back to supply runs and rounding up civilians? This place sucks."

Sheila lowered her rifle and started walking. Matt followed suit. Their squad had made a home in the holding cells, which was where Matt wanted to be, but it was their turn to patrol.

"It's only been one day since we got here," Sheila said. "Are you going to bitch the entire time we're here? Because if so, I'm requesting another patrol partner."

"That depends. How long are we going to be here?"

"Until further notice. At least that's what Roger says. Or until we all get killed by raccoons with opposable thumbs."

"You're hilarious," Matt said, then paused. "I just hate these middle-of-the-night patrols. They—"

"Because you're afraid of the dark. It's okay, you can admit it. You're a little bitch who's afraid of the dark."

"Am not."

"Are too."

"Am—" Matt stopped, turning back toward the rubble, raising his gun again. "Tell me you heard that one."

"I did," Sheila whispered. "Sounded like bricks shifting. That what you heard earlier?"

"Yeah."

They moved toward the rubble, rifles up, clicking their headlamps as they went. Twin pools of moving light shot out in front of them, illuminating nothing but broken stone and debris.

"You go around that way," Sheila said. "I'll go this way and we'll meet on the other side."

"Fuck that. We're staying together. Strength in numbers."

Sheila rolled her eyes. They were at the rear of the giant rubble pile, and they started to move around the side, toward the front.

Something moved just ahead of their lamplight. Something big.

"What the fuck was that?" Matt said, his voice high and trembling. "It was fuckin' big. Big as a man."

"Men can't move that fast. It was a deer or something," Sheila said, trying to keep her cool.

"You kiddin' me? Have you heard the stories of what the boss can do now? And what about that thing they removed from the rubble this morning? Just bursting into flames like that? Fucking screaming?"

"Just shut up, Matt."

"What bursts into flames in sunlight? Fucking vampires, that's what. I heard the boss threw a rock a mile last night. You know what else vampires have? Super strength."

"A mile? You sound like the biggest idiot in the world," Sheila said. "No one can throw anything a mile."

"I'm sayin'," Matt said, "that something weird is going on. I never thought zombies would exist, but they're out there all right. So, it's not a big leap to the boss having like . . . superpowers or something."

"Christ," Sheila said.

They turned the corner to what used to be the front of the mansion. Their headlamps illuminated a suave, pale-faced man dressed in all black. He stood there, not ten feet in front of them, like a statue.

Sheila and Matt froze, as if waiting for him to move, waiting to see if he was a statue or not.

The man smiled, his lips parting, revealing fangs the size of a wolf's. "Hello," he said.

Matt and Sheila both tried to shoot the dead man at the same time. Neither managed to get a shot off because they were yanked off their feet from behind. They found themselves on the ground, their weapons pulled from their hands.

The pale man stood over them, looking down with a hunger in his eyes. Next to him was a black woman with wide, bright eyes. They were both smiling.

"Where did they take him?" the man asked.

"Who? I don't know what you're talking about," Matt said.

"My turn or yours, Diirek?" the black woman asked. Diirek gestured at her with a tilt of his head. The woman bent down and moved her arm. A stream of blood shot from Matt's neck. The woman latched onto his neck and drank deeply as Matt convulsed.

Sheila looked up at the pale man, who seemed to be waiting for her to speak.

"I'll tell you everything I know," she said, getting the words out as fast as she could.

"Yes, you will," Diirek said.

UNDEAD EXTERMINATION TEASER

T he story isn't over yet! Read on to check out the first two chapters of the third and final installment in the Undead Trilogy.

PROLOGUE

THEN AND NOW

T HEN

***

"I stand before you today humbled. And I stand before you today grateful. Grateful that I could continue my father's legacy—my family's legacy—in assisting the United States government, and its allies, in helping make the world a safer place." Anders Revak paused for effect, looking around the room at the men in their tuxedos, dress blues, service uniforms, and mess dress uniforms, sitting at white-clothed tables. He looked at the women sitting next to them, wearing sparkling earrings, flattering dresses, and pearl necklaces. He shifted behind the podium, all eyes on him.

"Monsteranto's first government contract was signed by my great grandfather in 1909. Believe it or not, that contract was for pesticides derived from chrysanthemums, and mustard gas. It's a good thing we never forgot which was which." Anders paused for a smattering of laughter.

"We've come a long way since then, but the partnership between my company and the United States government has always been strong. And

I'm happy to report that we've just signed a new contract. For what exactly, I can't tell you. If I did, I would have to kill you, and then myself." There was more laughter at this. Anders had learned long ago that gallows humor was always a hit among military personnel.

"All I can say is that our advances in medical and nanotechnology have led to some remarkably interesting developments that are of particular interest to this great government of ours. Those of you who are directly involved in the project know to what I'm referring. The rest of you will have to wait, I'm afraid." Anders smiled, shaking his head sadly. This elicited a few chuckles from the crowd.

"Many of you know that Monsteranto's government contracts don't exactly pay the bills. But that's okay, because our chemical manufacturing is still at the forefront of the pesticide and insecticide markets. Our medical technology is gaining ground in the market. And that's what makes it possible for me to show my appreciation to you all tonight. Without you, the men and women of the armed services, our country would surely be a very different place. A very much worse place, I dare say. So, despite all the back-patting I've done up here so far, I really want to say thank you." A few people applauded, as he knew they would. Anders took the opportunity to look around the room again, seeing that the two dozen servants were ready, holding bottles of champagne in their white-gloved hands. "Thank you very much. I've taken the liberty of bringing out some of my personal bottles of Blanc de Blancs, 1995, for your pleasure." A few *ohs* and *ahs* floated up from the audience at the pronouncement of the expensive and famous champagne.

"Thank you again," he said. "And enjoy the rest of your evening." Polite applause rang throughout the large and lavish ballroom. Anders smiled and stepped back from the podium, one hand up, feigning modesty. *Fucking rats*, he thought as he stood there, looking around the room. *You're all fucking rats. I'll be rid of you soon.* He told himself that he'd tried—really tried—to be friends with these people. But it hadn't taken him long to realize that theirs was a group he would never be a part of. Not unless he joined the military. And he doubted even that would do it. There was a certain patronizing attitude all these military men and women carried. They would eat his food and drink his alcohol and smile at him and shake his hand, but they would never let him in. Too bad for them.

He watched a few specific servants pour champagne into glasses at a few specific tables, thinking about the billions of dollars in nanotech that was floating in the champagne. He stood there on the stage, watching as the powerful men and women at those tables drank down their bubbly, happy, and ignorant of what was coming.

He thought about the modified chemicals that had been mixed into the pesticides that every major agricultural producer in the world used. And he thought about how, in the next two days, another chemical would be mixed into major water supplies around the world through municipal waste treatment plants. When the two chemicals built up to sufficient levels in humanity's collective bloodstream, they would cause the dead to come back to life. He knew people well enough to know that many of them, when they realized the world was exploding, would kill themselves. If even ten percent of those suicides came back, they would spread their manufactured virus through saliva as easily as the Black Death on a rat-infested merchant ship.

Not long now, he thought. His plan was finally coming together. The work of decades of his life, coming to fruition. He looked around the ballroom in wonder, his heart swelling with pride. *The best investment I've ever made*, he thought. *After all, what's a few billion dollars spent if it gives you immortality and more power than anyone has ever had?*

***

Admiral Jacob B. Warren had no idea where the portable hard drive had come from. Panic gripped him as he realized that he was no longer in control of his own body. Something was very, seriously wrong.

It had been a normal day. Nothing eventful about his trip to work. His normal body men had picked him up in an armored SUV, as always. He'd arrived on time, as always. He'd grabbed a piece of fruit and a cup of coffee before heading to his office, as always. Nothing out of the ordinary. His day had been no more banal or exciting than any other day.

When his driver, a man named Reginald Jones, had come to see if he was ready to leave for the day, Warren said that he wasn't. That he would be staying late. But as soon as Jones left, Warren couldn't remember why he needed to stay.

After an hour of sitting at his desk, unmoving and unable to move, Warren was convinced he was having a stroke. Although his thoughts seemed clear—albeit tinged with growing hysteria—he couldn't make his body listen to him. Then, at 1900 hours, he opened his briefcase and pulled out a portable hard drive that he'd never seen before. He tried to stop his hands from moving toward the computer, but it wouldn't work. He tried to yell, to scream, to stand up and walk out of the office to find help, but he couldn't.

Presently, he signed into the Department of Defense's secure network using his own credentials. With a few clicks, the contents of the hard drive were uploading onto the DoD's network.

Warren had no way of knowing that other powerful men and women around the country were, at that moment, uploading similar viruses into other secure government networks. Or that those viruses would help bring about the end of the world as he knew it. But he wouldn't be around to see the world crumble.

When the detection systems started going off, warning of incoming missiles from countries around the world, defense agency intercept missiles launched. But there were no missiles coming in from around the world. Their computers had been corrupted by the virus. And so had the launch systems. Instead of speeding to meet nonexistent incoming missiles, the Missile Defense Agency's intercept missiles made their way to the major American cities they were designed to protect, the non-nuclear blasts leveling buildings and killing millions.

As American missiles were landing in American cities, intercontinental ballistic missiles launched from silos in Kansas, Wyoming, Montana, and a dozen other states. As these nuclear missiles raced to countries around the world, the individuals in charge of such things at those governments found themselves witnessing the end of the world, at a loss for what to do. The Americans had been attacked first—and by their own missiles. Now they were attacking the rest of the world.

A few countries decided to launch several of their own nuclear missiles. Some of these missiles landed on American cities and military bases, the nuclear blasts adding to the already extensive damage. Other nuclear explosions rocked Israel, Palestine, Iran, Russia, North Korea, South Korea, China, and India.

But before Admiral Jacob B. Warren had a chance to realize that the world was exploding with nuclear and non-nuclear ordnance, he opened a desk drawer, pulled out a gun safe, unlocked it, pulled out his Beretta 92FS, and shot himself through the roof of his mouth.

None of it was under his own power.

***

NOW

***

Why isn't this working? Anders Revak watched the recording of the man burning. Then he watched it again.

He moved his gaze to another of the three screens at his desk and pressed play. On the screen, another man was carted out into daylight on a steel gurney by four figures in full-body fire retardant gear. The man's feet touched sunlight first and began to smoke immediately. By the time the rest of his body was in full sunlight, his legs were on fire, the jeans he wore doing no more to stop the flames than a paper tissue on a campfire. He convulsed and screamed and fought against the reinforced steel straps holding him down.

Revak paused the video and turned to the third screen. He watched, for the second time, the video of a man in full fire gear being carted out into daylight. It took this man longer to start fire, but not by much. The fire gear did nothing to protect him. He, too, screamed and fought against the shackles. Anders glanced down at a tablet on his desk, studying the data that went along with the videos.

Why? What am I missing?

Anders stood up from his desk and walked toward the window and the darkness beyond it. As he looked out at the moon, his anger seemed to flare. He felt his fangs extend, pressing against his lips. *There has to be a way.*

He stomped back to his desk and picked up a tablet. He swiped and pressed a button.

"One," he said, trying to keep the edge out of his voice. He wanted to kill someone. "Come in here and give me an update."

"Yes, Master," One said from the tablet. Ten seconds passed. Anders stood at his desk, staring at the wood-paneled wall. The door to his study opened. One walked in, tablet in hand, eyes on the floor.

"Master," he said, "what would you like an update on?"

"The vampires," Anders said, still staring at the wall.

"Uh. Um, which vampires, Master?"

Anders spun to face One. "What do you mean, 'which vampires'? You know damn well who I am talking about."

"Right. Sorry, Master. No word yet. We have crews out looking for them every day and night. Everyone loyal to us in the city knows who to look for. It's just a matter of time, Master."

"Oh, is it? Is that what your data tells you? Is that based on some sort of scientific information? Tell me, One, if it's just a matter of time, tell me how long? How long until we find them?"

"No. Uh, sorry, Master. It is a figure of speech. I misspoke. I apologize."

Anders was happy to see that One was nearly crying. "And how about the cure for daylight? Is that 'just a matter of time' too? Nothing takes this fucking long, One. I should have it by now. I deserve it. So when will it be, One? When will it be?"

One said nothing, staring at the ground. Tears streamed down his cheeks as his upper body shook. Anders stepped up to One, grabbing him by the throat. "Tell me why our scientists can't find out what causes this. Tell me why nothing has worked. Tell me why I can't see the fucking sun." Anders paused as One let out a small, hopeless sound. "It makes no sense," he continued. "It defies logic. It's . . . It's fucking supernatural. But there's no such thing, is there, One?"

Anders expected some kind of answer but quickly realized that One was no longer capable of answering any questions. The man's face had turned purple and blue from a lack of oxygen. Anders had collapsed his windpipe with one hand.

Letting go, Anders watched One's body crumple to the ground. It was the fifth One he'd killed in as many months. Pretty soon he would run out of halfway competent slaves to promote. He stepped over One's body, thinking, *I used to be able to control my anger better than this.* He looked out at the night and felt his anger surge again.

I miss the sun, he thought. Then he turned back to drink One's blood while it was still warm.

CHAPTER 1

THE ASSHATS MUST DIE

She watched as the two gunmen stood at the gas station, leaning against the pumps and chatting in the shade of the large awning. A Humvee had just pulled away, taking with it a full tank of gas and four men dressed in fatigues and wearing olive-green masks—just like the two remaining men.

The girl was on her knees in the dilapidated fast-food joint across from the gas station. One of the gunmen levered himself off a pump and turned a lazy circle, looking her way. She dropped out of sight, heart thudding and cold sweat springing up under her sweatshirt. *He didn't see me*, she thought. *Or did he?* She brought her small caliber rifle up to her chest, holding it with both hands, finger inside the trigger guard. Once she felt secure with it, rehearsing in her head the movement she would make if she had to use it, she brought her head up to the bottom of the window, slowly, very slowly. *Bring it on, asshats*, she thought just as her eyes cleared the sill and she saw the two men still standing in front of the pumps, still talking, unaware of her presence. She was surprised to feel a little disappointed. But not too surprised.

She saw a thin and dark figure move quickly, darting back behind the gas station. She began sweating in earnest, despite the late October chill. The sun was still out. If she were caught—and with a gun, no less—she'd pay with her life. But who knows what they would do to her before they killed her. Nothing pleasant.

But she wasn't really worried about her. The more she did stuff like this, the more she grew to like it. As much as she didn't want to admit it, she was more concerned for another person than for herself. It was a relatively new feeling for her. It wasn't necessarily bad. Not necessarily. But it still made her want to barf in her mouth from time to time.

She watched one of the asshat soldiers turn around and head toward the gas station building. *Shit. Shit, shit, shit, shit*, Karina thought. *Shit.*

The other soldier stood where he was, looking around at the deserted road and the few empty buildings around the intersection. He rocked back and forth and swung his assault rifle lazily in front of him. Karina watched as the other soldier disappeared into the gas station.

Shit. Get out of there. Now.

She scrambled on the dirty linoleum past chairs and tables affixed to the ground. When she reached the order counter, she stood up and ran out the back of the fast-food restaurant. She came out into the crisp fall air, the sweat on her skin sending a chill through her body. Around the side of the restaurant was a small cinder-block u-shaped structure that held two dumpsters. She ran to it as fast as she could and slid to cover behind it. She poked her head around, looking from a different angle at the gas station.

Asshat One was still outside messing around. Asshat Two was nowhere to be seen. Still inside. Not good. The sound of a gunshot bounced around, echoing off the buildings. It had clearly come from inside the gas station. *Shit!*

Karina stepped out from behind the dumpster housing and knelt on her right knee, bringing the rifle fluidly up to her shoulder, placing her left elbow on top of her left knee for stability. Asshat One was looking dumbfoundedly toward the gas station. Karina got him in her sights, aiming at the center of his back.

She pulled the trigger, the familiar crack assaulting her and causing her to shut her eyes. But she didn't keep them closed for long. She opened them, seeing that the soldier had stumbled forward. But he wasn't down.

The front door of the gas station flew open, a dark and skinny figure running out. She watched him notice the still-standing soldier, but he didn't stop running. Even as the soldier lifted his gun drunkenly, he never stopped. Even as the wounded soldier aimed his high-powered rifle at him, he didn't stop.

Karina fired again, hitting the soldier for a second time somewhere in the back. The guy stumbled again as he pulled his trigger, his shots going wide and spraying into the pump right behind the sprinting figure.

Karina fired again, but this time she missed. She was paying too much attention to the black figure running toward her. Black mask covering his face, along with black jeans, a black hoodie, and black sneakers.

The soldier turned, leveling his rifle at the running figure.

"No!" Karina yelled, taking aim again.

A ball of bright orange flame shot out from inside the gas station, sending glass and shrapnel out, some of which pelted and pierced the soldier. But the fire wasn't done. A second, larger explosion rocked the structure, engulfing the four pumps outside and sending bits of debris raining down all around the black-clad figure.

The skinny runner looked behind him as his legs pumped, seeing his handiwork. He turned back toward Karina and ripped off his mask, slowing down as he approached her. A huge smile sat on his stupid, smug face. A smattering of peach fuzz coated his chin, and his brown hair was a matted mess from the mask.

"You little shit, Fred," Karina said, still in her kneeling firing position. "That wasn't the plan."

"Relax, little sister," Fred said, knowing full well that Karina hated when he called her that. He was breathing hard but was clearly amped up. "I had to improvise. Dipshit Two came inside and—"

"Asshat Two," Karina corrected.

"Right. Whatever." He used the opportunity to catch his breath, then seemed to change his train of thought. He looked behind him at the inferno that used to be the gas station, grinning. Black smoke poured into the dim and ashy sky. A flame-engulfed Asshat One stumbled out of the flames and fell flat on his face as the fire blackened his body.

Fred's smile faltered.

The sun would be setting soon. Then the real work would begin. All Karina could do was glare at his stupid face and say a silent thanks that he'd made it out alive.

"Let's get back," Fred said. "I want to be there when they wake up. Tell them what we found out today."

"Fine," she said. She was also excited about what they'd found out but refused to show it. "But you're making dinner tonight."

"Fine," Fred said, sticking out a hand to help her up. "Nice shooting, by the way. But we've got to get you a bigger gun."

"I think I'm ready for one."

"We'll see what they say. You're still just a kid, you know," Fred said as he pulled a 9mm Heckler & Koch USP from the pocket of his black hoodie. He held the gun at his side, comfortably and casually.

"Don't start with that shit again," Karina said as they walked away from the fast-food restaurant. "I'm only a year younger than you. And girls mature faster, you know. So maybe you should have the small gun. It'll match your other small gun."

At first, Fred didn't get the insult. She could tell from his face. Then it dawned on him, and his face went from pale white to lobster red in about a second.

"Shut—what—you," he stuttered.

Karina stifled a laugh. He was so predictable. Most of the time, any-way.

They walked through a thin alley between what used to be a doctor's office and a hair salon. It was overgrown with grass that had been green a month ago but was now yellowing. Before they reached the mouth of the alley, Fred dropped down, pulling his pistol up into a ready position.

Without a word, Karina did the same, bringing her rifle up. Then she heard it, the sound of a motor, getting closer. "Back up, back up," Fred whispered, scooting her back into the deepening shadows of the alley. A battered white pickup truck lumbered by on the street, about thirty yards away, past the parking lot that had served the businesses before the apocalypse.

Fred breathed an audible sigh of relief. "It's just the Whiteys," he said.

"Fucking Whiteys," Karina said. She hated the Whiteys more than any other gang in the area. They were a group of white supremacists who insisted on white everything. White clothes, white vehicles, white shoes, and, of course, white skin. They even went so far as to bleach their skin and hair to make themselves even whiter than they already were. Which was pretty damn white.

Their insistence on white everything wasn't very practical, considering the circumstances. Without running water to regularly wash their clothes and vehicles, they were more gray than anything. If she'd had her way, she would fire on them every time she saw one of those dirty pale idiots. But that wasn't the smart thing to do.

"They're ballsy today," she said. "It's not even dark yet."

"They're probably headed to the gas station," Fred said. "Drawn by the explosion. They won't find anything there, though."

They stayed in the alley for a little while longer just to make sure no one else was coming, then they ran across the street, entering a sprawling neighborhood through a hole in a wooden fence. Off in the distance, the cityscape sat on the horizon, the pale sun painting the buildings a watery orange.

Fred and Karina made their way into the neighborhood cautiously. They traveled between houses and only used streets when they had to cross one. They jumped small fences and ducked through previously made holes in larger ones. They ignored the moldering lawn furniture, the rusting playground equipment, and the few dead bodies decomposing here and there.

Their caution grew into paranoia as they approached their destination. They paused often, listening for anything out of the ordinary. They made sure to scan all sectors before entering the house. Then they went upstairs, each to a different room, and looked out, searching for movement. For any indication they'd been followed. They stayed in that house for ten minutes before moving slowly and quietly to the next house over.

They crept into the basement, each confident that the other could see without light as they went down the wooden stairs. They walked up to a large freezer placed against one concrete wall, each taking a side, and moved it. Behind the freezer there was a smooth hole in the concrete. It was about five feet tall and two-and-a-half feet wide. Fred had to duck to go through. Karina didn't. Fred turned around and pulled the freezer back into place, using makeshift metal handles that had been installed on the back of the appliance for that very reason.

Once the freezer was back in place, they pulled out and turned on their small flashlights. The fallout shelter's door was set at an angle into the floor. It reminded Karina of an exterior cellar door that she'd had in a house when she was a little girl. She had always been afraid to go down the rough concrete steps, past the willowy cobwebs, and into the pitch dark and organic musk of that cellar. She'd thought that monsters had lived down there.

Every time she came back to the old home base, she marveled again at how far she'd come since she'd been that little girl. *Turns out monsters are real. And I live with them*, she thought, reveling in the fact. She wasn't afraid of much. Even vampires stopped being scary once you got to know them.

The heavy-duty metal doors were secured with a chain and padlock on the outside, just in case. Fred levered off his right sneaker and dug his key out, then unlocked the padlock. He set the chain aside on the floor and lifted the doors. He could feel the seal break as he pulled, the flexible plastic foam around the edges of the door making a brief sucking sound as the doors lifted away from each other.

Karina stepped over the threshold and walked down a small flight of concrete steps, illuminating the way as she went. Fred waited for her to step off the stairs before he stepped down, turned around, and then closed the doors behind him while Karina shone her flashlight so he could see what he was doing. Once the doors were flush, Fred swung a large metal handle that locked the door from the inside. There was no way to unlock the door from the outside, so it was always left unlocked when anyone was out and about. Hence the chain and padlock.

Confident that the door was secure, Fred turned around and followed Karina down the low-ceiling hallway to another metal door, this one propped open. Battery-powered lanterns were blazing in what passed for a bomb-shelter living room. Fred and Karina switched their flashlights off and pocketed them as they entered the room, which doubled as an entryway. To their right was a rather large open kitchen. To the left, one of three bedrooms. Straight ahead, a stubby hallway that led to a bathroom and the two other bedrooms.

The whole place was utilitarian to the core. The only decorations had been brought in by the vampires, and those weren't decorations, per se. Instead, they were pages ripped from notebooks with diagrams, drawings, and scrawled information. There was, however, a bed in every bedroom and two couches in the living room. There was also a bookcase in the living room packed with books of all kinds.

Karina looked around. Binta sat on an arm of one of the couches, looking up at the two humans expectantly, fine as ever. Isabelle lay sprawled on the couch next to Binta, a book tented on her chest, staring in a very French manner at them, waiting. Jules and Jamie were sitting on the other couch, holding hands, looking cute enough to make Karina want to barf in her mouth. Gay vampires made her want to go all *"Awwwww."* Who knew?

Fred opened his mouth to say something, but Karina beat him to it, blurting out, "We think we found out where that dude Weller is today and we blew up a gas station and killed a couple of guys."

Fred half-turned and looked death at her. She smiled apologetically. Sometimes she just couldn't help herself.

"You're serious?" Binta asked without much intonation. "You think it's accurate this time?"

Fred nodded. "I need to go see Diirek."

***

To continue reading, get your copy of Undead Extermination now. Available for purchase on Amazon and free on Kindle Unlimited!

ALSO BY THE AUTHOR

Undead Extermination

It's a war of the undead as good and evil clash in the explosive conclusion to the Undead Trilogy.

The Devil's Playground: Tales of Terror to Keep You Up At Night

These collections of short stories will have you checking under your bed before you go to sleep. From serial killers and paranormal creatures to insanity-inducing experiences and monsters from parallel dimensions, these stories are perfect for horror fans everywhere. 20 chilling stories per volume!

Available on Amazon

The Trouble Thrillers

"Absolutely thrilling." -Amazon Customer.

Check out these adventure thrillers featuring Terrence "Trouble" Rubble fighting for justice in the streets of America. Read these standalone books in any order or start with the first!

- *Dead Man's Hatch* - Available on Amazon and Free on Kindle Unlimited

- *The Deadly Divine* - Available on Amazon and Free on Kindle Unlimited

- *The Death Dealers* - Available on Amazon and Free on Kindle Unlimited

- *Too Much Trouble* - Available on Amazon and Free on Kindle Unlimited

- *Trouble* - **Available for free at MatthewDoggettAuthor.com/Trouble**